DENIAL

FIRST EDITION

RICHARD STRIFE

Denial is a work of fiction. Names, characters, places, and incidents either are the product of the author's imagination or are used fictitiously. Any resemblance to actual persons, living or dead, events or locales is entirely coincidental.

PREFACE

I wrote this story because I could not find the one book I really wanted to read as a teenager. I wanted a coming of age story about a lesbian in a fantasy world - I wanted *her* to be my hero. Rebecca Silas is far from perfect, but she's the hero that I needed in my life when I was an angsty teenage girl. If her story helps to improve any other angsty teen's life for the better then I'll consider my mission a success.

It has taken eight years of learning, and applying what I've learned to make *Denial* what it is today. I have to thank both Lea Strife and Zachariah Strife for everything they did to help this book become a reality. Lea Strife edited the many drafts of *Denial* and she gave the gift of a unique voice to Rebecca Silas. When I struggled to formulate a unique style for Sebastian Madius, Zachariah Strife stepped in and helped me recreate his chapters with the exact voice I'd needed. It's thanks to their willingness to collaborate their voices to my story that it finally broke out of the box and became everything I had envisioned.

-Richard Strife

P.S. I've been told that the first several chapters are difficult to get through. This was reasonably intentional on my part; the girl telling you her story is depressed. Everything in depression is a terrible struggle. Stick with it, and I think you will be pleasantly surprised when it does get better.

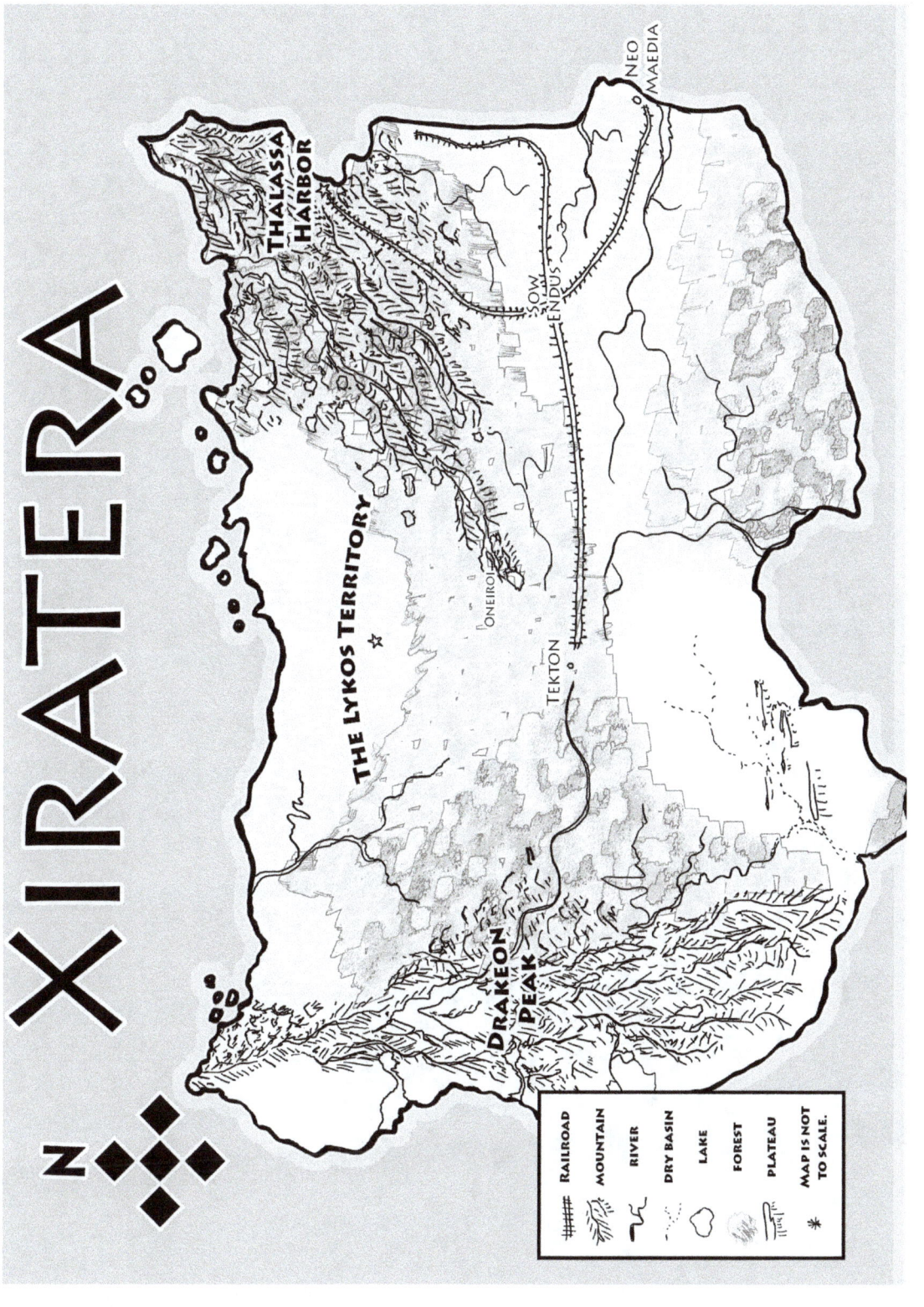

CHAPTER 1

As Rebecca knelt down to clean up the broken picture frame, she wondered if she was even really a person anymore. She felt like an empty shell. Anything real had long since suffocated under the weight of expectations that lingered longer than the person who'd set them. Expectations she couldn't shrug off, but that she couldn't force herself to meet, either. She picked up the photograph buried among the debris and frowned. She wanted to be the girl in the picture; she wanted to hold Monique the way she'd held her that day, and this was the only way she knew how.

In the photograph beside her, Brad stood awkwardly holding two enormous plush bears, while she and Monique had their arms around one another and faces full of laughter. Monique had insisted on tagging along on their date that day, although Rebecca didn't need any convincing. Brad surprised them both by winning not one, but two of those silly bears.

She couldn't remember the last time she'd laughed like that. She couldn't remember the last time she'd laughed at all, or even smiled a heartfelt smile. The memories of happiness, of being with Monique, pushed her heart up into her throat. Less than a year prior, during their senior year, Monique suddenly dropped out and left her alone, never to be heard from again. She swallowed, forcing the lump in her throat down as she stared at the vibrant, knowing smile of Monique's that filled her stomach with a mixture of butterflies and a sinking pit of despair. Rebecca wondered what had made Monique so happy in their Kodak moment. She told herself it didn't matter if Monique had shared the thrill she always felt with Monique – because it would never happen again. Monique disappeared from her life and left her with nothing more than the foundation of lies Rebecca had forged in order to be closer to her.

Brad stood at the base of that very foundation, just as he lurked in the background of their photo. His athletic build and defined muscles fit the bill for boyfriend material – the perfect topic of conversation every night over the phone. The perfect excuse to need Monique's help preparing for dates. Naturally, every girl wanted a strong, handsome jock, so of course her best friend devoted time and attention to Rebecca's cause. But then, as she played into the role of Brad's girlfriend, the half-truths and manipulations piled too thick to discern what was real from imaginary. She got lost in the certainty of being Brad's one and only. She said yes to his proposal with the sincerity Monique would have wanted to hear.

Surety had eluded her ever since she realized that she and Monique weren't inseparable. Their relationship proved to be just another lie in the book of lies, the eternally growing mountain of untruths that people dealt out in order to inspire false hope in others. Rebecca gazed at the photograph and considered how simple it would be to separate herself from Monique in the image, a permanent reminder of their friendship's fate. She took a shard of glass and sliced the ragged edge across the old photo. A self-satisfied smirk crept onto her face as she removed the extricated piece, crumpled it in her hand and tossed it into the waste bin under the sink.

With an eyeliner pencil, she scrawled "I'm sorry" across the back of the photograph that remained. She flipped the photo over again and wedged it into the frame of her bathroom mirror. Rebecca looked nothing like the girl in the picture anymore – she looked disheveled, and on the brink of tears. She didn't feel the tears constricting her chest, nor stinging her eyes; she didn't feel much of anything.

Behind her in the mirror's reflection, the pale fabric of the haunting wedding dress mimicked the bloodless pallor of her face. Silken perfection with a beautiful lace trim, the dress was supposed to be a dream come true. She would have sooner seen it torn apart by a starving coyote than worn. Yet, there it hung on the door, begging to be put on, to perpetuate exactly what she sought to escape. The silk cocoon would transform her web of lies into the misguided falsehood of a loveless marriage. That thought pushed motivation into her veins, the leaden weight of her body evanescing as she urged herself to finish what she'd started.

Rebecca pulled a white tank top on over her black bra. Then, she unfolded a pair of baggy jeans and stepped into them. She cinched a canvas belt around her waist and slipped a terrycloth armband onto her wrist. Her collection of jewelry lay strewn about haphazardly in the top drawer of the vanity; the glinting silver painfully reminded her of all the shopping excursions with her best friend. She dug through the jewelry until she found her favorite earrings – a pair of sterling silver hoops – and the wolf pendant her brother had given her for Christmas. Though it wasn't the nicest jewelry she had, it was what she felt best represented her. Carefully applied makeup and styled hair finished the look: the girl who stared out at her from the mirror's reflection more closely resembled the girl in the photograph.

She'd nearly transformed back into the Rebecca who still stood arm-in-arm with Monique – the Rebecca who had existed once, before Monique abandoned her. Rebecca sighed at the picture, and Monique's deep chocolate eyes stared back at her. The sensation of longing swallowed her whole. She wished that she'd thought of more to say but she couldn't figure out how else she could express all that she felt: the crushing weight of solitude, the atrocious knowledge of her freakishness, the insurmountable quantity of lies she'd hidden behind in order to deny it all. "I'm sorry" summed everything up without saying anything her mother would have to explain.

Satisfied with her message, with her appearance, she pushed the suffocating emotions aside. Behind the mirror, the medicine cabinet held the aspirin bottle she sought. Rebecca popped off the cap and shook out a handful of pills. Closing the cabinet, she gazed into her eyes and nodded. No fear, no regret, no excitement. She knew nothing in that moment but absolute apathy.

She swallowed the pills, then set the bottle on the counter and examined what remained of the shattered picture frame. Most of the glass seemed too small, too jagged to get a grip on. The large shard resting by the sink would have to suffice, she reasoned, it sliced through the photo with ease.

Rebecca swallowed against the burning in her chest and rolled up the sleeve of her pink hoodie. She took the shard in her hand, trying to decide where to start – where to finish.

A loud knock on the door startled her out of her contemplation.

"What?" She called.

"I want to talk to you."

It was her kid brother.

"I'm kind of busy, can we talk later?"

"No, there isn't a later," he retorted insistently through the door.

Anxiety laced itself through her lungs, constricting her throat – the sensation of panic made breathing difficult. How did Alex know what she was planning? She'd been so careful to mask her unhappiness, for Brad's sake, for her mother's sake. The last thing she wanted was to fail at upholding her facade. She exhaled as calmly as possible before she clutched the glass firmly in her palm, out of sight, and cracked open the door.

She peeked out at him, her foot pressed against the door to ensure he wouldn't burst in – he'd done it in the past, though usually to sneak a peek at Monique changing. "What do you mean?"

"The wedding," he pled with an urgency that shone in his eyes.

Rebecca frowned at her brother, less well-dressed than herself – complete with an uncombed mess of brown hair. His blue soccer jersey, khaki cargo shorts and untied tennis shoes told her that he anticipated her 'big moment' with even less eagerness than herself.

She wound up her best fake smile, the one she usually reserved for Brad. "What about the wedding?"

"I hate what he's done to you," Alex explained. When she didn't respond, he continued, "Come on, Rebecca! Now's your chance to get outta here. You never have to marry that loser, you can just take whatever you want and we can run away, me and you. I looked it up. It wouldn't even be illegal! Since you're eighteen, you can be my legal guardian. We could just get on a bus and go to L.A. or New York or even Mexico. Yeah, they'd never find us in Mexico, and American money would last us a long time as pesos. We should do that."

The panic subsided. Alex believed from day one that Brad was a brainless jock, just out to get a piece of the Silas family fortune. Similarly, Brad regarded her brother as a prepubescent annoyance, even though Alex would be starting his freshman year in the fall. It was a pissing contest between males that had little to do with her, and nothing at all to do with her immediate intentions.

Rebecca scoffed, "Why do you think I don't want to marry him?"

"Because you don't want to do *anything* anymore," he pressed. "You don't go anywhere, you don't talk to anyone, you never even come in for dinner. Even when you *do* leave your room, you're like some kind of zombie. It's like he ate your brain."

"That's so not true," she began, but her words failed her as she fought to keep the plastered-on smile in place.

"It is," Alex stated matter-of-factly. His eyebrows raised, a dare to prove otherwise.

Her defense amounted to an overwhelming nothing. He was right; it was all true. But running away wouldn't solve anything. The pouty-faced preteen standing in her room couldn't possibly begin to understand, even if she tried to express it. She was the problem – not Brad. How could she explain herself to him with words she didn't even have? The surroundings of her too-cramped room offered little solace; the converted garage hadn't changed since her father abandoned it, other than having acquired hand-me-down pieces of furniture that her mother wouldn't sell but no longer wanted. Not more than ten feet from her bed, the familiar whir of the old mini-refrigerator clicked on. Rebecca's gaze focused on the small black fridge until her eyelids grew heavy with its mechanical lullaby. She felt dimly aware of a nauseous sensation.

"See? You look like you're a million miles away."

Alex tried to force the door in, but her shoe stopped it from swinging open. He pushed hard a second time; his persistence caught her off guard. She rushed to hold the door shut against him, leaning in with her shoulder. In her sudden panic she clutched the glass too tight – it dug into her palm.

She bit back the yelp of pain and snapped, "Damn it, Alex. Go get ready."

"No, *you* get ready, and let's go to Mexico. I'm not gonna let you throw your life away like this."

Blood streamed down her hand and streaked the door – right beside the white dress. "Running away with you *is* throwing my life away. Get lost so I can have my happily ever after, okay?"

He let the door close and whimpered meekly through it, "You don't mean that..."

"I really do."

Silence.

Rebecca sighed and leaned back against the closed door. She felt exhausted, sick to her stomach, and ready to be done with everything. Drops of fresh blood splattered on the tile floor; the gash in her palm bled freely as she opened her hand to inspect the damage. It needed stitches – she imagined it would be one of many things they would sew shut before the wake.

She closed her hand around the blood-slicked glass shard again, then rested her forearm on the edge of the sink. As she drew in a deep breath, she pressed the edge of the glass into her wrist. The skin gave easier than she imagined; it pushed inward with the pressure, then began to split.

A thundering crash accompanied the sound of crunching metal; a car alarm sounded. The walls shook, the ground beneath her feet shuddered. Her hands reflexively gripped the edge of the sink, as the walls contorted with the vibration of the earth. The mirror cracked, splitting her face in half.

In the immediate aftermath, resolve burned through her – no amount of divine intervention could condemn her to live her miserable life of playing pretend any longer. She held her wound over the sink; the small gap of rent open flesh trickled crimson streaks across her palm. As the tiny droplets fell onto the shattered glass in the sink, she realized that she would need another instrument to rid her of this world.

Behind her, the door swung open. Before she could react, before she could even attempt to hide the glass or blood, Alex's shocked gasp filled her ears like poison.

"It was an accident. I was trying to clean it up when..." Her lie trailed off; she wasn't entirely sure what to call the ruckus from outside. She repeated, "It was just an accident."

Alex didn't say anything.

She watched his horrified expression as he stared at the blood all over her hands. "Just... Don't tell mom, okay? She'd freak."

He shook his head, wide-eyed. Without a word, he walked over to her and threw his arms around her. He buried his face in the shoulder of her hoodie.

Rebecca had nothing more to say. If he wasn't going to run off and blurt that she needed psychiatric attention, she just needed to follow through with her lie. Pulling away from his insistent, tear-soaked hug, she opened the medicine cabinet again, and retrieved the last gauze wrap from the shelf. While she wrapped her hand in gauze, she babbled quietly to herself.

"It *was* an accident... I just need to keep it covered and I'll be as good as new." She pulled the terrycloth armband down over the wound on her wrist. Her words felt foreign, rolling off her tongue like the venomous manipulations that got her into the mess to begin with. "You'll see."

Alex touched the picture of her and Monique, his finger trailing along the rough edge where Brad had been severed. Rebecca slammed the medicine cabinet shut, and snatched the photo from the mirror's frame, removing it from his prying hands. She didn't want to have to explain herself to him – she didn't want him asking why she left behind a picture of Monique as her suicide note.

Preempting the protest that would come with his incredulous look, she changed the subject. "We don't have natural disasters in Albuquerque. What was that – an earthquake? A bomb?"

"It was a pile of dinosaur bones falling out of the sky and crushing mom's car," Alex muttered.

The car alarm still blared right outside of her room. "No really. What happened?"

"That's what happened, I'll show you" he replied. He looped his arm through hers and led her through her room to the doorway of the converted garage. "I was standing right here, trying to think of a way to convince you to leave with me and like magic these giant bones dropped from heaven and ruined the wedding without me having to do anything at all."

From her door, they had a perfect view of the decimated wreckage that was once her mother's car. Enormous bones were scattered around the vehicle, but the majority of them were stacked on top of the car's body. An impossibly large reptilian skull with huge, curved horns rested on the engine block like an over-sized hood ornament. Deep brown fluids from the engine flooded from the mouth of the skull.

"Huh," Rebecca gaped. No amount of blinking alleviated the strangeness of the destruction. The bones were so grand in size, she couldn't fathom them belonging to anything but a dinosaur. Her mother, standing on the porch of the house, had obviously found someone to blame for the obliteration of her vehicle. Rebecca guessed it was an unsuspecting museum curator on the other end of her mother's screeching outrage.

"Yeah," Alex assented. "Mom's pissed. She probably wouldn't even care if I told her what you did."

The way every piece of the windshield and windows had exploded outward made Rebecca consider if she'd been in the car, she would have died by sheer accident, and she wouldn't have failed at ending her own life – she failed to kill herself the same way she'd failed to be a normal girl, failed at everything and failed everyone.

"I didn't *do* anything," she argued.

Alex's lower lip quivered and he clenched his fist as he stared forward at the chaotic disarray of bones. "I won't tell mom, but I have to tell someone. I don't want you to do it again."

Rebecca swallowed, unsure of whether she felt relieved or annoyed that she'd been caught. Alex hadn't spent that much time around her: how would he know what she did and didn't need? They hadn't been close since before Monique came into her life. She chewed on her lower lip and averted her eyes, instead staring at the ground. What would become of her now? She dreaded the idea of being psychoanalyzed in a white padded room.

A sudden, icy sensation washed over her – so cold it burned – then passed. The goosebumps raised on her skin made her wonder whether she'd imagined it, or if it was another sign of divine intervention trying to goad her into submission.

"Did you feel that?" Alex asked.

She tilted her head at him, quizzically.

His mouth hung open, aghast, shock etched into his face. He pointed past her into her room. "It's... It's... that thing's ghost!"

"There's no such thing as ghosts," she sighed.

6

"Then what do you call that?" He insisted, jabbing the air in the direction of her bathroom.

Big – too big to fit inside the tiny apartment – the ethereal form of what she could only think to call a dragon suspended her disbelief in ghosts. The spirit itself was constructed of bones, the same shape as the ones outside yet larger still, but translucent scaled flesh stretched tight over its ghastly skeleton. Its tremendous horned head disappeared into the bathroom, defying the very materiality of the solid walls as if they didn't exist. The forked serpent-like tongue flicked outward over the pool of Rebecca's blood on the floor.

"How do you get rid of ghosts?"

"Um..." Alex swallowed, his gaze fixated on the intruder.

"Come on, Alex. Aren't you the one who watches those paranormal TV shows? How do you get rid of ghosts?"

"Um," he furrowed his brow. "Salt, maybe?"

"Salt? Okay. I can do salt."

"Be careful," he warned as she crossed the room toward the small kitchenette, nearing the tremendous spirit dragon.

The words of caution seemed stupid coming from the little brother who was convinced she'd been trying to kill herself. Rebecca had no reason to be careful; she had nothing to lose. She pushed around the past-expired spices until she grasped the familiar cardboard cylinder of salt. She popped the metal pouring spout up and threw the container at the ethereal creature like a grenade.

Salt sprayed everywhere; the container erupted as it hit the ground. The salt granules fell through the spirit bones, as ineffectual as the walls at affecting it. The dragon raised its head from the drying blood, the eyeless sockets focusing on Rebecca. Those deep empty cavities burned with soft purple light. A hot rush of breath hit her face as the dragon roared. If the dragon was real enough to roar, was it real enough to hurt? Her gaze flicked to Alex and she decided that as long as he was safe, it didn't matter.

But the dragon followed her gaze; its enormous head swung toward Alex. Another earsplitting roar shook the room; loose debris from the quake fell from the ceiling. She rushed headlong for Alex at the same time the ethereal bone dragon charged him.

More than she'd ever wanted anything before in her life, she wanted to have made it in time. Her shoulder crashed into his chest as she knocked him through the doorway; she felt a frigid burning overwhelm her body when she collided with him. She squeezed her eyes shut against the pain of the bone-dragon's hot ice searing her body from the inside out. The stench of smoke and blood overtook her senses as the two of them hit the ground.

CHAPTER 2

"You're crushing me," Alex groaned.

Rebecca mumbled an apology and shifted her weight, supporting herself with a hand in the sun-warmed, fresh-watered lawn. She felt dazed, nauseous with a wave of shock that permeated her senses in response to the pain of the ghost passing through her.

The ghost. It had been inside of her room, nowhere near the lawn – they should've fallen onto the driveway – why was her arm soaked? She took in the cooling blood creeping up her sleeve.

"Alex?" She whimpered, afraid it was his blood.

His choked cry of horror matched her own terror as they realized the blood wasn't either of theirs, but instead that of the splayed corpse laying next to them. A dark pool of blood oozed from the gaping grin splitting open the stranger's throat; more blood had drained from other injuries Rebecca couldn't see beneath the mess of tattered clothing and blood-caked dirt. Breath caught in her throat when she found her fingers entangled in the chaotic fray. Damp, matted chest hair clung to her hand as she pulled back from what was definitely not the lawn she'd imagined. She gagged, her vision growing hazy and dark. Stomach acid burned the back of her throat, then her mouth. The pills she'd taken forced their way back up and into the mess of gore, leaving a bitter taste on her tongue.

"Where are we? What happened!" Alex cried.

She lifted her gaze from the worst sight of her life only to be met with absolute chaos. All around them, towering flames engulfed large wooden buildings; smoke and ash filled the air. Through the obscuring haze, the vague outlines of many more corpses littered the stretch of dirt road before them. The roar of fire drowned out the din of panic further down the road, where a tremendous, winged, reptilian monster loomed. Its massive fangs held a dead man's arm pulled taut. A pop that reverberated off the buildings echoed through the streets.

Unbelievable, but too real to ignore, Rebecca watched the charcoal-black dragon play with the disembodied arm like a rope-toy. The beast swung its ivory-horned head to the side, throwing the arm into the crowd of terrified villagers. They gasped, shrieked, and cried upon the impact of the torn limb. The way the creature watched the villagers' reaction made Rebecca feel as though it enjoyed feeding on their fear more than their flesh.

"Did you see that?" Alex gasped. "That dragon just ate that guy's arm!"

Rebecca winced; how could she miss it?

8

The beast bore down on the dismembered figure trapped beneath its monstrous talons. As its jaws closed around the limp body's head, Alex croaked, "It's going to decapitate him!"

"Stop yelling." Rebecca clamped her hand over his mouth and shoved him down against the ground.

When she looked back to the colossal terror, its glowing amaranthine eyes stared directly into hers. Alex spoke against her hand, probably some kind of protest to being held down, or a verbal notification that the beast was staring right at them – as if she hadn't noticed.

One of the villagers drove a pitchfork into its hind leg, but the archaic weapon stood no chance. The rusted metal snapped on impact, leaving the beast's scales virtually unscathed. The dragon snarled in rage.

Alex fist-pumped the air beside her, his cheer muffled by her hand.

"Stay down and shut up," Rebecca growled at him. Then she called out to the great beast. "Hey you! Yeah, that's right."

The creature's focus on Rebecca never wavered. Its blazing eyes narrowed; its head tilted slightly to one side. She pushed off the ground and backed away from the villagers, away from Alex.

"I'm the best tasting human here," she invited.

Those ominous purple eyes followed her as she stepped backwards. She retreated, one foot at a time, until the heat at her back from a burning building beaded sweat on her spine. Behind her, flames dominated the congregation of houses; in front, she could only see the vague silhouette of Alex, not far from the massive beast in the smoke.

"Come on," Rebecca taunted. "Don't you want a snack?"

The creature emerged from the haze, the crevices between its scales burning a hot orange, like breathing life into the dying embers of a fire. Its ribcage illuminated with the same flickering incandescence as it took a deep breath. A tribal pattern of chasms split open; first a horizontal line spread across its side, then four swirls swept outward from the line.

The orange glow culminated in its throat, blazing between its scales like a furnace. Mesmerized, Rebecca stared into the fiery sphere launched from the gaping jaws of the beast. Panicked yells filled the air

"Get down!"

Pressure on her shoulders forced Rebecca's knees to buckle, her balance thrown by the sudden weight. The hands held her steady, kept her from falling to the ground – someone had shielded her from the molten fire passing overhead. A shower of flames sprayed like viscous drops of lava around them. The sticky liquid heat clung to the cloak of her rescuer, which he hurriedly cast aside as the flames devoured the fabric.

The dragon roared again, stomping its claws against the earth; clouds of dust rose as the ground quaked with the beast's anger. Hatred flared in its eyes.

"Dragon!" Her hero shouted. His voice was calm, confident, as if unfazed by the reality of a dragon. "Listen to me," he commanded, the serenity of his voice infectious. The teenager stood with his legs firmly planted, his right hand fanned out in front of him. His shoulders were square, his posture perfectly straight – perfectly straight like the long ponytail of platinum blond hair that fell down his back. Perfect like the soft but defined jaw, smooth but angular face, the startling azure eyes that stared intently into those of the dragon.

Again the beast cocked its head, an ever-so-slight tilt from one side to the other as curiosity animated its features. They peered at each other, a nearly palpable tension between them like an elastic band pulled tight enough to snap.

The corpses near-by were catching fire as a result of the perpetually burning remains of the viscous fireball. Goosebumps pricked Rebecca's skin; how mutilated would the boy's pretty face have been if it had gotten on him? She doubted that he could just brush off the molten stuff – what had fallen on the ground glowed red-hot like melted glass.

"You will hear me out," her savior continued. "You will listen to my words, then you will share this message with your kin. The town of Sow Endus has paid an incalculable debt for your rage. I hold you and yours responsible for each and every Maedian life that was lost here today. Neither you, nor any other Drakeon, may ever come near a human settlement again. You will never return to this place. Your kind may never hunt again on land where humans dwell."

The dragon's lips pulled back in a frightening sneer; one eye twitched. Rebecca saw Alex moving, and tried to subtly gesture for him to stay. None of the villagers moved; they stood paralyzed, watching the teenage hero with starstruck awe.

"Dragon," he repeated, "You have caused enough destruction already. There will be no more of this ruinous behavior from you. Our alliance has been greatly compromised by your trespass. The next transgression from your kind against us will force us to divest you of your homeland, so Xiratera may be a safe and peaceful land for all. Now be gone!"

The dragon narrowed its eyes and snorted. Its black, leathery wings spread, spanning wide across the street, and extended over the burning debris. Then it flew away. Rebecca watched as it became smaller and smaller in the hazy sky created by its rampage on the town.

"Are you some kind of dragon tamer or something?" Alex excitedly questioned the youthful hero, "How did you make it listen to you? That rocked!"

She couldn't believe the first thing he did once they were safe was gleefully run over, like he was completely unperturbed with the burning village, the dead people, and the man-eating dragon. Of course her video-game addicted little brother would know exactly how to roll with being thrown headlong into some alternate reality. None of it made any sense, but to him it was probably crystal clear, like any number of fantastic lands he'd virtually visited for countless hours.

"I am a Madius," the stranger replied, as if that explained everything. He shifted and adjusted his shirt collar. "Sebastian Madius, heir to the throne of Maedia."

Rebecca bit her lower lip, trying not to give away the fact that his name meant nothing to her. She concentrated, instead, on the peculiarity of his clothes. He wore a pure white tunic with delicate gold embroidery. At his hip, a swept hilt rapier rested in a scabbard fastened to his belt. His dark canvas trousers were tucked into leather boots. Yet, the satchel, slung over his shoulder like a purse, shattered the illusion of a rugged adventurer. The purse and the strangely angelic perfection of his pale skin, anyhow – together, these two features implied he'd never seen a day of combat in his life.

He placed his hand on Rebecca again, resting it on her shoulder. Rather than showing her discomfort at his invasion of her space, she knew she ought to be grateful for his heroic display of protecting her from the dragon's fire.

She wound on the tight, forced smile she'd mastered, and tried to appreciate his palm on her arm as he spoke, "Correct me if I am mistaken, are you two Metakosmos?"

"I'm sorry?" She drew her eyebrows together.

"Unbelievable," he murmured. "I simply can't fathom how there were Metakosmos in Sow Endus and the palace was uninformed. How long have you been on this side of the Kosmos?"

Rebecca shook her head slowly. "I'm not sure what you're talking about, I don't know what a 'kosmos' is or how we even got here."

"We've been here for like five minutes," Alex offered. "A big ghost dragon attacked us! And when we tried to get away from it – cuz it was in Rebecca's room – we fell right over there." He pointed toward the spot in the middle of the avenue where they'd landed. "But then there was a *real* dragon."

"Fascinating," Sebastian mused, "the Kosmos is the very fabric of existence. It is the air we breathe, the water we drink." He gestured widely around him, indicating the bloodied and burning corpses, decimated buildings and smoke-filled sky. "The Kosmos is everything you see. As we understand, there is something of a distorted mirror in the Kosmos, the world in which you must have come from. On very rare and special occasions, there is a temporary rift in the Kosmos that allows one to travel to and from the Other Side."

Rebecca's smile wilted.

"Anyhow," he sighed, "I welcome you Metakosmos to Gaeadia... Any other day, this town would have been the wonderfully quaint Sow Endus, home to many of the farmers of Xiratera, as well as the major cross-roads of the two largest railways on the continent. As you can see," Sebastian gestured again with far less enthusiasm, "Something has gone terribly awry."

"What happened to this place?" Alex inquired.

While he and Gaeadia's resident prince discussed the blatant maladies of the dragon-obliterated town, Rebecca wandered away. She was more interested in finding a way to get back to the world where – even if they sucked – things made sense. She decided to test the theory that 'Kosmos rifts' were temporary. She figured, if she could find exactly where they had crossed over, there would be a portal, and like looking through a window, she should be able to see her room on the other side.

As she walked, she scanned the burning doorways, broken windows, and anything else that looked like it held the potential to be converted into a portal to another world. She passed the occasional villager searching the endless horde of contorted corpses lining the streets. Whether they searched for survivors or sought to identify fallen family members, Rebecca couldn't tell. She distracted herself from the thought of how many bodies she'd stepped over by focusing on the attire of the villagers. It equaled Sebastian's getup in peculiarity; every person she saw was clad in some variety of hand-stitched clothing she'd only seen in period films and mandatory field-trips to Popejoy Hall.

The further Rebecca strayed from Alex, the more hopelessness she felt mounting her shoulders. If the rift between Shakespearean Festival Hell and Earth was even remotely like Sebastian said it was, she should've already found the window into her reality. She breathed deep in exasperation and instantly regretted it. She coughed on smoke until her eyes watered.

"Fine," she peered up at the sky, straightening herself from the doubled-over position of hacking. "Fine, God, or who-ever you are. I repent. I've seen the error of my ways. I'm sorry that I was weak, and that I turned to suicide for the answer instead of you. I've learned my lesson. I'll go back home, and I'll pretend better than ever that I truly love Brad. I'll marry him if that's what you want!"

Only the crackle of fire in the surrounding buildings greeted her ears; the long stretch of lifeless avenue greeted her sight. Her plea obviously wasn't good enough to warrant a response.

"Okay! I get it, you want more. I'll go to church every Sunday."

A light breeze picked up, coaxing the lazy embers on wooden supports to brighten.

"Yeah. I'll go to church *every* Sunday." Hope crept into her voice, as she bribed the forces that be. "I'll contribute to overpopulation and make babies – lots and lots of babies with Brad. I'll be a good, obedient housewife who dies old, ugly and miserable, all *you* have to do is show me the portal. Or maybe make like the Wizard of Oz and wake me up from this nightmare. I'll do whatever you want for a one-way ticket back home."

Nothing changed. No magical portal appeared. There was no flash of light, no small voice in the back of her mind like her mother trying to shake her awake. Nothing happened.

Rebecca sighed, collapsing onto a yet-undestroyed wooden crate stacked beside one of the few houses still standing. She shouldn't have been surprised, though she couldn't shake the feeling of annoyance that no one listened to her cry for help. Why, after all, should Gaeadia be any different than Earth? Why would the divine powers intervene for any reason other than their own amusement? Surely even if they did, it wouldn't be for her benefit. If she were an omnipresent god, she certainly wouldn't help herself. Any all-knowing entity was bound to dig deep into her darkest secrets and learn things that would make anyone hate her.

"I deserve this," she groaned, hanging her head in her hands.

Someone chuckled, an abrupt snicker that preceded a voice laced with a velvety exoticism that sent a shiver down Rebecca's spine. "Ya got that right."

Looking into the alley, the first thing Rebecca noticed about her was her wide, yellow eyes encircled by thick, dark lashes. Those eyes, she was certain, could pierce into her very soul. She dropped her gaze and found herself studying the dark leather boots, fastened with brass buckles, that came up over the woman's ankles. It was difficult to tell where the boots ended and the thick leather that covered her from head to toe began. Rips, tears, and slashes in the leather exposed her rent open flesh. Her bloody calf was cleaved apart, straight down to the bone.

Rebecca gasped. Her chest ached inexplicably. This girl couldn't be more than a few years older than herself, was still alive, and too young to die. The pain in her expression, in those captivating yellow eyes, made Rebecca blurt, "You're hurt... I can get help."

"Ya need help to end me, eh? Coward, human." The young woman flashed a sneer, her lips curled back revealing four canines locked in a human-animal hybrid set of teeth. Her long black-streaked silver hair was uneven, plastered to the side of her head with blood.

It didn't matter to Rebecca that this woman was clearly not quite human – she was human enough to be hiding behind some junk in an alley waiting for death to take her. She struggled to find the right words, wrestling with the conflicting compulsions to blurt whatever the woman wanted to hear and to calculate her words carefully. She wanted to say the right thing.

"I'm really just trying to help... but... I don't know anything about first aid." She unraveled the gauze from her hand, "I, uh, don't have any diseases or anything. I mean, if you don't mind my blood on you?"

The woman arced an eyebrow, as if appraising her intentions. "Ya wanna bandage me?"

"Is that okay?" Rebecca asked. When the woman gave a small nod, she knelt down and feebly attempted to wrap the gauze around the massive calf wound. The bandage instantly saturated in blood. Rebecca's heart raced, pounding in her ears, as she unsuccessfully tried not to panic. "I'm sorry, I don't know what I'm doing, I don't want you to die, I... I can try to find something else."

"If ya really wanna help me," the woman started, stopping Rebecca in her frantic search for anything nearby that vaguely resembled bandaging. "I need to get outta here. I can take care of myself if I can get outta this damned town."

Rebecca nodded vigorously; she would do anything she could to help her. "Yeah, sure, yeah, I can do that. I met this guy, Sebastian... He's a prince or something, and he saved me, so I'm sure he'll help you, too. I can go find him?"

"A Madius?" She hissed through clenched teeth; her voice edging on anger.

"Yeah, that's what he called himself, Sebastian Madius."

"I don't know what kinda games you're playing at, human-girl," she rasped. "But if you're serious, only you can help, got it? I'll tell ya what I need from ya."

"Anything," Rebecca assented without hesitation. She wanted the woman to like her. She needed to earn her trust, to prove that she wasn't like other humans. She liked the idea that the woman did need her; it made her feel an almost foreign rush of excitement.

"The easiest way out is jus' down the main road, but there's Maedians out there. I can't move fast enough like this, and I can't sneak through as long as they're lookin' for me. If ya get them outta the way, I can escape with my life."

"Why would they hurt you?" Rebecca frowned.

"Because they're humans, *like you*," the woman spat. Her words dripped with hatred that made Rebecca's heart ache like acid had been poured on it.

"I'm not like them," she protested. "I'm not even one of them! Just... Give me a minute. You'll get the chance you need."

"Or you're exactly like the rest of 'em and I'll be dead soon. I'm not fooled."

Rebecca stood to prove herself different from those who would brutally attack a woman like her – tear her apart and leave her to die... No, she was nothing like them. She glanced back at the woman. "What's your name?"

She heard Alex's voice calling for her; he wasn't very far away.

The woman's mouth twitched, as if she'd debated whether or not to identify herself. Then, under her breath, she said, "Kaece."

Her name was Kaece. Rebecca's chest felt tight, swollen to a bursting point with nervous energy and those anxious jitters that came with trying to win someone's approval.

"Kaece," Rebecca repeated, unable to keep the awe from her voice. "I want you to know that I would never hurt you. I want to see you again, alive and well... So if all it takes is a distraction, maybe we can meet again some day?"

Kaece gave another small nod; her eyes flicked toward the entrance of the alley.

Rebecca heard the footsteps, the sound of rocks and dirt crunching under shoes. She was out of time. Bracing herself, she casually strolled out of the side-road to greet Alex and Sebastian.

"Were you calling me?" She asked innocently.

Alex snatched up her hand and scowled at the fresh blood-flow from her gauze-less wound. "You wouldn't just leave me here alone, would you?"

She could tell by the anger and sadness in his eyes that he was jumping to the wrong conclusion. "I told you it was an accident," she retorted. "I was just looking for a way back home."

"Your time would be better spent not dwelling any longer on such things," Sebastian chimed in. "It would be exceptionally unlikely that you could return to your world. The tears in the Kosmos last for only a moment and are unpredictable, random occurrences. They are impossible to track or to create. Some Metakosmos, and some Maedians as well, have spent their entire lives searching in vain for one of these gateways onto the Other Side.

"However," his tone shifted from something of a lamenting lecture to excitement. Rebecca couldn't help but think of when her high-school teachers got wildly passionate about some mundane topic, like math. "As I was telling Alex here, there is far more danger on the Wild Continent than merely that one dragon. I was hoping that the two of you might accompany me on a journey to Thalassa Harbor? I must travel to see the Overseer, and your eyewitness accounts of today's events would be most valuable."

"Um," she hesitated. Any moment, Kaece would be peeking out from around the corner and finding her hopes dashed because Rebecca couldn't think fast enough. She had to come up with something, some kind of diversion, and fast. The moment the thought hit her, she pointed skyward, to the opposite end of the town. "Oh my god! Look!"

Her brother and Sebastian both turned to look, but she knew that the panic in her voice didn't match the scene. There was nothing to look at, and they would quickly lose interest. Rather than wait for them to redirect their confusion to her, Rebecca started running across the boulevard from where she'd met Kaece and into a far catty-corner alley-way.

"Dragon!" She cried out, cupping her hands over her mouth to broadcast her message as she ran. Her coordination was no match for the tight alley cramped with crates and barrels intermittently dispersed throughout. The edge of a barrel struck her hip and thigh. Her forward momentum threw her backwards – and into the bloodied hands of a small group of bewildered men.

Alex and Sebastian weren't far behind. Her fictitious dragon may not have been convincing in itself, but at least it seemed to draw everyone's attention towards the running prince. Many of the villagers wandering the streets had curiously followed him into the alley. She realized the farmers holding her, though, all faced the direction Kaece would be coming from. Her heart raced; out of ideas, she needed to do something even more desperate.

When one of the men supporting her put his hands on her waist, she slapped him as hard as she could across the face. "Get your hands off of me!"

The man recoiled, his cheek reddening. Her wounded palm seared with pain. She pulled her hand back, cradling it against her body, but felt satisfied – the resounding gasps of the crowd meant the pain was worth the reaction.

The man snarled as he grabbed her by the wrist. He shook her violently, then backhanded her with his knuckles. Immediately, regret registered in his eyes. Rebecca's face hurt, but all of her thoughts were focused on one thing: Kaece.

She rubbed the swelling contusion, hiding the direction of her gaze by covering her face. Behind her toward the main road, far in the distance, hard to make out over the crowd, Rebecca could see Kaece's form, leaning on a makeshift crutch. A mixture of anxiety and relief flooded over her. If she could still see Kaece, any number of the villagers could too, but Kaece had gotten away from the alley that trapped her. All of the mingling sensations overwhelmed her and made Rebecca feel dazed to a point of numbness. The numbness echoed the feeling of emptiness she'd grown so accustomed to over the months prior to her wedding day.

"What in the name of Zeus is wrong with you?" Sebastian's eerily commanding voice filled the narrow lane. "This is an innocent Metakosmos, raised in a world of chaos ruled by violence – our ways are unbeknownst to her. You are not from the Other Side, you are Maedian. You should not be so weak as to give in to violent impulses. Each of you," he made a sweeping gesture, careful to look at every villager with those icy eyes and a stern, hard-set frown, "is a building block of society. Each one of you is a critical part of our way of life. You are each a representation of Maedia, of why humans are the superior sentient race of this world. Please, tell me your explanation for your behavior."

"Prince Madius," his friend interjected. "Sam didn't mean any harm. He's been fighting off monsters all day, it was but a reflex. Those monsters got to his family, sir."

"Sam," Sebastian addressed only the man who'd hit Rebecca. "What is your full name? And explain to me what it is I'm hearing about fighting."

The man stood, grounded like a rock, his face stone-still and carved with the expression of pride. He looked pleased with himself, but he avoided looking Rebecca in the eye. She wondered if the damage his knuckles had done would leave a bruise. At least she had created enough of a diversion that Sebastian harnessed everyone's full attention. Even Alex, standing between her and Sebastian, stood rapt, his eyes wide as if he were watching TV drama unfold.

"Samuel Miller," the man replied. "Less than an hour ago, I witnessed the slaughter of my wife and kids. I saw my neighbors, my friends from boyhood, torn apart by those *monsters*. My home, our fields – our food! – all ruined. But I stood strong, because I am Maedian. I know we'll rebuild our houses, we'll resow the fields... The work that I do keeps food on everyone's table, and because of that the Overseer would understand why we fought back. He would stand by me."

Sebastian looked skeptical, his eyebrows drawn up and his mouth closed, tight-lipped.

"What do *you* know of life here on Xiratera?" Samuel continued, pointing at Sebastian. "You've lived the pampered life of the Emperor's grandbaby – you've never had to do a lick of work."

Rebecca watched as several of the onlookers paled. They were mortified, embarrassed for – or by – Samuel's insult.

Sebastian calmly nodded. "I am but the grandson of the Emperor, and you are right to doubt my acquaintance with the wild land of Xiratera. I have been on this continent for a slight ten days. However, you have yet to repent for the lapse of judgment which caused you to act on your impulsive, heathenish display of violence."

"I'll never apologize," Samuel snorted. "Not for fighting off those monsters. I helped kill one of those beasts today, and for that I will never 'repent.' I should not have harmed this woman, but we should be allowed to protect ourselves. We should be allowed to fight to save our families and our land."

"Then, Samuel, you are a man corrupted by anger. Driven by such hatred, as none of those around you who have also suffered similar fates, you are a danger to this society. Your pure Maedian soul has been tainted, your goodness forever lost. From this moment forth, you are no longer Maedian. You will not enter a Maedian civilization; you will not speak nor correspond with Maedian citizens. You are to survive as an outcast of Maedia. You have your fate, Samuel Miller, now go."

The gloss that overcame Samuel's eyes seemed at first like tears of sorrow to Rebecca, but the rest of his face was just blank. His pupils dilated, then returned to normal, and the glassy look faded away. He nodded, then began walking, never once looking back or attempting to protest the condemnation. The man disappeared first from the street, then the wide avenue, walking into the distance and out of town. Through the haze of numbness, a thought struck Rebecca like a bolt of lightning that made her heart leap with fear; she prayed that Kaece was far away or that she'd hid somewhere Samuel wouldn't find her. Banished or not, he was still one of the humans she feared, and he walked away the very same direction Kaece'd left the village.

Sebastian breathed a deep sigh, watching Samuel go before he turned to the remaining villagers. "Let this man's fate serve as an example to any of you who may have hate brewing in your heart. It is your duty as upstanding citizens of Maedia to band together, to uphold our laws and the principals that govern society, while I get at the root of the cause for this atrocity. The future generations of Maedia depend on your diligence, we rely on you all to protect the delicate balance. And do not worry, I vow that I will exact justice for what has taken place here today. I will not rest; I will travel through light and darkness until I find the monsters responsible and restore peace to our nation."

The crowd erupted into applause, some cheering, a few whistling, and many with tears cutting through the dirt on their faces. Sebastian's way with words was increasingly daunting each time he opened his mouth. Sebastian led them away from the crowd, down the wide avenue the same direction Samuel had taken.

His exile weighed on Rebecca's mind. Anger burned in the pit of her stomach. He shouldn't have ever hit a woman – the violent act implicated him as someone who could've inflicted those injuries on Kaece. If he was abusive, he was a danger to society exactly like Sebastian said. There was no reason to feel bad about saving both Kaece and the other villagers from his unruly temper. She couldn't block out the fear of Kaece already having been found and murdered. Alex's voice derailed her troubling thoughts.

"Is that guy really never allowed to come back to his home?"

Sebastian nodded gravely, "That is precisely the aim of banishment."

"I'm sorry," Rebecca murmured, insincerely.

"Now, more than I had earlier, I believe that it is important for you to travel with me to Thalassa Harbor. It is apparent that you do not understand this world, and I would like to take it upon myself to teach you," he said as he raised Rebecca's wrist, and with a cringe he gestured to the cut on her palm. "You also seem to be exceptionally prone to danger. I have the supplies to clean and dress this wound on the Hadros. It would be a tragedy for you to become ill from infection."

"Um, Sure... Can I just talk to Alex for a sec?"

Sebastian let go of her wrist and gave a small bow before he continued forward ahead of them.

"You totally got that guy banished!" Alex exclaimed in a whisper, his face registering more excitement than upset. "What'd you hit him for?"

Exasperated, she sighed and shrugged with one shoulder. "I don't know, I didn't like his hands on me? But he shouldn't have hit me back, I guess. After all..." She trailed off, realizing she was letting Alex drag her off-topic. "Do you really trust this Sebastian guy? He's a little strange, I mean, the way people just listen to whatever he says and all."

"Are you kidding? You *have* to trust him! We fell into an alternate fantasy world with dragons and emperors; it's so obvious. I get to be the hero, and you're the damsel in distress who needs saving," he explained. "He is the knight in shining armor. You'll get to be his princess."

Rebecca hid the grimace at the idea of being just another man's woman behind a cheerful smile. "His princess, huh? I don't know..."

"Well, whatever, even if you don't want to be his princess," he shrugged.

She felt annoyed – she didn't say she didn't *want* to be his princess. Alex wasn't some all-knowing god or anything, shouldn't he just think she was being self-conscious?

"I think he's right about going to this Hadros place and cleaning up your hand. And about seeing Thalassa Harbor, because who knows? There may even be someone who knows something about how to get us back home."

She bit her lower lip; if she was back on Earth, she would stand no chance of ever seeing Kaece again.

"Or maybe," he continued, "You can get over this whole depression thing away from *Brad* – you know, get your head straight, cause I don't want you doing any of that creepy suicidal stuff again..."

"It was an accident," Rebecca insisted.

She closed her mouth and inhaled, considering. He still had it all wrong. Brad wasn't the problem; Brad had been the solution – was supposed to be the solution, anyway. One thing he was right about, though – she was glad to be away from the wedding, free of the marriage. And as long as she was in Gaeadia, she could find Kaece; she could know whether or not Kaece had lived, whether or not her attempt at heroics actually helped. She'd never get the opportunity to find out, to get a thank you, to have a friendship, if she didn't stay in this world.

Her gaze moved to Alex, up from her bloodied shoes, and she smiled a small, but genuine smile. "You're too immature to survive in this world without me. So I suppose as long as we're here, you've got my word: No more creepy suicide stuff. I promise. Not that I'm admitting to anything."

DENIAL III
On the Road to Thalassa Harbor

SEBASTIAN MADIUS
OF IDAN, OLD MAEDIA, GAEADIA
17 YEAR OLD HEIR TO THE THRONE
OF HUMAN CIVILIZATION.

REBECCA SILAS
OF ALBUQUERQUE, NEW
MEXICO, "THE OTHER SIDE"
18 YEAR OLD METAKOSMOS
DAMSEL IN DISTRESS

ALEXANDER SILAS
OF ALBUQUERQUE,
NEW MEXICO,
"THE OTHER SIDE"
13 YEAR OLD
METAKOSMOS **HERO**

Goodbye Earth & hello magical
alternate reality! We got on the
Hadros - Sebastian's awesome walking
machine - and haven't stopped traveling
in days, except to clean Rebecca's hand
and to sleep. Me and Rebecca never really
did road trips back on "The Other Side"
so I think it's pretty awesome. We traveled
through farmland (dull except for the
burning crops), some meadows with
buffalo, horses, and big cats, and now we
in a "dangerous" mountain region.
ever since his act of heroics in Sow Endus,
Sebastian's been pretty stuffy. He never
wants to leave the Hadros.
Rebecca hasn't even bothered looking
the window. She's all zombied out
again. We're in a magical land! Come on!
least I have tons of handwritten books
random Maedians who actually did
explore. I get to read all about the land
we've randomly dropped into. Just you
wait Gaeadia. When I get the chance, I'm
to get out there and see everything!
–Alex
P.S. The calendar says "195 under
Cancer in the Afternoon." I think
that means we're still in July.

20

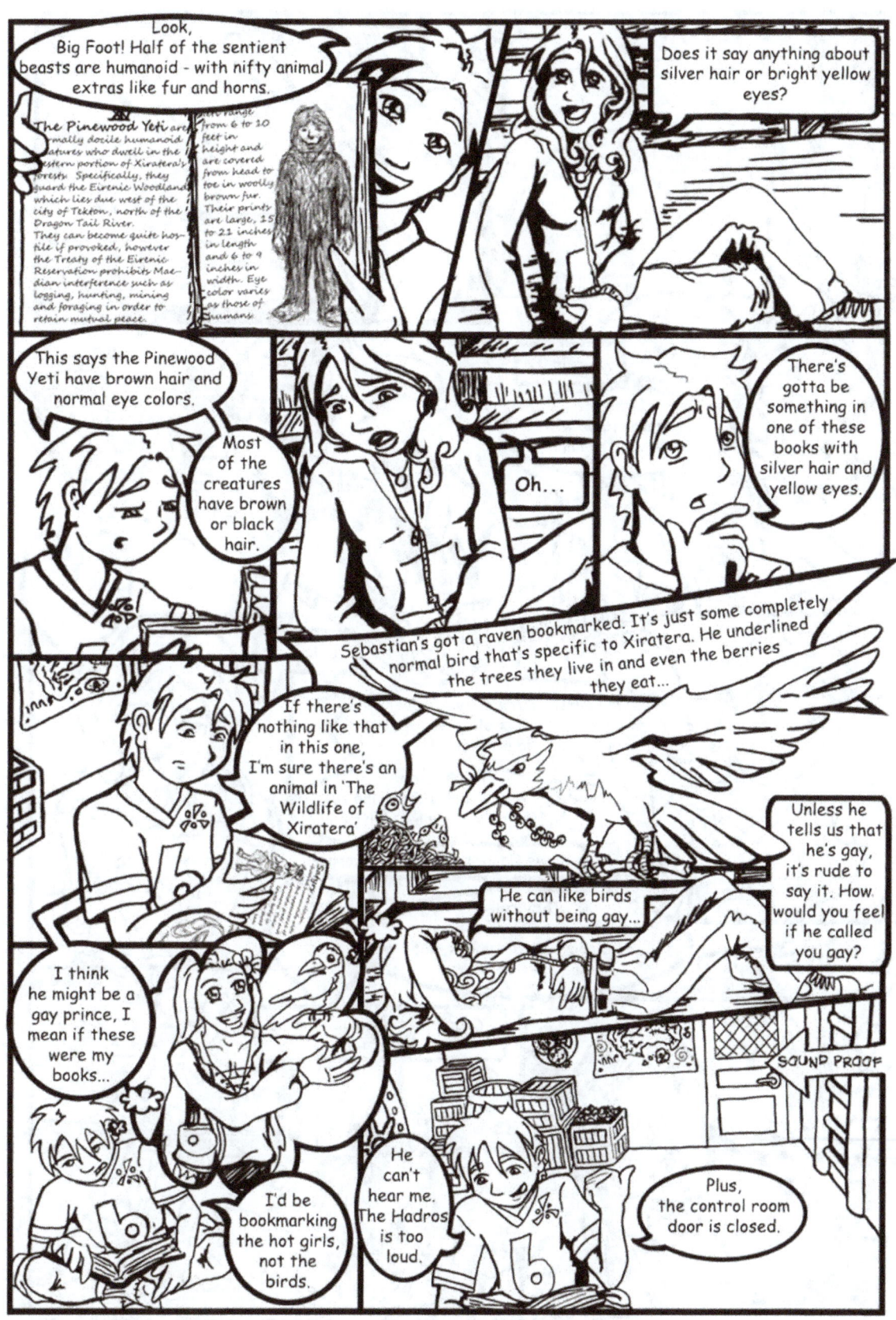

24

He's not talking about the men, he's advocating land massacre, pollution, and the destruction of the ozone layer. It's beautiful like a landfill is beautiful...

Do you think the pollution from this "better" world stacks with the pollution from our "corrupt" world, that is definately being destroyed like there's no tomorrow?

I'm not sure I understand your question, but for all intents and purposes, anything that exists in Gaeadia does not exist on the Other Side, and visa-versa, unless, of course, it crosses the Kosmos.

How about...

Anything can cross through a rift in the Kosmos, but there's no guarantee it could survive the dangers on the Other Side.

Haima Demons or Lykos? Can they cross over?

Even a creature as vile as this monstrosity here may not survive such an event. This Lykos may look human, but it is far from it. They are murderous beasts that know only violence and betrayal. We shall pray we never encounter one.

The Lykos

That's a little extreme, considering you've obviously never met one.

Our history with the Lykos is long and complicated, but I will summmarize: They were once regarded as our breathren, fellow Maedians, but they simply were not like us. Their wolf genetics drove them to horrible acts of violence and destruction. They had to be banished from Maedia, the Old Maedia long before we'd settled Neo Maedia, in order for Maedians to be safe from their beastial outbursts. Since Maedians settled on Xiratera, the Lykos have obliged to remain north of the very Skotos Mountains that we are currently traveling through.

SILAS

IV

As he guided the Hadros along the narrow path, as far away as the machine was able from the steep cliff, Sebastian reflected on the events of the recent days past. While his journey to Xiratera held the end goal of retrieving his father, he could not deny to himself a secondary motive lurking in his consciousness: adventure.

He had spent the greater portion of his seventeen years on the imperial isle of Idan. The small island held many wondrous things which, to him, held no interest. He could not wait to escape the sheltered world of manicured gardens and rigid architecture that had long become a lackluster manifestation of the culture he would be fated to preside over if his errand failed. From his boyhood, he had known the mundane life of an emperor was not for him. He longed for the excitement borne of exploration, the thrill of traversing an untamed land. All hope of that dream's fruition had vanished alongside Sebastian's father two constillaciouns prior, purloined so unjustly in the night's shadows, which seemed to swallow up the very memory of Stephan Madius' existence.

One could not simply disappear from Idan. An elite squadron of soldiers who surpassed in excellence all others on Gaeadia, known as the royal guard, was stationed at the palace. The palace itself spanned the entirety of the island, which, in combination with the Power of Madius, served to make it impenetrable, even to the shrewd and relentless Haima Demons. Yet, somehow his father had done the impossible and disappeared without a trace. His sire had been declared deceased, taken in the night by the bloodthirsty killers who had not infiltrated the palace in all of history. The likelihood of such an occurrence did not escape Sebastian; the odds were so impractical that he felt aghast at the ease with which such an explanation was accepted. Though Sebastian voiced his reservations regarding the future emperor's disappearance, his grandfather's attention was not kept long on such a matter. Sebastian's pleas to resume the search were greeted with nothing more than immediate dismissal from both the Emperor and his royal advisor, Vasilis. They refused even the simple task of acknowledging the marvel that Sebastian believed to be undeniable testimony to his father's whereabouts.

Sebastian's grandfather insisted that he 'put his father from his mind' and instead focus his energy on readying himself for the unjustly appointed task of assuming his place as the next emperor of Maedia. It did not take Sebastian more than the constillacioun of the Dioscuiri twins passing to decide that he would accept neither his grandfather's, nor the royal advisor's counsel. They were too stubborn to see the truth written in the vanes of the raven's unique feathers, and he was too devoted to the notion of an adventurous life unbridled by the chore of leadership. Oh, the disruption that such a fate would impart upon his personal ambitions! And thus, he surreptitiously boarded a ship traveling to the mainland of Old Maedia.

Safely away from the ever-watchful eyes of the palace's denizens, he was able to obtain a Hadros and the multitude of supplies he would require for the long excursion on the wild continent. He ordered the ros and his other goods be joined with the usual cargo of a soon-departing ship and, with it, he set sail for Xiratera.

The ship reached the port of Neo Maedia, at the southeastern tip of Xiratera, many days into the constillacioun of Karkinos. He disembarked rather than continue the maritime journey northward, in hopes of discovering clues of his father's whereabouts along the land route toward the central Polis, Thalassa Harbor. While his initial encounter with the locals proved to be little help in that regard, he found his disappointment assuaged by the grandeur of the country through which he traveled. Both the land's untamed beauty and the impressive engineering achievements manifested by the inhabitants' dedicated labor fascinated him.

Those living in Xiratera spent their entire lives from their infancy to senility toiling in interminable service to the greater good. Three generations past, the first immigrants from Old Maedia had arrived on Xiratera. Those initial laborers began the impressive network of railroads that spanned the entire eastern portion of the continent – from Thalassa Harbor in the north to Neo Maedia in the south. The railway eventually grew to encompass Sow Endus, then the westernmost settlement which later became the crossroads of Xiratera's civilization. The railway reached farther still, up to the eastern tip of the Dragon Tail River, an accomplishment greater than anyone had previously dreamed possible. Ever since the completion of this grandiose project, the Maedians of Xiratera endeavored to gather the abundant resources of the land. He wished the people of Idan could be as productive as these wondrous folk. Perhaps then, they wouldn't have so easily abandoned hope and pronounced with such definiteness his father's death even in the wake of the abysmal void of evidence.

One of the legs of the Hadros slid on a loose boulder, and the entire machine lurched towards the roiling waves far below. Sebastian pulled the control lever sharply to the left as the Hadros teetered one way and then the other before precariously rebalancing itself on the narrow ledge. To the west, mountains rose to majestic heights, snow dusting their upper ridges with a dazzling white that caught the sun's rays and multiplied them tenfold. To the east, the ocean rolled out from raucous breakers licking the coastline into the clear blue oblivion where sky and sea became indeterminable.

Sebastian sighed, reminding himself to be more cautious, then pushed the control levers forward again. If they were to reach Thalassa Harbor, he had no other choice but the ledge. The other pass through the Skotos Mountains was the tunnel through which the train tracks ran. That tunnel was not an option for the wide bodied, long-legged ros.

The control room door burst open and Alex entered the room babbling excitedly. He was a happy and curious boy, though he often seemed preoccupied by thoughts of violence. Sebastian suspected these violent tendencies sprang from the boy's desire to be heroic combined with the depraved influence of the barbaric world from which the Metakosmos had come. He rather enjoyed Alex's company, and as the boy was still young and impressionable, he theorized that a positive role model like himself might help quell Alex's darker tendencies.

"What happened? That felt like the Hadros almost flipped! All your books just pelted Rebecca again."

His words never seemed to make sense with the tone he used. Both he and Rebecca were often difficult for Sebastian to fully comprehend.

"It could have been far worse. Give Rebecca my apology if you would. And do return the books to their place on the shelf."

"Why do I always have to do it? I'm so bored! Rebecca does nothing, all the time, and I can only read so much in a day, you know? How about this: you put the books away and let me drive."

The Metakosmos knew nothing of how ros functioned, nor the countless hours of training someone must partake in to master the complex control mechanism. Sebastian wouldn't allow the only Hadros on this hemisphere to be rendered inert by untrained hands.

"I must concentrate, young Metakosmos. We are nearly to our destination. Do as I ask of you and keep our sleeping quarters tidy."

Frustration getting the best of him, he'd let the Power of Madius slip into his words once again. Had it any use, it would have been a small enough misuse of the Power to be admissible, but he reprimanded himself all the same.

As Alex departed, Sebastian considered the thought of Rebecca's continued listlessness. Rebecca had not taken the transition between worlds as well as her younger brother. She had been unenthusiastic and depressed since he first met her. In the coming and going moments of her alacrity, Sebastian found her detached friendliness and refusal to faun over him, regardless of his royal heritage, to be quite pleasant. Sebastian believed that if she were able to forget the savage world from which she hailed, she would come to love Gaeadia, and with that adoring acceptance of her magnificent new home she would find happiness.

Before he had traveling companions, the journey north towards Sow Endus had been largely uneventful. The southern lands had been a lush green punctuated by occasional patches of blue and purple wildflowers. Wheat fields had stretched to the horizon and rippled in the summer breeze around the villages of the countryside.

The sights had been amazing, but for the first time in his life, there had been no one there to share them with, not even a servant. By the time he reached Sow Endus, he had been desperate for human connection. Upon discovering Metakosmos, a rarity that few people were able to observe in their lifetimes, he believed it to be fate driving him on his adventure. His first act, as a great adventurer, would be to deliver the specimen of Metakosmos to safety in Thalassa Harbor, and eventually to Old Maedia.

The Hadros jolted, as if struck by an object overhead. He saw only the valley widening out below, the Polis of Thalassa Harbor spreading inward from the seaside. He cranked the valve that lowered the Hadros to the ground then turned towards the control room door. He had but made a step into the sleeping quarters when the sound of knocking came from the side of the Hadros.

Sebastian pulled the lever that opened the door's shutters. He was pleasantly surprised to see the familiar face of Clay Demarko beyond the slatted openings. Sebastian heaved open the door with eagerness.

"Overseer Demarko!"

His enthusiasm felt ill-met by the hard set lines of age around Demarko's mouth and eyes. The jaded expression he wore attested to the hardships he had seen since leaving Old Maedia, but otherwise he was the man Sebastian remembered, right down to his short, unruly, brown curls and bushy eyebrows complete with the matching mustache. On this day, unlike in the past, and much to Sebastian's curiosity, Demarko had donned a simple dockworker's uniform that failed to convey the position of power he held.

"Luck is on our side today! The good grace of Eos brought you on some business beyond the limits of your Polis. It was you with whom I have come to converse!"

"And here I was patrolling the area and spotted a Hadros, of all things peculiar. Now that I see that it is you, it explains how such a grand piece of machinery has come to my side of Gaeadia. Is your grandfather's presence among the day's miraculous oddities?"

Sebastian followed his gesture to the onyx Pegasus grazing serenely nearby right before Demarko leaned around him. The Overseer surveyed the inside of the Hadros and frowned at the sight of the two Metakosmos. Sebastian knew they were not the royal entourage that Demarko anticipated, but Sebastian was not visiting as a royal subject.

"No. He is not here with me. I have come on my own accord, in search of my father. He disappeared from the palace several constillaciouns past, and no one has had word of him since."

Demarko's expression drooped as Sebastian answered. He cleared his throat and scratched his mustache.

"That is unfortunate news, boy, on all accounts. Xiratera is no place for a young prince to play. If your father is dead, missing, what have you, then you are the next in line to become emperor. Last I heard, your grandfather, our emperor, had fallen ill"

His words bore a discernibly bitter undertone, but this news was hardly news at all. His grandfather's ailment was something of a chronic cough, an issue of the lungs that gave the doctors no pause. As they were not immensely worried, Sebastian too could excuse the illness.

"Gossip. He is ill, but not on his deathbed. He will survive long enough for me to locate my father."

"If you get yourself killed, there will be no Madius left to run the empire. All of Maedia will fall into chaos. Everything will be ruined."

The sharp note of anger in Demarko's voice concerned Sebastian. Wielders of the Power of Madius, be they so by birth or by selection, were intensively trained to control their emotions at all times. The tenet being that any powerful emotion, especially anger, could be extremely dangerous when paired with such power. This irked Sebastian greatly, especially since Demarko was not only a powerful Overseer, but also a family friend. They had a relationship of trust forged in a long standing history with one another; Sebastian felt wounded that Demarko would so harshly dismiss his attempt at locating his father, whom he had believed to also be Demarko's best friend.

In the days when his father was a young man pursuing his post-secondary studies, one of his teachers had been this man who, himself, had recently adopted the profession of educator and begun to teach philosophy of engineering. Stephan Madius was, as Demarko said often enough, the most intelligent student he'd ever been so well-fortuned to mentor. A friendship grew that would last for many years, and eventually lead to Demarko's assignment as Overseer of Mateopolis of Old Maedia. His competence as an overseer, and vast knowledge of modern technology, supported by a long list of literary works and advancements in engineering, led to his candidacy to the most coveted role in Maedian society, Overseer of the entire civilization of Neo Maedia.

Sebastian had been reading Demarko's theorems and poring over his contraption diagrams since he was a child. Some of his best reports had been on Demarko's theoretical schematics, up to and including the railway system of Xiratera. Free to exist in the world, unhindered by politics, he'd hoped to meet the man again as an intellectual on par with his father. It became apparent, that was not to be. Demarko was no different from his grandfather or Vasilis; he saw Sebastian not as a man of equal stature with whom to share ideas, but rather as a foolish child.

Sebastian gestured for the Metakosmos to wait, and then he followed Demarko down off of the Hadros to further the pressing conversation near the black flyer.

"Overseer, you must understand that I have come here to find my father, not to die myself, but to bring the empire to the best prosperity it can achieve. My father will make an excellent emperor, I believed you would understand that as you knew him well."

"Was is the key word, boy. Any Madius who has been missing for several constillaciouns past and sent no word is as good as dead, or he doesn't want to be found."

Demarko's utterance came with the feel of a heavy heart; he stared past Sebastian as the words left his lips, up over the Hadros, seemingly towards his own memories.

"I promise you, though, young prince, if you continue wandering around this untamed land, searching for your father, you will fail at your agenda and you will not leave this continent alive. You are prey to the creatures of this land, and they want your blood. It will be the deepest of tragedies, and I'd hate for it to come to such an outcome - but Xiratera is not a playground, and this is not a game."

Sebastian watched Demarko's drifting gaze shift from beyond him to refocus on Sebastian. He knew his own expression showed nothing, except perhaps his indifference to the Overseer's overly dramatic warning.

"I suggest you allow reason to absorb, take some time to consider before you say no. Come to my estate tonight. You will be my guests, and we can speak further. There is much out of place in Xiratera right now, as I'm sure you have learned in your travels."

"I accept your invitation, and look forward to a lively discussion. I am indeed more than a little curious about the Drakeon attacks."

Demarko bid Sebastian farewell, then mounted the Pegasus. The man Sebastian watched ascend into the sky was not the man he remembered so fondly. He sighed, and reminded himself to be patient.

Sebastian and the two Metakosmos set off on foot. They descended the ridge leading down into the Polis. Walking through Thalassa Harbor was moderately reminiscent of being home in Old Maedia. The buildings were constructed primarily of carved or cut stone, from marble to granite. Most were multi-storied, with ornate moldings and decorative trim in muted hues.

As they traveled deeper into the town, they passed the colosseum. It was constructed entirely of white stone, and supported by massive pillars. Each major Polis had a colosseum of similar construction, and held identical trials for contestants during the same time period.

"This is Xiratera's colosseum. All of Neo Maedia's youth partake in athletic training, making their bodies as fit as their minds, then every four years an Olympic game is held in which all graduates may compete for the title of champion. The entire territory gathers to watch. It is a time of great celebration. Isn't it a fantastic work of architecture?"

"So anyone who graduates high school can enter to become an Olympic gold medalist?"

As usual, Sebastian did not fully comprehend the meaning of Alex's question. He nodded with a smile of surety, though Rebecca had that look of skepticism she wore all too well.

"Colosseum means gladiators, right? Do you force people to fight criminals and caged animals?"

"Force? Most definitely not. Participation is not mandatory, but it is a great honor. And our criminals are banished from society, as you saw in Sow Endus - we do not kill them, even in gladiatorial matches."

"So you admit that you do have violent games."

"Traditions of old, I suppose it may seem somewhat violent, but not as violent as the games on the Other Side I am sure. They are never deadly, merely acts of competitive sport."

Rebecca huffed her discontent, while Alex looked onward to the colosseum with a sparkle in his eye that Sebastian assumed to reflect thoughts of victory. He found himself at a loss of words to convince them that civilized Gaeadia wasn't the horror they believed it to be.

As they crossed the railroad tracks, Sebastian noted the warehouses to their right, where the tracks ended. Here, he knew, resources were stored at the waterfront until they could be sent to Old Maedia via ship. He also noted that disheveled Maedians, refugees, were entering the town, walking along the railroad tracks. Their clothes were filthy, and riddled with unmended rips and tears. Their cheeks were hollow for want of food. He could only imagine how long they must have trudged to arrive in Thalassa Harbor from whatever location they began, not to mention the danger of the Skotos range in the night. Similarly to the fall of Sow Endus, it was a sorry sight to bear witness to and something he could have lived the rest of his days content to have never seen.

Buildings, divided up into shops and businesses offering every commodity and service to be found in the civilized world, lined the main street. As was typical in Maedia, the front of each shop was denoted by a sign, hung and masterfully carved or painted, proclaiming what was to be procured within. Porches boasting overhanging wooden roofs formed a covered walkway along both sides of the road.

The main street ended in a boardwalk leading out into the sea. Ships of various sizes and designs rested along its length. Two other boardwalks extended into the sea farther along the coast, allowing several large ships to be docked at one time. The boardwalk steps led down to a beautifully designed, yet weather-beaten, house. Over the door hung a sign bearing the title "Overseer." The house was built along the waterline, the landward side resting on the rocky shore and the seaward side on stilts.

The two Metakosmos paused to peer out across the vantage point. Sebastian observed their mesmerized gaze with a curious thought: had they never seen such beauty? Their world, a mirror of Gaeadia, would have had oceans, as far as he understood from lore.

"Wow. The ocean is crazy cool. I wish we had one near our house - look at those waves way out there! And seagulls! Look!"

"It's so vast... Endless. It makes you feel so small, like all of your problems are nothing in comparison. You'd just disappear into that void, and like your problems, you'd be nothing."

"That sounds morbid, like you're talking about dying. You promised you wouldn't leave me."

The way that the wind blew Rebecca's hair over her shoulder, giving Sebastian a perfect view of her wistful smile, made her look stunning. Any doubt that she had soul behind her sedentary nature vanished in those moments. The serenity in her voice as she replied made him feel that she could be the very visage of a goddess.

"No, it feels more like hope. In a world - two worlds - we can go anywhere. Anything is possible, right? This water that goes on forever, it's a reminder of just how possible it must be, somehow, someway. Like finding a needle in a haystack - I know that she is out there, alive and waiting."

"Okay, so that was less dark, but it was weird. Who are you talking about? Mom?"

Rebecca pouted and shrugged her shoulders, then ventured out onto the boardwalk, her sibling following on her heels.

"So not mom. Who then, Monique? I miss Monique. She was hot."

"Shut up, Alex. Just shut up."

Sebastian pitied the two Metakosmos. How naive they were, to think they would ever see anyone from their world again. The chance of encountering two rifts in the Kosmos in the same human lifetime was nonexistent. As the years passed, they would come to accept this, as Metakosmos before them had time and time again.

He knocked on the sturdy wooden door. Moments later, Demarko welcomed them in.

Cabinets and workbenches lined the walls; projects in progress and roughly sketched schematics covered nearly every available surface. The only clear area in the room was the long delicately carved dining table. Windows dominated the right wall of the room, framing a picturesque view of the sea.

While they took their seats, Demarko placed upon the table a steaming pot of stew, a loaf of bread, and a full mug for each of them. Demarko sat across from Sebastian, a harried expression on his face before he raised his mug and drained its contents. Sebastian cleared his throat.

"Before we speak further on any other matters, I must ask what you are doing to end the Drakeon attacks on this land. From what we saw traversing the town there are an alarming number of refugees in Thalassa Harbor. These attacks must be happening to a great many towns of Neo Maedia."

"Unfortunately that is the truth. The first attack happened over half a year back. As soon as I heard of the trouble, I sent messenger beasts to all the sentient natives of Xiratera, asking that they state their grievances, knowledge and allegiances so we may negotiate peacefully, and find a way to end these attacks."

"That is not sufficient action by any measure. These dragons have engendered casualties and destruction on our towns greater than even that of the Lykos revolt. They must be commanded to stop: you must go in person."

"I am following the same protocols in place in every Maedian territory, implemented by the Emperor. The only thing I must do is to be here in Thalassa Harbor to keep order when these refugees want services that Maedia doesn't offer in Xiratera. No, these people have no resolution here, and they've walked through the realm of Hades to get to this oblivion. And when people feel scorned, they can get a little unpredictable, a little uncaring, and – perhaps – turn to bite the very hand that feeds them. It no longer matters how loyal they may seem. That's my job, boy, to make sure order is kept, to make sure no one else gets hurt, here, in my Polis. It's the Emperor's duty to come command the dragons to stop attacking the towns and depleting his precious resources, you know it as well as I. My hands are tied in this matter."

"The resources are not significant to my grandfather. Nor are the lives of the replaceable workers of Xiratera. The travel is too far, and he is too old to concern himself with what he would likely consider petty. If he didn't care that my father went missing, why would he care about any of this? You are expected to deal with it, hands tied or not. When the problem is resolved, I'm sure he will order out a master crew of architects, builders, and more people for the jobs that are not being filled - but that is all you should expect."

"As I said, if I am to follow the laws of Maedia, I have done everything in my power to resolve the problem. I sincerely hope you are mistaken about Emperor Dorian's sense of mercy, for the fate of Maedia, of mankind, rests on his humanity. I pray he will come see to this side of Maedia and know their suffering."

"I will talk to the Drakeon, if you will not."

"Out of the question! You are to be the next emperor. Is your every idea fashioned out of sheer recklessness?"

For a second time this day, the man had raised his voice in an emotional rage, his scowl highly contrasted with Sebastian's impervious smile. Sebastian couldn't help but feel pride at his superior mask of stoicism. The man who he once held in such high regard perhaps was slipping too far from the rigorous standards set forth for Maedian rulers.

"My every idea is fashioned after doing what is right for all of Maedia"

"Whatever you do, may you do it prudently, and look to the end."

Demarko whispered the proverb, a suggestion that Sebastian use wisdom and consider the outcomes of his choices, and with it his display of anger waned to wariness. This quote, while insulting, was also puzzling. Sebastian believed he was doing what would be right for Maedia by finding and restoring its proper ruler. An individual like himself, who did not want to lead, leading the empire, would only create disorder. His acumen, though fine, paled in comparison to the capabilities of his father to see Maedia thrive. If, while accomplishing his task, he could also restore order to Neo Maedia by doing what the Overseer refused to do, there would be nothing but rejoicing for all of Maedia on all accounts. He couldn't fathom what other possible outcomes, what other end, could possibly exist. After all, even from his less careful decisions, good had already come. He had stumbled haphazardly upon the Metakosmos siblings.

"How rude of myself, I failed to give a proper introduction. These are my traveling companions, Rebecca and Alex Silas. They are Metakosmos who have recently arrived in our world. It was serendipitous that I stumbled upon them moments after their arrival and milliseconds before their would-be departure to the underworld. Had I not ventured to Xiratera, they would have been victims to the dangers of the wild continent."

"It is a dangerous place to fall into, especially in recent times. Your past experiences of luck, arriving unscathed, do not define your future survival here. This mission to find your father is foolhardy. You should have at least brought your grandfather and some of the royal guard."

"They wouldn't have come, or allowed me to do so, even if I pleaded. I am the best chance this side of Maedia has, and I am here. I am too young to be in charge of the empire, and I am not responsible enough to be an emperor. My father, however, is ready for it. I must find him. You have to understand."

"That is all well and good, boy, but your grandfather is ill, you admitted the truth behind the rumors yourself. If he dies, and you wind up dead because of this ridiculous search on a continent half a world away from where your father disappeared, what Madius will we have to be emperor then? None! Are you selfish enough to risk *that* for your childish ambitions? Do you think this is some kind of wives' tale? Accept that your father is dead. "

"You haven't even heard me out. I have good reason to believe my father is alive, and here on Xiratera. A raven, a sub-species found only on Xiratera, recently flew in through my window carrying a scrap of white cloth trimmed in silver, then promptly died. It was cloth from my father's royal robes; the material was exactly the same. There is no way a bird could, or would, make it across that sea without being commanded to do so. My father sent it to me as a sign that he is still alive, and I will not rest until I find him."

To Sebastian's surprise, Demarko snarled, slurring his rebuttal.

"Damned boy! It was but a bird that lost its course and became stranded at sea. It landed on the first land it could find – of course exhaustion took it. And a scrap of cloth means nothing. There is plenty of white and silver cloth in all of Gaeadia. You need to put this nonsense to rest."

Sebastian fell into wounded silence. There would be no convincing Demarko. He had come expecting aid and friendship, only to be rejected in the same unfeeling manner as he had been by the emperor. It was becoming abundantly clear that no one in a place of power would understand, let alone support, his quest. He felt betrayed, and utterly alone.

"Is this beer? It tastes way too good to be beer."

Alex cradled one of the mugs in both hands, a joyous smile lighting his face. Sebastian smelled his mug: it was indeed ale. Likely a sweet ale, honey-infused perhaps, from a local brewery. Such drinks gave workers a needed escape from the duress created by their intensive labor. As Sebastian returned his mug to the table, Rebecca snatched at her brother's cup. When he pulled out of her reach, she sat back in her chair with an angry huff.

"We're all underage, what kind of a person serves teenagers booze? He's just barely a teenager, even, he's just a kid."

"I can take it, lay off."

"He looks old enough to drink to me. You're not on the Other Side anymore, honey. It's a whole new world, forget all of the customs that held you back in that infernal place."

Rebecca stiffened and scowled at him.

Demarko only seemed to find the situation laughable, chuckling at their tense silence. It became clear to Sebastian in that moment how intoxicated Demarko was, and likely had been since their first meeting that day. He suddenly understood the rosy cheeks, nonsensical speech patterns and uncharacteristic aggression. It seemed that being Overseer of Xiratera had not gone well for him. It had worn him down, caused him to turn to drink, like a common worker. Being Overseer of this wild land, away from the careful watch of the Emperor and the stifling rules of the palace, seemed a dream come true to Sebastian. He had to assume it was the Drakeon attacks with no way to quell the fallout, which had driven the Overseer to this state of intoxication.

"Can I go look at your inventions, Mr. Demarko?"

"By all means. They exist to be viewed and toyed with."

Alex rose to his feet, still treating the ale as a coveted treasure. Seemingly rebellion fueled, he swaggered to the nearest wall and began admiring one of the half-finished contraptions. While he enjoyed his assault on his sister's authority, Rebecca paid him no heed. She did nothing and said nothing. Sebastian ate his soup, letting the weight of tension envelop the room.

When Alex returned, he had a small crossbow with a winding mechanism on the side gripped in his fist.

"This is awesome! The crank is suppose to make it auto fire, well.. semi-auto fire - right?"

"Hahah, there is no fire used in a mechanical device such as this! The crank is supposed to knock a small arrow in a single twist, the gears inside the body of it lever the high pressure needed. And it does do that, but the problem is the aim, the quick knock causes it to jolt - and then the damned thing can't hit a target the size of a bear with accuracy. Just as well use a normal bow, this design turned out so poorly."

"I bet mounted to a solid surface it wouldn't jerk much - couldn't really - like mounted machine guns. I bet I could figure out how to make it work better."

"An aspiring engineer, are we? Why don't you take it and try? It's useless to me. Send me word if you ever get it to function properly, and I'll make sure you get due credit for your part in its fabrication."

"Seriously? I can keep it? Cool!"

"Now you're giving him weapons? What next? Drugs?"

As much as Sebastian didn't understand her complaint with Alex having ale, he agreed about the issue of weapons. Weapons were not for civilian use. Only the Guard, meant to protect Maedians from the Haima Demons, were allowed to carry weapons. Sebastian's sword, while authentic and not exactly something he should be carrying, wasn't a weapon in his eyes. It was an artifact taken from the palace - Byran's sword, crafted by the Minotaur of Xiratera as a gift. To Sebastian it served as proof the man who wrote the journals was real and truly did all that his tales expressed. It was an inspiration.

"I have never seen a bow such as this. Is the design registered and approved by the scholars for production?"

"No. It wasn't designed for the Guard. It was merely an experiment meant for hunting here on Xiratera."

"Any weapon, even a nonfunctional one meant to serve as a tool for hunters, needs to be registered and approved by the scholars before a prototype should ever be created. This is immensely illegal."

"I know the laws. I'm an Overseer. The problem is, it takes longer than a constillacioun for the plans to be delivered to the scholars overseas, almost another for it to be reviewed - then most likely denied, with a request for changes before it's approved, and then another constillacioun passing before that denial reaches me. It was but an experiment, and this was the only one. There are much larger problems for Maedia to concern itself with than my failed experiments. Or do you disagree?"

"Alex. Weapons should never be used to harm, they are a symbol of violence - a descent into societal destruction. We must resolve our differences via amicable negotiation, not bloodshed. I suggest you leave the weapon here."

"You heard him, go put it back."

"No. He said I could have it. I just want to make it work better, I didn't say I was gonna go murder anyone jeez! If anything, I'd use it to protect us from the dragons."

"We must not slay the dragons, Alex. I am sure they are attacking with good reason. We must go and speak to their leader, listen to their grievances and resolve them. Then they will stop attacking."

Rebecca sat seething at her brother while Demarko sighed heavily.

"I already told you this is a foolish quest, Sebastian. But if you desire so strongly to disarm the boy, why not command him to leave the bow?"

"I would if I could. As you well know, many Metakosmos change, develop inhuman abilities when they cross through the magical barrier that separates our two worlds. *These* Metakosmos seem to have gained a total resistance to the Power of Madius. My power is completely ineffectual on either of them."

Demarko perked up at this statement, interested for what seemed like the first time since their arrival.

"If this is so, they can not be controlled. Immunity to the Power of Madius would make them quick enemies of the royal palace."

"I'm sure it must exist for a good means to an end, since all powers are gifts from the gods. Test it yourself, it's quite fascinating, albeit frustrating when they are so apt to continue the violent behavioral patterns of their world."

Demarko held out his empty mug to Rebecca and commanded her with the Power of Madius echoing in his voice to refill it. Sebastian watched with great fascination, excited to see another's Power fail. Demarko's Power arguably held greater strength than Sebastian's, since it came from the Emperor's ability, the most potent of all. Long ago, the Madius family had discovered that the eldest Madius always held the greatest sway of mind, and the less members with the Power, the stronger the Power of Madius held to the thoughts of those affected. Overseers like Demarko only harnessed the Power given them through the use of technology, a circumstance which Sebastian wasn't completely familiar with.

Rebecca raised her eyebrows, her irritation apparent, but she silently pushed her ale filled stein towards him. Sebastian wondered if she was slightly affected, having obliged to give him more ale, but rejected the idea of filling his mug.

Demarko took her drink, chugged it down, then slammed the stein on the table. He again, proffered his empty mug. "You will go fill my mug, girl. Get up."

"How about, no? You have legs. Fill it yourself."

She stood up as she spoke, her face twisted in a grimace of contempt. She walked towards the front door. Sebastian stood and called out after her.

"Rebecca, wait."

"I'm not an experiment, and I'm not doing anything for that jerkwad. He said forget about my social obligations, so consider this me taking his advice. Good luck

Sebastian."

She slammed the door behind herself hard enough to make the wall hangings wobble. Sebastian swallowed, he felt ashamed for having started such a disagreement. He apologized to Demarko.

"I should have warned you to be sensitive in how you tested the Power. She is quite strong willed, and is suffering depression from the transfer between worlds. I am sure she did not mean to dishonor your hospitality."

"Think nothing of it, her display of uncontrolled emotion was refreshing in a way. These Metakosmos are a most special gift to Gaeadia. You must make sure they do not become entangled in your fatal errand to track down a dead man."

"I have no intention of getting anyone, including myself, killed. Thank you for hosting us, Overseer. I am sorry we could not come to a better understanding, but I greatly enjoyed the stew."

Sebastian sighed, glancing out the seaward windows. The sky, which had darkened while they ate, had become close to black despite the Hemera guided sun. The tide had risen to the point that sprays of foam drenched the side of the house.

"Must you leave so soon? Tomorrow a shipment of lumber sails to Old Maedia, both you and your companions may decide to board it, were you to perhaps consider it overnight?"

"No, we'd best be going. I'd like to be on our journey eastbound before the storm breaks."

"The storm is a good reason to stay. One night, boy. I want you to reconsider this search for your father, and this mission to the Drakeon. I would highly prefer to see you again one day, alive and being crowned Emperor of Maedia."

He grasped Sebastian's shoulder in a fatherly way as he said this, reminding Sebastian of the past. But Sebastian hadn't forgotten in such short time, that this man was not the same man he'd known before. It struck him to wonder where Professor Clay Demarko's family had gone, he appeared to live in the Overseer's manor alone. The storm moved quickly, and if he wasted much more time he'd have to bunker down in Thalassa Harbor under Nyx.

"I will find my father and end this trouble with the Drakeon, we will talk more when I return."

"Sebastian, please, if you go to the Drakeon, you will most assuredly die... and Maedia will die with you."

"There has been no response to your messenger beasts. Even if I do not find my father, I must go to the Drakeon. These attacks must be stopped, or there will be few people left to rule, by me or anyone else. Goodbye friend."

Sebastian led the way out, Alex hovered behind long enough to thank Demarko for the weapon again.

"Don't worry Mr. Demarko, I will perfect the crossbow and protect Sebastian. You'll get to see him become Emperor someday, I promise."

"The tides of the Fates rise around us all, and I fear what has begun has no good end."

Once outside, they found Rebecca settled on the boardwalk watching the waves roll in. She didn't so much as glance at them as they approached her. Sebastian wished his last few hours with her had not been so filled with turmoil.

"I apologize for that situation, I meant no harm."

Sebastian offered Rebecca a hand. She took it and he pulled her to her feet.

"No big deal."

"The Overseer was right about one thing; my quest will be long and dangerous. The two of you should take a ship to Old Maedia tomorrow. This continent is not the place for someone who has barely entered Gaeadia. You should be somewhere safe, where you can learn the ways of peace and solidarity. I'd like to put you in a room at the tavern"

She looked him in the eyes, her determination and sincerity a reflection of his own. He felt his heart beating against his ribs, amazed at how much of a physical reaction she caused him by mere looks. He didn't want to see her go.

"We're not going to Old Maedia. I'm not leaving this continent. I want to be *here*, dangerous or not."

"We're from the Other Side, remember? Danger is nothing to us. If you're going on an epic quest, you're gonna need our help."

"You truly wish to help me find my father?"

"Hell yeah we do! And we want to make sure those dragons never torch another town again. We're in it to win it, Sebastian, like it or not."

Rebecca touched his shoulder and gave him a reassuring smile. Maybe it wasn't worth getting so excited over, but Sebastian beamed. He had come to Thalassa Harbor seeking friendship and aid from an old friend. Instead, two people who owed him nothing had chosen to become his friends and traveling companions. He wouldn't spend another day seeking his father in solitude with loneliness eating away at his sanity. In spite of the incoming storm and constant deterrents, he felt hopeful.

CHAPTER 5

Rebecca leaned against the earthen clay bricks of a building she assumed to be a bar of some sort. No one came or went from the plain oak door: the residents of Thalassa Harbor instead stood, sat, or aimlessly paced back and forth in the roads.

Sebastian and Alex had gone into the building across the street to get supplies for the "long journey ahead," but Rebecca opted out. She'd already had her fill of personal interactions with the Maedians. Their air of superiority reeked of imperialism, a holier-than-thou demeanor that seemed capable of justifying actions like slavery; at the same time, they preached love, peace, and fairness. Irritation crawled through her veins at the very thought of the Maedian paradox.

A group of them huddled together at the edge of the park catty-corner of the tavern, staring at her with an eerily passive curiosity. Their placated expressions were framed by unkempt hair. The thin torn fabrics they wore offered little protection from the icy gusts sweeping in from the ocean. They shivered like a collective entity when the chilling wind hit. Despite the Maedians' discomfort, they all wore a calm smile, a slight upward turn of their mouths, that made Rebecca shift her weight from one foot to the other. Was it Demarko's power that had swept over them like the cold breeze and stripped away their ability to concern themselves with worldly necessities? She wondered if they had any free will left, or if he'd managed to command away all capacity for desire. It wasn't hard to imagine them standing hunched against the elements, awaiting a long and excruciating starvation, free of complaints, with nothing more than a tranquil smile.

Rebecca shuddered and pulled up her hood, turning away from the crowded, grassy field in the city center. Demarko's house stood out in stark contrast against the horizon. Swirls of deep grey clouds marbled the sky behind floating seagulls on the ocean breeze above billowing sails. Rising waves and frothy foam cast a rough appearance across the water's surface. Lightning flashed in the distance, streaking the sky as it struck the ocean. Thunder followed, a low rumble that signaled the potential danger of the encroaching storm. That which Gaeadia considered dangerous seemed only to bring her solace. When the lightning struck the horizon again, the thunder echoed louder – closer than before.

"Did you require any other supplies?" Sebastian's voice cut through the elements' symphony. He held two crates of coal, while the torrent of wind whipped through his ponytail, which snapped back and forth in the tumult, striking his face and neck.

Rebecca shook her head.

When he started for the Hadros, Rebecca followed. Alex carried more supplies with a small box of mechanical parts balancing on top of them. That weapon Demarko had given him smacked against his thigh with each step he took, a soft thwap that perpetually reminded her of its existence.

"I can't believe that guy Demarko is in charge of anything. Does he get off on giving kids guns and beer? And what was that whole mind control thing he tried to pull on me? Is that what people in Gaeadia do when they want something? They just violate peoples' minds and rape them of their free will?"

"Violate...?" Sebastian puzzled aloud. "I think you may have the wrong impression. The Power of Madius is not mind control, it is merely a power that has the capacity to alter thoughts. To a Metakosmos, it may appear as mind control, but the speaker does not have the ability to control the individual receiving the command. It is more akin to an encouragement for the persons spoken to; something of an ardent desire to obey, really. They retain their will, and in fact use it to enact the criteria of the command. Even so, the Power of Madius is reserved only for circumstances of dire need."

She felt suddenly aware of the strange serenity that washed over Samuel Miller; she understood why Sebastian's words had such an inherently calming effect. He'd mind-controlled the man. Sebastian had robbed Samuel Miller of his identity; she'd heard him announce that Maedia was his life. Without thoughts of his home, what was left of the man she'd slapped? He probably sat on the outskirts of Sow Endus, picking blades of grass and awaiting the same starvation the mollified citizens of Thalassa Harbor could expect.

"That's awesome!" Alex interjected. "You have the ability to do mind tricks, like Jedi!"

"What is a Jedi?" Sebastian's eyebrows pressed together in confusion.

"It's not important," Rebecca asserted before Alex had the opportunity to geek out about *Star Wars* to an unknowing victim. "What *is* important is that you can't use that power anymore. You can't do that to people, it's wrong."

"As future Emperor, it is my duty to use my power in appropriate situations," he replied. "The Power of Madius is the means in which we maintain peace within the empire. Banishment, the ultimate punishment for those who disturb the social order, would not be possible without the influence of the Power's magic. It requires great consideration and responsibility to wield this Power, and the choice to do so is not made lightly."

"But you're not just *maintaining order*," she argued. "Those are *people*, they have thoughts and desires of their own. Making them forget or forcing them to do things that they don't believe in is worse than killing them – you're turning them into empty shells with no identity! And as if stealing their souls isn't bad enough, you have to go and do things like tell them to wait like cattle for slaughter with death looming over them every second of every day, or throw them from their homes like unwanted pets

45

when they do anything that doesn't match your perfect little utopia. I would choose being napalmed by a dragon fireball over the slow, torturous death by the Power of Madius."

Alex stared at her, a crooked smile on his face. He looked proud of her, which made her feel awkward. Sebastian's expression made her feel even more awkward. His face remained a blank, neutral slate as though he hadn't heard her. Was he seriously going to pretend she hadn't called him, Mr. Love and Peace, a murderer? The silence, what she took as an admission of guilt, lasted the rest of their walk into the outskirts of the city.

Once they arrived at the Hadros, Rebecca turned back toward Thalassa Harbor, taking one final moment to marvel at the churning sea – the chain lightning fragmenting the dark sky. Alex climbed into the Hadros and Sebastian passed the supplies up into the machine's belly.

After they finished shuffling supplies, Sebastian placed his hand on her shoulder. "I hope that on our journey together, you will see that I am honorable. I do not, will not, cause anyone harm. Samuel Miller was a danger to the good people of Sow Endus, and now they are safe and he has a good prospect of finding a home amongst the peaceful Pinewood Yeti to the west, or with the Minotaur in the deep south. He will live on and remain exactly who he was, barring the desire to return to Sow Endus, or any Maedian dwelling."

"I don't like it." She turned to him with a deliberate pout of her lips, her eyebrows raised to create the fool-proof puppy dog eyes. "Could you please not use your Power as long as I'm with you?"

"Well," he chuckled softly to himself and nodded. "Very well, I shall avoid it save life threatening situations during our travels."

"Thank you," Rebecca smiled.

"Though, I am obligated to inform you that our first destination beyond Maedian civilization is Drakeon Peak, and I will need to converse with the leader of these fire dragons. From what I have read, dragons can be very... intense... and more likely than not will require a bit of a nudge in the right direction from the Power. That is, of course, if we would like their full cooperation."

"I'm going to assume you mean they're life threateningly 'intense' because they're dragons, and not because you just need an excuse for another circumstance in which mind-control is 'non-harmful.' "

"I knew you would understand," Sebastian clapped her on the back. "Now, we must get traveling – dark is but a short while away and the storm is fast approaching."

Rebecca pondered, as Sebastian disappeared inside the Hadros, if the enormous bronze machine would heat like an oven and roast them if lightning struck it. Perhaps, she mused, it would just electrocute them. She gazed up the body of the Hadros, curious to know if there was anything on the roof to attract the lightning's strike. She contemplated climbing the thick cables running up one of the limbs to check, when the engine roared to life.

Alex leaned out of the machine, "What are you doing? Come on."

She shrugged half-heartedly and climbed into the Hadros. She lingered in the doorway looking at the ladder built into the wall between the doors to the bathroom and the engine room. It led directly to a hatch that opened onto the roof.

Rebecca wondered aloud while Sebastian pulled the big door closed behind her. "What is the roof of the Hadros like?"

"The roof? Rebecca, time is of the essence, why waste time on mundane subjects like the roof?" He sighed. "I will be happy to show you the emergency release, and the unremarkable plane of bronze that is the roof, in better weather and at a better time."

"Such as when we're at Dragon Peak?" She wondered how long the travel would take. When she'd examined the map beside the engine room she'd only bothered to take note of the Lykos territory in relation to Thalassa Harbor.

"Drakeon Peak," he corrected. "It is where the fire dragons born of the volcanoes, the Drakeon, dwell, not all dragons. But no, not there. Our next destination is the westernmost town in Xiratera. We must leave the Hadros there, in Tekton, and finish our travels on foot, but I will discuss more about that with you when we are closer. There is a long traverse west across the worst of the Skotos before I would consider us safe enough to make plans or waste time with the roof."

With those final words, he disappeared back into the engine room and closed the door behind him, creating a barrier that separated him from them until they stopped for the night. Alex studied her expression in silence. She felt like a guinea pig, some lab experiment being examined beneath the microscope; the sensation of his eyes boring into her soul, trying to read her thoughts, was disquieting.

The bed offered consolation as it always had. Sleep would spare her too much discomfort. The steady, sickening motion of the Hadros began and she closed her eyes.

"You promised," Alex griped. When Rebecca peeked with one eye from under her arm, she saw him sitting at the workbench still watching her. "You were thinking about trying to jump off the Hadros, weren't you?"

The accusation was so incredulous, that Rebecca snorted laughter. "Right."

"Don't laugh, and quit bullshitting me. You've been acting weird forever, but you're even weirder ever since we got here. It's like one minute you're that lump with its soul sucked out by Brad, and then suddenly you're smiling, excited and caring about stuff that you used to care about. Like the Rebecca that played with me and dad during game nights. Are you bi-polar or something?"

47

"No," she snapped defensively, sitting up. Annoyance burned in the pit of her stomach.

"Then you're up to something and I'm not letting it go until you tell me."

Her true reasoning, about conductivity and their odds of mortality in the storm, she would never tell him. So, instead, she changed the subject, "I saw a Lykos in Sow Endus."

"Really?" He perked up.

"Yeah," she nodded. "I helped her... She was injured. I bandaged her leg."

"A werewolf needed your help. Okay, yeah. In your dreams."

"Dreams and reality all blur together for me, especially since we got here," Rebecca assented, peeved that he didn't think she'd seen a Lykos but relieved he wouldn't go blabbing it to Sebastian.

"That's 'cause you sleep too much," he teased. "There's a pretty cool journal by one of the old emperors. His name was Byran Madius, the Explorer. That's what the book is called anyways. You should check it out, it's the closest thing to a novel Sebastian's got."

She shrugged, flopping back down and closing her eyes. So what if she'd made it up? How rapidly his interest dissipated was more frustrating than his accusatory stares.

"He has a chapter in there about the Lykos," he continued. "I think it's about the Lykos villages, I'm not sure, I just flipped through it. But I bet you'd like it if you're dreaming about werewolves. Like healing them and stuff. What happened next?"

"Well," Rebecca began, unable to keep the smile from her face at the opportunity to finally talk about Kaece to someone. "I didn't exactly *heal* her, I just tried to do what I could... I don't even know if I did enough, but I want to believe I did. I don't know if she lived, I'm so afraid for her I just can't stop thinking about it. I want to see her again." She finished, then added, "You know, to make sure she's okay."

"Yeah," Alex laughed. "Dreams are like that, like this one time - okay, that doesn't matter - The point is you can daydream her back. Then you can make up your own ending 'cause you control what happens."

Daydreaming about Kaece wouldn't bring her back, but she couldn't expect Alex to understand that. She shook her head, "I wish it were that easy."

"It is! It's easier if you have something to base it on, though. You could just close your eyes and pretend you and Monique are Lykos together, werewolves fighting crime and saving the helpless animals of Maedia!"

"You think Monique would give a damn about saving animals?" Rebecca had to laugh, a strained laugh that betrayed all of the despair she felt when Monique's name came up. Her heart ached in her chest, the slow blanket of suffocating pain all too eager to wrap her in its fatal embrace. The darkness that engulfed her after she'd lost the light of her best friend felt like perpetual nothingness.

"So maybe Monique wasn't into cute furry critters like you, but she *did* like to pick fights. And she always won somehow, like she had some kind of sneaky trick up her sleeve. I bet being a werewolf with superhuman speed and strength would be right up her alley. She could just take whatever she wanted and never have to fight for it, not like she did when she was human."

Rebecca could see his own fantasy had gone on long enough; the glazed look in his eyes giving away the daydream of Monique with black claws and long, silver hair. She rolled her eyes. "Why do I even try to talk to you?"

"Because you know I'm right," he snickered, "If Monique were here with us, she'd already have Sebastian wound around her finger and he'd be commanding armies to conquer all of Xiratera for her. Plus, I'm just pure awesome."

"Do the jokes never stop?" she groaned. Leaning across the bed, she grappled Alex into a head-hug and gave him a hard noogie. "Let's see how you like it when *I* pick a fight."

He yelped in surprise and started writhing to get out of her hold. With a little wiggling and smacking her hands, he escaped her barrage of head-knuckling and cheek-pinching. "Hey! Cut it out, I'm working here."

"Working?" Rebecca challenged, raising her eyebrow at him with a skeptical smirk.

"Yeah, working. I'm going to make this cross-bow shoot with better accuracy, and I want to switch up the way the lever pulls so I can mount it on my forearm. It'll be wicked cool once I'm done. But you gotta let me work."

Why were boys always so obsessed with weapons? Between Alex with his psuedo-gun and Sebastian's massive tree-crushing Hadros, she should've hardly been surprised Alex wanted her to read some dead guy's journal. After all, her proper place was reading about the daring tales of men, not experiencing them for herself. She may as well have been knitting like the good wench she'd sworn to be for to the god who wouldn't listen.

Then again, perhaps he'd been trying to egg her on – encourage her to act more like one of the guys and get impassioned about destroying something. Once upon a time, the time he'd referred to when he brought up game nights, she'd been more like one of the guys. She'd been oblivious to social stigmas, those stereotypes that governed every girl's way of life. Before her adolescence, animals both stuffed and real had been her favorite plaything, then she graduated to Legos, toy cars and 'Cops and Robbers.' The Barbies, fake plastic food and games of 'House' held little to no interest for her; it was easy to get into playing with her kid brother because they liked the same things.

———————————

Rebecca flipped through the sketchbook of terrible drawings and frowned at the howling coyote that looked like the scribbles of a five year old. She'd spent hours trying to perfect it, just the same as each previous drawing for the portfolio due one week into Freshman year, but she still wanted to flush it down the toilet.

"Oh. My. God," came the exaggerated words of someone truly shocked by a disgusting sight.

Rebecca snapped her book shut, looking up to see the teenage girl who confidently pushed the school dress-code with cut-off short-shorts that were just a tad too short, exposing the full length of both tanned, toned legs. Her long black mane of hair, perfectly styled to frame her face, hid her naked shoulders. The sparkle of the girl's jewelry paled in comparison to the mischievous glint in those shining dark eyes as she gave Rebecca a deliberate once-over.

"Are you *seriously* wearing *overalls*? What are you, a farmer?"

The two girls who stood behind Monique laughed, cruel and full of mockery. Rebecca's face felt hot from the sudden attention on her, because the eyes of everyone seemed to follow Monique wherever she went. She tried to hide her face with her hair, to not look the lioness in the eyes, and hoped the moment of derision would pass.

Too hopeful. Monique snatched the baseball cap from Rebecca's head. She placed the hat sideways atop her own head and rolled her eyes upward, and slouched exaggeratedly. "Hyuck, lookit me, aren't I a perty boy? Der-her! I wanna kiss girls!"

Rebecca's embarrassment evaporated, boiled away by the burning anger of sheer annoyance. A girl that bullied people was still just a girl underneath it all, regardless of what other people thought. What was scary about a girl? She stepped down from her seat on the concrete table and put her face right in front of Monique's.

Rebecca could feel the girl's hot breath on her, their eyes locked and she stood rigid. She could see, beneath the surface of cruel amusement, the surprise – the vulnerability in those dark eyes.

"Give that back," she demanded, keeping her voice even. "It's not yours, and you aren't funny."

Monique stepped back and threw the hat into the dirt. Scorn colored her frustrated tone as she scoffed. "Take it, then, loser."

But Rebecca refused to take the bait; she waited, staring Monique down. The glimmer in the girl's eyes told Rebecca a tale – she wasn't just surprised that Rebecca had fight in her. More than Monique had been beaten, she'd been impressed. Beyond the facade of unrelenting mockery, the most popular girl in school liked her – she liked this loser. That approval was something, once Rebecca could see it, that she wanted more sincerely than she'd ever wanted anything before. Fearful Monique would turn her back and forget the moment, remembering nothing but the tomboy who couldn't draw, Rebecca grasped for something – anything.

She blurted, "If I can be more like you, if I change.... Can I sit with you tomorrow?"

Monique's calculating gaze roamed over Rebecca's body, taking her in as a whole. Both eyebrows raised, her head bobbed from side to side as she appraised Rebecca. She clicked her tongue against her teeth, followed by a disbelieving "hmmm..." Once satisfied, she shrugged. "You could *never* be like us, Loser. Go ahead and try."

After countless hours poring over teen fashion magazines and endless dollars in wiped-away makeup, Rebecca knew she would be the girl Monique had challenged her to be. The need for Monique's approval drove her to transform herself; the tomboy Alex remembered with such fondness disappeared, replaced with a girl so femme no one would ever question her femininity again. She would sit down at their table with a confident smile and dare Monique to shoo her away the same way she'd been dared to become something more.

_____

Rebecca sighed, rolling onto her side. Thoughts, painful memories, of Monique plagued her. Their whole friendship was such a quick, hurtful blur that would never have happened if she hadn't won Monique's approval that day. They wouldn't have spent days on end together, practically attached at the hip – Monique went everywhere with the Silas family, and Rebecca went everywhere with her. They were inseparable, until one day Rebecca found herself to be the odd one out: she was the only single girl in the group.

In truth, she didn't want a boyfriend, nor did she like Monique having one. She reasoned that her boyfriends had gotten in the way of their friendship, occupying more and more of Monique's time in ways which Rebecca couldn't tag along. She tried to ignore the dysfunctional lack of desire to be with a boy, but she felt guilty – terrified that they would call her out as the extraneous factor in their equation of girl, boy, girl, boy... So when the nobody football player Bradley Logan asked her out, she agreed. He wasn't intelligent enough to realize he'd been caught in a trap, and as obsessive as he could get about Rebecca, he wasn't demanding enough to keep her from spending time with her friends. She'd kept him dangling for nearly two years when everything began to crumble around her.

It started with Monique's new boyfriend. The older guy wasn't a high schooler, Rebecca doubted that he even graduated. Monique came around less and less until the lunch table was nothing but Rebecca and the two girls she could hardly call friends. Then, when Monique officially dropped out in the middle of their senior year, they completely stopped talking to her. She'd been abandoned, left to suffer the smothering adoration of Brad with no reprise. Monique was gone, and with her went Rebecca's love for life. She slowly withered, existing as little more than her mother's rag-doll or Brad's pet, until even those duties felt trivial.

Though Kaece was nothing like Monique, she had done the very same thing Monique did that first fateful day; she looked Rebecca in the eye and dared her to prove her worth. The Lykos wasn't separated from her by social status like Monique was; Kaece was separated by a racial divide cleaved by fear that Rebecca had no idea how she would find her way across.

The divide was just another part of the challenge; to Rebecca, Kaece was just as human as Maedians and Metakosmos. The Lykos could be hurt, scared; she could be happy or in love. Rebecca refused to let a mere barrier stop her from following her heart the same way she'd devoted herself to winning over Monique. This new trial promised to be more intensive. If she put all of her energy, day in and day out, into finding Kaece, she was sure the friendship they would develop would reflect that investment. The transformation from loser to best friend happened quickly with Monique; the abandonment, too, had been sudden.

She had faith that, with enough time, she would find Kaece and have someone in the world who would never abandon her. She let the Hadros' sway pull her into an uncomfortable afternoon slumber, where even the hopelessly impossible could lay way to a happy ending.

CHAPTER 6

She awoke to the sound of a drawer closing. Her eyes fluttered open and darkness greeted them; it was still the middle of the night.

"Alex!" She scolded in a harsh whisper.

He shifted inside the cabinet, his pillow rustling against the interior. Sebastian snored lightly beside her. She strained to hear any other sounds but the blood pounding in her ears made it impossible.

Objects in the Hadros took shape as her eyes adjusted to the pitch-blackness. The vague form of an intruder stood stone-still, blending in with the shadows. Rebecca's heart raced – was it a criminal, a thief scouring the Hadros for valuables? A banished Maedian here to exact their revenge on the unsuspecting prince? As she struggled for answers, Alex's breathing fell into a rhythm of snores accompanying Sebastian's. The thief moved quickly, silently, up the ladder. They disappeared through the hatch in the roof.

The hatch, however, didn't close behind them. Rebecca wondered if they'd noticed her awake and waited atop the Hadros for her to fall asleep so they could sneak back in for more loot. Time dragged on, seconds ticked by then minutes passed. She lay awake, staring out the hole in the ceiling and watching the clouds part. Stars shone down on her, the black night growing lighter as the moon traversed the sky.

The robber hadn't come back – had they just panicked and ran with what they found? Curiosity piqued, Rebecca got out of bed and put on her shoes. Maybe, she thought, they left the hatch open intentionally. Maybe it was a trap. She knew she wouldn't be able to sleep if she didn't at least take a peek; she climbed the ladder.

Moonlight bathed the naked back of a woman. Her long silver hair, resting over one shoulder, gleamed in the moon's radiance. Her skin stretched like a canvas of perfection, marred only by subtle scars, over her athletic frame. The Lykos' nearly human ears, elongated into points, were covered in fine fur the color of the shadows. Rebecca felt light-headed and ashamed, a voyeur looking upon a goddess. Time continued without her while she remained, trapped, watching the ripple of muscles move across Kaece's back.

"You're a very strange human."

Heat flooded Rebecca's face. She swallowed against the panic rising in her chest. "I, uh," she stammered. "I was just– "

"Shh," Kaece interrupted, pulling the leather garment she'd been altering over her head as she spoke in a whisper, "Ya don't wanna wake the Madius, do ya?"

The shirt slung over Kaece's left shoulder with a simple strap; the material stopped short, cutting off below her breasts and leaving her midriff completely exposed. She stood, revealing the rest of her outfit as if taunting Rebecca for gawking. The

53

bodysuit of leather had been reduced to the top, a ragged knee-length loin-cloth skirt and discarded scraps. Only her thick knee-high boots remained as Rebecca had seen them first in Sow Endus, excepting the fresh layer of polish substituting for the layer of grime. Amongst the leather scraps, Rebecca noticed the sewing kit and pair of scissors from Sebastian's supply drawer.

The Lykos gestured for her to come up onto the roof. She hastily clambered up from the ladder and sat cross-legged beside the opening. Kaece pulled the hatch closed, the seal sliding into place without a sound.

Then Kaece glanced over her shoulder at Rebecca and smirked. "Ya must like the changes I made to my armor, eh? You're starin' more than ya stared at my wounds."

Shifting her gaze to the deep mazarine horizon, Rebecca defended, "I just can't believe you're here. I mean, like... Alive. Your injuries are..." She trailed off, her eyes wandering back to the Lykos. "They're gone."

Then her mind was off on another subject, words escaping wildly. "How did you find me?"

"Didn't," Kaece answered and reached over, lifting up the leather strap on the hatch to show a loop-knot. "Tied myself to this hunka metal before lettin' the regenerative coma work its magic."

Rebecca didn't know whether to feel hurt by the implication that Kaece wasn't looking for her, or ecstatic to know that Kaece'd been with her the whole time.

"I'm Rebecca, by the way." She held out her hand for a handshake.

Kaece cocked her head slightly in response – one eyebrow raised, her eyes scanning Rebecca's face.

Rebecca leaned forward and touched the tips of Kaece's hair where it'd been cut short. "Your hair didn't grow back."

"Regeneration's tricky. One of its many limitations is that it heals some injuries but not others. I'm jus' lucky that blow landed where it did an' not an inch more or I'd be forever known as One-Eye."

Rebecca fidgeted with a loose thread on her hoodie. What was the right thing to say? Worried there wasn't a right thing, that everything she said – being human, was the wrong thing.

"It's just useless plumage." Kaece grumbled.

"I could cut it for you," she offered. "Give you a kind of rugged, wolfish look... Well, even though it'll be short. You have a beautiful neckline, and it would add an edginess to your new risqué style."

Kaece swiped up the scissors and placed them into Rebecca's hand. "What, the claws and teeth aren't wolfish enough to be horrifying?"

"I don't think you're horrifying at all," Rebecca replied. She ran her fingers through Kaece's hair, delighted at the soft feel and the fact that Kaece didn't flinch

54

away from her touch. Giddiness bubbled up, nervousness springing to life inside her stomach.

She clipped the first strands of silver and immediately the fallen hair blackened. The tips of the freshly cut hair took on the same oxidized effect, the silver melting away into inky darkness.

"Your hair is amazing," she cooed when she finished, running her fingers through the short hair. "So soft, and this color... It must be magical."

Kaece leaned back into Rebecca's hand and shivered.

"Cold?" Rebecca thought to offer her hoodie. When she moved to unzip it, Kaece shook her head and stood abruptly.

"Do ya like hot springs?"

"Um, I've never been to any."

Kaece pulled Rebecca to her feet and turned toward the dark outline of the mountains. She closed her eyes and tilted her head up, giving the air a single, long sniff. She pointed out into the distance.

Rebecca squinted against the darkness, toward the dense forest at the foothills. The black silhouettes of towering pines and the jagged terrain of cliff-faces made themselves evident in the moonlight. Storm clouds hung in the distance as though they'd followed the Hadros over the days of travel from Thalassa Harbor. The warmth of Kaece's hand slipped from hers.

Kaece stood at the edge, balancing on the balls of her feet with her back to the drop. Her mischievous yellow eyes met with Rebecca's and she smirked. Then, she stepped backward. Startled, Rebecca rushed to the edge and looked down, hoping she wouldn't find Kaece with every bone in her body broken.

When she peered over the side, Kaece stood grinning up at her from the ground. "Jump," Kaece called to her. "You'll be alright."

Rebecca bit her lower lip: It was a drop she wasn't sure she'd survive. Her hesitation was enough, though, for Kaece to start walking away.

"Wait!" She closed her eyes and threw caution to the wind. She jumped off the roof and held her breath. Having just barely found the Lykos, she wasn't ready to lose her yet.

To her surprise, she never hit the ground. She'd landed safely in Kaece's arms.

"Not like other humans at all," Kaece chuckled and sat Rebecca down. She took Rebecca's hand in her own and pulled her forward towards the looming shadows of the forest.

Virtually blind in the underbrush of the soaring evergreens, Rebecca clung to the smooth, clawed hand: Kaece was her lifeline. The soft ferns tickled her ankles as they trudged through the darkness. Twigs snapped and dried leaves crunched under her feet, but all she could do was smile. Wrapped in a cloak of impulsivity, her rebellion amused her. The Prince of Maedia, subject to all the discrimination forced upon him by history, would be furious with her for wandering into the woods with a "dangerous" Lykos. Alex, too, would be frustrated for her lack of communication – she could almost hear him whining about missing out on a real adventure. Ultimately, though, both would demand to know what the Lykos wanted with her – of all people. Her smile split into a giddy grin; she didn't care what Kaece wanted with her. All that mattered was that she wanted Rebecca's attention. Weaving through the darkness of the forest, hand-in-hand, Rebecca realized she didn't care if all Kaece sought was a quiet place to murder her in cold blood.

Trotting along behind Kaece with the bounce in her step she'd been missing since Monique disappeared, she didn't notice when the Lykos stopped walking. Rebecca collided with her.

Her yellow eyes glinted in the faint starlight, contrasting the deep ocean of night. "Ya must smell delicious."

"What?"

Kaece crouched low to the ground. A deep, guttural growl seethed from her throat; a strange, rapid clicking, like a rattlesnake's tail, echoed dramatically in response. The putrid odor of sulfur filled the air around them. The stench assaulted Rebecca's nostrils and she clasped her hands to her face, gagging into her sleeve.

"There're at least three. Ya'd best watch your back, human," Kaece warned.

"Three what?" She felt bewildered, and increasingly nauseous; the stink of rotten eggs permeated the fabric of her hoodie.

But Kaece didn't answer – she took off into the woods and something, the size of a coyote and black like the shadows, bolted ahead. The Lykos pursued the creature and Rebecca lost sight of them.

She waited for the sound of the animal's capture, or Kaece's return from a failed hunt. Gasping as she removed her hand from her face, she coughed out, "Kaece?"

Leaves rustled behind her. She whirled to face the noise, stepping back and pressing her spine into the rough bark of a tree. Large, effulgent red eyes stared at her, the creature to which they belonged emerging from beneath the thick underbrush. The canine behind the glowing eyes looked dark as night. The strange rattling noise vibrated out from its chattering teeth. Rebecca's hair stood on end, her arms pricked with goosebumps and a shiver ran down her spine.

Three. Kaece had warned there were three of them. Adrenaline pumped through her veins; the one before her and the other Kaece chased away accounted for only two. The Lykos also told her to watch her back. She dove around the tree just in time to see the flash of red eyes, to hear the pads of its paws rebound off the trunk. A threatening, annoyed, rattle emanated from the beast as it landed on all fours. Different from the others, thick, jagged spikes burst forth from its spine from the base of its skull to its tail. The thing of nightmares that she only had one word for – Chupacabra, added to her mounting dread.

Rebecca stumbled backwards, tripping over a root and landing on the ground. Never taking her eyes off the four hungry demonic eyes, she tried to scurry away. The third beast erupted from the bushes and blocked the path behind her with its loud chatter. She swallowed, her fear tainted with fury – how had this *thing* bested the Lykos? Blindly she groped the forest floor; her fingers closed around a fallen branch. With a white-knuckled grip, she sprung to her feet and swung the small tree limb like a club at the nearest Chupacabra. One of the spinal protrusions snapped as she cracked the branch across its back.

The creature yelped and its companion lunged at Rebecca. But the demon-dog never found its target; Kaece's claws raked through its throat as she dropped from above, tearing its esophagus free. It crashed to the ground with a strangled gurgle as she drove her knee into its spine. The spiked Chupacabra, quick to retaliate, lunged at Kaece's exposed side.

Its glowing eyes extinguished, the red dissipating like quelled fire. Its teeth slipped from Kaece's leather bracer; its intestines spilled from its rent-apart belly, slopping to the ground. Kaece's gore-drenched claws lashed out at Rebecca and roughly threw her down. An abstract blur of demonic fangs flashed; the creature'd been seconds from sinking its teeth into her neck. Kaece snatched the last beast from the air by the leg and slammed its body into a rock beside Rebecca. With a loud crack, its neck twisted against the force of the impact.

The putrid stench of rotten egg and bowels married with the coppery scent of blood. Dark smears of the stuff covered the tree's trunk; black splatters colored the forest floor. Three mutant coyote corpses spread around them, disjointed and contorted in unnatural ways. Kaece's face, hands, body, everything was streaked with gore. Rebecca swallowed against the stink, covering her face with a bloodied sleeve.

"Are you okay?" She choked out. "I thought it got you."

Laughter erupted, unrestrained, from Kaece as she grabbed Rebecca's wrist and pulled her to her feet. As they walked away from the horrific scene Kaece answered, "Ha, normally a Haima Fox Demon would never even come near a Lykos, but with a tasty human-snack wanderin' alone through their territory at night... Well that's a different story."

"You used me as bait?" Rebecca demanded, the ridiculousness of Kaece's claim made her throat tight.

"Relax," Kaece snorted. "Ya did good. The spring is jus' through these trees and they'd have paced around us all night waitin' for a shot at ya. They had to be hungry, bein' that close to a Lykos means they're desperate."

"You make it sound like everything is afraid of you."

"Everything *is* afraid of me."

"I'm not."

Her confidence seemed to render Kaece speechless. She smiled to herself, following in comfortable silence. Not more than a few minutes passed before the dense thicket broke into a moonlit clearing. Steam billowed up from a large pool, nestled into a bed of mossy stone. Lush grass blanketed the ground, growing into tall yellow-flowered snapdragons around the edge of the bubbling spring. Across from them, a small stream cascaded down tiered rock crags, feeding into the water. Clear of the storm clouds, the sky above them gleamed with vibrant stars; the pale yellow of the moon at its apex cast an ethereal glow on the vapor that clung to the water's surface.

"This is beautiful," she whispered in awe.

Kaece glanced over her shoulder and smirked. "Yeah? Ya don't get out enough, human."

She frowned – there was a degree of truth in that. Partially, she could excuse her lack of experience in the wild on her city's lack of forest; in reality, she'd spent too much of the past year in bed instead of exploring the world.

Kaece'd started stripping. Rebecca turned away, yet still caught a glimpse of Kaece's skin. She stood so close that Rebecca could feel her movement as she discarded the rest of her clothes. Didn't Kaece have any sense of modesty?

The tips of the Lykos' claws brushed across her jaw, urging her face up. Rebecca took a measured breath then lifted her head – putting extra care into only looking into those captivating eyes. She felt lost in those eyes, another shiver rushing through her body; a tingling sensation lingered once the shiver passed. Their closeness, Kaece's warm breath on her, the touch of her fingers, felt like a waking dream – some convoluted fantasy – and she couldn't erase the thought of Kaece's lips from her mind.

"What're ya waitin' for?" Kaece mocked. "Ya can't enjoy the spring if ya stay dressed like that, eh?"

She blushed, the heat in her cheeks flaring painfully. The idea of getting naked in front of anyone on a normal day made her squirm; the idea of getting naked in front of Kaece frightened her beyond reason. She shifted her weight, trying to think of an excuse. Despite the feeling of vulnerability it caused, Kaece obviously didn't feel the same. She murmured, "I... don't know."

"Not afraid of a Lykos, but yer afraid of some... water?" Kaece taunted with a raised eyebrow, her smirk spreading into a wide grin.

"It's not the water."

Kaece scoffed and walked away to the water's edge.

Rebecca fidgeted; she hated Kaece turning her back on her. Kaece stalked forward into the hot spring until the water lapped at her thighs, then she sank down into

58

it and moaned. She closed her eyes and tilted her head back against the rocks, a pleased smile on her face.

"Ya were right to avoid it," she said, eyes still closed. "This is jus' terrible, all warm an' wet... Ya oughta stay cold and dirty over there."

"Is it really that good?"

Kaece replied with another pleased moan.

Rebecca stepped to the edge of the pool, then turned away from Kaece and hurriedly undressed. When she glanced back, Kaece hadn't budged, not an inch. Relief mingled with her discomfort and she quickly dropped into the hot water.

She groped around under the surface for a rock to sit on, but Kaece caught her by the arm and pulled her closer. The contact with the Lykos' bare skin surprised her. Rebecca swung her free arm, skimming the water's surface and splashed Kaece in the face.

Their laughter echoed through the clearing as a water fight ensued, ending when Kaece shook out her wet hair. Tiny, hard-hitting droplets barraged Rebecca and Kaece snickered victoriously.

Rebecca pushed Kaece up against the side of the pool, swept up in the moment. "That's not fair! I'd just whip myself in the eye if I tried that."

Kaece agreed with a grin. "I can see some advantages to havin' it short, but it'll take some gettin' used to. Its so light, my balance is off."

"I'm glad you like it," Rebecca smiled and brushed some of the wet, longer bangs from Kaece's face, then pushed her fingers back through the shorter hair.

Kaece grabbed the offending hand and Rebecca blushed immediately. She was mid-mumbling an apology for crossing Kaece's personal boundary when the Lykos forced her hand up, twisting Rebecca around by the wrist. She pulled Rebecca tight up against her, pinning Rebecca's arms. Her back pressed into Kaece's breasts, the Lykos' hands coming to rest on her abdomen. She felt awkwardly trapped, tense, pressed against Kaece's body.

The feel of Kaece's muscles relaxing made Rebecca take a deep breath to do the same. She closed her eyes and leaned her head back onto Kaece's shoulder, listening to the soothing babble of the small waterfall. Her fingers idly traced the back of the Lykos' hands as she sank into the comfortable embrace.

"*Rebecca*. What is it about you," Kaece whispered, her claws lightly raking across Rebecca's stomach.

The sound of her name, uttered in Kaece's strangely exotic dialect, thrilled her. A chill, more goosebumps, a tightening in her chest all worked against her, forcing her to have to remember to breathe. "What about me?"

"Exactly," Kaece purred. "Tell me, what is it that makes you so ... *Unique*."

Rebecca swallowed, furrowing her eyebrows together and looked up at Kaece. She searched those deep, yellow eyes. "I'm just me. What kind of an explanation are you looking for?"

The Lykos merely watched her.

Wrinkling her nose, Rebecca tried to think of answers to the too-broad question. "I'm a Cancer. My birthday is in June, which is unusual for a Cancer, I guess."

Her hobbies, pets, favorite colors or activities with friends should all have been readily available, but she found that she didn't have any of those. Without Monique, she'd had no friends and lost interest in activities. In Gaeadia, she had Sebastian – the Maedian whose very name had evoked something of a burning hatred in Kaece's voice. Well, she also had Alex, but he was just her annoying kid brother regardless of what world she existed in.

"My dad is a lawyer," she continued, since Kaece hadn't replied. "And my mother is an interior designer. I'm the oldest out of four kids... The youngest two are twins. I'm kind of letting them all down, though..." Rebecca sighed, thinking of her family back home reminded her of the wedding. She thought of how she'd disappeared not three hours before her wedding, and everything her mother invested into it. But she felt worse yet for not genuinely wishing she was anywhere other than Gaeadia, where happiness felt possible.

Kaece took in her reply by examining her facial expressions but showing no emotion of her own. When Rebecca failed to give more information, she said, "Is the Madius your mate?"

Unsure of whether to laugh or gag, she just stared at Kaece with wide eyes. Was she seriously asking if Sebastian was her soul mate? The nonsense Alex spewed about crossing the Kosmos to be with Sebastian made her stomach churn. He was, and always would be, far from her soul mate no matter what anyone thought. She couldn't figure out what caused Kaece's leap of logic, or why she'd brought up Sebastian when she'd reacted so poorly to his name in Sow Endus.

"I'm from Earth, the 'Other Side', or whatever." she defended, "Sebastian calls me a Metakosmos. I fell into Gaeadia like five minutes before I met you – there is no way me and Sebastian are soul mates"

The Lykos nodded slowly and Rebecca felt flustered, unsure of whether she'd understood that she wasn't with Sebastian.

"Ya arrived too late to get caught up in the destruction of Sow Endus, but just in time to help me get out of there?"

"That's right." Rebecca smiled.

"Wow," Kaece smirked. "Good timing."

Rebecca's smile broadened; she couldn't have agreed more. A few minutes earlier and she'd have been in the dragon's gullet before she had any opportunity to help anyone. A few minutes later and Kaece might've already been unconscious. The thought of Kaece at the mercy of those villagers made her pride wilt – she had no doubt they would've taken advantage of the incapacitated woman or taken it upon themselves to rid the world of a 'harmful' Lykos. The rift in the Kosmos in that exact moment had saved them both from dire, unspeakable fates.

"So how about you? What makes Kaece unique," she asked, teasingly. "Aside – of course – from you being an extremely agile Lykos who has an exceptional sense of smell... Saving a human girl from Chupacabras and expertly sniffing out a hot spring, and all."

Kaece's expression turned stony; she didn't seem to see the humor in Rebecca's question. "What has the Madius said about my kind?"

"He hasn't exactly said a whole lot," Rebecca shrugged. "Sebastian likes to talk about how Lykos are dangerous. He thinks they're savage, bloodthirsty beasts who lost their humanity and should be avoided at all costs. He only describes Lykos with words someone would use if they were talking about an animal, like bears or something. I think he's being melodramatic. You're perfectly level-headed and totally full of human cognition. If you were even half as monstrous as he believes you are, you'd have killed me already."

She gasped in surprise as Kaece's claws closed around her throat. The sharp points balanced on the surface of her skin, threatening to dig into her flesh. In an instant, just like she'd killed the Chupacabras, Kaece could end her life.

"Your precious Madius didn't tell ya *why* we're *beasts*," the Lykos snarled into her ear. "They created us, mutants! – So they could keep their peace. They made us to be violent where they, weak humans that they are, could not be. They had us so they could keep their precious conscience clean, but they destroyed their own unborn children to do it. They mutated them, infecting each one until the gene held fast – so many died – until they succeeded at makin' the monster – the Lykos – they needed to protect 'em. An' then they betrayed us. They banished us from *our* home. They ripped us from *our* lives, stole *our* purpose for existing."

The picture that Kaece's words painted in Rebecca's mind was full of horrific imagery, but she'd already heard some of Sebastian's take on their history, too. While it didn't seem at all un-Maedian to cast aside a population, she doubted it was completely unprovoked. Samuel Miller had, after all, hit a woman. She also doubted that either Sebastian or Kaece, distant descendants of this long quarrel between races, had any real clue about what happened. The war was long over and the claws fastened to her throat weren't meant for her. They were claws meant for Sebastian's long-since-dead ancestors.

"Listen," she said. "Every war has two sides, but this war is like ancient history, right? I think you and Sebastian should both just let the past stay in the past and forget about it."

Painful pressure constricted her throat; Kaece's fingertips pressed into her windpipe, making it hard to breathe or swallow, but her claws didn't bite into Rebecca's flesh.

"What you create doesn't jus' disappear when you're done with it," Kaece snarled. "We didn't just fade away!"

Rebecca choked against the hand crushing her throat, blinking away involuntary tears. The angry contortion of Kaece's face, her curled lips, bared fangs, narrowed eyebrows, didn't despoil her perfection. Her rage, intended for someone else, found Rebecca as a victim and she could only hope her death would bring Kaece peace of mind. She smiled at the Lykos, admiring the exotic woman for all that she was.

"I'm glad –" she croaked, "you didn't..."

Kaece's furious expression softened into confusion, her gaze darting from Rebecca's smile to her eyes. "Ya really aren't afraid of me."

Black spots dotted her vision, the air all but completely gone from her lungs. Still, Rebecca shook her head and forced out a strangled, "No."

Kaece released Rebecca's throat. She traced Rebecca's jawline with her fingers. Her hand trailed up her cheek, the warmth of her palm coming to rest against Rebecca's face. The intensity in Kaece's expression made Rebecca all too aware of the pounding of her heart. While moments before the Lykos had lacked a solid reason to rip out her throat, the very thought she surrendered to when the sheen of Kaece's moist lips pulled Rebecca's attention would be justification enough. She desperately wanted to find out if those lips were as soft as the rest of Kaece's body, or softer. But she resisted the impulse, holding her ground; she didn't want to give Kaece a reason to hate her.

"Rebecca," Kaece breathed, sliding her hand from Rebecca's face – exposing her cheek to the night air. "We oughta get ya back to that Maedian contraption soon. The sun's gonna be up before ya know it."

The sudden shift from 'we' to 'you' didn't escape Rebecca's notice. "But what about you?"

Silence.

Her mind raced, frantically trying to come up with a solid reason that Kaece shouldn't leave.

After a long moment, Kaece took a deep breath. Then she exhaled without a word, even though she seemed to have something to say.

Rebecca considered for the first time that Kaece didn't have anywhere to go; with the dragons destroying villages and the Maedians being far from hospitable, she had probably been rendered just as homeless as the villagers of Sow Endus.

"Come with us," she blurted. "Sebastian will let you stay, Lykos or not he needs all the help he can get. His father was kidnapped, and my brother and I aren't really much use... But you've lived here all your life. You can help us find him; you've got to know everything there is to know about Xiratera. Please?"

Kaece looked horrified by the proposal, her lips pulling back in disgust, but she quickly tried to hide the expression and instead looked away toward the bank.

"Please?" Rebecca asked again. "You found this hot spring, in the dark, and through the forest. And you knew about those Chupacabras. Have you spent a lot of time in these woods?"

Her question made Kaece glance back at her from the corners of her eyes, a smug smirk on her face. "I've seen twenty winters pass, but in all that time I've never seen this place. The Lykos territory only touches a small part of this forest on the other side of these mountains. Still, the smells are the same. Not that ya'd be able to tell, a Lykos' senses are far greater than your petty human senses."

"You're practically making my case for me," Rebecca urged. "Come with us."

The Lykos pushed Rebecca away and leapt from the water, crossing quickly to her clothes. She snatched up her leathers and pulled them on with such urgency, Rebecca could only hope her persistence hadn't caused it.

"What's wrong?"

Kaece glanced to Rebecca while she yanked her shirt over her head. "There's another Haima Fox Demon here."

Rebecca scanned the clearing; she didn't see it. But she knew it was there; she trusted Kaece.

When Kaece pointed towards a cluster of underbrush lining the edge of the clearing, Rebecca watched the leaves rustle in the wind. Then, low to the ground, she spotted them: the glowing eyes of a killer peered out from under a bush. A faint trail of red left its impression on her vision as she followed its movement from one shrub to another. It skirted the Lykos, dashing under the vegetation toward Rebecca – were it not for the demonic eyes moving ever-closer, she may never have seen it coming.

But something felt off; the creature was too low to the ground. When it bolted for another bush, Rebecca saw it – this demon looked much smaller than the rest. "That one isn't the same as the others," she noted aloud.

"Nah," Kaece agreed. "We could jus' ignore it, it's a young pup. It's too young to feed on its own, and with its mother dead it'll starve sooner than later."

Rebecca shook her head; she didn't want that.

"Would ya prefer I kill it now?"

"No!" She cried, hoping Kaece's stride toward the demon wouldn't be faster than her words.

Kaece stopped abruptly next to where the demon hid. "Lykos are not only quicker, but superior in strength and intellect to humans, too."

Frustrated and confused, Rebecca huffed. She couldn't fathom what Kaece's need to be better than the Maedians had to do with her offer to slaughter the helpless baby Chupacabra.

Answering her unspoken question, Kaece explained, "Humans adhere to the notion that compassion and the gift of life are one and the same. See how disgusted ya are when I offer a quick, nearly painless death – just because it's violent," she punctuated her statement by lashing out at the Haima Fox Demon; the bush it hid beneath exploded in a shower of leaves. The pup's teeth chattered and a noxious cloud of fear seeped from its fur. "It's in the animal's best interest. It'll starve to death, a slow and agonizing fate that ya think is better 'cause it'll be out of your sight."

The little demon shivered; Rebecca watched it cower, its fluffy black tail tucked tight between its hind legs. Its oversized triangular ears were folded back, pressed against its neck. Those enormous red eyes, devoid of malice, registered only fear.

"Turn around," Rebecca told Kaece.

As Rebecca dressed, she argued, "It doesn't have to be either one. Sure people can be horrible, but they don't have to be. We killed this baby's mother, so it's up to us to do the right thing – the not horrible thing. It's not hurting anyone, so it doesn't deserve to die, not quickly *or* slowly."

With a sideways glance at Rebecca and amusement coloring her expression, Kaece poked the little fox-demon between the eyes repeatedly. It hissed, but only shivered. It couldn't defend itself. "It's a she. The female pups don't have the start of those spinal ridges under their fur like the males do."

"Stop tormenting the poor thing." Rebecca knelt down in the grass near Kaece. She patted the ground gently in front of her and cooed in the tone that she'd use with a dog, "There, there, little one... The big bad wolf isn't going to bother you anymore."

"Haima Demons are humans' only natural predator," Kaece stood and took a step away from the demon. She watched curiously while Rebecca reached for it. "You are that pup's prey."

Rebecca cupped her hands around the furry little body. She could feel its tiny bones beneath its skin; the shivering, malnourished creature was more terrified of her than she was of it. "Do they only eat humans?"

"Nah. Anything with warm blood, even a Lykos, can be prey. Jus' one bite is guaranteed to end your life, even if they don't drain their victim completely dry," Kaece replied. "It's better for them to finish ya off, though, lest ya turn into a demonic blood sucker yourself. And they prefer humans, just as Lykos prefer red meat an' humans eat grains."

"Uck, grains," Rebecca groaned, sticking her tongue out at the little demon. Then she smiled. "People are friends, not food, okay little one? If you can learn that, then you've got an option other than death. Think you can do it?"

She cradled the creature in the bend of her arm, against her chest. It responded to her voice, comforted, by nuzzling itself into her warmth.

"Ya really are reckless." Kaece cocked her head to the side and smirked, one eyebrow raised. The expression seemed less mocking than before, and Rebecca knew – just like in her past – she'd impressed the Lykos.

Rebecca stroked the Haima Fox nestled against her heart and smiled at Kaece. "In my world, they say that when you hit rock bottom, you've got nothing to lose and everything to gain."

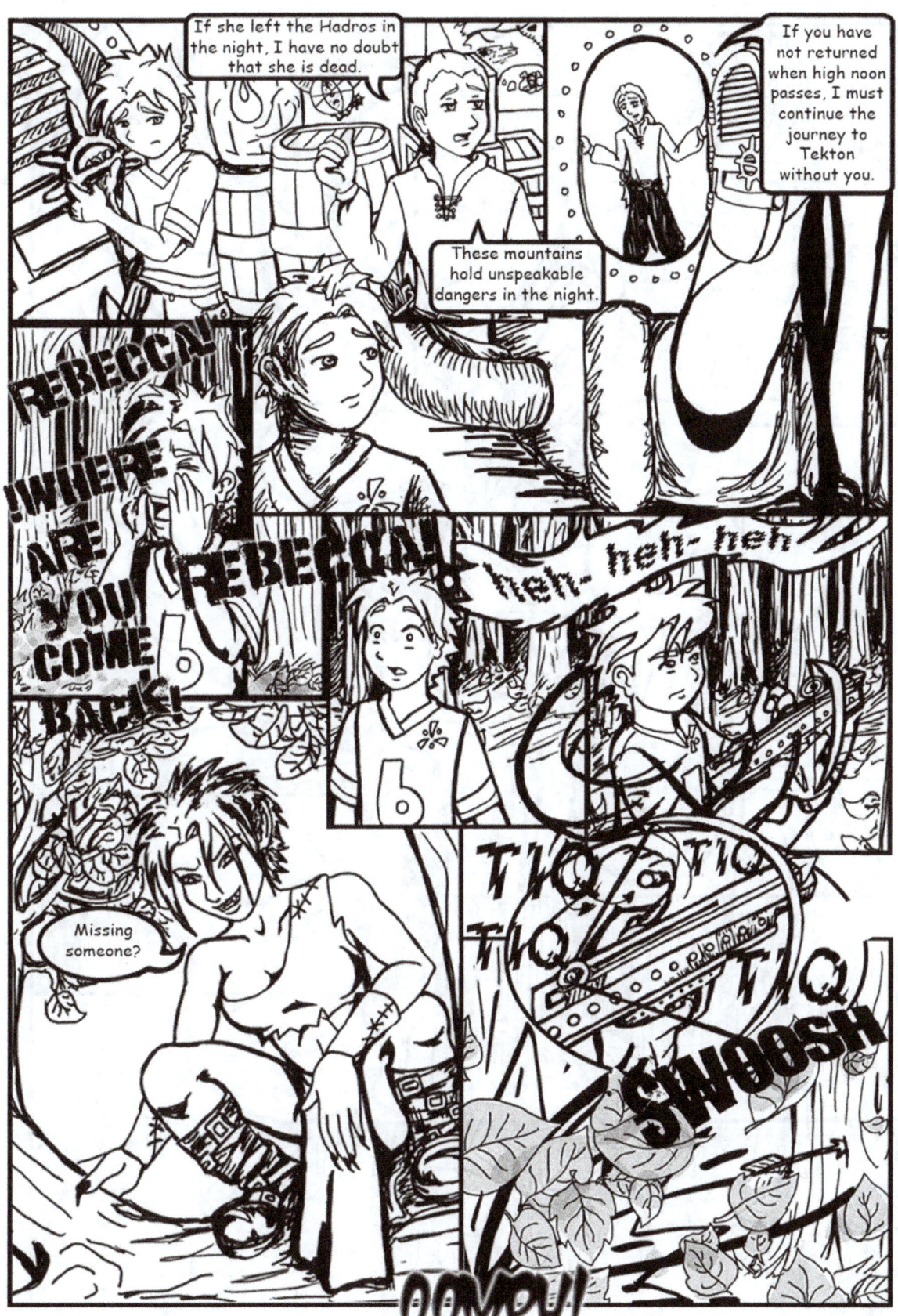

68

69

72

76

CHAPTER 8

Rebecca ran her fingers through Kaece's hair, relishing the downy softness. The comforting sensation tickled between her fingers, offering reprise from the knot of anxiety growing in her belly. She'd awoken that morning feeling uneasy. As she stroked her, Kaece's leg twitched restlessly – not her first mirroring of Rebecca's discomfort. Guilt seeped into the pangs of anxiety; Kaece's companionship didn't deserve to be rewarded by transferring her inexplicable upset through touch.

Kaece's occasional shifting and nervous rubbing of her hands, a reflection of Rebecca's anxiety, hardly surprised her: they'd clicked instantly. Like two old souls who'd shared a distant past, Rebecca and Kaece fell together in a comfortable silence. They both enjoyed lounging on the bed, taking pleasure in just relaxing and having each other's company. The day they were due to arrive in Tekton was no different.

Alex sat at his workbench, tinkering with his 'epic' weapon. Kaece's curious yellow eyes followed his movements while her hand idly traced her own abdomen. Rebecca's imagination ran wild with fantasies about the sensation of those claws brushing along her skin. She shivered, an electric tingle shooting down her back.

When Kaece looked up at her questioningly, heat flooded her face and she fumbled for an excuse. She knew how detrimental daydreaming about Kaece's hands all over her could be; those sorts of thoughts could only cause problems between them. Reaching down, Rebecca traced a faint, jagged scar along the Lykos' exposed midriff.

"Is this from Sow Endus?" She asked.

"No," Kaece replied, her expression unchanging – unreadable.

Rebecca's fingers traced back down the scar. "How did it happen?"

"Ah, ya gotta say first." Kaece snatched Rebecca's hand, touching the wound on her palm.

She shifted uncomfortably: though the slice healed into pink scar tissue, the memory of its cause hadn't faded. She frowned. "It was an accident."

"Strange accident," Kaece retorted, her smirk unwavering as she pushed up the sleeve of Rebecca's hoodie, revealing the irritated scab from her suicide attempt. "Liar."

"It *was* strange." She pulled her sleeve back down. Panic stirred inside her emotional cauldron of a stomach. She didn't want Kaece to get the impression she was crazy. The hole Monique had torn into her heart had begun healing, thanks to Kaece.

"I can hear it when ya lie. Your heart beats faster, and your breathing gets heavier. Even the smell of your perspiration changes. There's no point in lyin' to me."

Rebecca marveled at how tender Kaece's touch remained, even when she attempted to be intimidating. The silence lingered, Kaece breathed an amused huff, her challenge unanswered. Rebecca just smiled – a silent admittance that she knew she was a liar.

"But," Kaece mused, her thumb brushing across the mending wound on Rebecca's palm. "I don't s'pose there's a point in talkin' about the past either. Let sleepin' demons lie, yeah?"

Rebecca couldn't agree more. She welcomed the ability to dodge her precarious past with Monique, her slip into misery. She nodded. Despite her temptations, she needed to resist – resist asking about Kaece, no matter how desperately she wanted to get to know her better; resist succumbing to the physical impulses; resist exposing the perverse aspect of herself that she didn't know how to divert.

Her time with Monique taught her how to hide from the truth – how to hide behind the socially acceptable mask of normalcy. Her years in high school, safely hidden behind Brad, taught her she couldn't be wrong if she acted according to what she knew to be right. On Earth, she'd had Bradley Logan; on Gaeadia, she could secure Sebastian.

Slipping out from beneath Kaece, Rebecca got to her feet and strode over to the door of the control room. Turning the handle, she yanked the door open and instantly felt the blast of heat from within. Despite the uncomfortable warmth of the room, Rebecca persisted; she pulled the door closed behind her – that way she could at least maintain the illusion of privacy.

She couldn't imagine how Sebastian survived in the cramped space his control panel shared with the engine of the Hadros. The crackle of fire roared in her ears; flames licked wildly at the iron grate. He glanced over his shoulder and his eyes lit up at the sight of her. She smiled at him.

Sebastian faced forward, looking ahead through the windshield. "What a unique circumstance that your presences graces the control room."

"I, uh... Just thought you could use some company for a while."

"Thank you, though, we will come upon Tekton any moment now – it is nestled amongst some of these hills."

Rebecca placed her hand on the back of his chair, peering outside. Splintered trunks jutted out of arid ground, piercing the sky above with their jagged skeletons. The vast landscape of deforested hills stretched to the horizon. Shattered tree bark and fragmented branches littered the brown earth where nothing dared to grow.

Rebecca stared out at the destruction, wide-eyed, and swallowed hard against the lump in her throat. She imagined the landscape she'd left with Kaece, towering evergreens and thick, lush vegetation covering the forest floor, turning into this devastation.

"What... happened to this place?" She managed.

"Hmm?" Sebastian raised his eyebrows. "Oh, did I forget to mention, Tekton is a logging town. Some of the finest lumber comes from this town, and of course, the majority of the fuel Xiratera must use for the ros and trains."

"Ros?" Rebecca frowned.

"Of course. Ros are vessels that move us from one place to another, like the Hadros, Metaros or Pikros," he explained. "The people of Tekton use Pikros – very similar to a Hadros, though they are equipped with two extra limbs and are without a living quarter. One of these limbs is designed as a grasping claw for holding a tree trunk steady, while the other, a saw blade, releases the tree from its roots. The claw then places the log in a large bin atop the ros. Once the bin is full, the Pikros return to Tekton's lumber mill where the logs are processed into lumber."

"You're telling me that Maedians did this?" She sighed, "The effect of people on the environment never ceases to amaze me... It doesn't matter if it's in this world or the other... We're like leeches."

"Leeches?" Sebastian pulled his eyebrows together in confusion. "On Gaeadia, a leech is a small to medium worm that latches on to a host and feeds off its blood. They are really not at all unlike your pet Haima Fox, although most leeches do not tend to feed on humans."

For a well-read son of an emperor, Sebastian didn't understand similes. How he failed to make the connection between leeches and humans escaped her. Somehow, it felt beyond rude to spell it out for him...Why yes, Sebastian, leeches are the same on Earth. We are like small creatures that feed on our host, the planet, until every last drop of her resources is dried up – just like a Haima Fox.

She wound up a tight smile and changed the subject. "Hadn't you said something about not being able to use the Hadros once we got to Tekton?"

"Do not worry. Although the Pinewood Yeti forbid us to enter the Eirenic Forest with machinery, the terms of the treaty enable us to cross their boundary. They are a peaceful species that will not harm us while we travel through their territory, so long as we obey our agreement. Though the journey will take many more days than it would with the Hadros, it is better to travel at a dreadfully slow pace than to never arrive at Drakeon Peak.

"Thankfully," Sebastian continued. "This detour is also convenient. We will be able to gather more supplies in Tekton, and borrow enough Pegasi for us all to fly."

She doubted that Sebastian knew which creatures were truly peaceful. He'd sorely misjudged the Lykos. By the look of the decimated land around them, she found it difficult to believe the Yeti wouldn't be a little upset to find humans in their forest.

"I don't feel very good about this plan. Isn't there some other way we can get to Dragon Peak?"

"Drakeon Peak," he corrected, though she didn't see why it mattered. "And unfortunately, no. Tekton is part of the Dragon Tail river basin. The river leads directly toward Drakeon Peak which towers over the Unthrowlych Mountains. It is said to be a giant red peak, the first and largest volcano in all of Gaeadia. The mountains that surround it are ancient, highly eroded spires that make climbing to the Peak virtually impossible – "

"But not completely impossible?"

"We will need flyers to reach the snow-capped valley below the Peak," Sebastian asserted. "They should have a good selection of flyers in Tekton. There is no other way."

She placed her hand on his shoulder and smiled. Despite her unease, she wanted him to believe she agreed with his decision.

He expertly maneuvered the levers that worked the legs of the Hadros. Between the rhythmic shifts from one lever to another, he would turn a knob that caused the engine's furnace to flare up. A set of glass-encased meters registered read-outs she couldn't understand. The heat made her eyelids feel heavy; the rock in her stomach, the weight of the day – it lulled her with the sway she'd finally grown accustomed to over the weeks onboard.

The steady rhythm of the Hadros changed, a jolting of inertia that came whenever Sebastian applied the brakes. Rebecca gripped his shoulder tighter, using him as a crutch to keep her balance. She looked out at the town responsible for the forest's demise. In the foreground, framed by the desecrated hills surrounding it, stood a massive building. The entire factory was constructed from wood, save for a tall shining metal exhaust chimney. The machines Sebastian had described sat idle in front of a large open door; the interiors of both the Pikros and the building were piled high with unprocessed logs. Train tracks ran through the lumberyard, and beside them stacks of finished lumber awaited shipment to Thalassa Harbor.

Beyond the pointed roofs of a few buildings behind the lumber mill, Rebecca could see nothing of the town itself and even those disappeared as the Hadros sank to the ground.

"Something is wrong," Sebastian announced, a surplus of calm in his voice. "The sawmill is not in production. The Pikros are inactive...The mill should be operating until sundown; there should be workers here unloading those logs. I do not see a single man working."

"Maybe they're on break?" She suggested.

The engine of the Hadros fell silent.

"No," he replied. "That is not a possibility. This is not good. I need answers from the Lykos; Rebecca, this is a dire need. Do not hit me this time."

She grabbed his arm as he walked passed her and tugged, defiantly urging him to wait. He strode out of the room with such determination that he dragged her into the next room with him.

"Please don't go overboard?" She begged. He seemed dead serious that she'd face consequences if she slapped him – but she wouldn't stand idly by while he abused Kaece with his Power.

"Tell me what you know," Sebastian commanded Kaece, staring straight into her eyes.

Rebecca shifted her weight. While his words pricked her skin with the subtle traces of his Power, nothing seemed too mind-altering about the command. Kaece sat up and smirked tauntingly at him.

"This is gonna be an awfully long conversation, your highness. Where should I start? I think I'll start with what I know about the day of our kind's banishment. I know ya Maedians were the ones who started it, ya pushed us to hurt ya. You had jus' passed another rule, another petty law, that made Lykos less than Maedian. You took away our rights to our families, to our marriages. Ya ruled that we should be treated like animals before anyone ever laid a claw on your 'innocents.'"

Jaw clenched, Sebastian restrained his anger at her provocation. To Rebecca's surprise, he didn't attempt to deny the accusation, nor did he issue a new, more specific, command. "About Tekton, Lykos. Alex told me Rebecca first met you in Sow Endus – I know that you had been there. In light of that fact, I suspect you must know more about these attacks than you have conveyed. The time has come for you to tell me what you know."

"The human village is but a ghost town," Kaece said, her smirk hardening into a stoic expression. "The scent of burnt flesh lingers in the air; I've known it since the day's beginning."

"Are the attackers still near? Are there any... survivors?"

"Only burn and rot remain. This fight ended many days ago, I doubt anyone could survive in that stench – even your near worthless human senses would be overwhelmed by it."

"Is that all you can tell me, cur? The smell is all you know of Tekton, *nothing* more?" Sebastian's voice reflected his anger, but under that also pain.

Kaece glowered at Sebastian with a sinister sneer. Her eyes shifted from him to Rebecca and she breathed out a frustrated sigh, visibly calming.

"Jus' the smell," she affirmed.

"You," Sebastian paused as if reconsidering his tactic. "I would like you to remain in the Hadros and wait for us to return. Even if the town is nothing but ruins, it is on Maedian land, and you are a Lykos."

Were it not for the palpable tension, or the ominous prophecy from Kaece, Rebecca would have hugged him. He'd avoided altering Kaece's mind. The single command felt like such a tremendous step up on the Sebastian she'd met in Sow Endus. Though what Kaece had told them had explained her and Kaece's shared anxiety, it also meant that Sebastian needed friends more than ever. She slid her hand into his and gave it a reassuring squeeze.

Sebastian smiled – a weak smile that failed to mask his beaten expression. "The two of you do not need to accompany me into Tekton... I do not know what to expect, but I know that it will not be pleasant. I understand and do not fault you if you wish to remain in the safety of the Hadros while I search for the supplies we will need to continue our journey."

Alex seized the opportunity to stand and wave his crossbow. "Don't worry, Prince Sebastian, we won't abandon you. War isn't for the faint of heart!" Rebecca rolled her eyes as he continued. "I knew when I signed up for this mission that we'd probably face death, brutality and violence beyond the most AO rated video games."

"And sir," Alex saluted, "I stand by you no matter what. We will win this war."

"Thank you, Metakosmos." Sebastian nodded wearily.

Rebecca scolded, "You aren't fighting any wars or our deal is off, got it? You can just face this world alone."

"But..."

"I don't care," she preempted. "I can't handle losing you, either, okay? We're *all* in this together."

Defeated, Alex hung his head and sighed.

Sebastian turned to leave. Rebecca lingered by the bed next to where Kaece lounged while he and Alex climbed out of the Hadros.

"I'm sorry he's like that," she apologized. "Stupid Maedian laws that don't make any sense. I'll be back as soon as I can, I promise."

Kaece refused to look her in the eye.

Rebecca pursed her lips. Kaece's obvious upset added more stress to the perpetual ache in her gut, but she didn't have the time to soothe the Lykos' anger at Sebastian. Later, when they returned, she could figure everything out – including whether or not he expected Kaece to wait on the Hadros for the next few weeks.

She jogged to catch up with them, hearing nothing but the sound of her footfalls in the dirt. A noxious aroma hung in the air; with every breath, her lungs filled with the pungent stench of decay. The caw of a raven broke the unnatural quiet; another caw from a larger bird perched on the sawmill's roof echoed in response. A bloodied eyeball dangled by a nerve from the raven's beak. Biting back the impulse to vomit, Rebecca pulled off her hoodie and pressed it against her face. The bundle of fabric helped mask the odor of rot, helped keep the nausea from overwhelming her.

Alex held his jersey over his face while Sebastian pinched his nose. A few feet ahead of her, they both stopped dead in their tracks just around the side of the building. When she turned the corner and stepped up beside them, she understood why.

Bodies covered the road from the mill to the charred wooden houses and ransacked shops. The street was paved with heat-bloated corpses. Alien faces stared up at the sky – their eyes missing or mummified, their mouths alive with maggots. Flies swarmed festering wounds and buzzed through the air like a thick, cohesive entity. Trails of dried blood led to severed body parts and shriveled innards.

The concept of death seemed romantic, somehow enticing, until that moment. In Gaeadia, nothing about the death she'd witnessed felt romantic. Horrifying, gruesome; the decomposing flesh before her stood out as anything but enticing. Rebecca's realized that if Sebastian hadn't rescued them that day – if she hadn't rescued Kaece – their bodies would be sun-bleached and rotting in Sow Endus. The thought rendered her fragile and weak. Emotion overwhelmed her; tears threatened to escape. A sob choked in her throat, a strangled noise caught between panic and ironic laughter. Sebastian's comment, 'something is wrong,' couldn't have been more of an understatement. What was once Tekton stood before them, the antithesis of civilization. And she stood in the midst of it all, unable to think past the idea of her mortality.

"War," Alex whispered.

Sebastian replied, "This was not war. This was a massacre. These monsters are on a murderous rampage, but the real question remains: why? Why would anyone do this to the innocent people of Maedia?"

Alex swallowed, his voice trembling as he spoke "It doesn't matter why. What matters is that we find 'em and make 'em pay for what they're doing."

"We must find them and reason with them," Sebastian corrected. "We must discover what their quarrel is with us so we may resolve the qualm and restore peace to Xiratera. But that is a matter for a different time. Presently, we must hurry and be wary of what we touch. Disease is undoubtedly rampant in this refuse."

Sebastian trudged forward. His foot scraped against one of the distorted limbs as he entered the river of corpses. The flesh-feasting insects fell from their meal and slopped onto his boot. Rebecca whimpered, the acid of bile burned her throat. Tears streamed from her eyes while her focus shifted from not crying to not retching. Alex held both hands over his covered mouth and followed after Sebastian through the trail of death. Rebecca tried to force her foot forward, but her leg wouldn't respond. Through her hoodie, she called out that she couldn't do it.

Sebastian turned back and raised his eyebrows, removing his hand from his face to ask, "What was that, Rebecca?"

"I can't," she cried, dropping her jacket away just long enough to yell, "I'm scared. I can't – I just can't."

"If this scares you, perhaps you want to reconsider who you ally with," he said with a frown, gesturing to the once-Maedians at his feet. "These injuries were not caused by dragons alone. Many of these lacerations came from weapons, not talon or tooth. Just remember that she is a Lykos – a dangerous beast. As long as you are insistent she stay in our company, we await our inevitable slaughter."

She turned and ran, tears streaming down her face. Ignoring Alex's concerned cries after her, she ran. Rebecca ran back to the Hadros, back to the comfort of the woman she knew wasn't the monster Sebastian thought.

The bronze door waited, open. She climbed inside, hoping to find Kaece's arms waiting to embrace her. But Kaece wasn't on the bed. Immediately Rebecca searched the Hadros. Silence greeted her ears, contorted only by the sound of her uncontrollable sobbing.

The Hadros was empty; the Lykos was gone.

A heavy thought pelted her; could Kaece be guilty and running? Instantly Rebecca reprimanded herself – what could she be guilty of? They'd been together day and night since Sow Endus, though Rebecca herself hadn't been aware of it until a few days prior. She trusted Kaece not to lie to her, especially not about something so trite as how long she'd been around. Maybe she needed to get away from the stench – Rebecca certainly couldn't stand it, even with her weaker senses.

She took off running again, past the lumberyard and toward the fields of decimated land skirting the decimated town. The unyielding earth – compacted by so much machinery – pounded back against Rebecca's feet as she ran. She called the Lykos' name over and over. Nearly breathless, she tripped up the crest of the hill. Collapsed onto her hands and knees, she cried out for Kaece, her tears absorbing into the barren land as they fell.

From the hilltop, she could see Kaece. The Lykos stood still, a stark contrast against the cemetery of trees around her. The line between life and death blurred as Rebecca stared at Kaece, alive but emanating the solitude of one who had survived unbelievable suffering. Kaece waited while Rebecca ran down the hill and closed the distance between them.

When she collided with the statuesque Lykos, she pounded her fists against Kaece's collarbone. "You can't just abandon me!"

Kaece said nothing, nor showed any emotion. She blinked at Rebecca.

Rebecca smacked her again, trying to throw her off-balance. Kaece didn't budge. "Go on, tell me. Make an excuse! Tell me what's so important that you need to leave? Go on! Say *something*!"

Her eyebrow rose slightly as she took in Rebecca's tears. She whispered, "Ya chose to go with the Madius. He's who ya wanna be with."

"He's just some guy," Rebecca cried in protest, shaking her head. She threw her arms around Kaece and cried into her chest. "There's only one of you in all of two worlds..."

84

Kaece's warmth embraced her, those soft but muscular arms wrapping around her. She cried harder. Rebecca sobbed while Kaece stroked her hair.

Eventually, Kaece said, "Let's get ya back to the Hadros."

She nodded and numbly allowed the Lykos to lead her back toward the hell that was Tekton. Once on the Hadros, Kaece curled around her and held her while she cried, soothing Rebecca with loving touches. Taking such comfort in the Lykos, her mind circled back to Sebastian's accusation and a fresh flow of tears began.

"It was horrible," she whimpered. "Everyone was dead, everything was... The whole town... They're all torn open and covered in maggots and... they didn't even look like people anymore. They'd been people before, but... They had lives, with families and jobs and things they liked to do. Even if they did awful things... Like mistreat the Lykos or destroy the forest... they didn't deserve *this*. This is.... this...."

Kaece held her tight; Rebecca could hear her heart pounding in her chest. She could hear the Lykos' upset. She claimed she didn't care about people, she hated the humans, but the tough act wavered. If she'd been capable of the kind of brutality Sebastian alluded to, she couldn't hold Rebecca so tenderly. She wouldn't have slept those nights with her head resting on the bed, with Rebecca's hand tangled in her hair.

Choking down her sobs, Rebecca said, "These dragons – and whoever else is helping them – they're killing innocent people. They're killing defenseless women and children. They're heartless murderers. No... They're worse than that. I don't even have a word to describe how despicable they are."

"Monster," Kaece whispered solemnly. Her breath tickled Rebecca's ear, sending a shiver down her spine.

Rebecca shook her head; monster wasn't the right word either – too ambiguous. She hugged Kaece's arm against her body and closed her eyes, crying in her arms until she felt nothing.

DENIAL IX

From Tekton to the Eirenic Forest

KAECE

ALEX SILAS

SEBASTIAN MADIUS

REBECCA SILAS

206 Leo, daytime

Wow, over a week of walking through mountains and foothills just to find the one and only town way out here completely lifeless. Okay, 3 flyers survived, but they're almost dead too. Sebastian thinks others are helping the dragons, but the way everything is burned and the way all the people are mutilated - TORN limb from limb - I think dragons are definately responsible.
  -Dragons win the Battle for Sow Endus
  -Dragons win the Battle for Tekton
  -Alexander the Greatest will defeat the dragons at the Battle for Drakeon Peak and will restore peace and prosperity to all of Xiratera.

Goodbye Hadros! We're coming to take you dragons down!
                    -Alex

88

91

95

X

With closed eyes, Sebastian leaned against the rough cave wall and listened to the rhythmic grazing of the flyers a short distance away. He felt weary. The shallow cave, at the base of the Unthrowlych Mountains, where they had set up camp was the closest to real shelter they had come across since leaving the Hadros. He had never spent such a length of time deprived of basic human commodities, though he had expected sleeping under the stars to be enjoyable. Rather, the experience had been arduous: the wounded animals were cumbersome and slowed their travel, and his group squandered time each day setting up rudimentary camps only to stow them away after too few hours of rest on hard-packed earth. Until that very evening, even the stars evaded his ability to gaze upon them, for the dense vegetation through which he trekked had obscured them.

Directly above the cave, the mountain ascended skyward into steep cliffs adorned by ledges of coral sandstone. Sebastian had read tales of how Grufoi egg-gatherers met their untimely end when the delicate orange rock crumbled beneath their feet. Although the Grufoi-inhabited slopes were dangerous, the most perilous thing about Drakeon Peak would be the summit surrounding the peak itself. The mystic spire rose out of a deep volcanic crater at the place, already high above the snowy mountaintops, where the sandstone ended in flat-topped plateaus. There, far from the reach of man, the fire dragons dwelled for eons, and still to the day of Sebastian's advent they waited patiently for intruders to dispatch.

Many constillaciouns had passed since his father's signal had reached him. Sheer desperation pushed him toward what he feared could be certain death. He wore a mask of bravery, but in the long days of travel he had considered Demarko's words and come to conclude that if the Drakeon held his father captive, they were a foe more powerful than he could fathom. He would have appreciated the support of his new-found friends in his final exploit, but knew that their demise would be far more certain than his own. He intended to ascend the crimson mountain and alone meet the fate he had chosen.

His brow furrowed at the giggle from across the cave. It was Rebecca's laughter at some unknown humor she and the Lykos woman shared. He imagined the cause, perhaps a hushed hateful slander from the hybrid cur whose head rested in Rebecca's lap. An undesirable resentment burned in his chest.

As was the case of late: Rebecca would sit stroking and fondling the woman as if she were a companion animal rather than a monster. She cuddled and pet the Lykos, she spoke nonsensically in a soothing voice and slept curled up with her in the cold nights.

The scoundrel was not an innocent and sweet companion. She was rude and uncooperative, defying his every decree. She affronted his plans and ideas with her own which had no logic or scholarly support, yet Rebecca and Alex seemed inexplicably drawn to her irrational whims. He was the only one who saw the danger before them: the Lykos had hidden motives.

He felt vexed that he had not been left any opportunity to use the Power of Madius covertly, where Rebecca could not know, to subdue the threat and guarantee their safety. While he truly didn't want Rebecca to think poorly of him, nor hold the Power in ill regard, he could not ignore the devious smirk of the Lykos. Every time he made eye contact, she would glower at him in the most unsavory way. He believed she was well aware that he knew the falsehood in her guise of a friendly canine. There was a threat behind her intent, he was as sure of it as he was of his father's living existence on Xiratera. He knew he could not leave the Metakosmos in good faith without first halting the Lykos' plans, whatever they may be.

"Hey Rebecca, you ready to come with us? It's the perfect hunting night out here! It'll be quick and easy."

Alex called in from the mouth of the cave, huddled in a crouched stance. His eyes shimmered with excitement. Chupita stood behind him, clicking and chittering. Noises of Sebastian's nightmares reverberated along the granite walls. While seemingly harmless in appearance, and good mannered in comparison to the Lykos, the Haima Fox would never cease to terrify him.

"Is watching an animal eat another animal ever 'easy'? I think I'll pass."

"You said 'I'll come with you one time before we get to the dragons' - and this is our last night before we fly up to Drakeon Peak. This is the one time. Come on! It's not really gruesome or anything."

While Sebastian had no intention of allowing them to accompany his ascent, continuing to play into Alex's word of final opportunities would serve him well. With a subtle push, he knew Rebecca would succumb to her brother's insistence. He wished, however, that underhanded manipulations were not the best approach to make her do as needed.

"She should not have to witness such violence, Alex. If she does not wish to hunt, then she is a true Maedian at heart and you could learn well from her reasoning."

The Lykos shot upright with a sneer, and gave Rebecca a side-long glance that communicated her distaste without the use of words, for Rebecca sighed and began to raise from her seat against the cavern wall.

"A promise is a promise. I'll be right back... hopefully."

Rebecca tucked the creature's hair behind her bestial ear, before she followed the boy and his hungry demon out into the pitch of night. He listened to the footfalls fade until he could hear them no more, wanting to be sure Rebecca would not hear his command.

Too late, he realized the fallacy in his plan. Too late, he tried to utter his commanding power. Quicker than he could gasp at her closeness, at Kaece's sinister sneer of sharp teeth full of malice, her clawed hand closed around his throat. She slammed his head against the wall. On the force of the impact, he lost consciousness.

A youthful Sebastian sat on the bed in his bedchamber, looking up into his mother's smiling face. Her deep chestnut curls had fallen into her sparkling blue eyes, and he watched as she brushed the locks away. Her hands gently ruffled his hair. He realized why Rebecca comforted him so; she mirrored many of his mother's traits.

"And then Byran bowed to Elder Zakhar, and the great dragon patted him on the back with a giant talon. The treaty was made, and all of the world would be safe from further Drakeon attacks. Without the Power of Madius, the Drakeon would still hunt all of mankind, Maedians and others like us. Byran had changed the world. He wasn't done yet, as you well know, he went on to discover other lands, and peoples, and make many more friendships... but those will have to be tales for another day. Under the covers with you."

"But mother! I am not tired! Adventurers do not listen to anyone's rules, and they do not need sleep. Byran never sleeps in his adventures."

His mother cupped his chin as she smiled down at him. He felt a great love for her. Emotions that Sebastian felt estranged to flooded his senses as he took in the lost memory.

"You will always be my little adventurer. Someday you will grow big and strong, and then you won't have to listen to anyone's rules ever again. I only wish the same could be said for me... But even big adventurers need sleep, they don't write about it because it would be boring. Would you like to hear a story about Byran sleeping?"

"No."

"You see?"

She pulled the covers up and tucked them around his chin. When she stood to leave he whimpered, summoning her attention back.

"When I grow up, I am going to go on adventures all around the world like Byran, and I am going to take you with me. Then neither of us will have to obey anyone ever again."

"I would like that very much. For now, my little adventurer, you need to sleep."

"Yes, mother."

Sebastian closed his eyes obediently, and opened them to see the dimly lit cave walls behind the snarling Lykos. Her hand squeezed his throat. A torrent of long-forgotten memories flowed into his mind. His memories of his mother, who he had not so much as envisioned since he was a child, filled him with a terrible sense of dread.

He gasped desperately; his hands grabbed at her wrist, but her grip held like iron. The harder he pulled, the tighter she squeezed. He looked into her eyes and saw his own death reflected there. Her eyes were the eyes of a killer - cold, ruthless, emotionless.

"I am not the threat to Gaeadia, ya foolish Madius. It is you that is the threat, the Maedians are the plague of this world. Ya cry 'why would any creature harm us?' The question should be - why wouldn't they? No one likes humans. No one wants ya

99

here on Xiratera. If ya were smart, ya would have loaded up your mindless Maedian minions onto those ships in the harbor and sailed back to your resource-barren homeland, where ya belong."

He vowed a silent apology to his mother, his lovely mother - for with his memory of her surfaced a deep desire to see her again. He had failed at saving her, had failed at saving his father and had failed at saving himself.

"I am givin' ya one chance, Maedian filth. I'll let ya live, and in exchange for your continued heartbeat you will shut your damned poison-tongued mouth and leave me to do as I please. Do we have a 'treaty'?"

Sebastian nodded as best he could, considering only briefly what horrible demise he would allow to befall others with such an agreement. In that moment the selfish desire to live overrode any regard for their continued safety. Her grip loosened, and he collapsed to the cave floor.

She sat across the fire from him. He watched, coughing and dazed, as she unclenched her jaw and her expression slipped back into a neutral mask.

"One word about it and the agreement is over."

He rubbed his throat where his skin felt raw. The swirling chaos of thoughts barraged his mind. The memories, the threat, the implications seemed too much to comprehend. He sat motionless, staring into the fire.

The Metakosmos broke from the underbrush talking and laughing. Upon entering the cave, Rebecca cuddled up to the Lykos. The sinister canine began stroking Rebecca's skin, and Sebastian found he could not hold back his shudder. He dared not put imagery to the dark motive that had to lay behind her desire to do as she pleased with Rebecca without his intervention.

"Are you okay?"

Dear, sweet, Rebecca held such concern in her eyes when she looked upon him. It was as if he were transparent, her empathy quickly assessing his distress. He wished he could be candid with her, but he no longer held such liberty. He vowed that he would never again mention his rightful mistrust of her Lykos pet. It would be her responsibility alone to see through the lies and preserve herself.

"I am shaken, indeed. While you were gone, a vision of my mother came to me. This is a most disturbing occurrence, because until tonight I did not remember my mother at all, nor did I realize that I did not remember her. It is as if a large portion of my childhood was hidden from my mind, and has now been revealed once again."

He paused, looking up at his audience. All of them listened intently. The Lykos' glower seared with warning. The fire danced between them, throwing shadows of monsters and demons on the wall. He shifted and began again, speaking as he was trained: with suppressed emotions, he recalled his memory in a tone of indifference that betrayed no fear, no longing and no pain.

"She used to tell me stories about the adventures of Byran Madius. He was the first Maedian to venture out and explore the wild continent, despite having been born a

Madius. We made plans to go on adventures of our own someday, the two of us, away from all the petty rules and formalities that come with the Emperor's renown."

"What happened to her?"

"She died, or so they told me. I did not believe them, as one day she simply disappeared, much the same as my father has now. She was not ill in any fashion. If it were an accident, the details were never clearly expressed. No one had any knowledge of what fate fell upon her, only that she had died. I was told by everyone that I needed to accept it, to leave it be."

The similarity in his father's disappearance made the hair on his arms and neck stand on end.

"I went to the catacombs, alone, to bear witness to her grave as proof of her death. That dark, musty-smelling maze held seemingly endless vaults containing bodies of the dead from the imperial isles. I found her entombment; I remember tracing my fingers over the lettering in awe of her name beside the corpses of servants. And then I pried it open."

Rebecca sucked in air, her expression caught somewhere between shock and concern. Alex sat forward eager for the outcome of what lay in the tomb. He recalled feeling a similar eagerness while prying at the tomb.

"There was nothing in it. The vault was empty, clearly set up as an intricate deception. There was no body. I knew, and still feel the same, that she had not passed on. She could very well be out there in this world - or perhaps the Other Side, somewhere. But they were hiding that truth from me, and our people."

"Do you think she might have run away without you?"

"Perhaps. Perhaps she was taken, as my father has been all these years later."

"The plot thickens! The dragons are harvesting Maedian royalty!"

The boy certainly had an imagination. Sebastian's stomach ached, though, at the very thought. The Drakeon did harvest people for slaughter, and they seemed indisputably tied to the problems on Xiratera. His father's disappearance from Old Maedia would be no exception. These heavy thoughts made him feel hopeless, because such a case would be impossible to resolve alone.

"I doubt my mother was taken by the Drakeon, though if she was, she is not alive into the present. In my research, I saw nothing to inspire the thought that she may have departed to Xiratera. I spent weeks in the Scholar's Library, reviewing any report or record I could find that so much as mentioned her, seeking any clue that might lead me to her whereabouts, or even a confirmation that she did indeed still live. I recall a report having claimed a possible Haima Demon sighting the same night as her disappearance."

"Do you think she was attacked by the Haima Demons?"

"It is doubtful, to be honest. They claim the Haima Demons took my father but I do not believe it. How would the Demons get to the island undetected? And past all of the royal guard once there? My mother did favor venturing to the mainland, unlike my father, so perhaps it is slightly more possible. I was unable to confirm that she was on the mainland, that day, though - for my father discovered that I was searching for answers even after specifically forbidding me from investigating. He said that I would never be capable of leading our people if I could not learn how to discern the difference between worthwhile tasks that needed attention from those that are unchangeable and must be forgotten. To rule with selfish fulfillment, driven by sentimentality, would bring about the demise of the empire. And this search for what happened to my mother, he said, was a task of sentimental futility and an utter waste."

"So you gave up. Just like that. Maedians are so contradictory is hurts. How can you say that all you want in the world is love and peace, but as the ruler you have to be a cold-hearted ice king?"

The Lykos snickered at Rebecca's outburst. Sebastian had all the answers as to why, memorized, but trapped in the memory of a boy who loved his mother, he could only agree with her. The line between sentimentality and rationality was not as clear-cut as his father would have him believe.

"My father knew I would not stop. He did what should have never been done to me. He used the Power of Madius, and he commanded me to forget my mother. I knew that I had a mother, once upon a time, but I simply never thought of her or anything she and I shared. She, and my desire to find what happened to her, vanished from my worries and I was able to be the Maedian prince my father wanted me to be."

Sebastian's gaze met Rebecca's. His bitterness at being forced to be someone he had not chosen reminded him so strongly of her hatred of the Power of Madius. It was not overtly mind control, but she was right - it certainly had a life altering effect. He swallowed and felt the raw pain in his throat burn. He had not cried since he was a boy, but something welled up deep within him, threatening to undo his control.

"The effect of the power of Madius is linked to the patronage of the Power used. If my memories are returning, then my father's Power is fading. Time is short. If he is not here, if I do not find him tomorrow, I fear we have lost all hope of finding him alive."

What he could not bring himself to say was that at Drakeon Peak or not, he might already be dead. Sebastian simply would not say it for fear that would make it true, and all of his desperate desire - his sentimental fight against the unchangeable truth would be as everyone had told him - selfish and foolhardy. As his father would say: a waste.

"Don't give up now, not when we're so close! This is how stories go, it's just foreshadowing that he's being tortured and we will have to rush in and save him right in the nick of time. I've got my crossbow up in arms and locked and loaded. Tomorrow we vanquish Drakeon scum!"

"The only thing that'll be vanquished if we go up there is us. These zealots won't let ya leave with your life."

For once, Sebastian and the Lykos did agree on something. She knew her Drakeon lore well. Only leaders of a species would be allowed to trespass without forfeit of their lives. It was a treaty to live and let live, and the Drakeon would not take the lives of humans outside of the Drakeon summit.

"That may be accurate. While I have not given up, this is where we must part ways. I will ascend the peak and with the protection of the Power of Madius I will command they speak their grievances and allow a peace discussion. I will demand the return of my father."

"You can't leave us now... This is what we've been waiting weeks for."

Rebecca's mouth twitched, though she said nothing. Her eyes had never lost their compassionate hold on him. He wished he could read her mind.

"You have been excellent traveling companions, Alex, and I do thank you, but I can not be responsible for what would happen to you if I allowed you to accompany me further."

"... But we're your back-up in case something goes wrong."

"Your father was taken and he had the Power of Madius too. How can you expect to depend on that for protection? If they stopped him, they'll stop you too. At least with Alex's bow - which he is pretty good at shooting rabbits with, and Kaece's super-senses and fighting skills you'll have something to help you."

She spoke with such rationality; he felt at ease with her presence. She was the pillar supporting his world in that moment, even if she had no idea how significant she had become to him.

"I have considered that the Power may not protect me."

"How about this - we sneak up to the top and hide somewhere to watch the dragons for a while first. That way we can get a good idea of their habits and security before we do anything. You'll go in alone, or we'll all go in together, but either way we'll be making the best tactical decision because we'll have more information. And, like Rebecca said, that way we can be there to help get you out, if things look like they're getting too heated."

Sebastian considered the theoretical situation, fearful of the outcome of such a plan, but also appreciative of their fierce loyalty.

"I suppose you could come with me initially, if you promise to stay far out of harms way. And, the moment we come across any sign of a dragon near - you must descend from the summit immediately. Dire consequences, that I cannot stop, will follow if the Drakeon capture any of you while trespassing upon their land. I must talk to them alone."

"They'll know, you can't trick 'em. This is your fight Madius - your hands'll be stained with their blood if you allow this. Not the Drakeon's, yours."

Rebecca smacked the Lykos so hard on the leg that the cave resounded with the thwap. He frowned at the Metakosmos' unrelenting violent behaviors.

"This is our choice, not his. We're being supportive. That's what friends do - I'd do the same for you, after all. He said if we see a dragon we need to leave, and I get that - we can do that. So, you watch for dragons and let us know if one is coming and then we'll go. Hopefully *all of us*, after we've confirmed that Sebastian's dad is here and okay."

"He's dead. The Madius even knows it. Why get yourselves killed over a corpse?"

The Haima Fox chattered nervously. Sebastian grimaced in distaste. The sound of her chatter seemed to vibrate in his head, making his brain press against his skull painfully. Rebecca stood up and glowered at her Lykos pet.

"You don't have to stay with us, but you have no right to be so cruel when Sebastian has been so willing to try and be your friend. Think about it, and if you want to leave - fine. Go. But if you decide to stay, Kaece, then you need to watch what you say. Because he is my friend, and I promised to help him."

Curious enough, the Lykos wore an expression of fear. Rebecca jutted her hand out to help Sebastian to his feet and he willingly took the offer. She led him out of the cave and over to a group of large boulders that had tumbled down the mountain and wound up strewn helter-skelter at its base. They sat, and she touched his hand softly.

He felt the cool night air caress his skin, and let the silence between them be a calming point for his tortured mind. His entire life up until that moment had been built upon falsehoods and deceit. He'd been blind to rationality, headlong driven by sentimentality. Demarko had warned him, had told him he was treading on dangerous ground and he'd been too stubborn to see it. Awakened to the truth, he found himself wishing only that he could be brave and selfless enough to send these innocents away and face his fate alone. Rebecca rebuked his cowardice as if she could read it from the mere feel of his hand.

"We can't pretend like we know what we will find up there tomorrow, but I believe that there will be something up there. Your father, answers, whatever it is - it'll be there. Kaece is wrong. I know she is. You need to do this, and we're going to stand by you all the way."

As he stared up past Rebecca and into the endless darkness of the night, Sebastian slowly began to see the light in that all-consuming darkness. His eyes focused, the Metakosmos' hand still touching his own, and he saw the stars, really saw them, for the first time in his life. He saw that there was infinite light hidden within the endless darkness. He wondered if the Metakosmos would be the only light the Kosmos had to offer him. If she was, he thought perhaps that solace would be enough.

CHAPTER 11

They flew through the air. The Simurg's tangled mane billowed up around Rebecca's face while she hugged the beast's neck. Though she couldn't hear much beyond the sound of the wind, she could feel Kaece's heartbeat against her back. The Lykos rode behind her, her arms wrapped tightly around Rebecca's waist.

"Look," Rebecca pointed ahead, where a break in the clouds revealed a scape of spires piercing the sky. Grufoi nests hid in-between their crevices.

The Simurg swooped in closer. The distressed Grufoi screeched, tensely coiled muscles springing them into flight and away from their precious eggs as the Simurg touched down on one of the spires.

"They've been trained to land here by the Maedians," Kaece murmured.

"Follow Sebastian." Rebecca pointed the rainbow-feathered dog-beast back toward the thick fog of clouds.

Her mount veered away from the rock amidst the scattered Grufoi and rushed upward toward Drakeon peak. The nests disappeared from sight as the clouds swallowed them in white mist.

"I don't want to lose ya, Rebecca," Kaece breathed into her ear, in the hushed whisper of a forbidden lover.

With a hard swallow, Rebecca shuddered. She felt all too aware of Kaece's arms embracing her, of Kaece's body pressed against her own.

"Come away with me," the Lykos continued. "Let's go. It can jus' be the two of us for the rest of our lives... Good lives. Long ones. Together."

The world spun; her heart pounded; she couldn't breathe against the crushing weight of the thought: yes. Over and over in her head she repeated it, yes. The wind whooshed in her ears, a dull roar that filled her mind as the air around them grew ever colder. No matter how she tried to form the words, to utter what her heart ached to say, they clung to the back of her tongue.

"It's almost too late," Kaece warned. "I hear the wings of a dragon; we are not alone in these clouds. Say ya want me and I'll guide the Simurg away. Say ya want him, and we'll die together at the Drakeon summit."

Rebecca stumbled over the ultimatum, immersed in confusion. It didn't make sense; she didn't need to choose between them. But before she could argue or untangle the unfolding drama between Lykos and Maedian, she had to warn Alex and Sebastian about the dragon. "Simurg, take us to the others, quickly."

The Simurg grunted, a deep growl that rumbled in his throat and against her arms, then he ascended steeply through the clouds. They drew up next to Alex and the infant Gruy. Sebastian grasped the neck of his mount – the Pegasus began to fret at the nearness of the Lykos.

"There's a dragon up here," she shouted. "We need to do something."

Sebastian's eyes widened; his face contorted with anxiety. "If this is true, we must descend. The risk is too great; we will return to the Grufoi nesting area. We must get safely away from the Drakeon territory at once!"

"And give up?" Alex exclaimed. "No way! I'm not scared, we can't let them get away with this!"

Rebecca opened her mouth, but he willfully urged his Gruy down and escaped into the clouds before she could get a word out. She cursed and steered after him. He'd not gone far – he'd landed on a snow-blanketed plateau that jutted out of pale orange rock. In the distance, a deep reddish orange peak reached higher than any of the other spires. No snow rested on that tall peak; the thick clouds avoided it, as if its menacing appearance frightened even mother nature.

Alex dismounted his Gruy and sunk knee-deep into the snow. The Simurg plowed into the white powder in front of him.

Rebecca yelled, "Get back on the Gruy, Alex! We're NOT doing this."

"But look! It's *right there*. We're this close to getting Sebastian's dad back and ending this war."

"It's too late," Kaece stated quietly.

Sebastian left the Pegasus and approached her defiant brother. He placed a hand on Alex's shoulder as he spoke. "Metakosmos, you will never be a Guard for Maedian civilization if you cannot follow orders. As I told you before, if we were to encounter any dragons, it would be most vital for you and your sister to flee at once. The Drakeon treaty clearly states that human lives are forfeit if caught trespassing on this land. Return to your flyer at once. Go to the nests and wait, as we discussed. I will speak with the Drakeon alone, and if I do not return in two days, then you will return to Thalassa Harbor, and tell Demarko that he was right and I am but a dead fool boy."

"Not a chance," Alex argued, his eyes blazing; his fists balled tight. "We're in this together!"

Too late. Kaece's words echoed in her head; Sebastian's behavior reflected the truth she didn't want to believe. She peered into the stoic expression of the woman who'd lit up her life throughout their journey. The Lykos' regression to the cold, uncaring person – so unaffected by fear or compassion – she'd met in Sow Endus caught Rebecca off guard. Her brow furrowed and she grabbed Kaece's hand, encasing it in her own. She studied those yellow eyes for the warmth she'd become so used to having, and felt so desperate to keep. She squeezed Kaece's hand, pleadingly.

Kaece ignored her; her cold gaze focused on Sebastian.

The wind howled around them; flurries of snow lifted off the ground and swirled into the sky. She breathed a deep sigh – it figured that everything that could possibly go wrong would. Why not start snowing out of nowhere? Heck, why not have an avalanche? Kaece's arms encircled her, protectively.

"I wish ya hadn't chosen him," she whispered.

A torrent of ice and snow buffeted against their bodies. Rebecca squinted through the squall, hardly able to make out Sebastian or Alex in the pelting sleet. All three of the flyers fled.

"You need to get out of here now!" Sebastian cried.

"What's happening?" She screamed over the wind.

"Drakeon!" His voice boomed, "Cease this at once. Let us speak with one another as civilized creatures do."

"What was that, Madius?" A woman's voice answered, followed by her malefic cackle.

The woman's silhouette shone with pale light, illuminating her shape but nothing more. Though she seemed to float in mid-air, Rebecca knew she must have stood atop one of the snow-blanketed mesas corralling them. From the side of the steep wall below the woman, a deep chuckle rumbled through the wind; a luminescent orange tribal spiral flared outward like wings across a man's broad chest, burning like embers in the blizzard. His silhouette cast a fiery radiance that pulsed in time with the woman's eerie chant.

"I said, cease this at once!" Sebastian shouted, his power as palpable as the ice swirling around them.

The utter lack of response, the woman's continued murmurs into the wind, the resonating grumble of the man's amusement, frightened Rebecca. Who were these people? His Power had worked on everything – even dragons. Maybe these people weren't people at all, she considered. Maybe they were mindless dragon-familiars, poor brainwashed humans who had no mind left to command.

Pressing herself into Kaece, she surveyed the area for any possible escape route away from the Drakeon-people. She couldn't let them take Kaece to the dragons. She tried to think of something – anything.

The woman's voice hushed, trailing off as the storm passed. The flurries soothed, fluttering peacefully downward; as did the woman. Her red ombre hair twisted in neat curls around her face like coiled flames, and her deep purple eyes glimmered with mischief. For Rebecca, though, it was the thin black horns that spiraled back from the woman's hair that destroyed the illusion that she could be human. She had a feminine curve that led Rebecca's eyes from her breasts to her hips without a thought; black, skin-tight scaled fabric clung to her, leaving little to the imagination. Her exposed midriff and arms were toned like Kaece's, but her muscles less defined.

"Foolish little creatures," she chortled. "Though... I can't say I hadn't hoped you would trespass. It's been far too long since Typhos' last guests arrived."

The man closed in on Alex and Sebastian.

"Behind you, Alex!" Rebecca warned.

Alex ducked and rolled into the snow, a failed maneuver that only put a few steps between him and the bulky man.

Muscles rippled under his tightly stretched skin as he moved languidly forward after Alex; his massive chest heaved with every breath. He cracked his knuckles, his biceps flexing. The black scales covered little more than the man's groin. His hair, darker than his body, was cropped short enough that his thick horns jutted obviously, curving down like a ram's horns over his forehead. Set with intensity on Sebastian, his bluish purple eyes shone like tanzanite.

To Rebecca's surprise, Kaece's focus remained only on the woman. Sebastian, too, seemed to care more about her presence than the man towering behind them. Sebastian stepped toward her, his hand in front of him the same way he'd commanded the dragon in Sow Endus. "You will not harm these humans. You will take us to your Elder."

The woman twirled her fingers, a gesture that reminded Rebecca of stirring a cauldron. Glittering snow swirled with the motion. Steam hissed up from a melting patch of snow and an eyeless, mouthless black serpent lurched from the pool.

"She's casting black magic!" Alex cried. "Don't let it touch you!"

Kaece pushed Rebecca behind her and arched her back defensively, her claws and teeth bared – but the snake didn't come for them. It launched through the snow, slithering for Alex and Sebastian at an ethereal speed. Bolts from Alex's crossbow shot into the snow in a trail behind the snake as it lunged past him. Sebastian leapt back in fright, but too slow to keep away from the black serpent. It shot up the leg of his pants and Sebastian shrieked, jumping in a vain effort to shake it out. Alex's crossbow aimed at Sebastian.

Rebecca ran toward them – away from the protection of Kaece – and screamed, "Don't shoot him!"

Sebastian writhed in the snow, slapping frantically at himself before the featureless snake burst out of his shirt-collar. The black creature wrapped itself around Sebastian's neck, slithering up and into his mouth as he shouted futile commands at the dragon-people. It coiled around his head, covering his face so completely that his words became inaudible.

"Stop! It's not Sebastian's fault," Rebecca whimpered. She pushed Alex's crossbow down and stood in front of him.

The dragon-woman smirked, and then both she and the man removed plugs from their ears. "Were you speaking to me, human? I couldn't hear a word of it, Power driven or not. Ever since the last Madius visited, we've taken precautions in order to be better able to deal with his kind. Wasn't there something you've been waiting to tell the next one who came along, Magnus?"

A wide grin split his face while the man ran his fingers across his chest with pride. "Bring your weapons and armor, bring your machines of war, but be prepared for bloodshed – never again will the Drakeon succumb to manipulations."

Kaece laughed mockingly, an eruption of irony that gave Rebecca the sense that there were further politics she wasn't privy to. The man's response – his grin wilting into a rage-filled sneer – reinforced the sentiment. Rebecca let go of her brother's arm and jumped between Kaece and Magnus.

"We aren't here to fight," Rebecca pleaded. "We don't want any war. We just want you to give Sebastian's father back so we can all go home."

Magnus, face contorted with anger, looked past Rebecca to Kaece. "No war, eh Lykos? Maybe what she says is true, won't be any war for you now. Seeing you here brings me great joy; I will relish tearing off bit by bit of you while you cry out your repentance and beg for mercy."

"You're talking all big about fighting man-to-man but you're nothing but cowards!" Alex growled at Magnus, aiming his crossbow at him. "Trying to scare helpless women and hiding from silly words... You murdered innocent people, you don't fight like honorable warriors! Go on, put your magic tricks aside and face me, Alex the Greatest – you've met your match."

"Calm, child," the woman chided. "His quarrel is not with you, it is with the Lykos. He does not wish to, nor will he, kill you. I am the High Priestess of the Drakeon, my name is Ardin. Magnus here is the Warlord. While he is brutish and makes combat of every situation, that is far from my intention. You see, we've been watching you humans for many days now. The Drakeon do not kill simply for the sake of killing, nor do we eat the flesh of humanoids. This was merely an excursion to subdue the Madius," she smirked again. "And to provide a little entertainment."

"So you'll let us go?" Rebecca perked, hope seeping back into her chilled veins. "We can just leave the way we came and you'll never see us again. No harm no foul, right?"

Ardin laughed. "Well... We get so very few visitors anymore, and Typhos is waiting ever so patiently for the right one. We simply can't allow a possibility to slip by, can we, Magnus?"

The man assented with a grunt and a nod.

"But!" Ardin continued before Rebecca could argue. "I can also be reasonable. If you two humans cooperate, perhaps we can arrange for some of you to go free."

"No," Kaece snarled, sinking low into a crouch, poised to attack. "They're not going to work with ya and the pile of bone-dust ya zealots worship. The boy is right – your fight is here. Now!"

Kaece sprang toward the High Priestess at the same moment a bolt launched from Alex's crossbow. Rebecca wanted to scream – why was everyone being so difficult? She chased after Kaece, but tripped over her cold-numbed feet and toppled into the snow. Behind her, the outraged roar of a dragon echoed across the plateau. A rush of fire melted the snow around her.

The man had disappeared. In his stead stood an enormous dragon with coal-black scales. His thick horns curved downward in a spiral, the cracks in his scales flickered like hot cinder. The dragon's breast illuminated with an elaborate spiral that branched outward from his neck to his underbelly like the rays of the sun. Alex stood dumbfounded, his jaw slack as he gaped up at the impressive foe. Sebastian lay on the ground behind him, still clawing at the serpent coiled around his head. Rebecca twisted to find Kaece limp, a few feet in front of Ardin.

"No!" Rebecca raced to Kaece's side and dropped to her knees. She frantically felt for Kaece's pulse. The guilt of forcing the Lykos to come with her to die, instead of running away with her, pressed itself on her just before the faint throb of Kaece's veins greeted Rebecca's fingertips.

She glared up at Ardin, "What did you do to her?"

"And what does a human girl want with a Lykos?" Ardin taunted, her lips curved into a cruel smile. "Come, Magnus, take your toy. But don't kill her... Yet."

The dragon stepped forward – dangerously close to crushing Alex. He fired another bolt into the glowing chest above him. Like throwing a pebble at a mountain, the weapon was useless for even distracting the dragon. Ardin's rigid, cold hands pulled her away from Kaece's body.

She fought against Ardin's grip, as Magnus closed his huge taloned hand around Kaece and shook her limp body like a rag doll.

Rebecca screamed, "Please don't hurt her! Please..."

Without a response, the dragon plucked Sebastian off the ground with two talons. Magnus' wings spread; Rebecca watched helplessly while he took flight. Ardin's grip loosened. Furious, Rebecca spun on her heel and clenched her fists at her sides.

"Take me," she bargained. "Do whatever to me, okay? Just make him bring her back and let her go. I'll be a slave, a meal... an object. I don't care. Just bring her back."

Another bolt from Alex's crossbow whizzed by, inches from her arm. Not only was he dangerously close to hitting her, he also missed the dragon-woman.

"Alex!" She snapped, "You're more likely to kill me than she is at this rate! Will you put that thing away? I'm trying to get us out of here, okay?"

While he lowered his arm, his jaw set and hurt in his eyes, Ardin whispered into her ear. "You're not in a very good position to be bargaining, my precious human."

Precious. Rebecca didn't miss the implication. If Ardin considered her precious, she could use it to their advantage. "Didn't you say you wanted the two of us to cooperate? That you didn't want us dead? That means you're going to need us alive for something. I can deny you that. I will end my own life if you so much as hurt any of them."

"How impetuous." Ardin's tight-lipped frown betrayed her apparent indifference. "Stand back and I will take you to our Elder. Only he can choose to spare your friends."

Rebecca nodded then walked back to her brother. She put her arms around him.

"They're liars. They're going to kill us no matter what we do. We should just..." Alex swallowed. "Jump."

"No," she smiled gently. "It's not hopeless. Monique had the same kind of bravado, she liked to make everything seem impossible even when it wasn't. You know how she taunted people? It was just a tough act. I can work with this, I know I can. I'll get you and Kaece out of here."

"And you and Sebastian?"

"We'll deal with that once you guys are safe, okay?"

A pillar of flame erupted from where Ardin had stood; Rebecca and Alex shielded their faces from the sudden bright heat. The fire fanned and dissipated to reveal a slender dragon with thin black horns and a tribal crescent moon burning like molten lava across her lower back.

"I hate the dragons in this world," Alex muttered.

"I'm not fond of dragons in any world," Rebecca agreed as Ardin's claws enveloped them.

CHAPTER 12

Sunlight glared down on the snow at the cave's entrance; the light reflected into the cavernous interior. Deep-set concave walls, smoothed over by eons of erosion – or perhaps seconds of magic, Rebecca considered – were all that greeted her. Small tribal runes were etched into the walls, spiraling upward as they wrapped around the cave.

Rebecca touched one of the carved markings; she felt the rough edges in the neat, deliberate cuts. The petroglyphs looked like something created by humans, an idea she might've entertained if the etchings hadn't encircled even the apex of the high domed ceiling. As her gaze followed the ascending spiral, she mumbled, "Do you think humans and dragons once worked together?"

"No," Alex almost laughed from the cavern's entrance. He leaned up against thin air – the solid magical barrier that, in spite of the gaping cave mouth, kept them from leaving. "According to the books, people hadn't even discovered Xiratera up until a couple hundred years ago. The treaty with the Maedians is the only 'working together' they've ever done."

Rebecca frowned at his matter-of-fact tone, the all-knowing air about it reeked of Sebastian's influence on her little brother. "But look."

She pointed overhead to a cave painting of a spread-eagled human. It stood beneath a huge-horned, spiked dragon that bore a combination of the markings she'd seen on Ardin and Magnus. The dragon had more smears of tribal fire than even that covering its body, which she could see in entirety in the repeated depictions of the same dragon elsewhere in the cave.

"It looks like that ghost dragon that tried to eat us for breakfast," he gestured at it skeptically. "And that dragon in Sow Endus. And it looks like it wants to eat that guy, too. How does that look like working together to you?"

She could see why Alex would say that: the dragon's open jaws hovered dangerously close to the figure, who seemed to welcome the prospect of his demise. "I'm sure the writing explains it... Those history books didn't mention anything about these runes, did they?"

Alex shrugged, "There *is* a dragon language. Maybe this is what it looks like. But the book said they communicate through noises and body language, like most animals. Dragons don't use words. But they spoke in Common – English – to us, so maybe the books are wrong."

The magical barrier gave way as Ardin passed through, the air around her seared like embers creeping across burnt paper. It resealed behind her, the blazing edges seeping together and flickering out.

"Remove yourself from the Eolith," she snapped, then stared pointedly at Rebecca's fingertips until Rebecca dropped her hand away. "The Elder, Zakhar, will arrive shortly. He will listen to your plea, in spite of the rules clearly written upon these walls... But if I were you, I wouldn't anticipate anything by way of acquittance."

Alex snorted, but Rebecca stepped in before he could make matters worse with a rude retort. "What sort of rules?"

"Perhaps 'rules' was a poor choice of word. This writing," Ardin opened her arms out toward the walls of the cavern, a reverent tone infecting her voice, "tells the tale of Gaeadia, from its creation to this moment. Our Lord Typhos will rise again from the prison of his tomb; he will save our kind and all those worthy from the apocalypse threatening our world. That is, of course, only if we strictly adhere to his guidelines set forth in this history."

Apocalypse. Rebecca frowned, her brows furrowed as she recalled the desecrated landscape of her travels. The barren hills outside of Tekton, the strip-mined mountains on the way to Thalassa Harbor... Was the dragon about to devour the painted man because mankind would bring about the end of the world?

"Screw your history," Alex spat, kicking the wall. His shoe smudged one of the paintings: Ardin flinched. "You guys suck. You're suppose to be all-powerful, smart, and – most importantly – protect peoples' treasure and stuff. I saw what you did to those towns!"

"Is that so?" Ardin asked evenly. The upward turn of her sneer made Rebecca's blood feel like ice.

"He's just a kid."

"I'm not—"

"Alex. Just stop," she commanded, annoyance and desperation concentrated in her stern glower at him.

He folded his arms across his chest and sulked.

Rebecca gestured at the walls around her. "So where do we fit into these guidelines? I mean, why would your history say that we couldn't be allowed to leave? What about this dragon, he's with a man – is this where the rules are?"

Ardin glanced up to the glyph, a sincere smile lighting her face. "That's exactly right, human girl. That 'dragon' is no mere dragon, he is the great Typhos himself, and the scripture you see around him explains the process in which he most prefers to receive his guests."

One of the runes stood out in particular; it repeated more than Rebecca could hope to count throughout the room. She pointed to the rune, feeling that she knew its meaning. "That says 'Typhos,' right? Is his name another word for God?"

"Such interest in the Eolith, mortal. Do you believe that there is an answer to the predicament before you beyond suffering the consequences of your trespass? You will not discover any alternatives."

"No," Rebecca dismissed. "It's just that I'd like to know who my host is, if I'm going to be his guest and all."

"Very well, it would be a pleasure to oblige such a request if only you both can hold your tongues long enough to hear the tale. Our history is long, and you have little time..."

Rebecca nodded idly, ignoring the dragon's subtle threat. All she needed was time to find a loophole in their treaty, but the runes provided little counsel without being able to read them. She welcomed Ardin's willingness to share the secrets of their potential freedom, listening to the dragon's mythology with her full attention.

"Before the world fractured,
Before the great waters ran divides between dragon-kind,
Before warm-bloods walked Gaeadia,
There was a single land mass: ice, mountains, forest, drylands, all in order.
Dragons tended their own, fending off other dragons and lesser creatures.

The Drakeon born of the volcanic peaks, protected their homeland
They drove the Geodra to extinction long before Typhos' birth.
When he came to be, his empire was vast
When dragons stood as tall as the volcanic peaks,
He stood taller.
His body wore marks from arm to arm
His body glistened from leg to leg
His body bore embers from neck to tail tip.

For the thousand years between his birth and adolescence
The Elite marveled his strength and wisdom.
He was prophesied to conquer the world,
And bring the Drakeon to rule over all.
But when Typhos ascended as Elder,
He forsook the Prophecy.

Typhos looked upon the desert with great sadness.
Blood streaked, scattered with black scale and bones of the dead,
Once Geodra territory, the expanse served only as a combat arena.
'Look before you,' he'd told the Elite Council,
'Without the Geodra, this land has become barren.
These desert battles must cease.
The Drakeon are all to return to the red peaks.'
And then he broke off the tip of his right horn
He crushed it in his hand.
The wind carried the red bone dust out across the land,
To the north, the south, the east and the west.
'Red clay to honor the Geodra, scales and magic forever lost,'
With his words, the clay settled deep into the cracks.
And then he broke off the tip of his left horn

114

He crushed it in his hand.
The wind carried the white bone dust out across the land,
To the north, the south, the east and the west.
'White sand to honor the Geodra, their bones that serve as their grave stone,'
With his words, the sand settled into high dunes.
For centuries, none crossed into the sacred land of the Geodra.

Typhos ruled the Drakeon, independent of the Dragon Wars.
He would not agree with the Warlord's ploy to gain territory.
Even when the first of the strange reptilian Sauros appeared,
Typhos refused to fight.

As the years wore on,
Sauros swarmed the continent,
Sauros consumed everything in their path.
Meat, water, foliage – all was left to waste
As the carnal scourge rushed the land
Typhos watched,
Typhos listened,
But Typhos did not fight.

Words carried in the winds,
It was said that from a Sauros cut down,
Three sprang up in its place.
A hundred to one, the Sauros grew brave,
They killed dragons,
They consumed their flesh.

Typhos mourned his fallen brethren
His tears dripped into the volcanic ridges,
Geysers burst hot tears into the sky as his rage boiled.
'These hedonist beasts must be destroyed,
Without its guardians, like the barren desert,
Gaeadia will be no more.'
Typhos beckoned his Warlord, ready to listen,
The Warlord had only these words;
'There are too many, my wise Elder.
The Drakeon, and all dragon-kind are ill-fated.'
But Typhos would not hear this answer.

Typhos walked across the desert,
White sand blew his scales rugged,
Wind tattered his wings,
Sauros nipped at his body,
But Typhos trudged onward.

He reached the land of towering trees, jungles and forests alike,

Trees, formerly lush, stood like naked sticks.
Straight to the Elder of the Drakloron he went.
Typhos said, 'Set our physical differences aside,
Do we not all raise our young to be strong and wise?'
And the Jungle Lord listened with rapt attention
Surrounded by former enemies, Typhos stood tall and declared,
'Let Dragon-kind be one army and we will overcome the Sauros.'
The Great Green-scaled Elder bowed to Typhos,
And pledged, 'Lead us to Victory, Arbiter.'

Twice as far Typhos traveled to the next territory
Rain squelched his searing scales,
Cold mist obscured his vision,
Sauros leapt on his back,
But Typhos trudged onward.

He reached the land of expansive grass, marshes, and plains alike
Turf, once bountiful, lay crushed in waste.
Straight to the Elder of the Drakanthra he went
Typhos said, 'Set our physical differences aside,
Do we not all raise our young to be strong and wise?'
And the Plains Lord listened with rapt attention.
Surrounded by former enemies, Typhos stood tall and declared,
'Let Dragon-kind be one army and we will overcome the Sauros.'
The Great Golden-scaled Elder bowed to Typhos,
And pledged, 'Lead us to Victory, Arbiter.'

Typhos traversed the snow-capped mountains to the far reaches of the continent,
His body steamed in the snowfall,
He shivered as blizzards concealed his path,
The Sauros clawed him from beneath the snow,
But Typhos trudged onward.

He reached the land of glaciers and deep ice crags
Cold wind seeped through ice splintered with cracks,
Straight to the Elder of the Drakryon he went.
Typhos said, 'Set our physical differences aside,
Do we not all raise our young to be strong and wise?'
And the Ice Lord listened with rapt attention.
Surrounded by former enemies, Typhos stood tall and declared,
'Let Dragon-kind be one army and we will overcome the Sauros.'
The Great White-scaled Elder bowed to Typhos,
And pledged, 'Lead us to Victory, Arbiter.'

At the edge of the continent, Typhos traveled further still.
He swam into the deep ocean, which quiesced his inner-fire,
The water's weight began to crush him,

And still, the aquatic Sauros bit into his flesh.
But Typhos swam onward.

He reached the chromatic reefs at the ocean's bottom,
Paling coral and thrashed kelp forests,
All struggled to survive the hungering Sauros.
Straight to the Elder of the Hydrak he went.
Typhos said, 'Set our physical differences aside,
Do we not all raise our young to be strong and wise?'
And the Water Lord listened with rapt attention.
Surrounded by former enemies, Typhos stood tall and declared,
'Let Dragon-kind be one army and we will overcome the Sauros.'
The Great Blue-scaled Elder bowed to Typhos,
And pledged, 'Lead us to Victory, Arbiter.'

Typhos returned to the surface and took to the skies.
Months passed, searching without a perch for respite,
Fatigue encumbered him,
Lightning struck his horns,
Alate Sauros battered him with their bodies,
But Typhos flew onward.

After a seemingly timeless hunt,
He reached the ineffable sanctuary of the Psydrak,
Safe, and unharmed by the Sauros, Typhos feared their response to his call.
But still to the Elder of the Psydrak he went.
For one final time, he said, 'Set our physical differences aside,
Do we not all raise our young to be strong and wise?'
The Temporal Lord laughed and shook Typhos' hand,
'Young Dragon,' he said,
For the Psydrak lived many eons longer than Drakeon ever have,
'We have seen your journey across the land,
To the depths of the ocean,
To the furthest reaches of the sky.
You have brought unity to the world.
With that unity you will conquer all,
Just as was prophesied when you hatched.'
Dissatisfied, Typhos still rejected the idea of prophecy,
But he said, 'If that will make you join our cause,
And fight against the Sauros, Believe as you will.'
The Great Violet-scaled Elder bowed to Typhos,
And pledged, 'We complete your army, Typhos.
The prophecy is true - you will conquer the Sauros.
But in doing so, you will destroy Dragon-kind.
If Dragons are to live,
You have no choice but to believe in prophecy,
For yours will be our one chance at resurrection.'

'Lead us to victory, Arbiter, now and for Eons to come.'

Typhos lead his army, the greatest warriors of all Dragon-kind,
Into the endless waves of Sauros.
Each dragon's power was of use,
But collectively, their power was staggering.
Sauros fell, and in their cowardice,
They fell back,
Further and further from Dragon lands
The Sauros retreated.

But while the Dragons slept,
The Sauros multiplied and grew larger.
Every morning, the Dragons faced new Sauros,
Who were born of an indestructible quality.
No matter how many Sauros were destroyed over the years,
Countless more came in their place.

A hundred years of war passed,
And Typhos called the Elders together.
'We're at a stand-still' Typhos told to the Elders' Council, 'Tactics must change.'
'We've strangled them, and cut them.' The Jungle Elder growled,
'And still they return.'
'We've burned them, and buried them.' The Plains Elder snarled,
'And still they return.'
'We've frozen them, and shattered them.' The Ice Elder added,
'And still they return.'
'We've drowned them, and crushed them.' The Water Elder cried,
'And still they return.'
'We've tried weakening them, and controlling them.' The Psydrak concluded,
'And yet they will always return.'

Typhos abhorred violence,
Yet attack was all Dragon-kind knew to do.
His peaceful temperament begged for a way to banish the Sauros,
To send them to a different land,
Where they could pose no threat to Dragons.
'Of course!' The Psydrak Elder commended,
'But how will such a feat be accomplished?'
And Typhos allowed his instincts to answer for him,
'Our ancestors created the Volcanoes, the Jungles,
They created the Marshes, and the Ice.
Our ancestors created fire, water, air, and earth.
If Dragon-kind has the power to alter this world,
Why can we not create another?'

The Dragons, together, jumped at the center point of the continent.

Great cracks spread in all directions,
And water rushed to fill the gaps.
The world shook, and the continent broke apart.

They once again warred with the Sauros,
They pushed them together to one part of the broken land mass.
They cheered at their success as the Sauros drifted away.

Once the Sauros were vanquished
The Dragons went separate ways,
And again, the Dragons turned on each other.
Typhos pleaded,
'Do not let victory tear away our brotherhood,
We are kin.'
The Dragons replied, 'The War is over,
And now there is less land than before,
Each for himself.'
With righteous fury,
Typhos swore he'd never trust again.

Too soon, they'd celebrated.
Too soon, they'd disbanded.
Few years passed before, once again,
The divided continents each swarmed with Sauros.

The Elders crawled back,
Each from their separate territories in the broken lands.
The Elders came to Typhos' lair,
Each one begged for his forgiveness,
For his leadership,
For his help.
When all stood united before him, Typhos answered.
'You betrayed me.
You betrayed each other.
What's done has been done,
You deserve the fate the Sauros threaten.
But I will not betray you.
If you seek salvation,
You will find the Elder of the Psydrak.
You will meet me at the summit of the highest volcano.'

Five Elders did as Typhos requested.
Five Elders met Typhos inside of the red peak.
Five Elders sacrificed their lives.
None ever returned from the volcano.
Typhos burrowed into the magma-chamber, and bedded down.
How he took their power is unknown,

But that his body was not strong enough to contain it is certain

Typhos spoke through the rock walls,
And his voice, with so much power, caused earthquakes.
Mountains grew from the ground around his entombment.
His mental link with the Dragons spanned the entire world.
When his final words came, all heard his prophecy.

'Without their magic,
Sauros are destined to rest as nothing but bones embedded in rock.
Without our magic,
Dragons will fade from power.
Even the weakest of creatures will rule over the former gods of this world.
And creatures there will be many of in the years to come.
Fight, and you will die.
Cower, and you will die.
Kill only those that already walk the path of death.
Dragon-kind will cease to exist if you do not heed this:
When the Drakeon fall to darkness
When warm-blooded creatures control the world
You must open the seal on my tomb
All who enter will perish
The one who breaks the seal will release my power
They will bring the worlds together,
And restore the Dragons to their rightful place.
If the seal is not broken
The warm-blooded creatures will destroy both worlds,
All will die.'

The world fell silent with the great Typhos.
When his voice faded away,
Every Dragon's mind ached,
Every Dragon's body burned,
And Sauros vanished from the world."

"But as Typhos had prophesied, Dragon-kind is forever changed," Ardin laughed bitterly. "Always growing weaker, each generation smaller, living shorter life-spans, and hatchlings fewer. We must find the right sacrifice, or face extinction."

"We're sacrifices, then?" Rebecca asked rhetorically.

Ardin, seeming not to hear her, turned expectantly toward the entrance of the cave; no sooner than she turned, the body of a tremendous dragon appeared. He stood easily three times the size of any of the dragons Rebecca'd seen, and his fiery tribal design blazed glowing red-hot around his neck and down onto his breast like an elaborate flaming choker. The dragon bowed his head into the cave; his face was covered in greyish spikes that reminded her of an old man's beard. His horns were thick like Magnus', but curled in on themselves many times over.

"Elder Zakhar bids you welcome, though he does not shift to lesser forms. Dragon tongues do not permit for human speech. He requests that you answer what questions he has for you, and – if you cooperate – he will make an appropriate decision."

"This is total BS!" Alex snarled. "You know you're just gonna sacrifice us. We're not gonna tell you anything!"

"Elder Zakhar asks why you have come to Drakeon Peak, and from where you hail," Ardin continued in spite of Alex's outburst.

"We tried to tell you already," Rebecca answered. "We're here to get Sebastian's father. We started out in Sow Endus, where we were attacked by a Drakeon...But we're actually from Albuquerque...A place on Earth."

"You're giving the enemy information," Alex growled.

"Elder Zakhar apologizes for the behavior of the dragon that attacked you... However, the Madius' father is not here. Prior to your arrival, we had no knowledge of him at all. Unfortunately for you, you've chosen the wrong clan of dragons to visit. The Drakeon that attacked you, is in fact no longer are Drakeon at all – but a betrayer of our kind, a part of a cabal that left us some time ago. Tell us of this Lykos woman."

"She's..." Rebecca started, anxiety and hopelessness seeping in; what if Kaece was the one they wanted to sacrifice? "She's helping us. Please don't hurt her? She didn't even want to come here, it's all my fault."

"You're emotional about her," Ardin noted.

Heat crept into her cheeks. "She's my friend..."

"Lykos have made themselves the enemy of Drakeon. According to our ways, she should be destroyed."

"No!" Rebecca shouted, hoping that if she were loud enough, what Ardin said wouldn't be true. It felt irrational, but she couldn't stop herself.

Ardin sighed and rolled her eyes. "However. Zakhar sympathizes with your reason for trespassing, and will allow the Madius to resume his search for his father. He will also permit the Lykos to return to her pack, granted that she swears never to return again."

"Oh!" Rebecca smiled up at the huge, silent dragon in stunned appreciation. His eyes didn't hold the same cruel gleam that the eyes of the other dragons did. He gave Kaece her freedom back. "Thank you! Thank you, thank you, thank you!"

"What about us?" Alex asked.

"One of you must enter the tomb of Typhos at the summit of Drakeon Peak," Ardin replied, her tone filled with obvious discontent at the Elder's decision. "The other will be sent away with the Madius and the Lykos."

Alex and Rebecca both volunteered in unison.

Ardin held up her hands; wisps of magic trailed from her fingertips. "One at a time. You first. Speak your reasoning, child."

"It's obvious. I can't let you send my sister, I'm supposed to be the hero. I know it... So," he swallowed, then continued with the tough-guy act, "if somebody has to die, it's gotta be me."

With a nod, Ardin acknowledged his reply. Then she gestured for Rebecca to give her logic.

"Well," she began, smiling sadly at Alex before she looked to the Drakeon Elder. "He's right. He's young, smart, handsome, everything a good hero should be. He's meant to be a hero, and he's going to do great things in his life. Which is exactly why it can't end here... But me? There's nothing special to lose, I'm a terrible friend, girlfriend, daughter, sister... I did this —" Rebecca pushed up her wet sleeve to expose the raised pink scar, "just a few minutes before I fell into this world. I'm the person of least consequence of all of us... If you truly do sympathize with our cause, you'll sacrifice me."

The Elder raised his head out of sight, though his glowing chest remained visible outside in the setting darkness.

"He has chosen," Ardin waved them forward to the cave entrance. "Follow me."

As they reached the barrier, Rebecca stepped through as though it had never been in place. She glanced back to see Alex trapped behind the magical wall. He slammed his fists into the invisible barrier, tears cutting through the dirt in his face as he cried out words she couldn't hear.

"Once the moon has risen, you will begin your ascent. When you have passed into the tomb, your friends will be released and able to continue with their lives."

Rebecca nodded, unsure of which feeling was stronger – the wash of relief that she'd won their freedom, or the growing pit of fear in her stomach. "How can I trust that you'll let them go?"

"Simply have faith. Elder Zakhar believes that you are exactly the kind of sacrifice that Lord Typhos would have wanted. The child is too young, the Madius is an Arbiter as well, and the Lykos... Well, she's your personal passion. He trusts that you will willingly cross the seal into the tomb if we release her, no matter how it may irritate the Warlord. You, mortal, are troublesome. However, I doubt you will be anything more than a mere toy to our Lord Typhos, and you are correct that the world will suffer no loss when it loses you."

The mean jab felt unnecessary to Rebecca; she understood Ardin would have preferred multiple sacrifices. The pain, she reasoned, whether emotional or physical, was worth her friends freedom. "So... One more question. How will it happen? How am I going to die? Will it hurt?"

"That was three questions. Magnus will take you to the path, where you may choose to jump to your death if you wish – we will then have to send the young boy in your place. If you make the wise decision and continue into the tomb, there will be a barrier much like the one behind us."

Rebecca glanced back to the invisible wall, where Alex pounded and cried hopelessly. His pitiful struggle made her heart break.

"No one has ever returned from the tomb, so none could tell you what is on the other side. Though," Ardin smirked, "the screams have been heard from here, so you can expect that something frightening or painful lies in wait behind the seal. You have one last chance. Do you still wish to be the one who enters?"

She turned away from the sad sight of Alex and looked up at the towering peak – it no longer seemed red as the light faded away. She didn't wish to enter the tomb, no more than she wished they'd ever come up the mountain in the first place, but she knew the time for regrets had passed. All she could do in her final moments was hope for everyone's safety, hope the dragons would honor their bargain, and hope that Kaece could forgive her stupidity for dragging her up the mountain.

"Yes, I'll be your sacrifice."

Chapter 13

Warmth rushed over Rebecca; the numbing cold from her moonlit flight yielded instantly to a dull tingling sensation. The barrier she stepped through, into the tomb of the long-dead dragon god, kept out the cold.

Only a few steps inside, Rebecca noticed the first of the bones – huge and discolored – they could have belonged to dragons. The large bones decorated the cave floor just inside the entrance, more – smaller, but inhuman – were scattered a few paces beyond those. Farther ahead, the ivory remnants of countless creatures lined the walls of the corridor. But at the furthest point, the most disturbing remains lay in wait: a human skull balanced atop a slumped ribcage. All around it, the disjointed bones of past sacrifices existed where their living souls fell.

She felt sick, taking in the shapes of each fallen sacrifice who'd once walked the very same path of condemnation. Dread roused bile in the back of her throat, but she cringed and swallowed against it. She pressed herself to persevere – if dying would save Kaece and the others, she couldn't hesitate so close to their freedom. Only after she passed the last of the human remains did she realize that the warm tingling sensation no longer pricked her skin.

After all the destruction she'd witnessed in Sow Endus, the gore she'd seen in Tekton, the fate of collapsing into a pile of bones didn't seem so bad. Perhaps, she thought, it was so tame that she hadn't noticed it happen. She raised up her hands, examining herself with the expectation that she'd have skeletal fingers. Her palms were slick with sweat; she felt her heart racing and the breath filling her lungs – she hadn't crumbled like the others.

"Yet," she laughed bitterly to herself.

The sweltering heat of the cave felt oppressive; steam rose from the walls of the cavern. And the stench of something awful, of Haima Fox Demons – of death – filled the air. She looked back for the first time since she'd turned away from her little brother. The magical barrier burned with the brightness of a second sun, alive with dancing flames. One of the flames lashed out, licking the back of her right hand as she raised it to cover her eyes from the explosive blinding light. She yelped, scrambling backwards and clutching at the burn. It seared hotter than anything she'd ever felt.

Sweat trickled down her face. The heat intensified with each passing moment, making the cave feel like a sauna from hell; the beads of sweat on her skin began to evaporate into steam. Clamping her hand over the sharp pain of the burn, she struggled to breathe.

She turned back down the corridor, which opened up into a tunnel on a downgrade – an unavoidable ramp into the depths of the mountain she'd just ascended. She trudged onward. Far ahead, light flickered into view. Her determination to block out the pain in her hand kept her focused on the distant fire, kept her marching forward without heeding either the escalating heat nor the distance between her and the entrance. Unlike the all-consuming blaze of the barrier, the radiant design decorated the end of the tunnel in a way that reminded her of the etchings in the Eolith. She counted five large runic symbols that glowed like magma in the wall.

The floor of the cavern, visible as she drew near, flowed with intricate patterns. Interlocking circles formed of molten rock surrounded a bubbling ring of magma. Lava crawled through small jagged cracks into the tribal runes – repeated on the floor, each within a circle.

She realized that no one, nothing, had ever laid eyes upon those markings before. Thoughts buzzed in her head; confusion, fear, and more than anything – frustration. Typhos wasn't her responsibility – she was supposed to be a sacrifice. All she needed to do was climb into the tomb and die, just like every other sacrifice before her.

Pain shot through her hand and lashed out across her wrist, just above the burn. Her legs buckled; she collapsed against the wall as dizziness washed over her. Cradling her hand against her breast, she sank down onto the floor. The runes glowed in her eyes.

The longer she stared, the more some of the shapes began to look familiar. They seemed like runes from the story of Typhos, but none of them were the rune that said "Typhos." On the far left of the wall, three angled slashes formed an open triangle that encapsulated a spiral. The cracks that ran from the identical symbol on the floor reminded Rebecca of tribal fire.

"Like Magnus," she whispered. Her voice cracked – her tongue felt like a sun-scorched slug, her throat dry and rough like sandpaper.

The bright ember tattoo on Magnus' bare chest greeted her sight when she opened her eyes again. He lay stretched out on his side next to her, his head propped up by his hand. "Aww, did I interrupt your nap? Well, wakey wakey, little human."

Rebecca gasped. Words evaded her completely as the burning in her hand flared anew. The pain constricted like a molten wire biting deep into the flesh of her wrist. She rubbed at the lesion, but there was no wire – there wasn't even a mark.

"Poor frail thing," Magnus mocked. "Have a sprain in your tiny little wrist?"

She glowered at him, but he sat up and took her wrist in his hand. She couldn't feel his touch through the searing pain. Whether she could feel him or not, he was there. In Typhos' tomb.

"Is the seal broken?"

"Not even cracked," he answered with a lilt of amusement.

"Then what are you doing here? I thought..."

His hand engulfed hers; he lifted her onto her feet with ease. "You tell me, my tiny friend. You're the one who brought me here."

"You used the rune," she breathed. Eyebrows drawn together in a mixture of pain and confusion, she strode toward the mark on the wall. The rune against the far left side had burned out – nothing but a black mark remained on the wall. "It's not glowing anymore, but you are..."

With a proud smile, Magnus ran his hands down his chiseled pectorals and naked abdomen. "The embodiment of power, strength, and courage... I *am* Force."

"You forgot narcissism," Rebecca muttered. "But fine, okay – You showed up, the rune disappeared."

"It has begun," he replied.

"What's begun?"

"The end. The Sauros have returned, just as we should have expected... Most of Xiratera is at their mercy. They're climbing toward the Drakeon valley as we speak."

"The Sauros?" She repeated. "The ancient monsters that vanished with Typhos... are here?"

The seriousness in his deep purple eyes when he nodded wrenched Rebecca's attention from the numb, useless weight of her hand.

"But Kaece... Sebastian, Alex..." she protested. They would suffer in spite of her sacrifice.

"Everyone is in danger," he agreed. "We must act swiftly, with the hand of vengeance, and together with the power of Typhos we will be able to destroy everything in our wake. If you will it, I will decimate all who oppose you; in thy name, Gaeadia shall be saved."

"In my name? If *I* will it? What are you talking about?"

"Take my offer, unleash the power of Typhos and obliterate the Sauros before we've delayed too long. Do not repeat Typhos' mistake."

Panic struggled to the surface in shallow gasp after shallow gasp. "I just... want my friends... safe... I want her to be safe... That's why I did this!" She cried, wracked with anxiety.

"Every second lost to hesitation is one second closer to death."

"But what if, Magnus? What if –"

"I am Force." He patted the mark on his chest.

"Fine, *Force*. What if by agreeing to destroy the Sauros, I condemn everyone to something worse? They might have a fighting chance right now, but if we kill them all and the Sauros multiply – you know, three for every one that's cut down – they're going to be outnumbered. What if we just make them stronger? What if. We can't hope to have all the right information from down here in this stupid tomb. I need to know that I'm not hurting everyone more."

"Knowledge," he said, his voice contorting in an echo.

Once the resonating hum in her skull subsided, she opened her eyes. She was in the same place she'd fallen before crossing over the fiery pit. The sensation of an invisible red-hot wire fusing with her flesh seared all the way up her forearm. She gasped, hugging her arm close to her body, her knuckles white from clenching against the pain.

Force stood against the wall – a soldier awaiting his orders. A second rune had gone black; the rune of two curved lines bracketed a crescent moon arch over a small spiral. Positioned on her lower back, the tattooed symbol rested above Ardin's waistline.

"It's beyond me why it is that someone who denies their very thoughts would call upon the power of the mind to help them rescue the world from destruction," Ardin sighed, then placed her hands on her hips and turned to face Rebecca. She tipped her head to the side and frowned disapprovingly down at her. "Are you hoping that sitting around all day will stop the Sauros from devouring the bones of your loved ones?"

Rebecca shot to her feet; black spots filled her vision. She braced herself against the wall, crippled by the excruciating pain consuming her arm. "What can I do? What do we need to do...?"

"We need to acquire more information before we attempt to take any course of action. That's the reason you called upon Knowledge, is it not?" Knowledge. The rune embodied in Ardin's guise stepped forward to the small ring of magma in the center of the room and began chanting.

Trails of sparkly white smoke streamed from Knowledge's fingertips as she wove her hands through the air. Force's eyes reflected the swirling glow of lava in the center of the room. Knowledge churned the molten rock until the glassy surface cast the image of the world beyond the cave.

Rebecca peered into the pool. She wrapped her arms around herself, trying desperately to squeeze the burning sensation out of her arm as she took in the scene unfolding before her. Gaeadia rushed passed from a bird's-eye view; the forests and fields ablaze, the lakes polluted with decimated Maedian machinery, human and animal corpses alike dotted the ground. Then she saw them; colossal creatures clawing, biting, tearing at one another. Dinosaurs. Velociraptors, stegosaurus, allosaurus, even tyrannosaurus. Thousands upon thousands of them, each one crushing everything in its path, even others of its kind.

"Dinosaurs, Really? Dinosaurs."

"Sauros," Knowledge replied. "Their brains are underdeveloped, virtually non-existent. However, their bodies are unlike anything in this world or yours. They evolve rapidly to fit the changing demands of their environment, a process made easier by their asexual reproduction. The Sauros of your world were stagnant, weak and devoid of the magic that makes the Sauros formidable enemies."

The vision focused in on a territory dispute between Sauros. A large club-tailed dinosaur lashed out at a cluster of pterodactyls; the club smashed one of the bird-like dinosaurs against a rock. Then the bloodied abdomen of the pterodactyl split – from the lower half a head rapidly formed; from the head, a smaller, more agile body spawned. The new Sauros rejoined the attack; their claws raked across the thick-skinned back of the club-tail. An excruciating, pathetic noise emitted from its throat as the bird monsters dove in for the kill. Massive, serrated-toothed beaks tore into the fallen dinosaur's flesh until its back had been entirely picked clean. The frenzied pterodactyls dispersed.

The blood-drained corpse shifted and grew. The raw spine jutted out, the ribs flattened in tiers across its back like an armadillo shell. Vertebrae from the upper spine grew and molded with torn flesh to form a leathery armored helmet. She imagined the inside of the dinosaur mutating and filling out the interior of the new protective coverings. Right before her eyes, the dinosaur had recovered completely from its mortal wounds and half a dozen smaller club-tails had been borne of the unsalvageable bits of flesh. The reborn Sauros looked like a horror-movie rendition of an anklyosaurus, all jagged spikes and armor plates.

"This doesn't prove that incineration, an all consuming blast, wouldn't successfully destroy the Sauros army."

"He speaks the truth." Knowledge flicked her wrist; the jungle swirled like mist and dissipated, replaced by a view of the Drakeon territory. "Watch."

All sizes of Sauros rushed the protective cliffs around the peak – the largest head-butted the solid rock, while things resembling velociraptors scaled the mountainside with their hooked claws. Drakeon laid in wait for the climbers to reach the top. Viscous liquid fireballs exploded against the Sauros who ascended quickest. The velociraptor's feathers caught fire, then their entire bodies went up in flames and reduced to ash. Nothing rose. Still outnumbered, the Drakeon fell faster than the Sauros. Growing desperate, they resorted to tooth and claw in close combat – but every mortally wounded Sauros multiplied.

"No!" Rebecca whimpered.

"If you choose Force," Force offered, "the Sauros will be destroyed. All non-dragon-kin will die in the fire that consumes them, but the Drakeon shall continue on to witness the birth of a new world."

"We can't kill everyone," she objected. "They have a better chance against the dinosaurs than they do if we nuke them all... Why is this up to me anyways?"

"It is up to you, because you are here."

A riddle. She frowned at the vision of the Drakeon and Sauros engaged in a primal battle right in the very place her friends were trapped. She knew she had to think of a solution before it was too late.

Solution implied that there was a right answer, though. She looked to the symbols burning on the walls. Two down. Three more marks, three more possible ways to solve the paradox that weren't necessarily brute force. She pointed to the wall. "If Magnus represents the power to destroy, and you're the power to see what's happening, what are the other three for?"

A sly smile spread across Knowledge's lips, a shimmer of something – approval – glinted in her eyes. "There are five denominations of Drakeon; each bears its own rune. Which rune manifests determines where that Drakeon's power lies – a birthright. Priests, Arbiters, Protectors, Hunters and Warriors, each serves a specialized function."

"Which one are you?"

"Priest; the rune of Knowledge. Force," She gestured to Magnus, "signifies the Warrior. You have already expressed an understanding of what we do. An Arbiter, one who is born with the symbol of Arbitration, is destined to become a great Elder. The Protector is denoted by the rune of Trust and is the Drakeon who will rear, protect, and educate the generations to come. A Hunter bears the mark of Cunning; it will have the natural skill and instinct necessary to find food or other resources required for the well-being of the clan."

Rebecca nodded, teeth-gritting pain winding its way further up her arm. But the agony came second to her friend's safety. Force's solution couldn't be the only way – just because one thing wasn't true, she knew the immediate alternative wasn't true by default.

She tried a different approach. "Why are they on the wall?"

"Typhos embodies all aspects of Drakeon power; his power thus may take the form of your choosing, as you are the one who crossed the seal. Meanwhile, the problem at hand remains. I suggest we continue to wait – weakness will present itself in due time. Once the answer has surfaced, we may make our move."

"Wait for all of Dragon-kind to be destroyed, you mean," Force huffed. "We must act swiftly, not dally while all is lost."

"We need a leader," Rebecca sighed. "Someone else to make the right choice."

The air wavered; the steady rise of steam zig-zagged upward. Her stomach lurched and her head smacked into something hard.

She opened her eyes to see the two blazing runes aligned vertically; a third mark had extinguished. Groggily, she tried to puzzle through the sideways runes. When a lean, muscular man with a choker of tribal fire knelt down in front of her, it became clear: she was lying on the floor. Sweat trickled down her face, her teeth clenched so tight they might've cracked; her nails dug into the skin of her right arm. The searing wire had snaked up past her elbow.

"What's happening to me?"

"You look injured. We will have the Priestess examine you once the war is over," he replied. His firm tone held both kindness and finality. It brought her back to the choker emblazoned around his neck; it looked just like Zakhar's. It also looked somewhat like a W shape with horizontal notches above it – like the rune that had gone black.

"...War?"

"Yes. And if you leave the decisions in my hands, I will achieve victory. We will use every resource at our disposal and take the ground most beneficial to us. Of course, I will see to it that we do as little harm possible to the lesser inhabitants of Gaeadia."

"What about the Lykos?" Her head throbbed, her arm bled where she had clawed it open. She was ready to throw in the reigns if Kaece would be okay.

"They are our enemies, you know that. We will allow them to fight with the Sauros and buy us enough time to gather our forces. With any luck, they will take each other down. I am certain the Maedians will involve themselves, also, and in their machinery they may prove to be substantial fodder. Simply give me the go-ahead and our success is ensured."

"No," Rebecca whimpered again. "That is almost worse than Force."

"Finally!" Force exclaimed with a grin and rubbed his hands together. "The kid's got a sense of urgency. Let's do this."

"No," she repeated louder. "I'm still not going to agree to let you kill my friends, not any of you."

"What if we agree to take your friends into Drakeon protection, allow them to be guests during the war? They will be out of harms way,"Arbitration negotiated.

"And then allow you to kill all of Sebastian's family? All of Kaece's friends, her pack? No," Rebecca snarled. Her frustration and the immeasurable agony working its way up her arm, made the situation seem hopeless. Knowledge reinforced the impossibility of it all, and Arbitration only wanted to pressure her to make the wrong decision by not making her own decisions. Was there even a right answer to the puzzle? With only two marks left, Cunning and Trust, she didn't want to play anymore.

A Hunter, she sighed with the realization, would just side with Force and Arbitration. Everyone seemed eager to kill each other, to destroy as much as possible in the name of war. The quarrel between the Drakeon and Lykos reminded her of the feuding dragon factions; it made her weary.

Ardin explained to no one in particular what was lost; Magnus paced anxiously across the room and back; Zakhar waited patiently for Rebecca to answer a question she hadn't heard. She pushed herself up from the ground, letting her arm fall limp at her side while she slumped against the wall.

"Hey," she rasped, waving her left hand above her head to draw their attention to her. "I think I'm dying... And then you can do whatever you think is best, but –"

"You've decided to call upon the power of Typhos?" Knowledge inquired.

Rebecca nodded and instantly regretted it. She winced, her brain felt like it had come loose inside her skull. The invisible molten wire had embedded itself further up her arm, a sharp spike of pain jolting through her body with every centimeter it crept along.

"I choose the Protector, the rune of Trust, to save the world."

The diagonal wave of three interlocking spirals flared white-hot against the stone. The rock glowed red around the edges of the rune. White light melded into brilliant golden swirls of magma that ate through the wall and pooled into the elaborate design on the floor. Lava spewed from the growing pit in the wall, churning in the center of the room. Stone hissed and cracked; the cave rumbled and shook. The magma bore a hole deep into the floor and the cracks split wider, arcing like lightning straight for Rebecca.

The ground fissured and crumbled beneath her. She tumbled down an angled slab; the floor tilted toward the pit of lava. Frantically she groped for a handhold; palms slick with sweat, the ground slick with steam, refuge evaded her. She tumbled with the broken rocks down, down, down...

The thunder of boulders clamored all around her. The stone slab shattered beneath her, first a loud boom then a sickening crack reverberated throughout the chamber. Rebecca laid in the rubble, numb to everything but the blistering pain in her arm. A dull ache ebbed up her thigh. She glanced down to see the contorted limb, the glistening white of bone jutting from her bloody jeans. Her head spun and her stomach churned. Though she could see the injury, the pain – if there was any – paled in comparison to the phantom wire digging deeper into her flesh. Tears streamed down her face and dripped onto the debris beneath her. Each drip hissed as the tears steamed on hot rocks. She longed desperately for an end to the pain.

Kaece filled her thoughts; the Lykos injured in an alley, her leg bloodied and useless just like Rebecca's, hadn't given up. Rebecca heaved herself upright, and gasped in the hot, oxygen-poor air. She pushed off the ground with one leg, sliding her back up against the broken slab. She crawled to the apex and surveyed the scene.

She lay, alone, on an island. A vast emptiness stretched out all around her, blackness above with no hint of where she'd fallen from. Lava boiled below, a molten expanse that reached the bounds of the chamber and seemed to be rising.

"Protector?" Rebecca called out, her voice hoarse and faint.

Jets of magma shot up around the island; bones, each one large enough to support its own skyscraper, emerged from the pillars of liquid fire. First, five long, curved claws; then the phalanges; a disjointed hand preceded its carpals – all assembled themselves in order as if by a puppeteer. As the second set of claws protruded from the streams of magma, a horned skull larger than the island reared up out of the lava below. Spine, ribs, skeletal wings, all followed until a bone dragon towered high above her into the darkness.

Her breath caught in her throat, awe and fear momentarily tearing her away from thoughts of pain. Was this the Protector?

"You are the Protector," a loud, deep voice filled the cavern in reply. "You are the one prophesied to break the seal, for whom Dragon-kind has waited eons to welcome. Because of you, the Drakeon will once again rise to power and restore balance to Gaeadia."

Confirmation – she was the sacrifice Typhos wanted. At least, she sighed, his power would be released and stop the Sauros from their apocalyptic rampage.

"The dinosaurs are long extinct, Protector. The Sauros are nothing more than fossils – you should know that. The trial was but a ruse to test your will, a game of sorts. Human-kind are often quite insidious and only show their true nature under the most severe of emotional and physical strain. I've watched your kind evolve into guileful tricksters over the millennia – I had to be certain that the behaviors you exhibited on Earth would carry over when you crossed into the true world."

"The true world?" Rebecca frowned; staring up at – no, talking to – a great skeletal dragon, she was sure she'd succumbed to delirium. "This is just a fantasy world. ...Are you God?"

The chamber echoed with his deep, rumbling laughter. "I am Typhos – some may consider me a god, while others...They may consider me something of a monster. I am, after all, the cause of Gaeadia's state of decay; I am the reason my kind suffers degeneration in all aspects. For that, even those Drakeon who feel the truth of my existence often chose to deny it, and many failed to preserve the lives of those who did not already walk the path of death. No matter – they will know their mistake, just as I came to know my own.

"I used the power of the Elders to duplicate Gaeadia and create a mirror world – that which you call Earth. It is but a snapshot of the Gaeadia of the past, though it lacks the tapestry of magic that empowers the true world. The very spark of life, the frail remnants of magic that crossed into that realm, is so simplistic, so dim and faint... It is a wonder that life thrives in such a place. Earth evolved differently in the absence of magic, just as Gaeadia seems to you different for its abundance of magic. The crossing of the threshold often triggers changes in the fabric of the being that reflects the loss or gain of magic. A Haima Demon that crosses into your world develops an allergy to the sun, and thus inexplicable deaths by 'spontaneous combustion' occur. Though, a Haima Demon who enters the world at night may continue to enjoy the benefits of immortality by feasting on human blood, as they do here. Such a crossing gives rise to the legend of Vampires. Witches, werewolves, lake and sea monsters – all your lore holds truth, but their very existence is due to the accidental transference from this world into the other.

"Those who cross in the opposite manner may also develop side-effectual adaptation, though they are rarely so drastic as the transformation a Haima Demon undergoes. In the beginning, all humans were of Earth – you are not creatures of Gaeadia."

"But," Rebecca began, her head spun and she struggled to grasp on to some sense.

"The Madius line," Typhos answered before the question had even formed on her lips, "and all Maedians, came from a civilization that once thrived in your world – they crossed from an island in the center of the Atlantic Ocean some 12,000 years ago. With them came basic technologies, from which they built up an empire now called Maedia. Other humans have followed in their footsteps many a time since that age, although admittedly with my help more than once.

"I knew that the chosen one would be human, likely one who hadn't been raised surrounded by the wonders of magic – they had to be from the mirror world. Your confused apathy toward your own wellbeing drew my attention while you resided on Earth, but your display of devotion to others – absolutely casting aside any shred of self-preservation – at the point of Sow Endus' destruction couldn't have been more convincing. How many times did you throw yourself in harms way that day?

"I hoped you would follow that Drakeon to this mountain. And you did very well, Metakosmos. Most who cross over die a quick death, falling, drowning, or becoming prey to an inhabitant of Gaeadia. Some are less fortunate... starving, suffocating, succumbing to unusual disease. Few survive, and as you can tell – none have ever made it this far."

As Typhos spoke, the pain wrapped up her shoulder and squeezed tighter. The burning constricted her lungs. More tears welled up in her eyes. "How am I still alive?"

"The prophecy shall be fulfilled. It will run its course, precisely as preordained by those who foresaw it. How is but a petty question; the less you are told, the less your knowledge can meddle. What you may know is this: I am free of this prison, released at last – the prophecy is out of my claws now. The world's fate is a weight that rests solely upon you."

Rebecca grimaced as his laughter filled the chamber; she rolled onto her back and screamed. She clawed her flesh; her entire body felt consumed by the invisible flame. The burning spread throughout her chest and filled her lungs; her heart pumped boiling blood through her veins. The blistering liquid erupted from her mouth, searing her throat and burning her tongue. Her screams mutated into sputtering coughs, then her lungs refused to heave any more of the scalding blood from her body. Boiling tears streamed from her eyes, stripping the flesh from her face. Anywhere the seething blood could escape, it melted her skin, leaving the steaming muscle underneath bare.

"Poor, fragile creature... Calm yourself. Once your fallacious life-force has burned away, you will be free of the pain."

Lost in a torrent of suffering, her body convulsed. Eventually, the lava pooled around her paralyzed body, and as the scorching pain began anew, one regret filled her heart. Kaece. She would never know that Rebecca wanted to say yes. More than that, she would never know how badly Rebecca wished the heat of the viscous fluid enveloping her had been the warmth of Kaece's embrace.

133

135

136

137

138

139

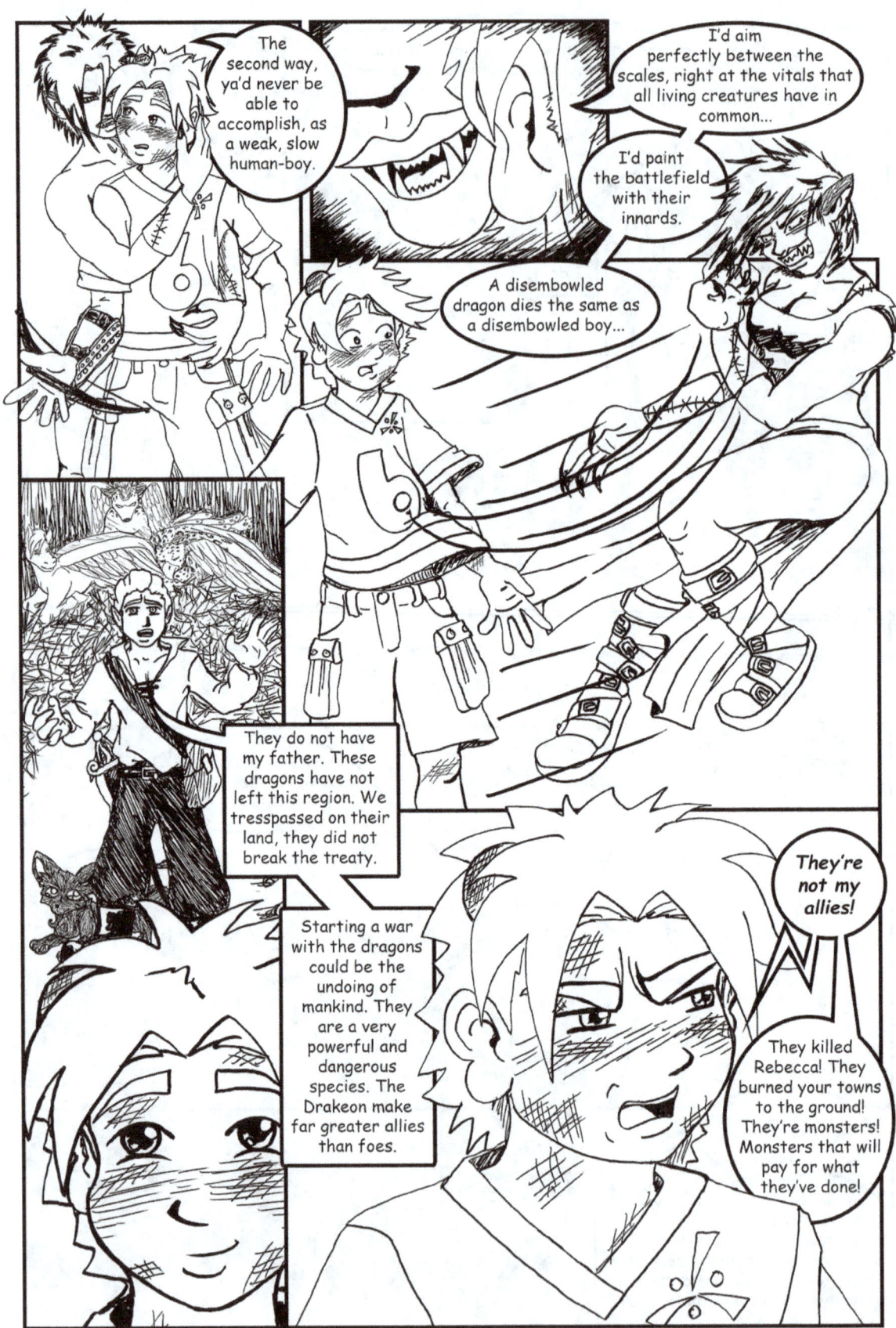

141

15

The ground shook and the Maedian spoke, but Kaece never took her eyes off of the High Priestess outside of the cave. After she'd announced, safely on the other side of the barrier, that they would be released, Ardin had spent the entire night staring up at the Drakeon tomb, watching, waiting.

When the earthquake hit, the High Priestess shifted from dragon form into her human guise and approached the holding chamber.

"It is done. The seal is broken. You are free. But if you stay here, you will die."

Egotistical dragons had told tales of an ancient dragon-god rising to destroy all who opposed Drakeon rule. They said the supposed dragon-god would rise when fed the right sacrifice. If the seal had broken, then all hope that Rebecca had escaped was lost. Rebecca, the one and only, had become that sacrifice.

"Of course it was her," Kaece whispered.

"The Elder and I hope we can continue our alliance with the Maedians, young Madius. The world will change, now that Typhos' power belongs to the great Zakhar. You would be wise to find your lost father and prepare for future negotiations. Beware of the Betrayers – do not underestimate how far the betrayal reaches." She looked to Kaece. "And who you trust."

"Like you?" Kaece sneered. She had more to say but the words caught in her throat. She hadn't cried since her days as a young pup, but in the wake of Rebecca's demise, she choked on repressed tears. She had told Rebecca that she would die atop the summit with her, and if Rebecca had died there, Kaece swore she would find a way to join her.

The ground roiled. Kaece had a front row view as the side of the enormous red peak crumbled in a disastrous slide of rock. Ash exploded upward from instantly crushed minerals and filled the sky in a giant plume. She knew the wave of heat, of pressure, the outward span of high-velocity debris, would cause a quick and nearly painless death. She vowed her love to Rebecca, and braced for her own end.

"Holy shit!" Alex cried out and blocked his body with criss-crossed arms. The debris shot upward and fanned out over the invisible barrier, over the cave.

Ardin shouted, "Come to me, you fools!" Her face strained with concentration; her body shook, lost to the power of holding the protective shield up around them. Kaece saw an opening, a perfect opportunity to kill the magic-wielding dragon.

But she refrained. To accomplish the goal of reaching Rebecca's remains, the High Priestess would be more useful to her alive. No sooner than the Madius had pushed Alex and the three flying beasts up next to Ardin, the back of the cave collapsed.

Kaece watched the ruination of the Drakeon tomb, watched for Rebecca's body, watched for any sign of the fabled Typhos. She didn't believe a god would rise from the mess, but she didn't want to be caught unguarded either. Lava spurted and poured from the decimated side of the mountain. The wave of destruction had passed, but noxious fumes and a cloud of ash rained from the sky.

The Warlord swooped down overhead, his hide covered in white ash.

"Quickly, mount your flyers and fly under Magnus. He will guide you to safety. I must not waste my time keeping you alive, I have a duty to greet the lord Typhos. Our deal is done – you must leave"

"This isn't over." Alex threatened Ardin as Sebastian pushed him down onto the Gruy youngling.

Sebastian scolded, while mounting his own beast. "Leave it, Alexander. We must take this opportunity to escape with our lives. Without the magic, we will surely die. We mustn't let what she did be in vain."

The Warlord tried to urge Kaece toward the Simurg with a claw, but she refused.

"I'm not goin' down. I'm goin' up, unless you're gonna stop me."

"Well then. Farewell humans, and good luck." Ardin nodded to Magnus. He spread his wings and guided the two flyers into the air. As they soared out into the hazy sky, Ardin dropped her magical barrier. Kaece gasped in the painful, heavy air.

"Elder Zakhar and I must examine the tomb. We could take you up with us, but chances are high that you will not be able to withstand the power atop the peak." Ardin tilted her head, "What is it you seek, that you would die trying to get your claws on, Lykos?"

"You know what I seek, Drakeon." Kaece replied in a low growl, "Your fictitious deity is of no interest to me."

"She is dead."

Kaece grimaced.

"Her screams, from the depths of the mountain, reached some of our ears. It sounded most dreadful. I assure you that she suffered for a very long time before she passed on."

Kaece's claws dug into her own palms with how tightly she clenched her fists. She loathed the Drakeon. The fact that they'd killed Rebecca was enough, but knowing that her end had been tortuous made Kaece shake with rage.

She snarled through bared teeth. "Quit speakin' my language, I'm not listenin' to what ya have to say. I'm goin' up with ya, and that's all I want."

"Your choice." Ardin shrugged. "I'm sure Magnus will be quite pleased that you've decided to sacrifice yourself."

Kaece despised being carried by a dragon, but it was quicker than climbing the molten peak. By the time they'd reached the mountain top, the lava had hardened into a dark black surface with deep orange streams running throughout. Various shaped rock protrusions ushered the winding lava flows.

Sweat dripped from Kaece's entire body, the heat almost unbearable. While she searched the area, she thought of all the ways she could have tried to keep Rebecca safe. It always came back to one regret – one regret she couldn't control: Rebecca had chosen the Madius.

The sun rose higher into the sky, nothing but a dim light beyond the dark clouds of ever-falling ash. Kaece relished her corroding senses, breathing in deep whiffs of the mephitic air. She blamed herself for Rebecca's death. She'd lost the only person she'd ever loved.

Standing on a large boulder that overlooked the destruction of the valley below, Kaece screamed. She screeched as loud as she could, willing the sound to drown her thoughts. The only person in the world that mattered to her was dead and gone forever. She was as dead as a Lykos' mother, as dead as Sebastian's father and as dead as the long-buried dragon Typhos. She couldn't escape the hurt that she felt, but she could scream until her chest burned as much as her heart. Heaving, she screamed again and again.

"Would you please stop doing that," Ardin chided

Kaece turned to face her. The silence rang in her ears.

"Thank you."

Kaece glowered; she'd resisted long enough. Believing that there was no part of Rebecca left to find, she leapt at Ardin. Her claws met nothing.

"You can not kill me, it is not even worth trying. I am the High Priestess, my magic is quicker than your claws." Ardin mocked from several feet behind her. She perched on the cliff's edge.

Snarling, Kaece dove again. She slammed into a magical shield between them. Having landed hard on the ground, she laid limp.

"Tisk, tisk. She would be ashamed of you." Ardin teased with a high pitched titter of cruelty. "Oh, right. That reminds me. She had a message for you."

"A message?" Kaece lifted herself up.

"She said she was sorry."

"Sorry for what?"

"She didn't say. I think she assumed you would know. She did say more, though, it wasn't part of the message."

Kaece snarled, with little patience for Drakeon head games. "Talk."

"'I wish I could have seen her one more time before' then she trailed off, unable to admit her own fate out loud. I forbade her from seeing anyone who might dissuade her from her sacrificial task."

Kaece threw herself at the shield with the full force of her body, but the barrier was gone. She slammed into the rock and rolled, toppling legs first, off of the cliff. She raked her claws into the rock. Blood oozed from her ripped nailbeds, as she clawed her way back up. She growled, "You're a coward, Drakeon. Fight me."

"Kill yourself, betrayer. Typhos' power must be found, and you are a pesky vermin."

She shouted after Ardin as the Drakeon walked away. "Ever consider there may not be a power? That maybe your old stories are jus' that, a myth?"

It gave the Drakeon pause, but she didn't take the bait. Ardin moved on, leaving Kaece to heave herself back onto solid ground. She swore that it would be the very last resort to take her own life. She was a Lykos born for combat: she wanted to die in a fight.

The Elder, old man Zakhar, still had potential. He'd been overturning boulders, scouring the magma, for hours with nothing to prove his 'lord Typhos' real. When he tossed back his head and roared his frustration as Kaece had screamed hers – she knew it was time to strike. She prepared to move closer, but instead hid when the priestess unexpectedly returned. The mole-guised Drakeon, her rune of Knowledge etched across her little black back, emerged from the caked lava flow. She pulled a glinting object toward the surface. The Elder reached in, and when his hand came up, the lava dripped from between his fingers. Pinched in his talons, two swords burned red hot.

In a burst of flame, Ardin returned to her human form, and took the cooling blades into her hands. Her eyes glossed over with a glaze of draconic telepathy. She held the swords by the hilts, twisted them, thrust them, shook them, and then frowned.

"Lykos, come here."

Of course the dragons knew of her presence. As she told Alex once before, one can't hide from dragons. She stepped out of her hiding place.

"Take this into your hand." She offered out a sword.

Kaece took the weapon – as soon as the hilt touched her palm, the damned thing heated. Pain lashed across her hand. She yelped and threw it down.

Ardin said, "Swords. Swords built for tiny humanoid hands. But the power of Typhos will burn any humanoid who touches it. I don't understand."

145

Kaece snarled. The white blister of a fatal burn colored her entire palm.

Elder Zakhar snorted, his only outward sign of his silent communications with the Priestess. Ardin picked up the sword Kaece'd dropped and shook her head, illustrating her disappointment and confusion. "This is it. This is the artifact we have waited eons to uncover. It's time to return to the valley. We need to figure out the purpose of such seemingly useless objects."

"They're swords. Seems rather obvious," Kaece jeered. "Ya stab, or slash with 'em. Why not give 'em a taste of Lykos blood in a fight, Priestess?"

Something familiar, something so faint under the fumes, she'd almost missed it, hit her senses. She raised her head and sniffed. It was the cloth 'jeans', as Rebecca had called it. Her heart beat rapidly in her chest, her breath all but lost in the sudden sensation of fear and excitement. She turned her back on the Drakeon.

As she circled around the far side of a crumpled boulder, she saw her. Not a scrap of cloth or a single disembodied limb, but the whole girl, intact and fully clothed, laid peacefully on the solidified magma's surface. As Kaece stepped closer, she eagerly sought the familiar smell of Rebecca's skin, her sweat, her pheromones, but they didn't come. Nor did the sound of a heartbeat. She looked as if she were sleeping, tucked in with a blanket of ashes.

Kaece whimpered and fell to her knees beside Rebecca's body. She brushed the ashes from Rebecca's lovely face, then traced a claw over Rebecca's lips. It hurt more than anything to know she'd never see a smile upon them again.

She gently lifted Rebecca into her arms, and held her to her chest. She kissed her hair and cried, "You were the only one who ever trusted me. You were such a fool. Ya shouldn'ta trusted me. Look at ya. I killed ya. I lied to ya... I was afraid."

She knew that Ardin and Zakhar listened from behind, and Rebecca couldn't hear her, but she couldn't stop. She wished desperately that she could undo it all and meet Rebecca in a good time, without war, without violence and lies. "Ya wouldn'ta looked at me like ya did. Ya wouldn'ta wanted me to touch ya. Ya wouldn'ta wanted me around at all. I was gonna kill ya that night in the woods. But I didn't... I don't know why. And instead, I fell in love with ya. Every moment with you was like living a life I never knew I could have... a life that's over now." She held Rebecca tighter. She whispered through her tears "Fight me Drakeon.... I want to die."

After a long moment of silence she said it again louder.

"Tell me what you smell." Ardin said in response.

Kaece sniffed. Through the acrid smoke, she could smell only the burning, the volcano and the dragons. She shook her head and nuzzled Rebecca.

"And what you see."

"I'm not interested in your riddles unless they end in a fight, Priestess."

"This is no riddle. The girl is uninjured, her clothes are unburned and she doesn't smell of death or human. She smells of dragon." Ardin sounded exasperated. "Your basic senses are greater than ours – tell me that I am wrong."

Kaece took a good long whiff of Rebecca's hair. Ardin wasn't wrong. "I don't... understand."

"We have to take her down to the valley with us."

"Over my dead body," Kaece snarled. "You're never touching her again."

"If we have to pry her from your cold dead grasp, we will. She will live and you will have accomplished your death wish."

"We'll rest eternally together, death suits me fine."

"You idiot creature. Your own species has an unconscious regenerative state – put together the pieces I've handed to you."

Disbelieving, Kaece pressed her ear to Rebecca's chest. Slow and faint, the heart barely beat – but again, Ardin wasn't wrong; Rebecca rested deep in a regenerative coma. Awestruck that Rebecca had survived, Kaece looked to the Drakeon Priestess for answers.

"I'm glad you have come to your senses. Do not ask what this means, I do not know. This is not what we expected. But her body could very well be a vessel to the lord Typhos himself. We'll have to see what happens when she wakes."

"I'll carry her down." Kaece replied, "Her body is not gonna be mishandled by ya zealots, vessel or not."

Ardin looked to the Elder for assent. After a long stare with his tired-old dragon eyes, he nodded at Kaece.

"See you at the bottom, Lykos. If I have to hunt you down, you will wish I'd killed you when you first requested it," Ardin said before the flames took her back into dragon form.

Tightly embracing Rebecca, Kaece waited for the two Drakeon to depart. Once they'd flown from sight, she whispered into Rebecca's ear, "If you come back to me, I'll never let anyone hurt ya again; I'll always protect ya. I promise."

She hoisted Rebecca up, so her body rested safely across her shoulders. As Kaece stepped up to the cliff face, she looked out at the grey-speckled sky. The gods, be it Typhos, those of the Maedians or those of the Lykos, fought in the fray of the haze and clouds, chaotic flashes marked each strike. Every few flashes, a streak of light arched down from the clouds. The air buzzed with a violent energy that filled Kaece with vigor. She relished the feel of Rebecca's weight and began her decent into the maelstrom.

XVI

Oneiroi Lake was north east of Tekton and took three days to reach when traveling by Hadros. At Alex's unsolicited request, Sebastian stopped before the tract of unkempt growth that led into the town of Oneiroi, so named for the fish which attributed to the small but successful population. The boy only demanded to be allowed privacy, a common desire since their departure from Drakeon Peak, yet he did not disclose when he intended to return. Perhaps, he desired one final opportunity to gather his wits before being faced again with Maedia's expectations after such a lengthy venture free of those constraints.

Companionless while Alex sought solace in the overgrown wilderness, Sebastian waited and looked out over the placid splendor of Oneiroi Lake. To the north, the lake stretched out before him like a sparkling aquamarine gem, its transparent surface unperturbed but for the occasional fish. Beyond the lake, lush fenlands merged into foothills carpeted in evergreen forests. The lake itself was fed by a clear mountain stream, which trickled from the snow-capped peaks of the Skotos mountain range. Many of the icy summits vanished into the pure white clouds that graced the bright Hemera lighted sky. Before recent events, Sebastian would have been entranced by its glory.

The eruption of Drakeon Peak and the ensuing escape from captivity had allowed them to continue the fruitless search for his father. The Lykos, though freed, remained at the volcanic mountain, devoted to Rebecca as a faithful companion pet willing to die waiting for its deceased master's inconceivable return. Such fraught memories stripped him of his typical awe.

When Alex returned to the lakeside, he startled Sebastian from his contemplations by dropping a small pile of roughly cut branches on the ground.

"These are going to be practice swords, and maybe we can make some real spears too. You don't know jack about fighting, and I don't know enough. So we're going to learn."

"I'm not-"

"Into violence. Blah blah blah - I've heard it all before. And you can shove it. Rebecca's dead. She died because we couldn't protect her. Your stupid peace preaching is useless. She's gone!

... She's dead because dragons aren't afraid to fight for what they believe in. They're not too afraid to kill. But you're too afraid to stand up and fight back while they murder everyone you care about! Or did you even care about her?"

Sebastian grimaced, the frustration at such an accusatory stance penetrating his emperor's tutelage. Rebecca had meant more to him than he could admit to anyone. Yet war had never achieved anything in all of known history, save bringing death to the masses.

"... Even if you didn't care about her, she's my sister. I loved her, and I'm going to avenge her. I'll make the dragons pay - I'll make them sorry. They need to know how it feels to have your family murdered! It's the only way justice will be served. If you're my friend you'll stop being such a coward and fight with me. If you don't, to hell with you - I don't need you."

Alex grabbed a stick from the pile and held it toward Sebastian. Sebastian took the mock sword into his hand. While he could not agree to such an ultimatum, he did not see any value in further ostracizing the hurting child either. He said nothing, but knew Alex accepted the gesture as submission. He helped Alex carry the sticks into the Hadros.

The rest of the journey to Oneiroi, he thought about how that fateful day, the dragons had taken something precious from them - the life of someone they both cared about. A primal, long-repressed part of himself cried out for vengeance, but that did not make it the correct path to take, nor the most prudent path. He could not, and would not make Rebecca's death yet another cog in the endless cycle of violence. One death never justified another.

He recalled how the Priestess deemed the bargain fulfilled moments before the eruption began. Rebecca's death earned their freedom, and given the opportunity to kill Sebastian and Alex, the Drakeon still did not. They were left to travel unattended once safely beyond the smoke billowing from the summit. The remainder of the day, they had flown by Pegasus and Gruy east towards Tekton and the Hadros.

By nightfall they had put a great distance between themselves and the Unthrowlych range. When the world fell silent and exhaustion should have taken him, Sebastian remained awake. A deep numb born of guilt filled his being. Sebastian could not fathom how or why they had survived such decimation. Nor could he believe Rebecca had left Gaeadia as swiftly and suddenly as she had come. In the darkness he saw the wetness glistening on Alex's cheeks. The boy had cried himself to sleep.

He had woken the next morning to Alex sobbing on a set of criss-crossed sticks that were fastened with twine. He watched him pile rocks at the cross's base before Alex collapsed with his head in his hands.

"I'm sorry I failed you, Rebecca. I was suppose to be the hero. I was suppose to save you. I led you into danger and did nothing when I should have rescued you from it. I'm going to put everything I've got into avenging you and I'm never gonna be caught off guard again. I'm going to kill every last dragon for what they did! They killed you. We came for their help and... And they killed you..."

"She walks with the gods now, young Metakosmos. They, and they alone will mark the Drakeon with what justice is due. We must continue our journey in her memory, and do what must be done so that her loss is with purpose."

Sebastian knew his words held little comfort, for he himself felt such angst at what he could not yet accept. Yet his words held truth. If they continued what they had begun, the small chance, a supposition given by the Priestess that his father could be held prisoner by the defecting Drakeon, would guide an otherwise aimless journey. The Priestess said the Betrayers inhabited the far northern foothills of the Unthrowlych range. What supplies he had salvaged from the remains of Tekton would not see them to the point of Xiratera where the mountains met the great northern sea. Such a realization brought them on the path to Oneiroi, the nearest Maedian civilization. Sebastian hoped the village would have enough supplies to allow them to see the journey to its end.

They left the Hadros just outside the village and continued on foot, leading the flyers behind them down the town's single earthen street as the sun set on the horizon. The size of the town hardly surprised Sebastian, as their continued existence depended entirely on the seasonal spawning of Oneiroi. Fewer than a hundred, including children and elders, could manage the harvest of the rare fish. The Oneiroi spawned exclusively in the lake on which the village was built, and were well-known throughout Maedia for the vivid dreams imparted upon those who consumed the fish. Only Oneiroi caught during a certain timeframe would induce the coveted effects. During this time, the people of Oneiroi led very busy lives, fishing from before sunrise to long after sunset. At another point in his journey, perhaps he might have been more elated about the chance meeting during one such rare occasion.

Villagers bustled about, entering or leaving single-roomed dwellings composed of sturdy branches and thatched roofs. When he and Alex entered the village proper, a group of wide-eyed children scattered away from them and ran north towards a single larger hut which stood at the road's end. But a few moments later, many of the children returned on the heels of the village patriarch.

The gnarled old man leaned on a carved wooden cane as he hobbled along. It did not take a practiced eye to see he had lived a rugged life, lacking many of the comforts of society. He was crippled from the weathering of age, yet he smiled such that he seemed a younger man. Sebastian had only on brief occasion seen such a genuine smile.

The patriarch bid them welcome to his hometown, and asked that they help themselves to whatever they might need during their stay. They tethered the Gruy and Pegasus behind his hut on long leads with every intention of leaving the animals at the village. Sebastian wasted no time with the niceties of his royal upbringing, stating that he needed from the town several weeks worth of preserved rations, as well the town's coal to continue fueling the Hadros. A wince flitted across the old man's face, yet he nodded wordlessly. He led Sebastian to a building near the center of the village that acted as both their storage room and trading outpost.

"Young Madius, you can take what you need from here. We only ask that you leave any coal that you can, eh, for the winters in these parts tend towards the harsher temperatures. You may need some help taking it back to your ros. Simply tell one of the fishermen that Galen asked that they assist you."

"Alex and I can manage. We shall take only what we must."

"Please do come back and rest for the evening with us. Many would love to hear the tales of a Madius."

Sebastian welcomed the ability to form a solid plan with a tangible inventory of supplies, not to mention indulge in the finery of a freshly cooked meal among fellow Maedians. An hour of palaver with Galen revealed that the village had not only been untouched by the dragon raids, but untouched by even the news of them. He dismissed the poor relay of information and explained that the town had very limited contact with external society. But, the news would have reached them eventually, he assured.

Hesperis's arrival in the heavens brought a dinner "worthy of the visit of a Madius." A great feast was served. The townsfolk brought varying contributions from their houses, which ranged from handmade tables to water barrels. The tables and chairs lined up along the village's single street. Each household donated a dish to the meal, each dish unique.

Both Sebastian and Alex ate heartily, enjoying the pleasure of good food. With the townsfolk laughing and fraternizing all around him, Sebastian's troubles lingered as a distant haze he could nearly ignore. When the time came to bid the villagers goodnight, he did so with great relief, as the clamor had grown irksome with their obliviousness to his longing for the companionship he witnessed all around him. He lingered while the villagers drifted in pairs to their huts. Children played in the shallow water at the edge of the lake. He watched in hope of quelling Rebecca from his mind. Only children, he surmised as they splashed about, could be so delighted by something so very simple. He had no memory of ever feeling as happy as those children appeared, even with the memories of his happiest years restored to him.

One of the younger children tripped and fell on a sharp rock. His squeals of delight turned to wails of agony. An older girl with the same dark hair gathered him into her arms. She struggled to hold him, as though she could barely lift his weight. Not the least dissuaded, she bounced him soothingly on her hip and sang a lullaby.

Awash with a wave of emotion which whispered that all was right in the world, Sebastian closed his eyes. Emotion, he knew, was a temptation to which he must not succumb as a Madius.

Realization set in as he watched the children return to their playmates. They were like Alex and Rebecca, children sharing the innate, unbreakable bond of siblings. They shared not only blood, but also experience and love from the time of their earliest memories. His agony, imagining the pain of those children suddenly torn from each other, seemed insignificant weighted against what Alex suffered. But not just Alex, for how many other siblings had been ruthlessly slaughtered in the Drakeon raids? How many other sons and daughters? How many other people, with lives and families and aspirations?

When he pulled himself from the sight of gleeful children destined to end in misery one day, he retired to the guest hut afforded him. He laid awake on his blankets and furs, tossing and turning as if he might turn away from the turmoil which plagued his mind. Nyx's watch passed by with interminable slowness. When he drifted at last to sleep, the Oneiroi elicited a restless slumber in which he dreamt a vivid, haunting, experience with Rebecca.

Rising with the first rays of Eos, Sebastian decided to remain for a few days in the company of the Oneiroi folk. He prayed the nearness of fellow Maedians would ground his irrational longings and remind him of his imperial duties. His royalty called for his father's rescue and to return to Old Maedia, not to get swept up in the torrent of chaos afoot on Xiratera.

Alex spent the time creating weapons. He carved multiple branches into rough practice swords. His second weapon, a water barrel with hoses and nozzles protruding from the top and one side, perplexed Sebastian.

"What is this?"

"I call it the 'Gaeadian Water Blaster.' Kaece said that water is the Drakeon's biggest weakness, so water it is. We'll take them down using this!"

"I wish you would not include me in these vengeful antics of yours. I have not agreed to come along. The people of Gaeadia consider these weapons barbaric. Violence does not solve any problem. It never has."

Galen, who stood nearby listening to their conversation, laughed.

"Violence never solves anything, eh? Is that what they teach you in the Poleis? Isn't violence the natural way of life? Do we not kill the fish for our own dinner? Does the wolf not hunt the deer?"

"Perhaps so, but that is different. Those acts are matters of survival, not revenge."

"Let me ask you this, then. Do the Haima Demons not hunt mankind? And does mankind not retaliate, if for no other reason than to show the Demons that you are not easy prey, that you are not weak?"

"We must protect ourselves from the Haima Demons, we are their prey and no treaty can ever be reached. Again, it is a matter of survival."

"How are the dragons not? It sounds to me like they are exterminating Maedians like vermin. Hunt or be hunted. It sounds to me, young prince, like these Drakeon no longer believe man is a species worthy of regard. It sounds to me like they need to be taught a lesson, not for the sake of revenge, but for the sake of the survival of the Maedians on this continent. They need to learn that we do not make easy prey.

...Why, I'd be tempted to come along and help myself, if 'twas still in my more sprightly days. But alas, it seems my hunting days are done for."

He looked pointedly at his cane with an expression somewhere between disgust and good humor. Galen and Alex shared a laugh.

Sebastian found it puzzling that he'd never questioned the violence against Haima Demons, how it fit seamlessly with the Maedian ideals of peace, yet defied those same teachings. The Haima Demons were sentient, as capable of a treaty as the Drakeon. The key difference – Maedians needed to defend themselves or all would perish.

The ash-laden Drakeon valley attested to the fact that the rules had changed. Rebecca's flame of life had been extinguished. If even the Elder Zahkar was powerless against the defecting Drakeon, who in Gaeadia could thwart Xiratera's new enemy? A fool's errand, perhaps, but the truth in the village patriarch's words did not elude Sebastian. He, the last left to speak for all of Maedia, must not let Rebecca's death, nor any of the other innocents who had been killed in the recent Drakeon rampages, go unaddressed.

He bowed out of the conversation which Alex and Galen so animatedly continued, and hurried to the Hadros. His palms perspired as he drew out his journal. Ink on paper would make irrevocable his decision. His rationality knew only harm could be the outcome, but he vowed silently to fight by Alex's side, in spite of all he had been taught. Revenge would be bittersweet for them and, if the battle ended in their favor, simply bitter for the rogue Drakeon. Revenge would be his destiny, for he would write his own rather than blindly obey the contradictions of the palace. He dipped his pen into the ink bottle and wrote:

My people are a great people, a wise people. Our society has endured for centuries because we abide by one simple fact: violence brings no good end. Revenge, even in the wily guise of justice, in the end brings death and nothing more.

I say 'we,' but perhaps should say 'they,' for today I turn my back on this very upbringing and forever alienate myself from those wise people who do not surrender to violent tantrums. There will be no successor to the Emperor's throne. My people must find another way. My mind is certain, my faith unwavering, and I know that it is better this way. One so weak as myself, so weak as to allow my emotions to control my actions so, is unfit to lead. I would have led my entire people down the path of destruction I now choose for myself, alone.

I know that this path is a path of death, of desolation. At its end, I will find myself alone, if even with myself for company. I suppose even that is not guaranteed. Yet what else am I to do? How far must the Drakeon travel with their murderous fires before we fight back? How many must perish before any will stand against them for our people? I refuse to be a coward in the name of peace any longer. I may die. Yet if it is so, I will die knowing that I fought and died for my people, and for those I have loved and lost. I have chosen my destiny.

- Sebastian Madius on Leo 234 under Hesperis

CHAPTER 17

Rebecca's naked body lay unconscious on a bed of straw tucked deep inside a Drakeon dwelling. Sometimes Kaece would wake, lean over, and stroke Rebecca's cold skin. She would watch the steady rise and fall of Rebecca's chest, or stare at the band of flames that licked up Rebecca's arm in a tribal wave of interlocking spirals. Those warm fingers would trace the glowing tattoo that fanned out from Rebecca's shoulder and onto her back, then fall motionless when the Lykos drifted off once again.

Folded and stacked, her clothes sat beside the straw mat. Only Kaece's warmth heated both bodies; Rebecca's blood ran cold. The Drakeon mark that spanned from her wrist to shoulder blade offered no heat of its own, despite the appearance of burning embers that illuminated the cavern. The Drakeon expected that Typhos would rise when Rebecca's eyes finally opened.

And five days after the Drakeon god had risen from the lava, those eyes did open. Vibrant purple infected her irises, their former hazel color consumed. The eye color, the living fire decorating her arm, and the perfection of her changed body would have made even Rebecca, herself, question her identity.

The warmth of Kaece's body – the sensation she'd died wishing to feel – registered first. She took in the high curved ceiling of the dimly lit room, then the features of the Lykos curled up against her side. The old cliché about people looking peaceful in their sleep didn't apply to Kaece; her brow creased and mouth parted, lips twitching in a frown, sneer, or snarl – Rebecca couldn't tell which. She brushed back the bangs from Kaece's forehead and rested her palm against Kaece's cheek.

The orange glow of the marking that traced up her right arm burned painlessly, exactly along the route the molten wire had taken to find her heart and kill her. She wondered if the beheaded bore tribal collars. Her own body's illumination cast soft light on Kaece's features, but more light seeped in from elsewhere. Dawn bled into the room from the wide cave mouth.

"Rebecca?" Kaece rasped.

Rebecca raised her eyebrows in question as Kaece searched her face with those yellow eyes. Fear, desperation, etched itself in Kaece's worried expression.

"Do ya– are ya..." She stumbled over her words. "Ya recognize me, right?"

She laughed. "Of course I do, Kaece."

I am pleased that you are awake, Agent of our Lord Typhos. What can you tell us? A foreign thought echoed in her head. She gasped in surprise just as Kaece threw her arms around her neck.

"Did I hurt ya?" Kaece pulled back.

"No, I just had a weird thought–"

Agent, I will be with you shortly. Kill the Lykos if her presence displeases you.

No! Rebecca thought against the voice; she heard the difference between them, slight. Something lurked in her mind. *I don't want this, get out of my head. It's none of your business what I do in my afterlife.*

Kaece shifted, crouching on the mat between Rebecca and the cave's entrance. "The High Priestess is coming," she warned.

Afterlife? The voice echoed again, puzzled. The perplexed tone matched the look on Ardin's face as she stepped into the room. She stared straight at on Rebecca. *This is no afterlife, Agent. Unless...* Her eyes widened. *No. You couldn't be the human girl. Is it even possible?*

Aghast, Rebecca realized without a doubt that – somehow – she was alive, and very much naked in a room with Kaece and Ardin. Her throat constricted and her chest felt tight, she thought she might actually die of embarrassment. She tried to hide herself behind Kaece while she fumbled for her clothes.

Answer me, Ardin demanded inside her thoughts.

Rebecca yanked on her clothes and snapped, "I don't know how you're doing that, but stop. I don't like it."

This?

"Stop!" She whirled on Ardin and glowered.

Ardin let out a clipped laugh, a cruel smile setting on her lips. "Then answer me. Did Lord Typhos speak to you? Do you have an explanation for why he has possessed your body, yet left your mind that of a human?"

Typhos. An image of the skeleton dragon looming over her rushed back; no words came, only memories of the pain. "I have no message. I don't even know why I'm here. I died. I'm suppose to be dead."

"You know nothing?" Ardin frowned; all traces of amusement faded. She reached down and a sword materialized from nothingness at her hip. With both hands, she reverently held the blade out toward Rebecca. "What of this?"

The sword's blade curved back like a saber; black dragon skin, cracked with veins of lava, wrapped the grip; a bone-colored hand-guard, studded by jagged dragon teeth, bracketed the hilt; a second, shorter blade protruded like a punching dagger from the pommel. She'd never seen anything like it in her life.

"You're certain?" Ardin asked.

Mind-reading, Rebecca decided immediately, was a curse. "I'm sure. I'd remember something like that."

What an enigma, Ardin sighed inside Rebecca's head as she slid the mysterious blade back into thin air. *When the sun has risen, you must seek Elder Zakhar in the clearing and tell him all that you have told me. If there is anything that you have not said, he must be made aware of it. Perhaps he will be more able to make sense of this than I.*

"Is it really that hard to open your mouth? We're in the same room."

This is how dragons communicate. Get used to it.

"Good thing I'm not a dragon, huh?" Rebecca rebuked.

"Typhos, what am I supposed to do with this?" Ardin pleaded to the ceiling before she turned and strode from the cave. Nothing happened when Ardin crossed the threshold; no magical barrier trapped them inside.

Kaece sat back, her tensed muscles relaxing. She glanced over her shoulder at Rebecca, amusement lighting her eyes. "You infuriate her."

"I could say the same thing about her," Rebecca shrugged. "You were right, though. They aren't about to help anyone, the Maedians or us. Let's find Alex and Sebastian and get as far away from this place as we can."

Kaece shook her head. "They're gone. They left when the dragons set us free, when... the day the tomb erupted."

"How long ago?"

"Days. Does it matter? You're different now. Purple eyes. Drakeon mark. Beautiful. If ya had horns, you'd look jus' like one of 'em. The Madius will treat you jus' the same as he treats everything that isn't like him – like a beast – if ya try and go back to him now."

Rebecca took in the glow edging out from under her cuff. She pushed her sleeve up and inspected the mark coiled around her arm. Just a tattoo, she tried to reason with herself – but this tattoo pulsated, it breathed embers in time with her breathing, cooling to a dull orange glow when she held her breath. Tattoos in Gaeadia, she suspected were supposed to be ink, like on Earth. Discomfort crept up her spine. She bore a mark that would forever identify her as abnormal; a queer mark. More than she felt horrified, she felt a smile fighting its way to the surface.

"Beautiful, huh?"

"I liked the way ya looked before." Kaece mirrored her smile as she entwined her fingers with Rebecca's. "But now, you're radiant. It's hard to look away."

She blushed, but heat didn't fill her cheeks. She sighed, "I'm different... freakish."

"Nah, come on. Walk with me. Bet your legs could use a good stretch after all that lyin' around unconscious, eh? Regenerative comas leave me stiff like nothin' else."

Kaece coaxed her outside. They walked hand-in-hand, comfortable in mutual silence. Together, they crossed the valley. The towering red peak lay in ruin, a heap of crimson and black rubble where the tomb once resided. An eruption she hadn't been alive to see created fresh layers of basalt on the valley floor, the black rock visible where her footprints disturbed the thick ash coating. Cracks marred many of the caves, and others had collapsed. Deep crags narrowed into thin fractures toward the edge of the valley, fissures that ran from the former peak.

Somehow, amidst all the wreckage, the beauty of nature still presented itself. The light of dawn cast down on the ash; flecks of mica glittered like snow, though snow was nowhere to be found. Clouds clung to the horizon, taking on the vivid pinks and oranges of the rising sun. Nothing disturbed the peaceful calm of the morning in the aftermath of the destruction. Nothing interrupted the wonderful heat of the sun on her back, nor the warmth of Kaece's hand in hers as they walked.

Typhos forgotten, the sight of Zakhar startled her. Kaece tightened her grip on Rebecca's hand and pulled them away from the Elder Drakeon.

You are late. Come, young one. Zakhar's voice filled her mind.

"No, it's okay," she told Kaece.

"Ya sure?" Her eyes darted from Rebecca to Zakhar and back.

Rebecca nodded. "I'm sure. I need to find out what's happened to me, and if anyone knows anything, it's him."

"But he doesn't talk."

"I'll be fine. I can hear him now," Rebecca tapped on the side of her head. "Different, remember?"

Kaece frowned in response, but said nothing. She loosened her grip on Rebecca, her tense body-language betraying her stoic expression as concern.

Rebecca gave her a reassuring smile and left her side. As she approached Zakhar, she thought, *I want answers. I want to know what's happening to me. I was a sacrifice. I shouldn't be alive.*

Answers are not always easy to find, came Zakhar's comforting, grandfatherly voice. *Sometimes what seem to be the most obvious of solutions could not be farther from the reality of a situation. Many are upset with what Typhos has done. However, I bear no hostility toward you; the prophecy stated "The one who breaks the seal will release my power." I consider your continued presence as a fulfillment of that prophecy. You are no longer of your species, nor are you of the Drakeon... You are something of a half-Dragon, and in being such a creature the next line of his prophecy also proves true: "They will bring the worlds together." None expected for the merging of worlds to be the merging of Drakeon and human within one vessel. But this only proves how complicated seeking answers can become.*

Perhaps, young one, the answer is that you are meant to be a mediator between the two species, one who may show the humans the truth of what they are doing to our world — to us. Typhos' power has been bestowed upon you. As it eventually destroyed him, it too killed you, and transformed you into this creature of two worlds. With this power, you will do as he foresaw.

"He called me Protector," Rebecca mused, rubbing the tattoo that resembled the rune of Truth that burned white-hot just before the tomb collapsed. Had she been marked as a Protector before she'd even chosen the rune? She wished she could remember what Typhos had said about the prophecy.

It is the appropriate salutation for the mark you bear. Do not fret, the importance is that his power has manifested, the seal has been broken. I hope that I will live to see the outcome, for I do not have more than a few centuries left before I must lay to rest and the next Elder will step into my place. Indeed, having the privilege to see this much of the prophecy come to pass is an honor great enough, and I must bow to you for having offered yourself as courageously as you did. Zakhar lowered his great horned head.

She scoffed, "It better happen a lot sooner than a couple hundred years, or he'll have gone through all this for nothing."

And why is that? You are no longer simply human. You are young and strong, with the blood of a powerful Drakeon coursing through your veins. It will bring you life for many thousands of years; the potency of your blood is extraordinary... Were you full dragon, I have no doubt that you would become the next Elder. But as our society works, you cannot be a true member of it, even if you are marked by the rune of the Protector. You cannot breed, nor lay eggs. You could not raise our young, nor teach them to fight, fly, and hunt. The question for which you should seek an answer is, Protector of what? That you are one in which we may have absolute faith is beyond doubt, the Protector is denoted by the rune of Trust: we shall rely on you to devote your power toward unselfish ends. The ultimate conclusion is an answer we shall not simply stumble upon, young one. It may not be easy to discover, but we must believe it is there.

Rebecca frowned, her head spun – how could she anticipate thousands of years of life, when she couldn't bear the thought of one more day with her fiancé?

I understand this must be a shock to a former human, one with such a very short lifespan. I feel your fear... I will do as much as I am able to answer what questions you have about this new life. We will all do our part in helping you with this transition.

"Thank you." She heard herself say it, but numbness had seeped into her brain. Ardin spoke of "necessity" and "importance," but Zakhar made her feel the weight of responsibility on her shoulders. The responsibility of prophecy, unlike a marriage to Brad, or keeping up the facade of normalcy, couldn't simply be shirked by suicide. According to the prophecy she would live out her destiny as a mutant superhero. Despite what Zakhar said about her blood, she didn't feel all that different. No psychic powers – beyond the sudden curse of telepathy – presented themselves, and her strength and senses paled in comparison to Kaece's. Where any of them expected the savior part to work its way in, she couldn't be sure.

Rebecca wondered why people always expected things from others; if no one ever had expectations, she wouldn't have been trapped in that awful predicament with Brad in the first place. She might've been free of the society pressuring her to behave a certain way, to be a certain kind of person – Like a superhero, or someone's wife.

"Are dragons supposed to get married?"

The Elder dragon chuckled. *No, dragons do not marry. They do not abide by the same mating rituals as humans, and in fact do not divide into pairs at all. Perhaps it is because our breeding cycle comes about rarely, or perhaps it is because our society is not individualistic – we each play a significant role in the structure of life here, no one Drakeon is more important than another. Though there are only a select few positions of noteworthiness, without each and every one of the other positions, there would be no order. If Magnus had no Warriors beneath him, he could not fight a war. If the Drakeon did not listen to my wisdom, it would be nothing more than idle chatter. Whatever the cause for the difference, humans choose instead to seek a mate and engage in ceremony to formalize the sexual relationship, possibly to make a show to the society of the desired mate's unavailability. This, however, is purely speculation. Maedians have participated in the ritual ceremony of marriage longer than I have been alive, so I can only venture to guess at its origin.*

She frowned, trying to imagine her mother fawning over the form-fitting silken dress while her tattoo glowed through the fabric. If, she thought, she was little more than a beast to the Maedians, she probably wasn't bound by their society either. No longer human, being half-dragon freed her from the ties of humanity. She wouldn't have to abide by the constraint of being Rebecca Silas, daughter of Emily Silas, bride-to-be of Bradley Logan. Nor would she be confused for Maedian. Marriage, she decided with satisfaction, no longer applied to her.

It seems to me as though you arrive at reasonable conclusions all on your own, Zakhar observed. *Your logic is sound, and your approach is very positive. I believe you will do well among us... However, the swords remain a mystery.*

"I don't know what to tell you," Rebecca shrugged with one shoulder. "I don't know anything about swords, I swear I hadn't seen anything like it, not until Ardin showed it to me."

I believe you, young Protector. They may be foreign to you now, as are the ways of magic, but I suspect that you will become well acquainted with these blades in due time.

"What do you mean?" She frowned, glancing back to Kaece and wishing that the Lykos could hear Zakhar and translate for her.

It is possible that these weapons were forged for you by Typhos himself; that, in essence, they are the embodiment of his abilities. Just as the Drakeon can sense the potency of your blood, we can feel the power emanating from the swords themselves. There seems to be an intimate connection between you and those blades, and if we are to have any faith that you will bring about the prophecy, you must learn what that connection is. Our fate lies in your ability to release – and control – the power of Typhos.

Control? Rebecca shifted her weight. What made Zakhar so sure she could handle that amount of power? It killed Typhos. It had killed her. Why wouldn't something like that just keep on killing?

I understand your concern, Zakhar chimed in, reminding Rebecca that her thoughts weren't private. *Seek out the High Priestess, she may have more to share regarding the power of the weapons, or an informed theory at the very least.*

"Isn't there someone else? I don't like Ardin. She's..." She paused, trying to encapsulate all of her frustration. Ardin drew lines that didn't exist, she wanted to make

159

everything a big deal or some kind of deep romance. Sebastian was just a friend; Alex was just her brother, Kaece just was. Her relationships were simple, like the words she could conjure up: mean, judgmental, a bully. "Rude."

It is in her nature to extricate all plausible solutions to a puzzle, even one that seems to have an obvious answer. As you have seen, the solution widely agreed upon can sometimes be the incorrect one. Do not fault her for the gift of seeing beyond what presents itself at face value. It is one of the gifts bestowed upon her by the rune of Knowledge, the rune which binds her to the Eolith. Ardin is one of few who has ardently devoted her life to preserving the legacy of Typhos,

Now, it is her very purpose to uncover the mystery of the power imbued within the swords, and in doing so she will better be able to assist you in your task. Perhaps she is more hostile than usual because of the series of unexpected events that have occurred in the recent past; please, I urge you to allow her the chance to reveal her true nature. I am sure you will warm up to one another, and in the meantime you would be wise to take the opportunity to benefit from her vast knowledge of Typhos. Once you have learned what potential the power of the swords may contain, you may pass a final judgment of your own on the High Priestess.

She agreed; his request felt reasonable. He didn't answer her questions with more questions; he didn't riddle with her like Typhos had. Thoughts of the dark, runed cave filled her vision. Ardin – Knowledge – and Magnus – Force – stood off to the side while Arbitration spoke down at her pain-wracked body. Zakhar behaved nothing like the rune of Arbitration behaved in the tomb. Maybe, she thought, she confused Ardin for the rune of Knowledge.

"Thank you." Rebecca smiled up at the great dragon and turned away. She walked straight to Kaece, who stood rigid where she'd been abandoned. Rebecca held out her hand.

Kaece tilted her head, raising her eyebrows and taking Rebecca's hand into hers.

"It went okay," Rebecca answered the unspoken question. "We need to go get harassed by Ardin some more. You with me?"

Kaece's expression shifted into mild confusion, masked with a smirk. "Always."

CHAPTER 18

Ardin and Magnus stood as humans in the center of the valley. Their audience looked on from every angle, many dragons hidden inside the damaged caverns – their blazing purple eyes glinted from the shadows. Rebecca shivered, nervous sweat intensifying the cold of her own body.

"Welcome back, friend," Magnus greeted.

The irony of his salutation grated on her nerves; the last time she'd seen Magnus, he'd flown her toward certain death. In spite of herself, she smiled a little and nodded to him.

"Hey, I, for one, am happy for you still being you. Dying from ritual sacrifice, well... That's not a dignified way to die."

Stone-faced and straight to business, Ardin settled her gaze on Rebecca. *Take the swords from him.*

Magnus raised the twin swords, both held in one hand. She took them, wondering if she'd ever grow fond of the icy Drakeon Priestess. It seemed as unlikely as thawing an iceberg with a Zippo.

At first, she held the swords limp at her sides. Lighter than she'd expected, she could ignore the weight forever if the dragons just wanted her to stand there. The grip felt uncomfortable though, backwards, like trying to put on the wrong shoe.

Rebecca closed her eyes and concentrated on the feel of the swords; awkwardness pervaded the entire experience. She wedged the tip of one blade into a crack in the ground, pushing until it stood on its own. She reversed her grip, her thumb and forefinger closest to the end with the punching dagger, and yanked the sword back out. The blade curved back against her forearm, resting comfortably against her skin; the dragon-toothed guard fit over her hand like brass knuckles. Holding the sword backward felt right. She repeated the gesture with the second sword and let her arms fall back to her sides.

Describe how you feel, Ardin interjected into her thoughts.

"Are you some kind of shrink too?" Rebecca retorted with a scowl. When Ardin didn't reply, she answered, "I don't know. Good, I guess."

They don't burn your hands? The grip isn't awkward? They don't seem too light?

I said it's fine, she snapped at the voice in her head, squeezing the sword hilts tighter. "What do you expect me to do with these, anyways?"

"Fight," Magnus replied. He raised an eyebrow. "Do you know how to use a sword?"

No, Rebecca admitted silently.

"Do you?" Kaece taunted Magnus.

He smirked. "You hold it, and thrust. She's holding them wrong."

Rebecca frowned.

"Yeah, wrong for thrusting," Kaece agreed with an air of smugness. "But these swords aren't meant for thrustin', they're slashin' weapons. See the curve to the blades? Some Lykos fight with lethal skill usin' swords just the way she's holdin' 'em now. She's a natural."

"Lykos stay out of this," Magnus snarled. "It has nothing to do with you or your deceitful ways."

"Aw, did I hurt the big dumb warrior's pride?" Kaece mocked; it reminded Rebecca of the way Force had mocked her in the tomb. "My mistake. Go ahead an' teach her all about something ya don't know, ya joke of a fighter."

Magnus sneered and leapt backward. He roared, flames engulfing his body. Moments later, the eruption of fire died away, revealing his dragon form.

Ardin spoke casually, "You'd best tread carefully, Lykos. Though Zakhar has permitted you to stay, it is against the wishes of many. Magnus holds a grudge against you and your kind for all that has been done. He is not wrong to do so, though your death would be a sorrowful loss for Rebecca."

"Let them teach me," Rebecca pleaded with Kaece. "I'll be okay, just... Stand back for a while, okay?"

"Dragons don't use weapons, they use tooth, claw, and their damnable fire and magic. They can't *teach* what they don't know. But," Kaece trailed off, her tone quieting as her temper cooled. She stepped back, moving away from both Rebecca and the Drakeon. "I'll be right here if ya need me..."

Rebecca smiled and said, "Thank you"

Ardin stood with her hands on her hips, expectation plain on her face. *Use the swords; attack Magnus.*

"What? But I don't –"

He's a resilient Drakeon. He could use a little softening up. Now attack him.

Rebecca frowned at the swords; she knew she couldn't fight the warrior dragon.

Magnus roared again. He raised his talons and crushed a boulder. The rock exploded into a cloud of dust. His gaze shifted, behind Rebecca, to Kaece. Rebecca swallowed and tightened her grip on the swords; her palms slicked with sweat – the threat made her heart thunder in her chest.

Muscles coiled like springs, Rebecca launched herself forward, running at Magnus with full force. Blindly, she swung the blades at his massive leg. The dragon made no attempt to dodge; her sword slashed through the air and the side of the blade slapped against his scales.

Pain shot through her arm; her wrist twisted back at the force of the impact. The Drakeon onlookers laughed at her ineptitude, at her failure. Frustrated, she tried again. She braced the blade against her forearm and swung from the shoulder. Her second attempt succeeded no more than the first; the sword ricocheted off Magnus' scales again.

Her lungs constricted and her jaw tightened as annoyance threatened to burst from her chest. What did they expect from her? If standing back and snorting uproariously while she dulled the blades on a rock-solid dragon was their idea of training, the world was doomed.

Good, harness that anger. Use it to release the power of Typhos.

Rebecca closed her eyes and felt the anger burning in her chest. Once more, she launched herself at Magnus. Once more, the assault culminated in nothing. For what felt like hours, she persisted; each attack offered the same results. When Ardin interjected, Rebecca was ready to take the swords to her own chest, since she felt like she'd only ever succeed at causing herself harm with them.

"This isn't working," the Priestess sighed. Her tone reflected the boredom in Magnus' eyes, the frustration in Kaece's expression; Rebecca managed to disappoint everyone. "You aren't taking this seriously. Fine. If you won't spar for the sake of releasing the power, perhaps you'll fight for the sake of avoiding pain – Magnus, hurt her. Tear her limbs off, and we can see if they grow back."

Magnus' mouth split into a wicked, fanged grin. His eyes burned with maleficence, the boredom snuffed out by the promise of violence. The earth shook when the dragon stamped like a dog excited to play. His claws came at her; she cowered, shielding herself with the artifact weapons.

On the ground, off her feet, her mobility completely inhibited, Rebecca couldn't dodge the attack. She closed her eyes and shakily held the swords over her head, hoping the useless blades would be a match for dragon talons or that the threat of damaging Typhos' swords would keep Magnus from tearing into her flesh. A shriek pierced her mind – to her surprise, it wasn't her own; Magnus' scream echoed in her head.

The dragon's pained roar filled the air: her eyes shot open to take in Kaece, who stood with her arm drenched to the shoulder in blood. Magnus reared his head, more blood sprayed from his gouged eye-socket. He swiped at Kaece, but she hopped over his arm with ease.

"Kaece!" Rebecca cried, "Stop!"

The Lykos didn't listen. Instead, Kaece backflipped onto the dragon's wrist and used his body as leverage to propel herself forward in one smooth motion. She leapt up and drove her claws into his underbelly. Just as her fingers plunged between Magnus' scales, Kaece went limp. Her unconscious body fell to the ground with a hard thud – her head lolled back.

Rebecca heard herself scream; she felt her legs moving. Time seemed to grind to a halt as she ran toward the helpless Lykos. As if in slow motion, Magnus' weight shifted with sinister intent to crush Kaece under his colossal body. His hand plummeted unbelievably fast. She pushed her burning muscles to reach Kaece in time.

Sheer desperation fueled her instincts; power flooded her veins. Rushing to protect Kaece, she raised the swords, not yet knowing her next move. Rebecca slid between Magnus' hand and the Lykos about to be squashed beneath him. She crossed the blades and held them firm, pushing up against the momentum of his crushing weight as it came down.

Aided by the magic of Typhos, Rebecca's swords bit into the thick stone scales, then cut straight through them. Steel sliced deep into muscle, then tendon and bone. The force of Magnus' stomp cleanly severed two fingers and a thumb; half of his palm flopped into the ash-strewn ground. Blood oozed from the twitching, dismembered digits and pooled around Kaece.

Magnus' cry echoed throughout the valley and her head in unison. He recoiled, his tail thrashing against the earth. Two of the spectating Drakeon, each bearing the rune of Force, restrained Magnus and dragged him away. Rebecca dropped to her knees beside Kaece. Her swords clattered to the ground as she checked for a pulse. She breathed a deep sigh of relief when she felt the vein throbbing against her fingers; Kaece was alive.

Don't you dare kill her. If you kill her, I swear that I will never do as Typhos wants. I promise you, I'll live out my days doing everything within my power – and his – to see that his Prophecy fails you all. I won't let anything stop me from making sure the Drakeon die out, Rebecca threatened.

You're bluffing, Ardin retorted. *Nonetheless, she will not be killed. So long as she is a guest of Zakhar, she is... safe. However, if she pulls another stunt like that, she will be removed from our territory. Make her understand this, or you will have to live on without her.*

"Fine," Rebecca agreed. "I'll talk to her."

The shimmer of magic weaved through the air, trailing behind Ardin's fingertips as she waved her hand. At Rebecca's feet, Kaece gasped.

The Lykos took in the sight of Rebecca, but wasted no time kipping up and whirling on the Drakeon. "Ya hide behind your magic. Jus' wait, Priestess, there'll be a time that ya don't see me coming."

"And once you've succeeded at that, what then?"

Kaece responded with a deep-throated growl, her muscles visibly tensing.

"Hey now, calm down," Rebecca soothed. She stroked the nape of Kaece's neck with her knuckles.

Kaece's growl faded away into silence as she leaned back against Rebecca's hand.   Rebecca upheld her end of the bargain with Ardin. Each word came, one after the other, each more forced than the last. "Listen... You can't do that again, Kaece. You have to... could you... Respect them? They're my people now. Magnus wouldn't actually hurt me."

Is any of that even true? She sought validation from Ardin.

He would not have caused you any harm that you couldn't have healed from, I'm sure. That will be all today. Food will come to you.

Ardin's reply only nettled her. She hoped Kaece wasn't upset with her for the reprimand. Tentatively, she spread her hands across Kaece's shoulders and traced her fingers down the Lykos' back, expressing her apology through touch.

Feeling a twinge of sorrow for Magnus, she took up her swords and grabbed hold of Kaece's blood-caked hand. As she led Kaece toward the cave they'd left together earlier that morning, she wondered if Magnus would fully heal from those wounds. Though she recovered from death, something about Zakhar's awe at the power of Typhos' blood in her veins made her suspect not every dragon could.

Back in the cave, Kaece walked straight to the ceramic water basin. It struck Rebecca as strange that the dragons used human tools, if they truly viewed their human form as "lesser," but the basin looked undeniably old. Perhaps, she thought, the Madius who came long ago had been more welcomed than Sebastian. She sat on the straw bed while Kaece washed the blood from her hands, blood that wouldn't have been shed if it weren't for Rebecca's ineptitude.

With a sigh, she set the swords at her feet. The reflection that stared up at her from the Drakeon blades frowned disapprovingly. The girl she saw didn't look quite like her, but moved as she moved. When she tilted her head, the reflection mimicked her; when she sighed, the lips of the purple-eyed girl also parted. She marveled at the idea that this mirror-girl would live for thousands of years. The thought horrified her, but so did the concept of dying while fighting to save a world that wasn't hers. She shook her head at her strange new reflection and kicked the swords aside.

Rebecca smiled as she watched Kaece's arms glisten with water. Kaece's muscles worked just below the surface while she scrubbed her face. Her toned body and soft skin betrayed her youth in spite of her numerous scars.

"You said you were like twenty, right?"

Kaece paused her scrubbing to glance at Rebecca. The water ran down her face and dripped back into the basin, stained red. She studied Rebecca's expression, cocking her head questioningly.

Rebecca shrugged. "How old is the oldest Lykos?"

"Age." Kaece scrunched her nose. "What's it matter?"

"I just..." She fumbled for the words to express why she wanted to know Kaece's life expectancy. But she could only shrug again – she shouldn't have to explain herself in order to get an answer. "Never mind. Is it really so wrong that I want to know more about you?"

"No." Kaece shook her head before she resumed washing. She submerged her face and splashed water up into her hair. Her fingers massaged her scalp. She flipped her hair back and shook her head wildly, just like she had the night they shared together in the hot springs.

Maybe, Rebecca reasoned, she didn't have to have all the answers. They didn't need words. Moments like that night – moments like watching Kaece enjoy something as simple as bathing – were all she needed. Being close to Kaece, spending time in her company, brought her a warm satisfaction. More than that, happiness worked its way into her heart every time Kaece looked at her, spoke to her, touched her.

That very emotion seeped up into her cheeks when Kaece finished shaking herself dry and abandoned the ceramic basin. She joined Rebecca on the bed of straw, sitting beside her. Rebecca pulled her legs up and laid out behind Kaece, curling around Kaece's back and propping herself up on her side with one arm. She used her free hand to trace up Kaece's arm, enjoying the feel of her skin and all its familiar imperfections.

Kaece's smile tinged with sadness, but her eyes held the soft shimmer of adoration that nourished Rebecca's very soul. "The oldest Lykos saw over eighty winters. Some thought of him as a well of wisdom for all the things he'd witnessed in his lifetime... But even so, most pitied him."

"Why?"

"'Cause he was too old to hunt. Too old to fight. He was destined to die without glory, without honor."

"Most people want to die from old age where I come from."

Kaece closed her eyes as if she were looking deep into the past, "His cough rattled like an angry wind... I remember the sound of it. For endless nights, I'd sit awake an' listen, waiting for the earth to take him an' stop his suffering." She opened her eyes, her lip curled into a sneer. "Few males die like that. It's the females that're destined to die in pain outside of combat."

Sympathy and excitement washed over Rebecca in a confusing muddle; at once, she felt sorrow for the fate of the old man and a rush of enthusiasm because she'd been given a piece of Kaece's past. "So men and women have different roles, then? Like men hunt and women gather...? Except that can't be right... I mean, I know you, and you're not a berry gatherer. So the men gather and the women must hunt."

"No," Kaece frowned. "Everyone hunts. Everyone gathers what is needed. The difference is... The... the females..."

Her concern roused when Kaece faltered. Her hand trailed across Kaece's back as she sat up then slid into Kaece's lap. She leaned into her warmth;. the feel of her bare skin almost invited a kiss. Kaece wrapped her arms around her waist and held her; Rebecca relaxed into the embrace.

"Well," she tried to divert the subject from whatever made Kaece so uncomfortable. "I think it's cool that all Lykos are equals. Because even though Sebastian *says* that Maedians are all equals, it's such an obvious patriarchy. I mean, his father's father and his father and now him, all lined up to be Emperor? Even Demarko, the king of the "wild land," is a man. And a schmuck at that."

Kaece chuckled, raising an eyebrow. "Not a fan of alphas, eh?"

"Alphas? Like a pack leader? I'm not really sure I'd consider a king the same thing... Do you like your alpha? Or do you even have one?"

She tightened her arms around Rebecca and, still smiling, rested her head on Rebecca's. "She is the only Lykos worthy of her position. Most despise her, though none understand her. But what's more – not one can best her. I think you're wrong, an' she has more in common with this Maedian 'king' than you'd think."

"Is she a drunkard who condemns people to an agonizing death by starvation?"

"Nah, starvation is too slow. Ya'd have to wait too many days for their death."

Rebecca didn't know what to say, whether to laugh or frown; of course Kaece only jested, but her tone made it impossible to be sure. Kaece seemed to understand the distastefulness of her humor, offering instead to steer the conversation in a new direction.

She murmured into Rebecca's hair, "I don't know you, either. Tell me somethin' you've kept hidden."

"What?"

"Tell me a secret. Anything ya wouldn't want to admit to me. Just one."

The first thought that flashed in her mind was Monique and the smile that stole hearts. She couldn't tell Kaece about her friendship with Monique, couldn't tell her how an obsessiveness crept into their relationship. She couldn't explain how much Monique had meant to her, because it was Kaece who filled the gaping wound of the past. Kaece showed Rebecca the unrestrained affection she'd only dreamed of with Monique.

She traced the edge of her tattoo, trying desperately to think of something else she'd kept hidden; something she could expose without destroying their friendship. "In my world, I was engaged... You know, to be married?"

"Maedian's have marriage, too," Kaece replied evenly.

"Oh. Right. Okay. Well," She took a deep breath and forced herself to continue, "I tried to kill myself on the day of our wedding... So I wouldn't have to marry him."

Rebecca hid her face so she wouldn't have to see the disgust. She didn't want to hear Kaece's disapproval. When Kaece didn't respond immediately, she assumed the worst. Of course, she sighed, why wouldn't Kaece find her deplorable?

After a long silence Kaece asked, "Why'd you choose him as your mate? Did he change after the arrangement?"

"He chose me, really... I just didn't say no."

Kaece pulled her back, out of hiding, and peered at her with those captivating dark-rimmed yellow eyes. "Ya never liked him?"

"Not really, no."

"Don't be so frightened," Kaece purred, taking Rebecca's hands in hers and entwining their fingers. "My mate an' I have differences that can't ever be reconciled. I prefer this, here," she squeezed Rebecca's hands. "Maleless."

Rebecca nodded absently, a nervous laugh accompanying her response. "Yeah, less drama this way, right?"

Kaece smirked.

"So..." Rebecca pried, "You have a mate then? What's his name? How long have you guys been together?"

Kaece's eyes shifted, as if contemplating whether or not to answer. "Kym," she said much like she'd originally said her own name. "We're not exactly 'together,' but If I were to return, it would be to him. Having offspring requires mating."

"You're with a guy just to have kids?"

Kaece shrugged. "If it comes to that."

"Brad wanted children. He wanted this picture perfect life complete with a wife, four kids and a white picket fence. Cats, too... He loved cats. And probably a tire swing in his overly-watered lawn... I had nightmares about it. The idea of something foreign growing inside of you, leeching off your nutrients and becoming a person... That you then have to take responsibility for, for *eighteen years*. It's terrifying. Why do men get the easy job?"

Kaece snorted, then laughed. An infectious smile lit up her face. She hugged Rebecca tight and flopped over onto the bed, pulling Rebecca down with her. Laying beside her, Kaece took Rebecca's hand and gazed into her eyes. The feel of Kaece's breath tickling her neck made Rebecca giddy.

"That's what he wanted... Tell me, what is it that you want?" Kaece asked.

The answer came easily. She knew what she wanted more than she'd ever known anything in her entire life; she wanted Kaece. She just wanted to be left in peace, alone with her, forever. But a thought nagged at her: she'd wanted her forever with Monique, too. Her former friend's taunt echoed in her memory, *you'd better take a picture, it'll last longer*. She swallowed, thinking about the photograph she'd scribbled her suicide note on. In Gaeadia, she had no way to preserve the moment. She knew, forever was impossible, everything always had an end.

"I don't know," she sighed.

"If ya didn't want his fence or cats, ya had to want something."

Rebecca sighed; clearly Kaece wouldn't drop it. She thought carefully about how to word her answer. "It just wasn't possible. I wanted to love being with him, everywhere...Anywhere. I wanted something mutual. But that's it, really. Love. Trust. That sort of stuff."

"Ya said wasn't." Kaece's smile broadened. "Is it possible without him?"

"I hope so," Rebecca answered without thinking. She felt the charge of excitement when her skin brushed against Kaece, the surge of emotion each touch gave her. The feel of the Lykos on her fingertips drove her to say more than she'd ever intended to tell anyone. "But you can't attack any more dragons, okay?"

"Because they're your people?"

"Because I'm begging you. I want you to be here with me, you're my friend. I want to trust you. But I need you to promise me, and mean it."

Kaece took a deep breath, a shiver making her whole body shudder as she exhaled. Rebecca pressed herself against Kaece, the Lykos' warmth eased the setting cold of dusk.

"Alright," Kaece rasped, "for you, I'll never hurt a dragon again. I promise."

Denial XIX
The Cavern of the Drakeon Betrayers

SEBASTIAN MADIUS

ALEX SILAS

244 Virgo in the afternoon

Rebecca's been dead for almost a month. I can't believe it took me over a week just to convince Sebastian that we needed to avenge her death - but I DID convince him. We trained every day for at least 2 hours after he agreed. We are totally prepared for these dragons... and even if they do kill us, we'll at least hurt them. We left the flyers, safe, in Oneiroi, and traveled by Hadros far north to the foothill caverns. We're parking out in the middle of nowhere so the dragons won't hear us coming. We'll sneak up in the grass, pop up and squirt the hell outta them with my Gaeadian Water Blaster, then while they are weakened, we'll wipe them out. Rebecca, this is for you.

I loved my sister,

–Alexander the Greatest

170

174

175

178

179

That is the determination that defines you so aptly. We will be out of this cave before you know it.

WHAT ABOUT YOUR PATRON MADIUS? LEAVE THE BOY AND PERHAPS I'LL GIVE YOU THE MAN YOU SEEK

AND HERE I HEARD THAT YOU WERE FIXATED ON FINDING YOUR OLD MAN, WILLING TO DIE TRYING.

Did the Lykos tell you that somehow, dragon?

Come on man, you said it was just head games.

Tell me from who you have heard of my journey, dragon. Tell me how she had contact with you. How did she do it?

No reply means the Power is no longer working. He resisted, we must go quickly.

If your Power doesn't work, his threats are probably real. He'll be back before we get out.

We'll have to stay on guard.

CHAPTER 20

Rebecca hopped back, dodging Kaece's claws. Her ankle rolled beneath her then she fell backwards, landing on her butt.

"Ya couldn't hit an animal that wanted to die," Kaece teased.

"At least I can play dead."

"Ya gotta work on that, too - the dead don't usually talk."

Rebecca swung her leg to trip her, but Kaece stepped over the kick. Throwing her hands up in playful surrender, Rebecca flopped over onto her back. She stared up at the early morning sky. Every day, from dawn 'til dusk, she and Kaece would come out to the field and train. No matter how long they fought, Rebecca still couldn't get the Lykos to break a sweat – Kaece dodged her attacks with ease. Each passing day, Kaece continued to tell her she was doing well; she kept saying Rebecca was a natural with the swords. She didn't see it – since Magnus lost his fingers, she hadn't managed to so much as strike her opponent, be it Kaece or another Drakeon.

"Get up, lazy. A warrior never rests."

"Good thing I'm not a Warrior," Rebecca retorted, sitting up. "I'm a Protector."

"Ya keep sayin' that, but I don't see the difference." Kaece snatched Rebecca by the wrist and pulled her to her feet, then leapt backwards and snarled.

She couldn't help but smile at Kaece's insincere threat; she knew Kaece would never hurt her. She grudgingly picked up her swords. "Protectors take care of the clan... I think 'teacher' is a better word, but Ardin insists that's not quite right either. I guess when I go back to the moment when I actually hit Magnus, I don't remember it at all. I was so busy thinking about protecting you."

"But ya can't protect yourself. Not yet," Kaece said. "Come at me, you've almost got it."

"If I *needed* to protect myself, I could. The swords would do it for me."

She lunged at Kaece, though Kaece sidestepped the sword thrust effortlessly. Dropping to a knee, she grabbed Rebecca's ankle and pulled it out from under her. Rebecca fell backward again, landing on her back and winced.

"Ya weren't supposed to fall that easy. Ya usually see that move comin'." Kaece crawled onto Rebecca and peered down at her with concern. "You're not hurt, are ya?"

Rebecca grinned and smacked Kaece in the side with the flat of her blade. "Gotcha!"

"You sneak! Ya tricked me... "

As Rebecca laughed, the invasive voice of Ardin interrupted her thoughts. *Zakhar has approved your request, though he will not be bidding you farewell. We are prepared for your departure. Come when you please.*

"I'm so done," she said. "Trickery or not, I totally hit you. I win."

"Ya can't be done," Kaece protested, moving to stand. "We've got a long time 'til dark."

Rebecca pulled Kaece back and pinned her. "Actually," she sighed, "I need to tell you something."

Kaece smiled up at her; the contentment on her face made Rebecca wonder what she expected to hear.

"We're leaving."

Kaece's smile wilted. "Leaving?"

"Alex and Sebastian are still out there, somewhere..." She slid off of Kaece, using physical distance to ease the sudden tension. "We should be with them, not just letting them go wander into some deathtrap."

"The dragons won't like that idea," Kaece said evenly after a long pause.

"I've already talked with them."

Those deep yellow eyes widened as Kaece peered at Rebecca, as if measuring her expression for honesty – or sincerity. "When?"

"A few days ago." Rebecca tapped the side of her head. "Mind-speak..."

Kaece's eyebrows scrunched together, her jaw tensed; the corners of her mouth formed a subtle frown. The glassy sheen of her eyes exposed the truth behind her mask of anger: she looked hurt. Rebecca's heart ached – she'd anticipated an argument, but not hurt. She reached out to touch Kaece's shoulder, but Kaece avoided her and stood swiftly.

"I need you to help me find them," Rebecca pleaded, pulling leaves of grass out by their roots. "You know this world, and even places you've never been you know all about. You have super senses... Besides, we'll still be together."

Kaece nodded and extended her hand.

As she took Kaece's hand, Rebecca sighed. Kaece's upset pervaded the atmosphere, the air grew thick with her disapproval. Even though she didn't voice her protest, Rebecca could hear the argument: Kaece detested Sebastian. Rebecca had kept their inevitable departure to herself because of Kaece's sensitivity about the subject.

"Listen, it's been great here. We have our own room, and the dragons make sure we have plenty of food, and they treat us *both* kind of like friends. We get to play around out here all day and call it work... But that's exactly it. Something is wrong, and it bothers me. Every day it bothers me, Kaece. All the time. The dragons know it, they understand. That's why they're choosing to let us go. Can't you understand, too?"

"Something's wrong," Kaece repeated, her tone matter-of-fact.

Rebecca swallowed, annoyance crawling across her skin and seeping into her voice. "Yes. Something's wrong. I care about my friends, about my *brother*. They're out there chasing traitorous dragons and god knows what else, while I'm living my life as if everything's all peachy."

Again, Kaece nodded, but she didn't speak. She said nothing on their trek back into the heart of the valley, and each moment of silence grated on Rebecca's nerves. Where was her fight? Why couldn't she just admit that she didn't want to help find Sebastian? She knew that Kaece didn't want to leave – that she wanted to keep Rebecca all to herself.

How can you be so certain that isn't simply your own desire speaking in place of hers?

Tell me I'm wrong, Ardin, Rebecca dared. *I know her, and I know how she feels. I just wish she'd show it.*

By arguing with you? What faulty logic you have, Protector. Still so human. Are you sure that you are ready to leave us?

The Priestess stood in human form, surrounded by other Drakeon who remained dragons.

"Yes," Rebecca asserted as she approached. "I need to find Alex and Sebastian before anything bad happens to them."

Do what you feel you must; our future is in your hands. Perhaps the Drakeon Betrayers will offer a clue about the prophecy that we have overlooked. There is no way to be certain. However, we will always be here to assist you in whatever way we can.

"Thank you, Priestess." She bowed her head at first, but the looming threat of final parting made Rebecca abandon formality. She threw her arms around Ardin, hugging her just in case she never came back.

I have a gift for you. Ardin pulled back from the embrace. She raised her seemingly empty hand. *Or, rather, I have a gift to protect the artifacts bestowed upon you by Typhos.*

I don't see anything.

Ardin laughed. "It's an enchanted sheath – a bag imbued with magic. It will hold any item that has been attuned to it, such as the swords. The magic will keep them secure – in another dimension, where they are safe from the hands of others until you draw them from it. Anyone can use the sheath, though it will only hold one thing: the swords of Typhos. Please, keep them well protected. I imagine many creatures will covet them."

"Covet a good burn," Kaece remarked, flashing the faint scar across her palm.

"Neither you, nor I, believe that such a petty wound would stop someone who desires them."

Kaece shrugged. "True."

"So..." Rebecca interrupted their stare-down. "Show me how it works."

Ardin obliged by placing the bag in Rebecca's outstretched hand. The sensation of a real object surprised her – it felt like a small square of silken cloth resting in her palm. She groped it; soft leather ties protruded from one end.

Would you tie it to my belt? I don't want to lose it, she asked Ardin.

The Priestess took the silken bag and did as she asked. Once the sheath was secured, Rebecca ran her fingers along her belt until she felt the ties. She thanked Ardin while she pushed a finger inside the small pouch. The opening stretched only as wide as her hand.

It will do exactly what it should, Ardin answered her unasked question. Then she showed Rebecca how to draw and sheath the swords.

Rebecca practiced pulling Typhos' weapons from another dimension. Many of the dragons she and Kaece befriended during their stay said farewell. Even Magnus came to see them off, though he remained dragon rather than taking on a human form.

"I'm sorry," she apologized for the hundredth time since the day she crippled him. Rebecca stroked his big snout. The dragons had managed to reattach his fingers but, his gouged eye still stood out like a black hole in his face.

He dismissed her concern, instead wishing her a fun and eventful journey. Then he walked away, just as each Drakeon before him.

"Lots of them are saying goodbye to you, too," she told Kaece. "Magnus said he was wrong about you."

Kaece forced a smile. "Good to know."

"Actually," Ardin corrected, "he said maybe he was wrong about you. The truth is, Lykos, you and your people are very smart. Most of your kind don't cause our world any harm, and if dragon's power is restored, then the Lykos and Drakeon should no longer be warring over ideologies."

"Just admit ya dragons are afraid of me." Kaece winked, a cocky smirk replacing the sad excuse for a smile she'd conjured for Rebecca.

Seeing Kaece get along with the Drakeon, even smiling at Ardin, made Rebecca's chest feel near-bursting with adoration for her. Knowing that Ardin approved, that Magnus could forgive, only proved what Rebecca had known all along: everything people assumed about Kaece was wrong. The Lykos she'd grown to love stood apart from the horrible tales of Lykos that Sebastian told.

The snarl of the Simurg pulled Rebecca from her thoughts. She looked to the sound; a humanoid dragon, disgruntled to be in his 'lesser' form, lead the Simurg toward them. The animal's eyes were wild, frantic with so many dragons nearby. Rebecca'd hoped he would warm up to the Drakeon like Kaece had, but he never did. No amount of feeding or grooming soothed the poor creature's nerves once a dragon got too close. She could only be thankful she and Kaece had been allowed to care for him during their stay – she couldn't imagine the Simurg would have fared well without a break from all the distress.

"Hey," Rebecca cooed, petting the Simurg. "How are you?"

"Unfortunately," Ardin lamented, "the beast still isn't fond of us. Best to remember that you also smell like one of us now. It wouldn't do at all for the heir of Typhos to die by falling from the sky."

"Yeah yeah," Rebecca dismissed the caution with a wave of her hand. She climbed on the Simurg and said, "Come on, we'll leave the scary dragons behind."

"Wait." Kaece shifted, her amusement melting into the wounded expression she'd had before.

Rebecca glanced to Ardin with a knowing look; *see?* she thought. *Here's the fight.*

"This'll change everything," Kaece whispered.

"What?" Rebecca's confidence faltered. The protest hardly echoed the argument she'd rehearsed defending against.

"If ya make this decision, which... ya already have... And we go through with it..." Kaece's voice cracked. She paused to gather herself, staring down at her hands, flexing her fingers and watching her tendons contract. "I'm afraid for us. I'm terrified, Rebecca. Please don't... let's don't go after them?"

"If *you're* afraid, can you imagine how they must feel? They need us right now. Just let your issues with Sebastian go, okay? I know you can befriend him, too, if you just try like you did here."

"I don't want to be friends with the Madius," Kaece snarled. "I want him to stop this inane search for a dead man so I can live at peace, with you. What happened to our 'better maleless' plan?"

"I'm going to save him, with or without you. So make your choice. Help me save Sebastian or stay behind."

Kaece reluctantly climbed onto the Simurg. She licked her lips, her eyes darted from Rebecca to Ardin. "Priestess please, can ya make her understand... Somehow?"

"I don't have a love life, Lykos. I'm sorry."

A shiver shot down Rebecca's spine, and she blushed. "We're *friends.*"

Before Ardin could make any more inappropriate insinuations, Rebecca urged the Simurg to fly. She hated how Ardin talked about them like lovers – couldn't two girls be close? So what if they were friends who trusted each other? Sharing love between them didn't make them intimate. There was a line between loving someone and being their lover; there was a boundary between friend and significant other. Even if Rebecca wanted to sometimes, she never kissed Kaece, because that would be crossing the line.

I shouldn't bother, Ardin projected into her thoughts, *but I will say this: someone like her does not beg easily. You may consider appraising her actions and emotions from outside of your own insecurities.*

You're right, you shouldn't have bothered. Don't worry about us.

Ardin's warning was the last thing she heard from the Drakeon before they hit open skies, and flew north along the mountain's edge. Rebecca couldn't make sense of it, beyond the obvious insult. Kaece needed to acclimate to the situation - male or not, Sebastian was a friend too. Determination creased her brow as the Simurg's prismacolored wings beat, pushing them to where she would hopefully find Alex and Sebastian, alive, intact and well.

21

The sun hovered on the west horizon, just barely peeking over the foothills. Kaece scowled down at the Maedian contraption below them with as much loathing as she had the day she tied herself to its roof. Were it not for bad luck, they would have missed it. Rebecca's heart quickened and Kaece knew she'd spotted it.

The Hadros, a physical representation of broken dreams, confirmed that her days alone with Rebecca were in the past. It meant Rebecca could, and would, strengthen her bond with the Madius. Her nemesis sought the one weapon Kaece could not defend against: the truth. She tried to stifle her fears, but as Rebecca's command urged the Simurg into a steep dive, her skin chilled with the terror of losing Rebecca again.

They climbed off of the Simurg and Rebecca ran to the door. Kaece could tell by their fading stench that the two humans had left recently. She took a deep, calming breath and stretched her stiff muscles.

"They're not here," Rebecca called out to her from the doorway.

"I know."

"How long have they been gone? Can you follow them?"

Something about Rebecca always made her want to tell the truth; the seriousness and trust in her body-language begged for it with desperation. But, for Kaece, the truth was the end of the game, and revealing it herself would be forfeit. Losing would be acceptable, though an undesirable outcome, but forfeit - she would never.

She sniffed the air dramatically, though she already knew the trail led due west toward the setting sun. With feigned sincerity she lied, "The smell is faint, they've been gone from here for many days. If there's a trail to find, I'll find it for ya."

Rebecca gave her a weak smile, thanked her then disappeared back inside the machine.

Kaece walked north and took a wide loop around the east side of the Hadros. Dry grass and salt water fragranced the air. The Madius' scent led toward the Betrayers nesting cave. Kaece had to trust that the few Drakeon that had remained in the cave would swiftly slay or capture the boys.

"Can't trust 'em to do anythin'," Kaece sighed into the wind.

The breeze caressed her face and ran through her hair, beckoning her to have patience.

Every moment with Rebecca was a precious gift, a gift in life that she'd never expected to experience. She despised the fact that the game to win Rebecca was a game she couldn't win unless she cheated. If she'd been quicker on her wit, she'd have followed the trail and killed them instead of waiting for the Drakeon to do it.

She stalled her return until the stars illuminated the sky above, then she returned.

Once the scent of Rebecca hit her nose, she grinned and ran. She leapt up into the Hadros, causing Rebecca to startle. Shooting upright, Rebecca pressed her hand to her chest as if pressure could slow her rapidly beating heart. Kaece chuckled while she closed the distance between them.

"You were gone for so long... you had me worried."

"Jus' didn't wanna give up." Kaece slid her hands under Rebecca's hooded jacket, and rested them on her waistline. She loved the way Rebecca's hips felt in her palms.

Rebecca leaned into the touch, her fingers brushed Kaece's cheek as she tucked a strand of hair behind her ear.

"You can't give up," she replied after such a long pause that Kaece'd almost forgotten what she'd said. "They were here."

"The trail ends. I'm thinkin' they musta discovered the dragons were gone or somethin' 'cause the trail heads east a ways, then it's gone. They might have taken the flyers back toward the Maedian Polis, toward Thalassa Harbor. That's not too far from here." Kaece faltered. Rebecca could disprove her lie with a map. Thalassa Harbor wasn't close - it lay across the entire span of the continent and in the exact opposite direction of the Drakeon nest. Kaece clenched her jaw, trying to suppress her anger at herself for the mistake.

Rebecca frowned, her skepticism plain on her face as the oil lamp's light flickered across her features.

Kaece didn't like the feeling of tension behind the look. Words created such a tangled mess, but the way they communicated through the feel of each other's body had never lied. Kaece didn't want to talk with fallible words, so she urged Rebecca toward the bed and then gently leaned her down.

She climbed atop her and whispered into her ear, "They're long gone. Let's forget about it, yeah?"

"You're absolutely sure they've been gone for days?"

"I'm sure they're gone, yeah."

Rebecca's hair tickled her nose as she breathed. She relished in Rebecca's quickening heartbeat and the rush of her blood. She could smell the girl's anxiety, and she could feel her muscles tight with anticipation.

Kaece planted a light kiss behind Rebecca's ear. Rebecca swooned, leaving herself open for Kaece's advance. Kaece trailed light kisses down, and then slowly back up her neck, ending at Rebecca's lips. Softer than the finest cloth, Kaece couldn't resist indulging in the delicacy. She kissed her deeply, a kiss that Rebecca returned with lustful vigor. Kaece'd never felt so alive, or so madly in love. Passion drowned her senses. She'd become so lost in the moment that she didn't understand why Rebecca whimpered and shoved her away. Sliding out from under Kaece, Rebecca tumbled to the floor.

Her crazed, wide-eyes shined with tears as she cried, "You lied. You lied to me!"

Kaece sat and waited. A confusing array of smells and sensations flowed from Rebecca. Kaece's throat constricted, but she resisted the natural reflex of swallowing. She knew that guilt shown at Rebecca's accusation would only set ablaze the vast dry land of deceit. She watched, not reacting, and hoped like in her past outbursts, Rebecca would calm herself.

Rebecca pulled herself upright using the workbench, then snatched up a Maedian book from its surface. As she flipped through the book, her anger overwhelmed the mixture of arousal, fear and guilt. Her lip curled into a sneer and her voice wavered as she read aloud, "If anyone should find this, know that I am dead. This journal should be returned to the Isle of Idan, to whomever is in charge, immediately. Today is my last opportunity to do what is right and not let the hurt in my soul decay my moral essence to that of the inhuman beasts that took her from us."

"It's jus' Maedian babble," Kaece growled.

Rebecca continued reading, faster. "My choice was made many days ago, but today I make it irrevocable. Maedia must not let the monsters of this world force us to cower behind the walls of the palace for safety. If we are to live truly at peace, then the creatures who would harm us must come to regard us as a people worthy of their respect. I set out to do the impossible; alone, the Metakosmos Alexander Silas and I must attempt an attack on the Drakeon Betrayers and strike fear into the hearts of those predators. We may kill none, we may kill many. Whatever transpires, I know that each act of violence I commit will bring me further from my homeland. In honesty, I hope you find this, whoever you are. I must admit that I take this journey to a sure death because I long for the reprise of it; when I am no longer of this world, perhaps the gods will see to it that Rebecca and I can meet each other once again. Only in this fate can my turmoil be set to rest. I am very sorry that I have failed you grandfather, and all of Maedia. Sebastian Madius, 244 Parthenos under Hesperis.

"Alright, they didn't go to Thalassa Harbor. It was a guess - why are ya so upset at me? I didn't tell 'em to go die fightin' dragons."

Rebecca flung the book at Kaece. "It has today's date on it! It was written today - *this* afternoon! Like within a few hours of when we landed. Before you wandered off to who-knows-where! You lied to me - and it's not just the lie Kaece, it's how *easily* you lied to me. How much of what you say is fake? How can I trust anything that comes out of your mouth?"

The book missed, but the words hit her like a fatal blow. Her facade, her act of indifference that had allowed Rebecca to create a lovable Kaece, shattered. She'd come to adore how Rebecca looked at her with compassion and trust. It had given her a reason to attempt change, to attempt being worthy of that love. She had no defense, no words could express her fear or sorrow. She reached toward Rebecca, to show her what she was bad at saying - that she loved her.

"Don't touch me!" Rebecca screamed, slapping Kaece's hands away. "Talk. Or just stay silent and I'll know that everything you've ever said was complete and utter bull."

Kaece grumbled, "If ya hadn't been so insistent on findin' him, this wouldn't have happened."

"You'd lie to me forever then?"

"That's not what I was sayin'."

"No? Because that's exactly what I just heard. And to top it off, that... thing you just did. Did you do that to distract me? I trusted you. You lied to me, and then when you knew I wasn't going to let it go... you *kissed me*? And you think that's okay?"

"Aw, come on Rebecca. Ya wanted it, didn't ya? I know ya liked it." Kaece gave her a playful smile.

Rebecca didn't soften. With clenched teeth, and eyes burning with rage, she shook her head. Then she turned and walked away. She climbed down from the Hadros and wandered outside into the grassy plains without another word.

Kaece let out a ragged breath; she felt tense, yet exhausted, like she had always felt after a difficult Trial. She picked up the Maedian book and flipped through the pages. Page after page of squiggly marks filled the book. She had no idea what any of it said, or why the Maedians felt so compelled to record everything in ink. A tear dripped onto a page, and only after studying the splotch it left did she realize the tear was hers. For a second time, Rebecca had made her cry. She watched several more drops drip onto the page. Their kiss had been magical, like the kind of kiss the female Lykos would tell of in stories of romance - kisses with the power to move the heart, not just the body. If Rebecca didn't feel the same, Kaece doubted she could ever win Rebecca's heart in full. She ached with the reaffirmation that someone as good as Rebecca could never love as despicable of a monster as herself.

She gently closed the book and returned it to the workbench. A satisfied smile crept onto her lips. The Madius had walked into an unescapable trap; Rebecca wasn't hers, but she'd never belong to him either.

After she snuffed the light, a sudden sharp stink overcame the oil, books, bronze and wood. Outside, in the grass, a Haima Fox lurked. Kaece shot to her feet. Before she'd even cleared the door, the Haima Fox had closed in on Rebecca.

CHAPTER 22

Her head felt like static – no thoughts came, just wave after wave of conflicting emotion. She stared out at the vast plains and watched the silhouettes of grass dance in the wind, while she struggled against her confusion. No matter how many times she replayed the scene in her head, she couldn't get past the fact that she was making out with Kaece while Alex and Sebastian were either dying or dead. Neither outrage nor justification surfaced; only white noise filled the void of her mind.

The Lykos just proved to be everything Rebecca had defended her against. But the truth came bubbling up from the fountain of Kaece's never-ending lies, and all Rebecca wanted was the time to sort through her thoughts. She needed to know if she could ever forgive herself for turning a blind eye to Kaece's deceit – for all that may have happened behind Rebecca's back because she'd been Kaece's ignorant accomplice.

In the midst of her rising irritation, she almost didn't notice when something hit her shin. She crouched down, pushing aside the tall blades of grass to reveal the big red eyes of a young Haima Fox. Since the Demon didn't take the opportunity to latch onto her jugular, she reached out and ran her fingers through its coarse fur. It clicked its teeth, then hopped up onto her knee just like Chupita.

The pup licked her hand; its tongue felt sandpaper rough. Then it jumped down from her knee. Before the pup trotted too far, it doubled back and threw itself at her leg in full force. It looked over its shoulder at her, and chattered.

"Oh my god," she gasped. Chupita had grown much larger, but she was unmistakably Alex's puppy. "Go on, go! I'm with you."

She had no concept of how long she'd been chasing after Chupita when Kaece made herself known. The Lykos ran beside her, too close. Rebecca wanted to yell at her to just go away. The way Kaece acted as if nothing changed made her skin crawl; how could she pretend like nothing happened? She couldn't afford to stop and bicker. She tried to outpace the Lykos, ignoring the burning in her lungs.

Outrunning Kaece proved impossible, but in her desperation Rebecca tripped forward and landed on her face.

Kaece chuckled, "I can carry ya, if ya want."

She didn't want Kaece's help. She ignored her and stood up. The pain in her ankle was just another annoyance. One step at a time, she continued.

Kaece's words echoed in her head: *You wanted it. I know you liked it.* She clenched her teeth, picking up her pace as she trudged onward. Kaece had played her for a fool; she had crossed the boundary of friendship in an act of manipulation – she used Rebecca's desire for trickery. She loathed the possibility of Kaece's love being insincere, of Kaece being a monster who would give Rebecca what she 'wanted' to keep her off the trail of lies.

Not long after Rebecca began running again, Kaece disappeared in the darkness. The field ended abruptly and Rebecca burst through the tall grass; she emerged onto hard-packed dirt where the deep black form of the mountain dominated the horizon and blocked out the starry sky. Sounds echoed in the vast emptiness, reverberating through the foothills. She'd lost Chupita.

She heard a roar, then a clatter.

"Not Alex!" Sebastian cried somewhere in the distance; an echo distorted the direction of his voice.

She scanned the darkness again and again, watching for any sign of either Sebastian or Alex. Flame erupted from the ground at the base of the mountain; fire and smoke burst out like a propane explosion. Black against the blaze, the silhouette of a limp body catapulted into the sky. Rebecca's lungs constricted, her heart frozen in her chest as a loud thud filled her ears – the sound of Alex's impact.

She whimpered and raced toward the place he'd hit the ground.

Rebecca collapsed to her knees the moment she reached him, but her attention split – Sebastian, shirtless and running, followed by a Drakeon Warrior burst from a cave. Without taking her eyes from the scene, she pressed her head against Alex's chest.

When Sebastian laid eyes on her, he stumbled and stopped in his tracks. Rebecca's momentary relief at hearing her brother's faint heartbeat shattered as the Drakeon swiped at Sebastian. The dragon swatted him with its palm. Like an eager cat toying with a mouse, the Warrior pursued its disoriented prey.

The feeling she'd searched for since the day she fought Magnus filled her with confidence. Power coursed through her veins. The air felt thick with magic, not suffocating but instead fueling her in a way oxygen never could. She pushed off the ground into a sprint as she unsheathed the magical blades. The swords resonated with her need to protect Sebastian. She whirled them around, gripping them backwards with the blades resting against her forearms. With the power of the fire dragon god guiding her, she knew she wouldn't miss.

Just before she lunged, the Drakeon twisted toward her, away from Sebastian. His sword glinted in the moonlight; the blade stuck out from the left side of the dragon's chest, wedged between the scales of its breast. She leapt an impossibly long distance and, using the hilt of Sebastian's sword, sprang toward the dragon's wing.

She led with her swords, lodging one into the dragon's back just above its shoulder blade. Her other sword slashed open the base of its left wing. The Drakeon wailed. Rebecca shuddered against the tortured scream: evil or not, she hated the sound of suffering.

Her voice trembled with uncertainty as she commanded, "Kneel or I will kill you, Warrior."

The dragon sank to the ground and bowed his head. She sat on his back, patting the scales surrounding the saber that pierced his flesh.

"Rebecca?" Sebastian cautiously approached the dragon from the side. "Is it really you? You were inside the tomb during the volcanic eruption. How can this be?"

"Now's not the time. Is your father here?" She avoided his question.

"The dragon knows where he is. It offered the information in exchange for your brother, but I doubted that it would trade an emperor for a teenage boy. There was no possible logic behind such an offer, unless my father is but a corpse inside of that cave."

"Warrior, answer Sebastian's questions honestly, and I'll put in a good word with Elder Zakhar for the day you face judgment by the Drakeon for all that you've done. Just shake your head for no, nod for yes. Make your gestures clear."

She knew she could open the pathway between them and speak to him directly. Though it would be faster, she never learned how to block her thoughts from Ardin – the dragon would have access to her mind just as she would to his. Besides, if she didn't communicate with the dragon any differently than Sebastian would, he might not notice she *was* different. He might not hate her after all.

"Do you know where my father is?"

The Drakeon nodded.

"Is my father here in these cave dwellings – or nearby?"

The Drakeon shook his head.

"Does the Lykos know where my father is?"

The Drakeon paused; he made no gesture.

Rebecca felt annoyed that Sebastian had the nerve to ask such a question, but worse that even she considered it a possibility. After all, Kaece had exposed herself as a blatant liar. As if summoned by her mention, Kaece stepped out from the shadows behind Sebastian, her cruel glare fixated on him.

A spike of fear struck Rebecca; the Lykos, set with a deadly expression might actually kill him. "Watch out, Kaece's behind you."

Sebastian half-turned and hurriedly backed away. Kaece looked up at her and Rebecca realized instantly that her instincts were wrong. The hurt in Kaece's eyes told her all the trust she'd worked to build for months between them was destroyed in that one sentence.

"Your answer, dragon," Sebastian prompted. "You never gave it. Does the Lykos know where my father is?"

The Drakeon raised his head, uncurling from the bowed position. Kaece nodded to him and walked toward him.

"What are you doing?" Rebecca frowned at Kaece. She smacked the hilt of the saber buried in the dragon's scales. "Eyes on Sebastian, Warrior. Answer him."

Rebecca cried out as the dragon whipped his tail at her. Nearly knocked from his back, she gripped the sword lodged inside his body. The force of her weight dragged the blade down, tearing muscle and ligament while she struggled to regain her footing. A second time, the dragon brought his tail around. She raised her other sword; the spiked hand-guard bit into the dragon's flesh.

I doubt Typhos would appreciate your disrespect. She forced her thoughts at the reeling dragon. *I want you to tell Sebastian where he can find his father. Now. Nod, or shake your head.*

The Drakeon sat motionless, his marvel loud in his head. Then, he nodded. *Typhos has risen? That explains why you lack the stench of human, why you possess such inhuman combat ability. You're the – Beware the Lykos!*

The dragon convulsed; a loud gurgling noise bubbled into the quiet night air as Kaece ripped the Drakeon's esophagus from his throat. She'd rent his scales apart so fast, Rebecca hadn't seen it happen. The Drakeon barely had the time to warn her in a thought. His mind wracked with pain, panic, and fear of the unknown.

His death came swiftly – yet slow enough for him to force Rebecca a strangled message; the voice of his thoughts grew fainter with each word. *Kill the Crimson Whirlwind...stop her...before...the Madius... Save Gaeadia, Typhos...*

Then his thoughts fell silent; his body became still.

"No..." Rebecca whimpered. "No.. No!"

She reclaimed her sword then slid down the limp dragon's side. She ran to his front and shoved Kaece. Throwing her swords to the ground, she frantically tried to shove the enormous, bloody mass back inside his throat. The slick, rubbery tube slipped from her hands; the slimy thing fell back into the dirt. She tried again, knowing despite her effort she couldn't bring the Drakeon back to life.

The gaping hole in the dragon's throat wouldn't be filled. Rebecca stood numbly for a moment, covered in a mixture of his blood and dirt. His blood was on her hands – but it was on Kaece's, too. Her jaw set, teeth clenched; anger burned anew.

"You!" She screamed at Kaece. "You're *everything* that everyone says about you. You're a lying, murdering, heartless, back-stabbing bitch. Inhuman. You're just a dumb beast."

The Drakeon's blood coated Kaece almost completely; drying blood clung to her arms up to the elbows. Her entire body, right down to her skimpy leather outfit, was stained with the deep red of her crime. No emotion showed; Kaece stood, cold and silent.

"Where is my father, Kaece?" Sebastian asked. His eyes shone with the concern she wished she'd seen in Kaece's expression.

"For the hundredth time," Kaece snarled, her lips pulled back into a sneer, revealing her fangs. "I don't know a damn thing about your worthless father."

"I'm sorry," Rebecca cried. "He was about to tell us...This is all my fault."

"You didn't kill him," Sebastian consoled, stepping up beside Rebecca and putting his hand on her shoulder.

Kaece shifted her weight, her deadly glare fixated on Sebastian again. Rebecca noted where she'd dropped her swords, just in case. She couldn't imagine Kaece would be that stupid, but she'd been wrong about the Lykos all along. Deep down, she wanted to see if Kaece would pounce.

"It's not my fault because I killed him," Rebecca explained. "It's my fault that I didn't listen to you sooner, about the Lykos woman. She *is* dangerous. It was wrong of me to keep her with us. That's why it's my fault... and why I'm sorry."

Kaece's death glare transformed, her eyes wide and focused on Rebecca.

"It burdens me to know that Rebecca trusted you, and still you betrayed her. Now she has witnessed first-hand the very reason that Maedians and Lykos cannot co-exist. You, Lykos, are no one's friend."

Rebecca retrieved her swords: keeping them close ensured her ability to protect Sebastian, who seemed all too eager to provoke the Lykos. Kaece walked past him, grabbed Rebecca's arm and forced Rebecca to look into her eyes.

"You're the only one that knows me. Ya don't mean any of that, do ya?"

The dark-rimmed, bright yellow eyes peering at her in the moonlight reminded Rebecca of the first night they spent together. The night they shared at the hot springs, where Kaece saved her life, felt so long ago. She fought against the fond memory, instead remembering a night much less distant – a night when Kaece, with those beautiful eyes, promised she would never harm another dragon.

Rebecca swallowed, steeling herself. She pulled her arm free of Kaece's grasp. "You're a liar. You lie any chance you get – I know that. What else is there underneath all the lies you've heaped on me? I don't really know anything about you."

The Lykos exhaled an exasperated breath, accompanied by absolutely no show of emotion beyond the wide-eyed stare of a lost puppy.

"Don't give me that look." She heard her mother's voice leave her lips. "Heck, what *haven't* you lied about? Because if you even dare to talk about any of your promises or declarations to me, just forget about it. They're all voided. See Exhibit A – DEAD DRAGON!"

Kaece winced and took a step back. "I... I was tryin' to protect you."

"Protect me?" Rebecca laughed. "I don't need your protection any more. I don't need you. Quit pretending like I do – you're only lying to yourself. You killed this dragon for you, not me. You needed to save your own ass, not mine."

Wild-eyed, Kaece took another step back. Her chest heaved, her eyes glistened with unshed tears, her teeth clenched – all the signs of guilt compounded in her behavior. She was caught. Rebecca reveled in the surge of pride at her success; Kaece actually felt some emotion.

"So why'd you do it?" She continued, "what did this dragon know about you that you didn't want us to hear? What could be worse than knowing where Sebastian's father was all this time?"

"Nothing!" Kaece hissed, "there's nothin' to know."

"Hah. That was defensive," Rebecca scoffed. The memory of Monique, the girl always on the tail of truth, always digging into people's secrets just to watch them squirm, empowered Rebecca in the moment. "It must be pretty big, whatever you're hiding. Huge. Maybe it's Emperor huge. Is that it? Do *you* have Sebastian's father hidden somewhere?"

"Leave it before ya regret it," Kaece snarled. She sank down into a crouch, making a point of readying her claws. "Ya don't wanna make this uncontrollable *beast* attack, do ya?"

"No one makes you do anything, Kaece, but you're right about one thing – you are uncontrollable. You can't even control yourself. You don't think, do you?"

Kaece dove at her. She blocked Kaece's claws with the flat of her blade. As she deflected the blow, she sidestepped out of Kaece's range. With a loud snarl, Kaece whirled back on Rebecca – eyes dilated with rage.

"It's funny how ya block all of the sudden, when ya spend weeks fightin' me and ya couldn't defend yourself against a single move. That makes us both liars."

When Kaece lunged for the second attack, she moved so fast that Rebecca feared she'd been hit. She threw herself to the ground, somersaulting to get back onto her feet. As she stood, she checked herself – Kaece'd missed.

"I think I almost felt that one," she taunted. "And you called yourself a fighter?"

Kaece's maniacal laughter rang out in the night. "I'm jus' gettin' started. Quit while you're still breathing, because once I take you down, I'm going to gut this Maedian alive and tie his intestines to a tree. I'll let the birds do the rest."

With the threat, Sebastian shrank back further away from the quarrel. Kaece circled around Rebecca, looking for an opening. Each step she took to the side, Rebecca mirrored the movement. She kept her eyes on Kaece, ready for the attack.

"How many other people have you gutted like that, huh? All those people in Sow Endus?"

"That would make me quite talented, wouldn't it!" Kaece lunged again, but as Rebecca blocked, she threw another attack.

Rebecca leapt back, again using the side of her sword to smack down the claws. Kaece winced at the force of the blow. If Rebecca'd used the blade, Kaece would have lost her hand. The thought scared Rebecca and suddenly, she didn't know what she was doing. How would causing more bloodshed make her feel any better about Kaece stomping on her heart? Kaece betrayed her trust, made a mockery of her love, but in the end, she didn't love Kaece any less. She was just angry. Picking a fight had only made it worse, because Kaece was angry, too.

"I'm sorry, okay?" She lowered her swords, letting her arms hang limp at her sides. "There, I said it. I don't know why you're trying to be such a bad person. I just want to hear the truth from you."

"The truth, is that I'm a bad Lykos."

Kaece attacked again; Rebecca started to dodge; every muscle in her body told her to move, but she stopped herself. Kaece's claws ripped into her side. Rebecca's muscles spasmed; she gasped at the sharp pain. Kaece froze, stunned, mid-attack. Her hand lingered, claws in Rebecca's torso. The blood washed over Kaece's arm, down Rebecca's side. It felt strangely warm as it rushed from the injury and soaked into the fabric of her jeans. Each beat of her heart brought a new gush of blood – she never felt more acutely aware of her own heartbeat. She could almost hear Kaece's heart, throbbing in unison with her own. The Lykos held stone-still, as Rebecca relished the feeling of Kaece's hesitation, of her hand buried in her side. Kaece hadn't killed her. Kaece would never kill her – Rebecca regretted having doubted it.

"I love you," Rebecca whispered into her ear.

Rebecca gasped as Kaece's claws slid out of the gaping wound

Kaece backed away and, aghast, she stared down at her bloody claws.

"It's okay," Rebecca breathed, reaching out for her. "I know you aren't any more of a monster than I am. I'm with you."

Kaece shook her head and continued to back away. When Sebastian reached them, Kaece ran.

"You will be alright," he said, but he couldn't mask his surprise.

Rebecca leaned against him. Dizziness pervaded her senses; she slumped down, sliding onto the ground until she could only clutch Sebastian's leg. She rested her head against his thigh and closed her eyes: she knew she was losing a lot of blood. Sebastian babbled about medical supplies, something about using his shirt to bandage Alex, but she knew she'd heal. Half-Drakeon, she'd be fine.

She lifted her shirt: Four deep gouges ran diagonal down her ribcage, deepening just below the bone and sinking into her abdomen. Raw tissue glistened inside the slashes; a pale mass of organ beneath her skin struggled toward the gaping hole in her body with each breath she took. She grabbed a handful of dirt and pushed it into the wound. Pain seared through her left side and she bit her lip to keep from screaming. Once the pain subsided, she packed more earth into the injury; it stopped the blood flow – if only temporarily.

She looked to Sebastian, who stood with his jaw slack.

"What?" She countered. "I have to go after her."

Sebastian shook his head slowly, looking dumbfounded and unable to close his mouth. She knew he wouldn't understand, but she had to hurry. She couldn't believe she let Kaece get so much of a head start.

Rebecca pushed herself to her feet, using Sebastian to stand upright. Shakily, she stepped forward and away from his support. He called after her, but she ignored him. She hurried across the grassland, sometimes running, sometimes stumbling, sometimes crawling, but always calling out for Kaece. No matter how much the wound hurt, no matter how much blood drained from her body, she wouldn't be able to give up. She'd never forgive herself if she actually lost Kaece.

XXIII

The moon had set long before, leaving Sebastian to wait in utter darkness. Without light, he had limited ability to assess the extent of Alex's injuries. Sebastian prayed to Nyx, begging for safe passage through the long stretch of night. The last echoes of Rebecca's calls for Kaece had long since faded into eerie silence. Even Chupita remained inactive, curled close to her beloved boy as if to lend him her warmth. The Haima Fox's exocrine glands excreted her anxiety, the nauseating sulfurous smell diffused as it ascended out over the plains.

He wished somehow he would wake and realize he had dreamt everything from the moment they left Oneiroi. The whole experience was vivid, real but unfathomable, much like his dream of Rebecca induced by the fish. Yet time stood still. His chest throbbed with pain, his muscles ached. He could not deny that he had fought the dragon. Rebecca's intervention had halted a battle that likely would have continued until exhaustion took him. The dragon had not wanted him dead, though why his continued breath was of value could be known only by the gods.

He laid beside Alex and looked to the sky. The stars shone with the brightness he'd taken in a constillacioun prior, at the base of Drakeon peak. He could see the long shimmering belt of a far away galaxy. Dazedly, he pondered how Rebecca had returned from the dead, not only alive and in good health, but almost luminescent with vitality. She had attacked the Drakeon with the grace and fluidity of a highly trained guard - or worse, that of the blood thirsty Haima Demon. He swallowed hard against the thought. Rather immediately, he realized he could not bring himself to loathe Rebecca, even in the worst possible circumstance. Perhaps, he mused, the Haima Demons were a misunderstood gift bestowed upon humankind.

Sebastian awakened to Alex's high-pitched wail of agony. The first orange rays of Eos lit the horizon and he graciously thanked Nyx for heeding his prayers. He sat up and placed his hands on Alex's shoulders.

"Alex. Alex, calm yourself. You must not move until I have the opportunity to assess the damage caused by your second fall. Be strong. What is it that hurts?"

"My leg! It's all my leg. It hurts. It hurts way worse than... Than... Where am I? What happened?"

"Lay down and breathe. I will explain what I witnessed - though I hardly believe it myself."

Alex closed his eyes, seeming to focus on breathing while Sebastian inspected the boy's wounds in the dim light of predawn. Much to his relief, further blood loss had been minimal. In his appraisal he concluded Alex may have sustained a concussion, but otherwise the Metakosmos would be capable of recovery. Of course, recovery could not happen if Alex became ill from infection. The deep gash from his initial fall remained exposed to open air and without medical supplies, Sebastian could do nothing more than stop the bleeding.

"Do you recall anything?"

"I remember fighting the dragon, and I ran out of bolts. We were running away, and then the dragon came at me."

"Indeed, he did. He threw you, as an athlete throws a shot-put, straight up and out of the cave. I feared you'd died on impact, and I am grateful that you did not. That, however, is not the most surprising of last night's miracles. Rebecca is alive. She has returned to us, and took it upon herself to subdue the dragon."

"Are you sure the dragon didn't knock you out too? That's impossible."

"Impossible as it may seem, I assure you it is true. The dragon is dead, and your sister is alive."

Sebastian gestured to the Drakeon corpse. The smell of rot, if decay had begun, was undetectable beyond the stink of the Haima Fox quivering in the boy's lap. Alex took in the sight with tear brimmed eyes, whether from pain or sadness Sebastian could not tell.

"Rebecca did that? How? Where is she now?"

"She and the Lykos engaged in a rather impassioned altercation immediately after the dragon was subdued. The Lykos attacked her, as I always warned that she someday would, then ran out that direction. Rebecca followed after, though it was quite dark and she was bleeding profusely from the Lykos' attack. We could not possibly know when, or even if, she may return."

"We can't just lay here if she's out there bleeding to death! We have to find her."

Though clearly pained, Alex thrashed to get to his feet. In light of the boy's persistent effort, Sebastian did what he could to help and gave him a shoulder to lean upon. Alex inspected the dried blood pooled around the Drakeon before he pointed toward the savannah. Ravaged blades of grass bore the mark of Rebecca's passing. They followed the trail.

"How do you know it was Rebecca, and not one of those Drakeon posing as her to spy on us? That would explain why Kaece attacked her, right?"

"It was Rebecca, your sister, I am sure of it. She is like no creature of this world, and could not be mimicked... though she was a bit strange for herself."

"Shh! Listen. Do you hear that?"

A faint sob resonated in the near-silence. With renewed determination, Alex pulled Sebastian toward the sound. They found her curled in a fetal position. Her shirt, jacket and pants were saturated with her own blood. Alex, undaunted by the ghastly sight, dropped to his knees and nuzzled her as she cried. Sebastian waited, unsure of how to proceed: he wanted to get them both treated as soon as possible, but couldn't bring himself to interrupt their reunion.

"You *are* a dragon!"

Alex jerked upright, and as Rebecca sat Sebastian saw her purple eyes in the light of Eos. She tried to smile, but sadness tainted her expression.

"I broke open Typhos' tomb. There were... Side effects to surviving."

"A dragon would say that, too. Say something that proves you're my sister."

"Like what? I can't prove I'm me - anything I say you'll just come up with some kind of sci-fi conspiracy theory excuse as to why I would know myself. Believe me, or don't. I'm not proving myself to anyone."

"You're right Sebastian, it's her in there alright. I thought I'd never see you again - and he said that you somehow killed the dragon. You couldn't kill a dragon."

"And I didn't kill him. Kaece did. He'd surrendered and he was telling me about Sebastian's father. She was so upset about me wanting to find Sebastian, she just... Went crazy. I don't know..."

Rebecca touched her bloodied side with her bloodied hands. Sebastian cleared his throat. The wound still bled freely, unlike Alex's tourniquetted leg.

"Ew! We need to get you back to the Hadros, that looks bad. Did you see my leg? That dragon threw me! Twice!"

Rebecca listened as Alex recounted his version of how the events had occurred while they walked east. She supported him, and he supported her as they moved along. Trailing behind, Sebastian noticed a stretch of valeriana. The medicinal herb, native to the northern plains of Xiratera, bore clusters of tiny white flowers on long stalks, making it stand out amongst the homogeneous tall grass surrounding them. He told the Metakosmos to continue and wait for him in the safety of the Hadros.

He knelt in the patch of valeriana and salvaged the soothing medicine. As he stripped the stalks of the potent flower, he contemplated the most recent developments. At long last, the Lykos' true nature had shown through in Rebecca's presence. Rebecca's reaction to the unveiling of her canine companion's cruelty, however, puzzled him. She had acted with outrage, uncharacteristically overemphasized and quite opposite of the passive yet distant girl he'd come to know. Both behaved during the quarrel much like lovers. He considered the possibility of having misread their behavior from the beginning. All along it may have been a mating ritual that had never happened before - between Lykos and Metakosmos.

He tried to banish the confounding speculation as he returned to the Hadros with quarry in hand. There was no merit in guessing at Rebecca's words or actions, nor those of the Lykos. In extricating herself, the Lykos had proven the depth of the monstrous betrayal that flowed in her bloodline.

Upon arriving at the Hadros, Sebastian prepared a healing salve and a sedative. Rebecca's brow furrowed as she paced, as if she were deep in thought. After some time, she paused in front of the map adhered to the wall and studied it. She pointed to the area, north of the Skotos range and south of the Krygefyra sea. The primarily nomadic Lykos had nearly half of Xiratera dedicated solely to their tribes. Only one group, Pack Prime as they called themselves, remained in a fixed location, exactly where Rebecca pointed.

"The Lykos territory."

"We need to get moving. And you'll drive as long as there's any light to see by, even if it's moon light."

"I understand that if we are to draw conclusions from the information given us by the Drakeon Betrayer, it is the logical next step in our search for answers... But after all that has transpired, may we not consider that each step of this journey brings us not only closer to the answers we seek, but also ever closer to the confirmation of our own mortality. The Lykos territory will be the most dangerous, and unpredictable habitat we have encountered yet. You have now seen first hand how a Lykos truly behaves. I imagine that Kaece is a mild beast in comparison to the males."

Alex scoffed loudly, though the sedating pain relief concoction rendered him unable to articulate his disdain.

"I keep telling him notsh to talk like that. We're never giving up. We're gonna finishhh our mishon in Gaeadia and put everything right. Tell him."

"Shh. You just rest and get better so you can finish this quest with us, okay? I won't let him quit. Not now."

Rebecca placed a hand on Alex's cheek.

Sebastian took hold of Rebecca's wrist, then raised her arm up and inspected the wounds on her abdomen. The Lykos had not shown restraint; her claws had left five gaping slashes behind. Sebastian could see how, with the Lykos' inhuman strength, the gashes could have turned into a quick disembowlment. He swallowed hard against a wash of nausea.

"What?"

"You are lucky to not be dead twice over. If you would remove that filthy shirt and let me tend to those wounds, I can cleanse the bacteria from your body before infection becomes an inevitability."

She pulled free and shrank away from him as though he threatened to wound her further. He watched in horror as she clamped her hand over the wound and squeezed out dirt and fresh blood. It gushed from between her fingers, flowing anew down her side. Never had he seen her do something so directly self-harming. Thoughts of disease and death raced through his mind. He could not challenge himself to display the calm stoicism of an emperor, for instead he cried out as a parent overcome by the fear of losing their offspring to an act of folly.

"By the gods! Do not cause yourself further harm! I merely wish to help."

"My wounds aren't your problem; they're mine. I want the pain. I deserve it. You can help me by getting into that drivers seat and taking us to the Lykos territory."

Rebecca retreated another step and Alex whimpered a protest to her declaration of entitlement to pain and suffering. His words slurred together, becoming little more than jibberish as the sedative put his mind and body at ease. She glowered at Sebastian, walked around the bed and seated herself beside Alex.

"I was a jerk, and I hurt her. I really, really hurt her. I think I hurt her like Monique hurt me... or worse. Don't worry about me. I'm past the suicidal stuff, I promise."

"...You promised beforet..."

"This time I mean it, though. I'm done pretending to be happy when I'm not. I'm done wearing a mask and hiding just so people won't judge me. I'm not depressed anymore. I'm just mad at myself for a bunch of stuff I did and said. Before... I was afraid. Afraid of a lot of stuff."

"Like... Shpensing life wish Brad?"

"Hah, Brad. I was so bad for both of us. He didn't deserve to suffer me any more than I deserved to suffer him. Poor guy."

Alex's next reply was a clipped snore. Rebecca moved to ruffle his hair, but stopped just short of rubbing her own bodily fluids on him. Sebastian offered her a towel, tentatively. She took it and cleaned off her hands.

"He will peacefully rest for a long while now. Please allow me to treat your wounds. Neglecting to care for them properly could lead to infection, and possibly death. You may never see the Lykos village if you have fallen ill."

"I'm not gonna die. You're being incredibly dramatic, considering you have plenty of scrapes yourself. Let's go already."

Sebastian obeyed her command, given that he had no use of his Power over her or any hope in making her see reason when she simply refused. He had shown a similar willfulness when he disregarded his elder's wisdom and left to find his father. He still believed he was right, and that his father had come to Xiratera. But how had he thought he would be capable of saving the man from the unknown force that had stolen him in the night? As they all repeatedly said, what good could a fool boy do? And they had been right.

He pondered how far he would go, how much he would outgrow the bright-eyed eager-for-adventure boy he'd been, in his reckless abandon of his duties. The boy he had been never would have fought a dragon. Could manhood be the fall from accepting the world as a just place? He knew, at this point, that he no longer expected to find his father alive. He also accepted that he may never find him at all. Those who ignored Stephan Madius' demise would never be punished, nor have any reason to answer for their part in his father's death. There would be no justice. Sebastian could no longer expect any good from his journey to Xiratera, save perhaps survival.

He still desired to know how and why it happened above all else, the same desire he had about his mother. As a child, his insistence had been stopped by the Power of Madius, and if he ever did return home he would continue his search for that truth as well. In regard to his father's end, he would find the answers he sought or die on the path for truth. He knew his father must be a keystone in the disarrayed puzzle of violence and betrayal that had overwhelmed Xiratera. His were the questions that begged for answers, and while he knew it was foolhardy to seek those answers, he had ceased to care if an ill fate befell him.

Rebecca entered the control room after a long while. She said nothing at first and leaned against the back wall. When he glanced back, she refused the smile he had become so accustomed to seeing when he looked to her. She had used the facilities to cleanse herself and her clothes. Her skin looked as pristine as the false skin of a porcelain doll. She seemed, not a girl wandering the wilds of Xiratera, but rather a princess whose servants continually pampered her with the finest of beauty treatments. She had always fascinated him, but that which she referred to as "side effects" of draconic magic had changed her in such a way that he felt almost frightened by her stunning beauty and temperament. He wondered if the radiance he perceived the night before had been a material manifestation of the changes she had undergone, or simply an immaterial glow attributed to her by his own bewildered mind.

"What I said to Alex back there... About how sorry I am - I meant it. I was blind to so much, especially about myself. I'm sorry for all the stuff I said and did to you too, like... About Kaece... And slapping you and... Everything."

"We all can behave unpleasantly from time to time. It is a part of life and of being human. I hold no ill regard toward you for anything you have said or done in my presence, I assure you. I am nothing but grateful to have you back with us."

"A part of living, of being human. Heh. I was too afraid to live, while I could. I was afraid to experience anything real, *and* afraid I wouldn't ever experience anything real. Like, real, head-over-heels love. Like, real, jumping-for-joy excitement. I wouldn't let myself do it, and yet that's all I ever wanted. It's ridiculous, really."

He studied Rebecca's face for a moment, hoping for some hint at the true meaning of her words. They seemed to Sebastian to be nothing more than her thinking aloud, a monologue understood only by her.

"How is it ridiculous, exactly?"

"I just fell into it, like I fell into Gaeadia. I had everything I ever wanted... and I was still afraid, I guess I still am. I reacted out of fear. She reacted out of jealousy. We hurt each other... I can't let these wounds heal, because I can't ever forget. I made a mistake. They can heal when I've apologized, when it's over."

"For all of our sakes, do not allow one mistake to facilitate another. Our journey, thus far, seems to have been a progression of such mistakes, on all of our parts, though, chiefly my own."

"That sounds more like a definition of life: A series of mistakes. What good would a life be if everything was always peaceful and perfect? Here we are, different from yesterday, better, because we're always learning from our mistakes."

"There may not be a better, tomorrow, if you do not treat your wounds properly."

"Here's the thing. I've been through worse - way worse, and these really are just scratches - so no matter how bad you think they are - I really just don't care. So quit worrying about how I'm bleeding or infected and worry about what I tell you is wrong: I need to find Kaece, and I need to find her before it's too late. When she looked at me last night, before she ran away, I could see how much I'd hurt her - and I wanted to die when I hurt like that. Do you understand?"

"You do not want to treat your wounds because you are afraid the Lykos will bring herself to harm?"

"Exactly."

Sebastian fell silent, and looked forward to the next stage of their journey. Rebecca's logic remained an enigma. He could not fathom fearing that the Lykos would bring harm to herself. Kaece had acted out of an obsession with Rebecca's affection, with exception of the time she had threatened him before they ascended Drakeon Peak. The one time when she almost outright admitted that Lykos had partnered with many other species of Xiratera to exterminate the Maedians... In hindsight he would have been right to walk away from the Unthrowlych and return to Overseer Demarko with the new information. A plotted assault, a plan to conquer and extinguish all of Neo Maedia would have been enough to gain response from the Overseer of Xiratera. It would be enough to gain response from the Emperor himself.

CHAPTER 24

At the end of five days of travel – four long sleepless nights – they'd finally arrived at the heart of the Lykos territory. Rebecca had vied for pushing onward in spite of the darkness, but Sebastian had explained that the Hadros could go no further – and, of course, traveling at night on foot would be taking unnecessary risk. Thus Rebecca remained awake, impatiently awaiting the moment she could pursue Kaece.

That moment arrived when Sebastian's snoring began. Sure both of the boys were sound asleep, she quietly opened the Hadros door and slipped out into the night. The moon had already risen, crested and began its slow descent across the sky. It cast a pale light on the vast expanse of savanna; Rebecca wasn't afraid.

Kaece could smell them from a mile away – why wouldn't the other Lykos? Since they had no hope of sneaking into the territory, it seemed obsolete to worry about what time of day they made their foolish attempt. She held her hands out and let the top of the waist-high grass brush across her palms while she walked. The soft vegetation tickled like Kaece's hair between her fingers.

The countless nights she'd spent with Kaece, feeling every hair, touching nearly every inch of skin, felt wasted. They could have been so much more. She'd let the weeks pass – days of travel with Sebastian and her brother; days of training with the Drakeon – without fully appreciating their time together. Instead, she let her preoccupation with normalcy taint everything. Ruin everything.

Tall, thin-trunked trees with long, gnarled branches interspersed among the thicket of grass. A cool breeze breathed across her skin, reminding her that she was still alive. As long as that was true, she could continue to search for Kaece – no amount of distance between them would dissuade her need to make amends. She wondered if she'd had the persistence to find Monique, if she might've been able to right the wrong of their broken relationship.

Monique laid across Rebecca's bed, reading a fashion magazine. Her feet kicked back and forth in the air; Rebecca watched her fidget, pretending to read a magazine of her own. They'd barely spoken since Monique showed up at the door after missing a week of school. As Monique read, Rebecca could only sit in stunned silence – the aftermath of hearing "I moved in with my boyfriend."

The boyfriend Monique spoke of was a mechanic, too old for her, covered in too many tattoos, with too much facial hair. She had sounded excited, enthusiastic, but her body-language told another story. Rebecca hoped Monique's nervousness meant that she'd come to ask for help.

"You've really got to learn how to stop staring like that," Monique chided. "Brad may be slow, but not everyone's been hit one-too-many times in the head."

Rebecca blushed and shifted her attention to a photograph of a too-perfect model. "I just can't believe that you're living with him. What did your parents say? And what about school? And, well... Why?"

"My parents?" Monique scoffed. "You don't understand the real world, do you, hon? I belong there, with him. He's not like the guys at school. He's the real deal. I'm dropping out. He makes enough money to take care of us, so why bother?"

"Your parents don't know."

"And they're not going to know. It's none of their business what I'm doing with my life, and it's not your business to tell them. I thought you'd be happy for me, but I guess I was wrong. Who I'm living with isn't any of your business, either."

Rebecca's throat constricted, her chest tightened – she couldn't breathe past the panic. It was her business: if Monique moved to Las Cruses, they'd be nowhere near each other. How often would she ever see her?

"I can make it my business," Rebecca countered. "If you come live with me. I'm moving into the garage soon – you always told me you wished you could live there. Now you can."

Monique laughed, and her laugh told Rebecca more than words ever could. That laugh conveyed all the years of judgments Monique silently made when Rebecca poured her heart out, all the marks of inadequacy against her. There, in her own room, Monique told her without saying anything exactly what she thought of Rebecca: she was never going to be anything to Monique but the joke she was on the day they met.

"Fine. But don't think he's any better," she snapped. She pointed at the bruise on Monique's wrist. "He doesn't even treat you right. How many bruises are you hiding? This is just sick, Monique, he's like ten years older than you *and* he's hurting you. He doesn't love you, and I bet the cops would agree with me."

"You wouldn't dare."

"I would, for you. To keep you safe. Someone has to. I care about you. It's not like I want to hurt you."

"No, of course not," Monique sneered, "You just want to fuck me."

Rebecca's blood ran cold.

"So. If you feel like telling anyone about me, or my man, then you'd better be prepared for me to expose each and every one of your dirty little secrets to the whole world."

Monique stood up and shuffled her makeup into her purse; brush, eyeliner pencil, lipstick – each one clacked as she slowly, deliberately tossed them in the purse. Every clack only served to emphasize her point; how many secrets had Rebecca spilled to Monique over their years of friendship?

"You know that you're not normal. And if I told Brad, he wouldn't be around to protect you anymore. Let's face it, Rebecca, without him you're nothing but a freak show. Maybe *I* wouldn't be hurting you, but you'd still just be vulture food at the end of the day, after they raped you and broke your skull open with a tire-iron. That's what they do to people with secrets like yours."

A shiver shot down Rebecca's spine; goosebumps prickled her skin. Her thoughts gave way to numbness, because she knew Monique wasn't exaggerating. She'd heard the stories about Monique's brother and his friends beating guys who wore girls' clothing. She swallowed back the tears; if she cried, she'd be admitting guilt for something. Brad was her only defense, and Monique had already disarmed her.

In the silence, Monique smiled a cruel, satisfied smile. She pulled her purse strap over her shoulder, smoothed out her shirt and made for the door.

Rebecca croaked, "Don't go..."

"Oh, I'm already gone. I tried to be understanding, but don't you get it? You'll *never* understand. I backed you up, and you can't even support me being happy for once! So I'm out, just forget I ever existed. You've got no right thinking you can tell me the right way to live my life when you can't even figure out how to live. Good luck finding anyone who will ever be nearly as sympathetic as I was."

Monique slammed the door behind her. Rebecca pulled it open and hurried after, down the stairs and to the front door. "Stop! Wait. I just... It was a joke."

"You're a joke." Monique whirled on Rebecca, a glower darkening her face. "You'd better figure out how to cover up your tracks – learn how to lie better or you're going to lose that 'perfect' boyfriend of yours. You'll be all alone with no one to fake it with. As for me, well, you lost me. I'm not going to miss you at all, because unlike you, I have a life. A real life, where I get that my man isn't perfect, but love is enough. And he loves me. He's willing to support me *and* our baby. So get over yourself, grow up, and stop daydreaming about a world that doesn't exist. Dreams don't come true, you just learn to appreciate what you've got."

"I appreciate you," Rebecca cried out as Monique walked away.

"You don't have me," Monique yelled, not looking back. "You never did! This friendship is over."

———————————————

Rebecca had no idea how long she roamed or how far she'd strayed from the Hadros. The sky had begun to lighten with predawn when she noticed the wisps of smoke. She squinted at the horizon; she could make out dark conical roofs in the distance. Her pace quickened with her heartbeat, excitement and dread both rushing her forward.

The hint of civilization could mean she'd found Kaece; the trails of smoke could mean she was too late. She raced toward the village, praying that when she found Kaece, she'd be alive.

Rebecca burst into the village, looking for signs of life – or death. The smoke rose from fire pits, not dwellings. As she moved through the camp, the intricacy of the fire pits astonished her. Smooth, uniformly-shaped stones encircled the dying embers.

She found herself drawn to a large detailed carving of a wolf over a door frame. The wolf's eyes peered down at her, a look of pride etched into its features. He guarded a log cabin, which stood two stories high. A metal dome capped the top of the second floor, creating the impression of a third. The bottom of the metal hemisphere fanned out into a large awning with wooden supports. A wide ramp curved out from the balcony on the second level and wrapped forward to the ground. Along the sides of the lodge, carved wood framed large glass windows. The glass panes had a natural greenish tint, though designs – the moon, the sun, stars – in each pane were brightly colored.

The circular layout to the camp made Rebecca realize that she'd followed the footpath straight into the center of the village. Unlike the intricate wooden lodge, the smaller, yurt-like huts all shared a simple similar form to each other, but each one seemed constructed a little differently from the next. Each hut had been built of a mud and straw mixture; the adobe walls looked expertly crafted, with wooden supports in the openings for windows or doors. They all had thatched roofs that formed conical points. The windows varied from hut to hut – very few had glass like the log cabin. Every window was covered, sealed off with blinds or curtains.

"Hail, visitor."

Rebecca jolted and turned to face the voice. Just a couple feet away, a slim, well-toned man leaned on a staff. His hazel eyes glinted with a golden sheen, providing a stark contrast with his dark, nearly black, hair. His dark tan chest stood bare, nearly hairless, though a thin, well-groomed beard lined his jaw. The long ponytail of black hair left his ears – human ears – exposed; his smile revealed sharp Lykos teeth. Like Kaece, he had claws instead of nails. Unlike Kaece, a long black wolf tail swished behind him.

"What brings you here...Human? Dragon? Human-dragon." He beamed, tilting his head with each question. "We've never seen a human-dragon before."

Rebecca felt flabbergasted. Some Lykos emerged from the dwellings. Though they clearly noticed her, none looked upset by her presence. The Lykos' reputation, once again, appeared to do them no justice.

He cocked his head again; the curiosity in his expression only deepened as he awaited her reply.

"Uh," Rebecca stumbled, "I'm looking for a Lykos."

"Ah..." He nodded gravely and jabbed his staff in her direction "Then you!"
Rebecca jumped, fearful she'd made a wrong move.

"You," he repeated, then his serious expression cracked. He laughed, "are in luck! We're all Lykos here."

He looked to the other Lykos for approval. They responded with insincere titters. A couple of the Lykos women winked at her as they walked past, preparing for breakfast around the fire pit. One Lykos unashamedly brushed against her as she stepped up next to the pit and dropped in firewood.

Her tawny braid fell forward over her shoulder while she bent down. A darker brown tinted the ends of her hair. The delicacy of her soft features lent to the illusion of frailty; her high cheekbones and round jaw gave her an excessively feminine appearance.

As Rebecca concluded the Lykos woman looked nothing like Kaece, the male Lykos stepped up beside her. He, too, silently stared at the female Lykos; his head cocked as Rebecca's had, watching the woman as she arranged the wood. He tilted his head back then howled. The long wolf-howl startled her. Though painful, it sounded musical, beautiful.

Once he had everyone's attention, his howl died off and he took Rebecca by the wrist. He held up her arm, pointed to her with his free hand and announced proudly, "Everyone, we have another guest. This is one of the great and unusual human-dragon breed...."

He hesitated, then whispered to her, "What are you called?"

"Rebecca Silas. I'm a Metakosmos, I guess..."

"Ah! She is a Rabekasylus, and she comes to us from the Other Side. She came here to see a Lykos, so make a good impression!"

The moment he closed his mouth, the whole village sprang to life. Ruckus began in all corners; Lykos came in and out of their dwellings, tidying up, gathering jars and jugs. Cooking fires roared to life all around, and the wonderful aroma of meat filled the air.

"Rabekasylus." Another man's voice addressed her.

She looked in his direction; he stepped out from the doorway of the lodge. His muscles drew her attention first; his chest and abs looked rock-hard, firm and well-defined. His biceps, calves, each part of his body seemed carved to perfection like a marble statue. The yellow in his amber eyes reminded her of Kaece. A thin beard decorated his jaw; his short, dark brown hair had pitch black tips. He stood tall, his broad shoulders squared – he walked with an air of authority that left no doubt in Rebecca's mind that he was Alpha.

"Are you common in your world? I'm in awe of your uniqueness."

"Thanks... I think," she said. "But it's just Rebecca. Silas is my last name."

"I see, it is your name, not your species. Is Silas your family name, or a title?"

"Family name."

"Ah, then, we'll disregard that. We've given up some Maedian traditions, and bearing the weight of your father's reputation is one of those. While you're with us, you make your own name." He smiled, then placed his hand on the other male's shoulder. "We shall call her Rebecca, for now."

"Rebecca it is," the other Lykos assented with an excited head bob and a grin. "It sounds like a human name, doesn't it? But her arrival is spectacular. Does this mean we can have a gathering? I could go get the others. I'd like that."

The Alpha gestured for the enthusiastic Lykos to be calm, then asked Rebecca, "Won't you have some breakfast with us?"

She nodded and took a seat on one of the carved wooden benches surrounding the fire pit. The flames warmed her cold skin, raising the hair on the back of her neck. She leaned in, holding her hands out to the fire. The smell of fresh bread mingled with the meat roasting over an open flame. The Alpha sniffed the air and smiled appreciatively as he sat across from her, while the other Lykos plopped down beside her.

A female Lykos brought them each a wooden cup full of warm tea; she served the Alpha first, then Rebecca and the other male. Her wolf ears and blonde hair streaked with black reminded her of Kaece.

"Thank you," she told the girl.

"My pleasure," the girl replied and smirked something like Kaece would, then walked away.

Rebecca drank the tea, so thirsty she forgot to taste it. She let the cup rest in her lap and relaxed. Everything felt so strange, almost like a dream. The hospitality of the Lykos seemed unreal – she'd anticipated another encounter like the one with the Drakeon. No one had asked her to explain herself, nor where she came from.

"My brother and my friend Sebastian Madius will be coming here later today," she said. "I hope that isn't a problem."

The Alpha simply nodded and sipped his tea. "Sebastian Madius, hmmm... He's the youngest one, isn't he?"

"Yeah," chimed in the black-haired Lykos. "The last Madius, but I heard he was dead. It's funny how we still call them Madius even though we don't use family names, don't you think?"

"Focus, Asher," the Alpha scolded. "Are you sure? When did you hear this?"

Asher wiggled anxiously in his seat, his tail swishing behind him. "About a moon ago. But I'm not sure, it was a he-said-she-said kind of thing, so maybe not."

"And when did you last see your companion alive, Rebecca?"

"I just left them last night." She blinked.

211

"Then you must have misheard your informant," the Alpha told Asher. His amber eyes then focused on Rebecca; though his lashes weren't as long or dark as Kaece's, she couldn't deny his eyes were still exceptionally attractive. "It's been a long time since we've seen a Madius, but it would be quite a pleasure to have him as our guest."

She nodded. "You won't hurt him, will you?"

"Heavens no," he laughed. "Our territory is, perhaps, the safest place on Xiratera for the young emperor to be. There's been a great ruckus about Maedian rule in this land, and what Asher likely misunderstood was that the Madius line is wanted dead by a great many. Hm, I suppose that in and of itself is reason enough to call the others. The more Lykos, the better he will be protected if his presence here becomes known."

"A Festival of Unity?" Asher perked.

"Yes, and go quickly. Take the news to the south, have the other scouts take the news east and west."

Asher sprang from his seat and started to bound away, then froze mid-stride, ran back and patted Rebecca on the top of the head. "Thanks for stopping by! I'll see you in a couple days."

Rebecca shrugged, ducking away from the pats thumping on her head. His lack of personal boundaries, touching her like they were old friends, grated on her nerves. "I may not be here that long."

"You'd better be, or I'll be running all over the territory for nothing!"

"I suggest you start running now, or she may be gone before you leave."

Rebecca smiled at the Alpha, grateful for his interjection. Asher's tail drooped and he looked to the Alpha with a hurt expression before he bolted down a footpath and away from the village.

"Most Lykos listen the first time," he apologized. "He's always pushing his limits, thinking he can get away with more than the others because he is kin."

"Aren't all of you kin?" Rebecca asked, raising her eyebrow.

"I mean that he and I were born of the same litter." He paused, then laughed. "I forgot to introduce myself. Everyone around here knows me, so I don't get to often – my name is Kym, Alpha Prime for five winters and counting."

Kym. The man before her, Kaece's boyfriend, was Alpha Prime. That kind of status meant that if anyone could help her find Kaece, it would be him. She needed his help, but at the same time she desperately wanted to find his shortcomings. Something about him, beneath his kind eyes and warm smile, beneath the beautiful surface, had to be Brad-like. There was a reason he wasn't so great – a reason Kaece didn't want to be with him. Rebecca just had to dig deep enough to figure out the flaw.

When Rebecca didn't respond, he continued, "Alpha Prime is a title that means I'm the toughest Lykos amongst all the packs. I've only ever lost one sanctioned fight. That's how we make our name – earn our titles – in the ring of combat. I see that you've recently been injured... Are you a fighter as well?"

"I'm a Protector... I protect the people I care about."

"Rebecca the Protector," Kym repeated. "That rolls off the tongue nicely."

The blonde Lykos returned, carrying two plates of the freshly cooked meats and bread. She handed one first to Kym, then gave the second plate to Rebecca, and winked. "Let me know if I can do anything else for you."

Rebecca's stomach growled as the immediacy of the food overwhelmed her senses. Dodging the need for a proper reply, she started eating. But no matter how starved she felt, one thing pressed on her mind with more urgency – Kaece.

"So," she swallowed. "Do you know Kaece?"

An array of emotions washed over Kym's face; sadness gave way to anger, which smoothed over into a stony expression of apathy. "I do not."

The blatant lie irritated her; she'd known beforehand that Kym and Kaece more than just knew each other. Hiding her indignance, she played into his lie. "She's a Lykos. I came here looking for her – I just need to talk to her... Maybe you know her by a different name?"

His jaw tightened and his face set into a serious glower. "There is no Kaece here. No Lykos in our packs go by that name. Perhaps once upon a time, but not anymore."

Kym set his plate on the bench and stood abruptly.

"Wait," Rebecca pleaded. "I need to find her. Anything you can tell me, anything at all, would be a great help."

"Our internal affairs do not concern you. I'm sorry, but with this, I cannot help you."

Internal affairs. She thought of the Drakeon, of Ardin's hesitation to disclose the meaning behind the Eolith even though she shared Typhos' lore. Ultimately, she'd won their favor and become a member of the Drakeon family; Zakhar, Ardin and Magnus regarded her with respect, which had to count for something. She'd learned their secrets. If the Drakeon Elder could bow before her, she would do whatever it took to make the Alpha Prime treat her with the same respect.

"How can I become worthy of your help? Can I become a Lykos somehow?"

He shrugged. "Join the festivities. If you are a Protector as you claim, then you will be worthy. Until you've proven yourself, do not utter that name again. My pack does not need the undue grievance."

His words stung; they meant Kaece wouldn't arrive with the other packs when Asher returned.

213

"I understand," she nodded. "Likewise...Could my dragonness not be mentioned around my friends?"

Kym's eyes roamed over her expression, scanning her face the same way Kaece had countless times. Rebecca never knew what her expression said, but he looked satisfied. He sat back down. "Very well. Now, before you go into the trial, you will need to have those wounds treated. With such an injury, you will be little more than a helpless fawn in combat."

"I'm fine. What Trial?"

"The Trial of Dominance. It is the central event during our Festival of Unity – the gathering that we have called on behalf of yourself and the Madius. You must compete in the arena in order to earn the title you believe is rightfully yours. If you don't wish to fight, that is well enough, but know the answers you seek will not be found here."

"If I fight, you'll tell me about Kae- the Lykos I asked about?"

"If you win. Though, the odds are not in your favor with that wound. Please, Hani the Shaman is among us. He claims that he can heal any mortal wound."

"He says he has even brought the dead back to life," the red-haired Lykos giggled as she added more wood to the roaring flames. She glanced at Rebecca, her eyebrow raised questioningly. "Your blood runs fresh... Do you wish to die?"

Rebecca startled, pulling her hand away from her side. She hadn't noticed herself idly picking at the scabs, but just as the Lykos said, fresh blood seeped from the wound.

"If you came seeking a Lykos to kill you, then you've come to the wrong place," Kym spat.

She didn't want to die. But she also didn't want Hani's healing touch or magical balms, nor Sebastian's blue disinfectant or Alex's hugs. She didn't want to heal.

"These wounds have meaning to me ...Do you understand? I'm afraid I won't scar ...and if I can't scar, I can't let them heal. This may be all that's left, a memento... A memory sealed with my blood. A reminder of my mistakes..." She trailed off, though countless thoughts and defenses circled in her head. She knew that she sounded insane.

"Hm," Kym sighed. "If you aren't toying with death, then the very least you could do is refrain from spilling too much of your own blood. The smell does rile up the pack, and by sunset there will be many more of us to arouse. Will you be participating even with your injury?"

"What other choice do I have?"

The female Lykos spoke, "You could allow us to repair your armor, or perhaps equip you with something that may be more fitting for combat, easier to move in – with more padding?"

"Shanan's suggestion is a good one," Kym added as if he sensed her uncertainty.

Shanan smirked, "It would be lovely to see the beauty that's surely hiding beneath all that fabric and grime."

214

CHAPTER 25

Long before she'd gotten dressed, Shanan disappeared with Rebecca's outfit. She was grateful that she'd managed to snatch up her belt before the Lykos darted out of the room. Though Rebecca couldn't deny the leather skirt and tan leather boots could provide more protection from weapons, she couldn't shake the sensation of being exposed.

A light breeze tickled the back of her neck and across her naked back. The air caressed her scabbing wound, her burning ember tattoo, both uncomfortably on display. She'd tried to double up the leather bracers Shanan provided, wrapping one around her forearm and the other above – but no amount of stuffing cloth between the bracers covered the full extent of the Drakeon marking. In the end, she'd had to reason with herself that Sebastian and Alex would eventually see it anyways. She couldn't hide from the truth forever.

She heard Sebastian say, "Tell me what you've done with Rebecca," as she walked back to the center of the camp

"Here she comes now," Kym answered.

Sebastian and Alex both waited on a bench at the central fire. Kym sat in the same place as when Shanan took her to the bathhouse, but a number of Lykos had gathered around him. They gawked at Sebastian; the awe in their expressions reminded her of the villagers from Sow Endus.

Kym gestured toward her with a smile.

Rebecca nodded, nervously clutching her hands in front of her; she felt so naked. Sebastian's eyes instantly glued to her, following her every motion while she sat beside Alex. His face blanched, then his cheeks burned red. She rolled her eyes.

Alex hoisted his injured leg onto the bench and glowered at her. "You ditched us again! Are you ever going to stop trying to bail on me? You promised you'd stay with me..."

"I wasn't trying to ditch you," Rebecca defended. How could she even begin to express the need to go on, continue the hunt for Kaece, even if it meant going on alone? It had nothing to do with Alex, and everything to do with the guilt gnawing at the back of her mind. A hundred lies came easily to the tip of her tongue: nonsense about needing water, a tantalizing smell in the distance, all plausible excuses for why she walked to the Lykos village in the middle of the night spawned before she spoke. She settled on the truth, "I couldn't sleep knowing the Lykos were so close."

He reached out and rubbed his hand across the illusion of glowing embers. "What's this?"

"A side effect of surviving the Drakeon."

"You keep saying that." He examined her arm tattoo in entirety, from wrist to shoulder blade.

"Surviving certain death is bound to have side effects. Lots of side effects. So I'll probably keep saying it."

He let her arm fall back to her side, but then he winced at the sight of her gashes. "It's getting worse."

The wounds from Kaece's claws looked ragged, deep and infected. She knew it looked bad, but she also knew rot could eat a hole in her ribcage and she still wouldn't die. Allowing the injury to scab felt like sacrifice enough – the wound represented the wound in her heart, a gaping hole always flowing with fresh blood. Her exterior no longer matched the aching in her chest; even if the claw marks healed over, the pain in her core wouldn't. She needed Kaece to undo the damage, and until she found her, she wanted to leave the hurt where the whole world could see it.

"I know." Rebecca smiled

Alex sighed in defeat and shook his head, "You're a jerk."

She shrugged. "I'm sorry."

"Well," Kym interjected. "Now that you've seen for yourself that she is alive and in the condition in which you last saw her, will you accept our invitation?"

Sebastian blinked, seeming to have difficulty tearing his eyes away from Rebecca. "This is most unusual."

"Unusual? How so?" This came from an older Lykos with a nearly bald head and a long grey, braided beard. His brown eyes and human ears contrasted sharply with his pointed fangs and the long, gnarled claws that clutched an old wooden staff. His wrinkles stirred Kaece's story of the Lykos with a rattling cough fresh in Rebecca's mind.

The old man sat beside Kym, who introduced him affectionately. "This is Tryst, our Loremaster. He guards the tales of generations past, as far back as our birth in Old Maedia. Sebastian Madius, we would love to hear your tale and learn how our homeland fares."

Sebastian nodded. "I had not anticipated such hospitality from Lykos. After all, your reputation is one of uncontrollable rage and senseless bloodshed. "

"Now that you're here, I hope you see that you're perfectly safe," Kym said, unfazed by Sebastian's open derision for their people. "Not all Lykos are predestined with a violent nature, the same as not all Maedians are violent. In fact, you'll find that a delightfully small number of either exist. None of the Lykos here, nor any who will be arriving over the next few days, are given to fits of rage or acts of aggression. All of our combat is sanctioned, and purely for determination of rank."

"If the number is minuscule as you say, how do you explain the Maedians your kind murdered? We shared our homes, our way of life, with you, and that graciousness was repaid with the brutality recorded in eyewitness accounts, and detailed autopsies."

"We can't dispute the murder you speak of," Tryst agreed with a nod. "However, I must ask, does your history ever express that Lykos harmed the Maedians – beyond the usual mistake that both Lykos and Maedian make – prior to the day of our banishment?"

"I could not answer with certainty."

Kym chuckled. "Certainty is not something that applies to what is hundreds of years behind us, as is the event we speak of now. Give us a guess."

"Honestly," Sebastian faltered. "Most of the accounts I have read do not have a time associated with them, unless they were eyewitness accounts from that day. The detailed records are, I am... rather certain, all from the murders that took place – it was, after all, the only massacre in our history. The Lykos caused more damage in one single day than the Haima Demons have ever harmed us."

"How many Maedians do the Haima Demons take in a full season's turn, would you say?" Tryst asked.

"It depends. We have the guards to protect as many people as possible, as you well know." When neither Lykos replied, both patiently awaiting an estimate, he continued. "A handful every time they come. Perhaps as many as fifty are lost each year."

"And yet the lore states fewer than ten Maedians were lost in a year to the demons while the Lykos stood watch," Tryst countered. "How many years do you suppose we guarded Old Maedia – forty Maedians a year saved from such a terrible fate? And how many were slain by our claws, perhaps a few hundred?"

"That may be true," Sebastian frowned, defensively. "It does not change the law, which you blood-thirsty beasts so openly defiled. The law you callously broke, time and again that day."

"We don't dispute that we deserved punishment for our actions," Kym said. "In fact, we agree that our banishment was a necessary step. It has been difficult, at times, to live away from Maedia, but we have the blood of the Great Wolf Fenris. We are strong. It is you, our ancestors, that we've worried for. You are aware, I'm sure, many of the Banished had husbands, wives and children who were not considered Lykos enough to be banished."

"Interracial breeding was forbidden. If a Lykos was discovered or came to be from a union with a part-Lykos, then it was banished to the south, to a life in Renatera with the other Maedian outlaws. They are given a second opportunity to make a life for themselves there, in Renatera. To this day, we are still trying to cleanse Maedia of the gene responsible for the Lykos' uncontrollable violence. Rest assured, you have no family in Maedia."

Kym shook his head. "I didn't mean to imply that we only cared for our blood relatives. Though, it saddens me deeply to learn that our lapse in judgment has burdened our children's children to be banished from Maedia as well. How many generations must pass to undo the damage done in a single day?"

"Hang on," Alex interjected. "So if I have this right, the Maedians *made* the Lykos to protect them from the Haima Demons... And the Lykos turned on their Maedian creators even though they had Maedian families? Like, you guys had Maedian wives and stuff and you killed them anyways?"

Sebastian and Tryst both opened their mouths to speak at the same time; they both paused to wait for the other to begin. After a moment, Tryst said, "May I?"

Sebastian nodded.

"In the beginning, there was no segregation between the Lykos and the Maedians. We were all considered Maedian, treated as equal. As time went on, it became apparent that any field requiring a specialized skill was dominated by Lykos. Maedian humans became concerned that the Lykos would overrun the city, and the council passed a great many laws over the years to increase the segregation. At first, Lykos were banned from certain high ranking positions. Then, strict regulations were enforced; only physical labor and guard positions were suitable for Lykos. Eventually, it became such that Lykos could only become guards. Not long before the uprising, the city council passed a law to criminalize interracial marriages. Any preexisting Maedian human-Lykos marriages were dissolved. Lykos could only marry other Lykos."

"There is perfectly sound, logical reasoning behind that decision," Sebastian huffed. "Interracial relations are dangerous, and more than that, the Lykos were dangerous. Can you imagine what would have become of Maedia if they ran the empire? Where would our society be? Likely in huts like this."

"We weren't running the empire, nor pushing the Maedian humans out — we have always identified as human," Kym said. "Altered humans, yes... Perhaps Lykos is a fair name, but until the day of our banishment, Lykos were Maedians first and foremost."

"Then why are Lykos killing people on Xiratera?" Alex blurted. "Your words are pretty, but we've seen more than one town that you guys have decimated."

Kym sighed. "You may doubt our loyalty to Maedia, and for that I can't blame you. I beg you, stay and enjoy our company. Take the time to fill your hearts and bellies. It'll be a much needed rest, from the looks of you all, and if at the end of the games in three days you still don't trust us, there will be no harm done. If we have earned your trust, perhaps we can begin anew and dissolve the Treaty which prevents us from forging a bond with the Maedians on Xiratera. We can begin trading goods and knowledge; I imagine there are a great many things the Maedians have encountered and perhaps we've survival skills that could prove useful."

"Speaking of the peace treaties, I would like to know what you know of my father's whereabouts, as well as the attacks on our towns."

"Yes, yes. Of course," Kym nodded gravely. "But that's all such dreadful business... At the end of the gathering, I will tell you everything I know."

"Everything?" Rebecca asked. "As in absolutely *anything* you know?"

Kym's expression darkened, as if he knew the thoughts racing through her mind: where can I find Kaece? Why do you refuse to talk about her? Are you in love with her? What's with the qualifiers about the Lykos we will meet verses what...Other hidden Lykos? She shifted in her seat, glad he wasn't a Drakeon.

"As I said, at the conclusion of the Festival, all shall be revealed."

"I could simply use my power, you know," Sebastian stated. "Three days is a long time to demand a Madius stay among outlaws."

"But you are the future Emperor," Kym responded with amusement. He shrugged, palms up. "To abuse your power in such a manner would be going against our ancestors – defying your people and your laws, as they are now."

"Fascinating," Sebastian mused. His eyes went wide and his stern expression cracked into a smirk. "Your sophistication has truly taken me by surprise. Few Maedians, whether from Neo Maedia or Old Maedia, would have been able to counter such a threat with my royal obligation."

To Rebecca it seemed as though Sebastian's lightheartedness was the shift in mood that finally broke the ice. Within minutes, Kym and Sebastian found common ground talking about leadership and responsibility. Rebecca couldn't fathom where the joy laid in that kind of conversation, but it felt rude to get up and wander away. She counted the Lykos, who bustled about the camp working to build makeshift tents and fire pits for the soon-to-arrive packs.

Nineteen males, not including the Alpha Prime, his brother, or the Loremaster; eight females, all of which she'd already seen throughout the day. Eleven of the Lykos had tails – twelve if she counted Asher, who would be back before the festival's end. Only three of the twenty-seven had hair anything like Kaece's – only two had a silver base to their hair, while the third was the blonde that had served them.

Rebecca wondered if the men with silver hair were Kaece's brothers, if they'd come from the same litter; on the other hand, Asher and Kym had very different hair color. Kaece never made it sound like she had immediate relatives. Though, if she did, they'd probably disowned her. What could Kaece have done to make her own mate deny her very existence? As she watched the Lykos of varying shapes and sizes all working together, laughing and smiling, she couldn't make sense of it.

Kaece's differences with Kym stood out like a sore thumb in her speculation. Kaece, quick to turn to her claws to solve her problems – all the way back on the night of the hot springs – probably fell under the category of 'too Lykos.' Her reliance on violent methods had rubbed Sebastian the wrong way, and as Rebecca watched Sebastian and Kym getting along like long-lost friends, she imagined it would have irked Kym as well. Maybe he'd banished her 'for the good of the pack,' or maybe – she hoped and feared at the same time – their difference in attitude just caused irreconcilable relationship problems.

Motion on the roof of the lodge's first floor caught Rebecca's eye. Colorful sashes, belts, satchels and glass bottles decorated yet another shirtless man's torso and hips. As the figure sauntered to the balcony railing and leaned over, Rebecca furrowed her eyebrows. Something about the way he walked seemed off. Short, tan horns curved back from his hairline like goat horns, the tips of his ears looked pointed – but not wolfish like the Lykos. His dirty blonde goatee matched the color of his chaotic, curly hair.

The man's steel blue eyes shifted from Kym and Sebastian to Rebecca. He winked at her, then pushed off the railing and strolled down the wide ramp that lead to the front of the lodge. His lower half wasn't human at all – he walked on caprine legs covered in a fine tan fur. Black cloven hooves existed where she'd anticipated feet. The disturbing nature of his gait didn't end there; he sauntered as if drunk, but with such deliberate movement that she thought he might be pretending. When he flashed a charming smile at a passing Lykos male, a rock of anxiety formed in the pit of her stomach. Something more than being half goat bothered her about him.

"Rebecca," Alex snapped.

"Huh?" She tore her eyes from the satyr like people had to force themselves not to stare at a car wreck. The entire congregation of Lykos around the fire stared at her expectantly. They'd asked her a question; she'd missed it completely.

"Will you be fighting for honor and the title of Champion?" Kym repeated his question politely, though she guessed it was more for a show than because he really wanted to know. They'd already had this conversation, before Sebastian and Alex's arrival.

"Yeah," she shrugged. "It'll be easy."

The lie seared her tongue like acid. It would be impossible to concentrate knowing that Kaece was out there somewhere. While the Lykos partied for three days, keeping her and her friends by the warmth of the fire, Kaece would be sleeping cold and alone. She wanted the information from Kym so they could move on, but there didn't seem to be an ethical way around the formality of wasting time.

"It's true," Alex chimed in with a proud announcement. "She killed a dragon! But only because me and Sebastian weakened it first."

"Combat and murder. How very un-Maedian. Hm, does this mean the two of you may also participate in the Trials of Dominance?"

"Oh, heavens no." Sebastian frowned, the shame plain on his face.

"I'm so in!" Alex's enthusiasm bubbled up, then fizzled out as he looked down at his injured thigh. "Aw man... I guess I can't."

"Hani the shaman is staying with us. If you wish to take part in the Puppy Trial of Dominance, he can surely see to your wound," Kym offered.

"Puppy trial? Why would I want to fight puppies?"

Rebecca stifled a laugh.

"It's a side event for the youth," Tryst explained. "It is a series of sanctioned fights in the Ring of Combat, like the other Trials, but the combatants are all prepubescent. It serves as practice for the Trial of Dominance in adulthood."

"So... I'd be one of the oldest puppies in the ring?" Alex asked with a grin.

Kym nodded.

"Sweet! Hook me up with Hani! I wanna fight."

Tryst stood and strolled towards the lodge, Rebecca assumed to fetch Hani.

"In order to win the title of Champion, Rebecca, you'll first need to become champion of the females," Kym explained. "After you've defeated the final female, you graduate into the male Trials. It's rare, but not completely unheard of, for a female to take both championships."

"I'm ready whenever you are," Rebecca agreed distractedly. Tryst approached the eerie goat-man and began talking to him. She hoped he wasn't Hani, but as soon as she had the thought, Tryst lead him toward their fire.

"Patience," Kym chuckled. "Many of the other packs will arrive tonight, and a few stragglers will continue to arrive late into tomorrow. The Festival of Unity begins at sunset. The Trials of Dominance will start at high noon – there should be enough combatants by then. The female Trials are first, so get some rest and be prepared for a good fight."

"I hear there's a boy in need of some servicing," the satyr breathed seductively.

Rebecca swallowed. Gay. From the moment she saw him, she'd known something was off – it was his sexuality. She didn't know how she knew, but as certain as the sky being blue or the ocean being salty, she was certain the satyr was gay. The fact that she knew meant danger – maybe the Lykos were clueless for now, but if they found out... She shivered, afraid to see him roughed up and afraid to be near him.

"Let's do this inside," Kym nodded to Hani, then looked to Alex. "Can you walk?"

Alex said he could, but flinched when he tried to put his weight on the injured leg. Sebastian pulled Alex's arm over his shoulder and supported him. Rebecca wanted to tell him not to leave, not to go with the gay satyr into a private place, but she couldn't find a reasonable argument.

"I'm going to stay out here, if that's okay?" She said. If she could avoid being around Hani, she would.

"Of course," Kym agreed. "You've got free reign of the village. Our home is your home for as long as you please. Help yourself to anything you'd like."

"And what a glorious array of goods to choose from," Hani winked at Kym.

The Lykos and Hani chuckled together as the group of men disappeared into the lodge. They all seemed so utterly clueless, it made Rebecca's stomach churn. She got up from the fire and turned the opposite direction of Kym's lodge.

As she walked past an open-walled structure, she overheard the titter of gossip inside. She eavesdropped, just out of sight.

"There *could* be a chance that he'll take on the Champion of Dominance as his new mate," said one woman.

"Yeah right," another woman laughed. "We oughta call you Jyn the Dreamer – that'll be your title. He has a mate, and he's never so much as mentioned a Trial to replace her."

Rebecca swallowed – were they talking about Kaece? She stepped inside the shelter, making her presence known. An array of craft materials crowded the space; hammers and tongs and tools were crammed around four huge hornos. Each one seemed to have a different purpose, different materials surrounding each oven: food, glass, metal, and ceramics. Stretched across the ceiling were three differently sized animal hides, drying out.

"Hi," she said to announce herself. "It's Shanan, right?"

"Shanan the young and titleless," the blonde server Lykos, Jyn, jeered.

"Yes, that's right," Shanan answered Rebecca as she jabbed her elbow into Jyn's side. "Did you need something?"

"Oh, no, thanks... I just overheard you talking about the Alpha Prime. He's something, huh?"

Jyn swooned, visibly melting at the mention of Kym. "He's something alright. I'd lay down my life for that man without a second thought. Or have his litter."

"All three brothers from his litter really are handsome," Shanan added, rolling her eyes at Jyn. "Are you after the title of Champion so you can win his heart like Jyn here? That would explain a lot. There's been quite a fuss about you joining the TOD"

"Do you think it's possible?" Rebecca feigned excitement. "Could an alpha like him fall for a pathetic human girl?"

"Give up now," Jyn snapped. "It's not possible. He's not available. He already has a mate. She may be on hiatus, but she's still alive. She'll be back. So even if by some miracle you did win, she would gut you if you tried to take him."

Rebecca reflexively touched the wound on her side. The threat of Kaece gutting her made her smile – if only Jyn had any grasp of her comment's irony. "It's okay. If I won the championship, and his heart, I think I'd just use him for a little while. He may be something, but I've met somethings better than him. If I'm gone before she gets back, I'll be safe, right?"

Shanan laughed. "Use him for a while. You're too funny."

"You wouldn't want to risk it," Jyn persisted. Her tone changed from defensive to desperate. "It's possible that she'll be back any day now, and beating Kym is nothing compared to trying to beat her. She totally humiliated him, completely defiled his Alpha Prime title... Everyone knows that Kym isn't the true Alpha Prime, but we haven't got anyone else to lead us. There isn't a fighter in this world who could stop her from getting what she wanted. You definitely wouldn't want her to be seeking your blood on her claws. Do the smart thing, stay away from him."

"She says fervently, all while hoping one day he'll wake up and ask her to lay with him," Shanan rolled her eyes again. "Don't even worry about that, kitten, I'm sure the only one who'd mind if you used our Alpha Prime for a little while is Jyn."

The blonde Lykos blushed and murmured some kind of half-hearted protest into her hands.

"So," Rebecca pried, "What was her name?"

The two women exchanged looks of terror. Their sudden transformation from amused, giggling girls to silent, stony-faced sentries made Rebecca frown. Obviously she'd asked the wrong question; the Kaece panic button was larger than she'd thought.

"Who?" Shanan asked after a few moments.

"Kym's mate."

"I don't remember," she replied too quickly, then looked to Jyn again. "Do you?"

"No, I can't recall," Jyn lied. "Isn't that strange?"

Rebecca sighed – stonewalled. She wished she'd managed to navigate around the precarious subject of Kaece better. If she could've gotten any more information out of them, she might've been a step closer to finding the Lykos she truly wanted to be with – without needing to waste the time among the Lykos who'd exiled her. But as disheartened as she felt, standing there with the suddenly amnesiac Lykos, she held out hope. Shanan and Jyn eagerly divulged information about Kaece, so long as Rebecca pretended to be investigating Kym. She would snoop around the Lykos camp and sucker information out of the gossip hounds. Maybe, she thought, she could uncover their secrets and leave before three days passed.

DENIAL XXVI
The Lykos Village Part 1

ALEX SILAS

REBECCA SILAS

249 Virgo in the Evening

Honestly I have no idea what's even going on anu[...]
Rebecca's not dead, but she's different. She has
Drakeon eyes and her arm freaking glows! And for
some reason we're looking for Kaece instead of
Sebastian's dad. Either way, no one we're looking fo[...]
here. but I'm glad WE are because the Lykos fixed n[...]
leg with magic, and I get to enter a big fighting
tournament. Rebecca too. Is it dumb that I'm exci[...]
but terrified of losing her again at the same time?
Even if the dragons did something horrible to her, sh[...]
still alive and she's still my sister and I worry about
her. She's just as reckless as before. Well... here's to luck
being on our side for once! -Alexander the greatest

226

227

228

229

230

231

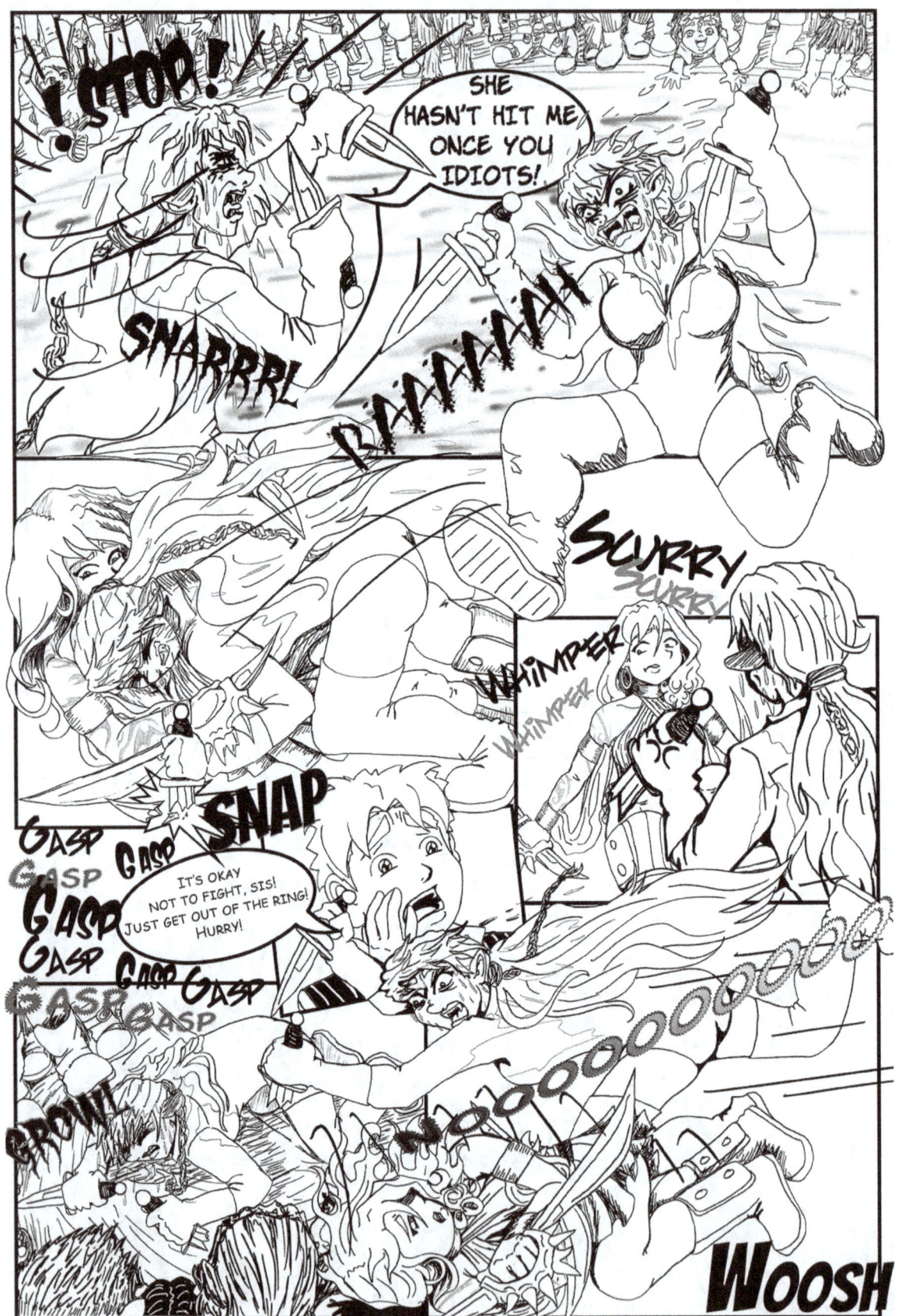

232

233

CHAPTER 27

Sweat beaded on her spine; hot, sticky blood seeped from her side. Blinding light glared down from the bright sun overhead. The vast savanna stretched endlessly, the tall grass drooped a sad, brittle yellow. Exhaustion weighed on her every muscle; gravity beckoned her to give up. Days had gone by while she searched. Each passing moment quickened her weary heart.

"Kaece!" She cried out into the emptiness. Her throat burned. Blistered. Hoarse. But the Lykos was out there, somewhere.

Laughter echoed, carried in the wind. Rebecca whirled around, searching the horizon. Nothing. No one. The presence of the ghost laughter lingered, and she couldn't shake the feeling: Kaece didn't want to be found. If she didn't hurry, if she didn't try harder, Kaece would disappear forever.

More laughter; then the roar of the crowd filled her ears. The onlookers surrounding the combat ring cheered, hooted, hollered, all expressing their pleasure at her opponent's defeat. A Lykos woman lay face down just outside the boundary, too humiliated to stand. Rebecca squeezed the hilts of her swords tighter.

"Next up, the Crimson Whirlwind – the final challenger!"

She planted her feet firmly on the ground; her jaw clenched. At long last, the villain who puppeteered Kaece would come forward, show herself, and be defeated. She'd earn Kaece's freedom from the overlord who manipulated her into slaughter, who took advantage of her natural aggression and misused her.

"Just how naïve are you?"

Monique stood with hands on her hips, beside Rebecca. Her perfect hair, perfect complexion, perfect everything – it all paled against that all-knowing smile. Even phantom Monique knew secrets she would only share if she felt like it.

"Go away."

"You're bleeding."

"I know."

"She hurt you," Monique continued.

"I deserved it," she defended. "I was acting like you."

"Tell yourself whatever makes you feel better. Either way, you're never going to see her again." Monique traced her hand across Rebecca's side. The wound burned at her touch, then cooled. The sensation relaxed her, soothed the pain, and she knew it was healing. "It's probably for the better you know."

Rebecca cried, pushing Monique away – but it was like trying to move a wall. Rebecca's muscles felt useless and weak. Monique's hand stayed firmly pressed against her injury, her arm unwavering. "Don't take away all that I have left of her."

"Forget her."

"I can't!"

"You should. She's just a Lykos, and a bad one at that. You know first-hand what she's capable of."

Rebecca opened her mouth to protest, but her words strangled in her throat. Droplets of hot blood rained from the sky; red mist thickened the air. Each drop scalded as it broke against her skin. The slick blood coated her, drenching her hair and clothes.

Panic squeezed her like a vise; her breath came ragged as her opponent, a black silhouette dripping with blood in the red fog, approached. The Crimson Whirlwind.

Kaece stepped through the obscuring mist and into the combat ring. In her claws, she held Kym by the hair. She dragged the Alpha Prime through the blood-saturated dirt, a sinister smirk lighting her features. An animal craze glinted in her golden eyes – the craze that overtook her when she murdered the dragon – the craze that possessed her when she sank her claws into Rebecca.

"Murderer," Rebecca whispered.

The weight of the word carried like a feather in the wind; Kaece looked tickled by the sentiment. She knew exactly what Kaece could do without showing a hint of remorse.

Rebecca searched Kaece's expression for a sign of validation. The Lykos' cold, hard eyes stared back at her. Her fingers flexed, her muscles tensed, eager for the fight – for the bloodshed. The woman Rebecca thought she knew stood ready to destroy everything, wanting for power badly enough to take the life of a prince, of a helpless boy, of Rebecca.

"You know what to do." Sebastian stepped up beside her. He took her hand in his, and closed her fingers around her sword.

The blood-slicked weapon fell to the ground. "I can't."

Rebecca entwined her fingers with Sebastian's. Holding his hand, she stepped outside of the circle etched in the deep crimson mud. Frothy waves lapped up onto the sand, the surf washing over her feet – washing away the blood. The blood dissolved into the clear water, disappearing into the stormy grey horizon.

"When I'm with you, I'll be thinking of her," she whispered.

He smiled a handsome, warm smile, then stroked her cheek the way Kaece used to before he planted a kiss on her lips.

Rebecca woke in a cold sweat. Her skin chilled like ice despite the heavy blankets covering her from neck to toe. When she opened her eyes, only darkness greeted her vision. The laughter and ruckus of merriment filtered in from outside. She felt the warmth of someone's hand in hers. Tentatively, she squeezed it.

"Are you awake?" Sebastian asked.

She nodded, then realized he – unlike Kaece – wouldn't be able to see the motion. Moments later, the small flame of an oil lamp flickered to life. Rebecca winced against the dim light permeating the room; she felt like someone jammed her brain full of cotton. Her head throbbed, pulsating of pain and dizziness.

Sebastian's eyebrows creased, his mouth set in a worried frown. "I am relieved that you regained consciousness. Kym tried to warn us that you were pushing mortal limits, but you seemed so eager to continue... Everyone was very worried when you fainted. Even Hani graciously cast a healing charm on you to speed your recovery."

Rebecca mirrored his frown, trying to ignore the fact that Hani put his hands on her. She struggled to remember what happened before the dream. Lykos – so many Lykos. Once the sun had peaked in the sky, Kym announced the beginning of the games. It hadn't been long before someone called her name and she entered the Ring of Combat.

The female Lykos eagerly dove into battle at first, striking at Rebecca with an onslaught of blows. Each attack, regardless of how carefully timed or well-placed, failed to hit home. The swords of Typhos led Rebecca through an intricate dance of defense but she never struck back. The woman's irritation grew with each blow blocked or dodged. That frustration became recklessness and Rebecca used it to trip the Lykos out of the ring.

Match after match ended in a disqualification. She developed a pattern, a method for causing the least amount of harm to each opponent she faced. Only a few of the women persisted like the first, attacking with stubborn finesse until Rebecca wore them to exhaustion. Before mid-afternoon, she'd defeated all of the females. The males, too, were tricked out of bounds without bloodshed. The matches passed quicker and quicker, a confusing blur of exhaustion and pain working against her. The magic of Typhos carried her through each bout, even after she couldn't feel her muscles moving with the swords. The magic of the Protector fueled her body long after fatigue should have pulled her under; her need to find Kaece burned too great to allow them to stop.

When twilight set in, no combatants stood – none wanted to be humiliated in the ring after all they had witnessed. Kym remained, her only opponent, but he cowardly insisted he would not fight until noon the next day. He distracted the attention away from his fear of another defeat, instead suggesting they enjoy the festivities of the evening. She wanted an earlier match, but he hid behind the necessity to keep to a schedule of sorts – the Olympic-style games commenced in the morning hours, and he said there would be plenty of time for combat to be had afterward. She remembered trying to goad him into a fight, but little more before waking up in the hut.

In the faint light of the flame, Rebecca studied Sebastian's features. Those striking blue eyes, his platinum blond hair, even his complexion, flawless as Monique's, all worked together to make him charming. Charming and silent, just like the resolute man who stood with her in the cleansing surf. She touched the cloth bandage laid over her wound, feeling the oil of an ointment, instead of her blood.

"Do you..." She stumbled. "...want to be with me?"

"I'm with you now," Sebastian replied with a warm smile of unconditional love.

The simplicity of his answer, the fact that he took her question at face value – even if she'd meant more – made her smile back. She could imagine herself with him; she loved him more than she'd ever loved Brad, even if it was platonic love. She shook her head. "I mean *with* me with me. As my boyfriend. My lover. Like people assume."

He flushed up to his ears; his whole face turned bright red.

"Am I too crazy for you?"

"No," he stammered quickly. "I mean – yes. And no. Er... Wait. I mean –"

"Shhh." Rebecca laid her fingertips against his lips. "I understood, it's okay. ...Hold me?"

Sebastian nodded, then kissed the back of her hand. He watched her, proceeding cautiously as if scanning her face for signs of hesitation. In response, she smiled and moved over on the bed, inviting him to lay with her.

She nuzzled into the pillow and closed her eyes, trying desperately to block out the memories of that dream. His arms wrapped around her, lukewarm in comparison to the heat of Kaece's body. Satisfied with any warmth at all, Rebecca cuddled into his embrace.

"You're so cold." Sebastian rubbed her arm for a few moments before he pulled the blankets over them. His hands rested on her sides, careful to avoid the wound and poultice.

Outside, the laughter and commotion continued. The liveliness of the Lykos celebration should have been enticing, but her motivation was gone. A gaping hole in her heart where Kaece once lived allowed her newfound vigor to drain away. Instead, she lay in Sebastian's arms, in near silence, listening to his even breathing. She wondered what it would feel like to pass every night for the rest of his life in his arms. Sebastian couldn't ever stack up to Brad's irksome behavior – nor could he measure up to Kaece's passion. Regardless, he was a hero, a prince, the perfect knight in shining armor who – she knew – could love her in spite of her glowing arm and cold skin.

Pondering the depths of her love for Sebastian, Rebecca succumbed to the pull of her nightmares and gave in to another restless slumber.

ALEX SILAS

REBECCA SILAS

250 Virgo in the morning

is the day I make history. I will be the
human to win a Trial of Dominance
becca doesn't count, because I'll win before
fights Kym.) It feels a little bit unfair,
ce I'm up against children... but there's no
y the children's fights could be anywhere
ar as brutal as the women's fights before
ca started fighting. I figure only bad
would hurt children, so it has to be safe.
        The point is:
ecca and Sebastian and the Lykos will see
for the hero I'm meant to be. No one will
tion me or laugh at me anymore. If the
gons could see me now, they'd quiver with
and fly away to the furthest reaches of
adia.
ey'll tell stories about me forever. Last
ht Rebecca's fights were all anyone wanted
talk about. She beat 50 Lykos without
lling a drop of blood. I've got to be even
more impressive, or I'm just going to be
forgotten. I can do it, I believe in me even if
no one else does,

                            Alexander the greatest

        Lykos are strange. A bunch of them
m to be gay. I haven't had a chance to
talk to Sebastian in private, but he probably
knows why. I'm thinking it's one of those
adverse side-effects to their mutations.

238

239

240

AROOOOOOOOOOOOOOO
GROWL
SQUISH
YIPE!
I did it! I actually did it! I get another round! Yeah!
WOAH! AH!
GUSH
But... I was finally going to win... owww.
With a successful disarm, Jak is the winner! Honor for Jak!
No one moves on to the next round....
Spirits welcome another home Guide and protect him
Rest eternally with your honor, young one.

242

My sister treats me like I don't exist because I'm four years younger than her. She's always so caught up in herself that she doesn't even take the time of day to acknowledge me.

Until this Trial of Dominance people could only brag about winning a championship without accidentally killing someone. She won the entire female and male championship in a single day without hurting anyone! It was the most amazing thing any of us have ever seen, ever.

She is pretty great. She sacrificed herself to save my life....

She was thrown into a live volcano, and then the volcano erupted - but not before she escaped, and ran far and fast away from the villains who tried to destroy us all.

Yeah it was crazy. In the meantime, me and Sebastian were fighting a huge dragon. We had it cornered, and then Rebecca showed up outta nowhere and she put her sword straight through its heart while Kaece tore its throat out.

Wow!

Then Kaece attacked Rebecca and ran off... That's why we're here, looking for Kaece.

Kaece. Hm. That's not a familiar name.

But I don't know everyone in all of the Packs, and I don't know any of the names of the Supremacists. No one can say their names or titles because it gives them respect they don't deserve.

Supremacists? Like... Nazis?

You don't know what that is. Uhm - How can you tell if someone is a Supremacist?

We all look the same, we're all Lykos. They used to be part of our collective packs, but there was something that happened and they left.

It's not how a Lykos looks...

It's how a Lykos thinks.

244

246

247

CHAPTER 29

Asher's staff blazed while he danced in time with the drums. The flames twirled, decorating the black night with luminescent spirals. Bonfires roared throughout the camp – the heat of the flames and the warmth of so many Lykos had finally been enough to thaw Rebecca's icy skin.

Her whole body tingled with the sensation of heat inside and out; the potent drink loosened her muscles, it made her head spin like the fire spinners' batons. An arm encircled her waist; she leaned into the comfortable touch of Lykos claws. She closed her eyes, the feel of hot skin against hers more enticing than the swirling flames.

The voice of a female Lykos rasped in her ear, "Ya look like ya could use to lay down."

Rebecca giggled. The forward line reminded her of Kaece's bluntness. It made her wonder if all those special things she loved about Kaece weren't so unique among Lykos. "I've already spent enough time on my back for one day."

"Don't let it get to ya," the woman soothed, tracing her fingers up Rebecca's side. "Kym's our Alpha Prime because he's got superior strength and agility. But ya seem to have a lot of untapped potential yourself."

Neither Kym's speed nor strength caused her to lose the match. The power of Typhos disappeared in the wake of her nightmare. Without the need to protect Kaece, Rebecca felt like she existed without a purpose. The magic of the Protector abandoned her, and so she'd lost the claim to the title she'd been given by the Drakeon.

"Go away," she slurred.

"Humor me, Drakeonette. There's something I want to show ya."

Rebecca's heart knocked against her ribs; painful longing constricted her lungs. From the playful yet smug expression to her seductive whispers, the Lykos refused to stop reminding Rebecca of Kaece. Everything about her stirred the ache in Rebecca's soul and reaffirmed that she had lost Kaece. The Lykos grabbed her by the belt and pulled her off the bench.

She led Rebecca through the village to the outskirts of the encampment, where only a few fires still burned. Rebecca felt grateful for the hand guiding her; her clumsy feet wobbled like jello beneath her numb legs. Dimly, she wondered what lay beyond the camp, but the Lykos acted with enough urgency to make Rebecca believe something important existed there.

The fading flames of a campfire cast light on two Lykos locked in an embrace. Skin-to-skin, lips-to-lips, their hands roamed unashamedly over every part of the other's body – exposed or not. She openly gaped, resisting the insistent yanking on her belt. How could they be so overt in such a public place? Maybe they thought everyone was asleep, or maybe that no one would notice them in the dark.

Their lips parted and one of the Lykos tilted her head back and moaned. The loud, throaty sound of pleasure caused a wave of hot embarrassment to rush over Rebecca. Her gaze trailed down the body of the moaning Lykos, following the hands of her partner toward the short leather skirt. Unable to tear herself away from the searing vision, she swallowed

The moans grew louder; One Lykos leaned down and pressed her lips against the other's open mouth. She kissed her cheek, jaw, neck, further and further...

Rebecca's muscles tensed; her abdomen tingled with the same heat flooding her cheeks. Had she and Kaece almost been entwined like these two, before she pushed Kaece away forever? She longed to know the answer – longed to be the girl pleasured by Kaece's confident touch.

"C'mon, snapdragon, I can see you're all riled up," the Lykos behind her cooed. "Let me relieve ya."

She squeezed her eyes shut against the world. The darkness behind her eyelids spun, a disorienting blackness. Everything seemed unreal and when she opened her eyes she couldn't sort reality from fantasy. Who could know right from wrong? Nothing was what it should have been.

"I hate how you Lykos do that," she whispered.

Frustration roiled just below the surface, masked by her confusion and despair. The conflicting emotions overwhelmed her, so she pulled away from the woman.

"Wait," the Lykos called after her. "Don't leave yet, this is where the thing I wanted to show ya is... It's a surprise you'll regret not seein'."

Rebecca rolled her eyes and kept walking. The Lykos village surrounding her radiated too much sexual energy.

"It's related to what ya seek."

She marched back, her stare fixed on the Lykos who promised her something of Kaece.

The Lykos turned and, lifting the patchwork leather curtain of a makeshift dwelling, invited Rebecca inside.

"I am Talia Springs, ya can use either name, title or both as ya please."

Rebecca watched as Talia unfastened a bedroll and removed a bundle of blankets from within it. The Lykos looked over her shoulder at the door; her eyes glinted with anxiety. She peeled the layer of blankets back to reveal a weapon, which she lifted from its sanctuary with reverence. It looked like a headsman's axe. At both ends, curved and rusted double blades protruded from the leather-wrapped wooden haft.

"This axe was stolen from the Supremacists," Talia explained, offering the weapon to Rebecca. "It was Alpha Whirlwind's. My brother from the Northwest Pack took it – but the Alpha Prime doesn't know some of us have been raiding their camp."

Rebecca felt mesmerized by the smooth wood and soft feel of the leather against her palms. She wanted to believe she held where Kaece's hands held, disregarding the dark bloodstains coating the shaft. Dried blood had caked into the deep etchings of words she couldn't understand.

Talia's hands cupped her breasts, underneath the thin fabric over her nipples. Shocked out of her rapt state, Rebecca whirled on Talia and swung the axe at her. The Lykos dodged, of course.

"Not funny," Talia hissed. "That thing might be cursed."

"Oh yeah? What do you even know about it?" Rebecca snapped. "What makes you think it's Kaece's?"

"Her title. It's etched on the blade," she grumbled. "It's a combination of 'Whirlwind', and the color of blood."

"Crimson Whirlwind," Rebecca whispered. The Drakeon warning. Needles of comprehension shot through her brain, numbing and painful all at once. The weapon had belonged to Kaece.

"The blood on it is probably all Maedian blood, from executions. It's not really a fighting weapon, and she'd never fight with it anyways. It was probably used to torture prisoners, break them mentally, ya know? Maybe by beheading family or friends. Maybe she made the prisoners do it themselves. I can only imagine the stories this weapon must hold."

Rebecca's awe broke and gave way to a rush of nausea. Maedian blood. The blood splattered across the buildings and soaked into the streets of Sow Endus washed into her memory. Innocent women and children, gored and splayed open by the very weapon in her hands. She knew the stories the weapon contained – tales of disemboweled workers, gutted dragons, rent-apart and contorted bodies left to bloat in the heat of the sun. Behind it all, wielding the axe that ruined everything, had been Kaece. She threw the weapon onto the heap of blankets, then sank to the floor and cradled her stomach.

"It was meant to bring you joy, not make you cry," Talia sighed, her voice tainted with confused annoyance.

The tears rolled down Rebecca's cheeks. She touched her face – her whole body felt disconnected, foreign. She couldn't feel anything – moreso, she couldn't trust in anything she felt to be real. Her confusion, torn apart by the extremity of murder, gave way to need. Caught in a haze, she forced herself to her feet and groped at the heavy curtain.

"What's wrong? I don't understand."

Rebecca pulled against the weight of the curtain, frantic to get out. She yanked it back, pushed through the opening and broke into a run. She ran through the village, clumsily crunching belongings under her feet. She needed to find Sebastian.

She felt so stupid for loving Kaece. The instant she fell into Gaeadia, Sebastian had saved her. Like Alex had ordained, fate bound their romance, sealed their destiny together. The tears kept falling freely as she combated her intoxication, while she searched the encampment for her knight in shining armor.

When she found him, his melancholy expression split into a smile lit with the sparkle of adoration in his eyes. His unmasked infatuation was exactly what she sought. She hoped that Sebastian could make her feel normal.

"Come on," she panted, grabbing him by the tunic and hoisting him up.

Surprised by her authority but unobjecting, Sebastian followed her into her room. She pulled the door closed behind them and pushed him onto the bed.

"What has possessed you so?"

Rebecca ignored his question, refusing to think of what. She pushed the bloody axe, the Crimson Whirlwind, the overly affectionate Lykos, the fire-lit homosexuality – all of it, she forced from her mind. She wanted nothing but to think of Sebastian and how good he felt.

"I need you," she replied as she sat in his lap. She pulled his belt free and thrust her hands up under his tunic. He flinched at the cold touch of her hands, but she fanned her fingers out and explored his chest. "Don't you want me?"

"I – uh..." His words stumbled over themselves, jumbling in his mouth and escaping as bewildered noises. His surprise married with fear and she realized that he was a virgin.

She smiled and pressed her lips against his. He swallowed audibly, then meekly kissed back. Her tongue slid into his mouth while her hands roamed. When she realized he still looked frightened, she playfully bit his lip. He gasped, and she knew she'd succeeded.

Rebecca pulled his tunic off and threw it aside. She kissed down his neck and exposed collar. She rubbed her body against him, begging to be touched, but his hands remained awkwardly stiff at his sides.

"Don't," he whimpered as she moved to untie the string at the back of her neck. His cheeks burned a rosy red, his entire body rigid.

"Don't what, Sebastian?" She purred seductively in his ear, then unfastened her shirt and let it fall away. His eyes moved over her body like she wished his hands would. As he took in her nudity, she wondered if he might faint. "It's just sex, don't be so nervous."

"No," he protested. His chivalry was so cute; she found the dumbfounded argument adorable.

"Yes. I want you. Right now."

His mouth moved, but he couldn't manage to form words. She trailed her hand up his thigh. Her palm found the firm bulge in his pants; he gasped again.

"Why are you pretending you don't want me?" She smirked and squeezed, eliciting another ragged breath from him. "You've given yourself away."

"It's not that," he stammered. She reached down with both hands and unfastened his pants. "I want to...to..."

"So do I."

She sat back in his lap and rubbed herself against the hardness between his legs. The wet cloth of her panties slid on his bare skin

He shook his head, and when she tried to kiss him, he pulled away.

Rebecca froze, annoyed at his persistent reluctance. She growled, "Why are you being difficult? Are you gay?"

He plead, "I want to be in love. I want to be married."

"You don't love me?"

"Well yes... I do." His face reddened more.

She rolled her eyes. "Then what's wrong? We can get married. I want this – us. Just you and me, like this, forever."

Skepticism lingered in his face, but he moved to touch her for the first time since he'd been pushed onto the bed. He tentatively brushed his fingers against her side, up her ribcage and stopped short of her breasts. She moved into the touch, pressing the full front of her body against his. Then she reached down and moved her underwear aside, pushing him inside of her. He slid in with ease, the wetness between her legs making it easier than it had ever been with Brad. She closed her eyes and moved her body with his.

The rhythm of his thrusts felt awkward. The thumping of his sheath against the floor and slapping of her skin on his became too apparent. Too mechanical.

Rebecca pushed against his chest and sighed with frustration. It wasn't working – she felt nothing. She wanted to like being with Sebastian. She couldn't handle another Brad.

"I'm not comfortable with this," he said and tried to get free from beneath her.

"I don't care. I want you to do it. Don't stop."

She ground her hips against him, pinning him against the wall.

It felt like an eternity passed before a rush of wetness flooded out from between her legs and she knew he'd finally come. She climbed off his lap. He seemed just as eager as she'd been for the end; he hurriedly stood and pulled his pants up. He rushed outside, the redness in his face replaced with a pallor. She didn't know why he left, but she didn't care, either.

Disgusted with herself, sticky fluid clinging to her thighs, she hugged her knees to her chest. Numbness overtook her and she wondered if it might have been a dream. Nothing felt right; nothing had been repaired. Everything felt just pointless, distant, and lost.

CHAPTER 30

The sound of dripping water roused Rebecca from the deep, dreamless sleep brought on by her exhaustion. She winced against the light burning through her eyelids and pulled the blanket over her head. Her muscles moved like pulverized meat. Pain radiated between her eyes, a sharp ache that throbbed with each beat of her heart.

"How do you feel?" Sebastian asked from beside her.

Heat flooded her cheeks and her stomach tightened, guilt and embarrassment working together to render her speechless.

"You had a lot to drink. I have heard that it can make people behave very strangely, uncharacteristic of themselves... But I have never witnessed anyone affected quite so."

"Are you okay?" She croaked.

"I worry about you."

Rebecca peeked out from the blanket. His sad smile when he looked at her wrenched her insides. "Don't worry, you didn't do anything I didn't ask for."

"Yes. However, your actions were guided by something darker than alcohol, by the invisible scars you carry from the terrors on The Other Side. You are not well, Rebecca." He tapped his temple meaningfully. "Those scars become more apparent as time passes."

"I miss her," she defended. She seemed insane to him and though she felt indignant at his accusation, she felt worse for agreeing with him.

It seemed to her, that he knew the truth and wanted her confession. She took a deep breath.

"I don't think I'm into men. I think I'm –" Her voice cracked, she faltered.

The words wouldn't come, but Sebastian nodded as if he heard what she couldn't say. "I assumed as much after you became involved with Kaece."

"Involved in what?"

"One another. Were you not? Your relationship with her is something I detested – even tried to deny. But your preoccupation with finding her, and your determination to keep the wound inflicted by her claws left me little room for an alternative answer. She has always been the one, I was not a true contender," he explained, an unreasonable calm in his voice. She wondered what he really felt beneath the controlled tone.

"We weren't involved."

"No? Tell me, how do you feel about her then?"

Rebecca bit back the tears, masking the pain with laughter. Her chest ached from the hole her feelings had bored into her heart; she wanted to feel betrayed by

Kaece. Instead she felt the swollen sense of longing, the gaping wound Kaece left in her absence, and she wished her Lykos would return – to fill the void she'd created.

"I want to see her again," she whispered. "More than I've ever wanted anything in the world. In either world."

"That commitment you made to me, that you wanted to be with me forever... I believe it, and everything you said was meant for her."

"How are you staying so calm? Shouldn't you be grossed out right now? It should bother you that I want to be with another girl. Doesn't that make me abnormal? Some kind of freak?"

Sebastian smiled, an amused turn of his lips accompanied by raised eyebrows – the expression of someone talking to a slow-learning child. "In Maedia, many women choose to live with other women. It is simply less common than male and female coupling, not so much abnormal. I honestly have taken no notice of their behavior or lifestyle in contrast to that of other Maedian women. I gather from your expectation, however, that women do not often have romantic relationships with one another in your world?"

"They do, I guess. They're called lesbians. Or gays, or homos, or any number of other derogatory names. It's just not right, and I don't want to be one of them."

"Forgive me, but I do not think that you know what you want." When Rebecca opened her mouth to protest, Sebastian held up his hand and continued to speak, "You seem to fight against what you want at every possible turn. You want to be with Kaece, yet you do not want to be with a woman. You want to conform to the expectations of your society, yet you cannot truly be happy fulfilling the role someone else has designated for you. If for only a moment you could set aside politics, what is it that you would desire?"

"I'm so in love with her," she breathed. "I have been from the first moment I laid eyes on her. I could be gay... I could be okay with it – for her, I could."

"Love is a beautiful thing," he assented. "Especially when it is mutual attraction. You two share a very special connection, and for that I can set my feelings aside."

"But how?" Rebecca protested. Sebastian's support meant the world to her, but it didn't change the truth of Kaece's identity. "She's a murderer. A psychopathic murderer. She slaughtered your people – she practically admitted it. Then there's everything else she's ever done: threatening to kill you, destroying Sow Endus...She is the Crimson Whirlwind... Crimson, for blood. Don't you get it? It'll only get worse after the Lykos tell me what they know, too."

"Do not mistake my desire for your happiness as condoning what the Lykos has done. Though I am certain she was the villain you describe, and that she is a blood thirsty beast who has committed countless atrocities, I have to ask you something. Why, if that is all she is, would she have done all that she did while she traveled with us? Why did she not kill the three of us, then continue to massacre yet more towns? She certainly had the opportunity. Only one thing stopped her, Rebecca. You."

Though she wanted to argue, to say she wasn't the only reason, she remembered the hateful look in Kaece's eyes when she had looked at Sebastian – the crazed glower that had softened when she saw Rebecca. Her heart sank a little deeper and her lungs constricted as she heard the ghost of Kaece's desperate voice in the wind, begging her to run away with her. She'd felt the tenderness in Kaece's touch when she woke up from death. It was true: Kaece had only been with them for her, and as long as she had stayed with them she hadn't killed anyone. Except for the Warrior.

"Except, she killed that dragon," she frowned. "She swore to me she wouldn't hurt them."

"I do not understand your love for those dragons. The Lykos, of all the beasts on Xiratera – the Lykos! – have been more hospitable than those scaled creatures. Let us not forget the Drakeon you speak of almost killed Alex and I. And their very species attempted to sacrifice you."

"She made a promise," Rebecca snapped. "And still she killed him. I wanted to believe she's not the monster I knew in my heart she was, but you were right. She's everything you ever said about the Lykos, maybe worse."

He sighed again, the weariness in his voice showing on his face. "In my opinion, she most likely slew that dragon in order to prevent it from warning you about her dark history. The Drakeon at Drakeon Peak recognized her, they openly called her a betrayer – the same word they used for the banished Drakeon. If she was instrumental in a war against my people, do you not think that that information is the last thing she would want you to know? If she loved you, she would have done anything to keep you from learning the truth. As you have witnessed, with these Lykos, those who are the enemy cannot be involved with a member of the community.

"According to this society, her culture, you two would have been unable to keep your relationship."

Sebastian's logic made sense go her: if Kaece knew being her enemy voided their romance, then lying condemned her less than the consequences of letting the Drakeon live. Rebecca'd lied often enough to keep herself close to Monique: she'd even committed herself to Brad for the sake of their friendship. Not even a sliver of doubt existed in her mind that she'd lie for Kaece.

"My opinion may not have much value to you, but it is true to Maedia," Sebastian continued when she didn't reply. "Love, rather than violence, is what holds Gaeadia together. Regardless of what she may have done, if peace can be made, it is the better option. She, perhaps, was less of a monster while the two of you were involved."

"You keep saying involved. We were never official," Rebecca defended. "It would've meant we both had to admit to things we didn't want to talk about. We agreed to let sleeping dogs lie. But I sort of ignored it when she broke her promise not to hurt any more dragons."

"Secrets have a tendency to surface, regardless of the measures taken to keep them buried. Even the secrets we hide from ourselves, or the lies inscribed on the pages of history books, emerge one day. Truth cannot be suppressed forever. The true measure of character is how one chooses to deal with that truth. And so, it is up to you. The truth lies less than a full day away, at the conclusion of this ridiculous celebration. Are you prepared to discover whatever it is that we do not yet know about Kaece?"

She hesitated, considering all she'd learned during the past three days. Could she ever be ready to find out something worse?

"The Kaece they knew wouldn't ever follow anyone... The woman they whisper about was menacing, fearless. We don't need to know any secrets to know that."

"Hmm." Sebastian stood and crossed the room toward the door. "Perhaps that is something to consider. People do change. Somewhat, at least."

As she groggily readied herself for the last day of 'Unity,' she considered just how much Kaece had changed in their woefully short time together. The fierce beastial nature behind that passionate gaze had been what made Kaece unforgettable. She wore her scars proudly, like a badge of dignity – something Rebecca had always admired, but never examined too closely. For both of them, the love they shared had been transformative, but her experience with Kaece couldn't undo all the pain that Monique had caused. Rebecca vowed that, if she found Kaece, she would have the patience and understanding that Sebastian had shown to her. She would love Kaece unconditionally, and do everything possible to smooth over the battle scars that Kaece hid behind to deny her suffering – suffering that created and powered the monster.

The familiar sensation of Typhos' power prickled along her skin. She needed to be with Kaece; she knew it was a step toward peace. Casting off the Lykos garb, she pulled out her mended clothes. She hurriedly dressed, knowing a rematch with Kym stood between her and finding her way back to Kaece.

Alex trotted up next to her. "What's wrong? Why do you look like you're about to kill someone?"

Rebecca ignored him, her intent focused on getting Kym into the arena. She stepped over the line etched deep into the blood-soaked sand and drew her swords.

"Alpha Prime Kym Timbercut, I challenge you to a rematch!" She yelled, "enter the Circle of Combat and prove the worth of your title!"

Kym stepped through the quickly gathering crowd of Lykos and answered from the boundary of the ring, "When I defeat you, you may never challenge me again, Rebecca."

"Bring it."

He lunged. His smugness didn't waiver as she sidestepped his sword. She wanted to laugh; he didn't realize the magic of Typhos fueled her. Kym stood between her and Kaece.

She saw his next attack before it happened, saw the tension in his muscles building in preparation for a second slash. When his blow came, Rebecca deflected it as easily as she breathed the air. His second sword followed up, but she twisted away and caught the blade with her spiked guard. Then she thrust at him with her other sword. He abandoned the sword she'd snagged. It clattered to the ground as he jumped back.

Rebecca used the momentum of her thrust to tuck and roll, then swept his legs out from under him. While he lay dazed, she stood and planted a foot firmly on his chest. She leveled the tip of her sword against his throat.

"Give up. I don't want to hurt you."

He grabbed for her ankle, but she leapt away before his hands could touch her. He came at her with another clumsy swing. She held fast, fighting against the urge to dodge his attack just as she'd fought the urge to block Kaece's claws. She waited until his blade had almost made contact, then she brought her sword up in defense. The position promised equal injury, or worse, to Kym if he followed through. He recognized the threat, falling away but off balance from the sudden shift in momentum.

As Kym stumbled past her, trying to escape and regain his footing, Rebecca whirled on him. She slammed the dagger pommel of her sword into his exposed back. She heard a collective gasp from the crowd. Blood burbled from the wound, as she slid the dagger's blade from his shoulder.

Rebecca jumped back and sank low to the ground, blocking defensively with her swords. Only the bleeding wound and his clouded gaze betrayed the severity of his injury. She remained guarded and kept her eyes trained on the sword in his right hand.

He raised the blade, then thrust his sword into the dirt. Another gasp echoed throughout the crowd. Tryst stepped into the ring, his hands held high into the air. He spoke as he approached Rebecca, "Packs, from far and wide, the games are over! A new Champion of Domination is named: Rebecca One Strike, the Protector.

She has earned the highest of honor, and deserves our utmost respect. None shall forget this."

Tryst took her by the wrist, lifting her arm up above her head. The stunned silence gave way to cheers. The old man held her in that celebratory stance for only a few moments before he abandoned her and knelt at Kym's side.

"Is the wound too grave?" He asked in a hushed tone.

Kym nodded; blood colored his chin, it oozed from his nostrils and the corners of his mouth. "It's nothing a little sleep can't fix," he joked in a strained whisper. "Though when I rise, there will be much talk of how I should've fought to the death, you know. My pride won't recover with my body."

"Gophers! Let them talk," Tryst replied, while he helped Kym stand. "The Metakosmos are mysterious beings, even disregarding the fact this one is also a Drakeon-mix. No one will speak long of such nonsense. She has simply proven that she's special – something to be respected – just as we suspected on the day our guests arrived."

"If I'm so special, why did you make me wait three days?" Rebecca scoffed. "I've got important things to do, things that concern all of Gaeadia."

"Restraint can teach us valuable lessons. Do you not see how you've changed in these three short days?"

Rebecca scowled at Tryst for answering her question with a question. The time wasted not searching for Kaece was anything but "short." She inhaled sharply through her clenched teeth.

"She hasn't got the patience for it today, Loremaster." Kym supported himself on Tryst's shoulder. "She's won our respect and concluded the Trials by defeating me – the gathering is over. Some day, she'll understand what purpose the event served for her, but for now tell her of the Supremacists. Do not omit the rumors, or my lost mate."

Kym choked on the word 'mate,' a profound sorrow haunted his tone. Though he grew paler by the moment, she knew the pain that registered on his face couldn't entirely be blamed on his physical injury.

"Use Hani for your health while he is with us," Tryst advised.

"No need." Kym shook his head. "Fare well on your journey, One-Strike, Protector. I hope the answers you seek won't hinder your ambition."

As Kym turned away, Rebecca blurted, "Wait, you can't leave. What if you know something Tryst doesn't?"

Kym smirked. "Tryst knows everything. Keeping the knowledge of the packs is what he does – hence his title. May we meet again some day. And when we do, we shall have another match in the ring, yes?"

"Fine," Rebecca shrugged. Anger festered just below the surface: she wanted to hear the details of Kaece's history from the person closest to Kaece, and he shirked the responsibility.

Cheers erupted from the crowd once again as they passed through the village. Eventually, the cheers died off and the noise from the camp faded away.

The wind rustled the tall grass and eased wisps of pale clouds across the sky. Tryst's robes flapped in the breeze as he traversed further from the camp. Rebecca began to wonder where they were headed, and just how far from prying ears they needed to go before they could "remember" Kaece's existence. She realized the middle of nowhere wasn't their destination when she saw the Hadros.

She grabbed Tryst's arm and pulled him back. "Wait. We aren't going anywhere until you tell me everything."

"You said you were in a hurry." he explained, "I can answer your questions here. Once your curiosities have been satisfied, you'll be free to begin your journey without any further ado."

"Where is Sebastian's father?"

"We have not seen him, though there are rumors – simply rumors, mind you – that he is dead. Others have said he's a captive of the Supremacists. A few even whisper that the Maedian may be the one orchestrating the operation against his own people."

"He would never!" Sebastian exclaimed. "I received a message from him; he is being held captive."

Tryst shrugged. "Then you already knew more than we did."

"But where is he being held captive?" Rebecca asked, wishing Sebastian would let her handle things. "According to your rumors, that is."

"North, toward the coast. Then east, toward the Prism Forest. There, along the beach you will find a driftwood village. The Supremacists have claimed the coastline. Their territory spans from the foothills in the far west to the far east, where the Maedians' metal tracks mark Maedian territory. Our Lykos tribes are forbidden from either territory by the command of the Alpha Prime. The Supremacists have no qualms killing a Calyxist outside of sanctioned combat. The Supremacists view us Calyxists as Maedian-lovers, as inferior, as their enemy. If you cross into their territory, you are at their mercy."

"So he'd be in their village...? Or a cave, or what?"

"It is most probable that they harbor prisoners in the village. There are rumors that many Maedians are kept as slaves and abused greatly..." Tryst's weathered face creased with sadness, tears in his old eyes. "He may be among them. The Supremacist Lykos you asked of – she is their Alpha. That much is not rumor: she commands her forces to capture, rape, murder, and torture..."

His bluntness hit her like a slap in the face; Rebecca blinked against the shock. She expected to need to pry the truth from him. "Kaece?"

"Kaece was her name in youth," he confirmed. "Whirlwind was her title as Alpha. Crimson Whirlwind seems to be her salutation as the Supremacists' Alpha Prime. She has always been drawn to violence, her path is paved with anger and hatred. She blamed the Maedians for some of the more unfortunate happenstances that we must live with. There have been two sects of Lykos, two ideologies, since our ancestors first arrived on Xiratera after our banishment. Calyx was the Alpha Prime, a title he won with strength and wit. He left behind his wife, whom he loved dearly, in Maedia, and reminded us not all Maedians willed our banishment. Many Maedians fought for Lykos rights, and the followers of Calyx believe that we have brethren in Maedia.

"The Supremacists believed that Calyx was no more than a puppet, planted by the Maedians to keep us placated and naïve. They believed Lykos were the superior race and regarded the Maedians as cowards. They were quick to suggest retaliation for our treatment – there had been a Supremacist Alpha Prime not long before Timbercut's reign. Under his command, we were instructed to slaughter any Maedians who crossed into our territory. Though his reign only lasted a short time, the Maedians on this land feared us more than ever. The tension grew between the sects, Calyxists were uneasy with what had been done, while the Supremacists felt justified. Our tribes lived divided and restless, up until Alpha Whirlwind defeated Kym. Rather than commanding us all to do harm as the previous Supremacist Alpha had, she only took those who craved revenge, and decreed those who opposed it remain with Timbercut. For the first time, we had two Alpha Primes, and two disparaged territories. This separation is why we no longer consider her one of our own. It is by her will."

Rebecca's head spun, a confusing whirl of politics and static she couldn't think past.

"Wow! We had the evil mastermind with us the whole time." Alex blurted, "Talk about back-stabbing..."

"Do not make assumptions," Sebastian rebuked. "We do not have all of the information yet. The Drakeon would never obey a Lykos – you saw as much for yourself. Loremaster Tryst, what is the connection between Kaece and the Drakeon?"

"Hm. We believe the Supremacists and the Drakeon are working toward a common goal – eradicating all of the Maedians on the continent. They seem to have an alliance, though it is a fragile one at best - the Supremacists know they are as much a target as the humans to the dragons of this land, and the Drakeon, no offense to you, want utter dominion of this world."

Rebecca scowled.

Sebastian pursed his lips, his brow furrowed.

"We have to convince the Supremacists to stop helping them," Alex said. "If the dragons win, they'll totally destroy everything."

"Look, Tryst. This is important – why is Kaece doing this? You knew her once... Put Calyxists and all that aside. Why is *Kaece*, as a person, doing this?"

"I can tell you a story, if you like."

"Quickly," she sighed. "Please."

The old Lykos nodded. "One day, when she was a young pup – she couldn't have yet seen her fifth winter at the time – she came to me with tears in her eyes. She said, 'You know why everything is the way it is, right?' I told her I knew as much as there was to be told, and asked what she wanted to know.

"'Why must all female Lykos die?' she asked. I replied that all Lykos must die, that mortality is what separates us from the undead creatures of Thanos. Those tears fell and she shook her head, then she screamed, 'No! Males don't have to give birth.

260

Males get to die honorable deaths, not having litters too large for them to survive. We kill our mothers! I don't want Dara to die, Tryst!'

"You see, Dara was the midwife who raised many litters the age of both Kym and Kaece. She cared for them as her own pups, but she'd recently mated and was carrying a large litter of her own. The physical strain of the pregnancy kept her bedridden. Her chance of surviving the birth was very slight, and I suppose she'd just told Kaece as much. Here, I made the mistake of sparking the flame that became her burning hatred for Maedians.

"I said, 'Our creators created us in the image of themselves, crafted us from their flesh with the blood of the great wolf. But they did not have foresight when they used the great wolf's magic. His magic is what makes the females carry wolves, humans, and Lykos alike, often one or many of each. The size of a wolf's litter mixed with the size of human children too often results in a litter far too large for our human bodies to survive. We pay the price for our greatness with equal frailty, but you are wrong about one thing Kaece. Females do die honorable deaths. There is no death more honorable than one which brings life into the world. Dara is a great Lykos, and she will die as a great Lykos performing a great deed.'

"Then Kaece began to hit me. I allowed her to punch me repeatedly, passive for the sake of her own learning experience. When she finally stopped, I asked if venting her anger had made her feel any better. I could never forget the look in those golden eyes, the darkness in them when she looked up at me. I have no words to describe such a look. But she sensed my fear, and smiled a wicked smile. This young pup said, 'They made us to fight. If I'm going to die because of how they made me, then I'm going to die doing what they made me to do. If you were our creator, I wouldn't have stopped until you were dead.'

"Her words chilled my blood, but from that day she progressed as a rather normal young Lykos. Though she behaved more as a male when she could, our conversation seemed to be behind us. I knew she saw the female role as a curse of death, and she never mated with Kym in spite of how much she loved him. It seems as though her fear of pregnancy may have led to all of this. War is a temporary escape from her commitment, an escape she created for herself. She knows as well as Kym does, though, that they have a destiny so long as they both continue to live. She will mate with him, it is her fate."

"Fuck that," Rebecca spat. "If I want to find her, where would she most likely be?"

"She likely would have returned to her territory. Find the driftwood village."

"You heard him, Sebastian. Let's go."

Rebecca walked away, still feeling as though the past three days held little meaning. She'd lost precious time finding out that she agreed with Chupita about the Lykos – especially Kaece's 'mate.' If anything, she learned that Sebastian could never be more than a friend, but he would always be the best friend she ever had.

31

Kaece crouched in the shadow of a tree and watched the tide rise. Time, the supposed healer of all wounds, gnawed and distorted her sanity. Regrets filled her to the brim. The person she had once been no longer seemed valid, no longer seemed viable; how could she return to the life that she'd abandoned for Rebecca? She'd paced the beaches, mulling over her two choices: die alone, forgotten, or die as Fenris intended, as a warrior fighting for a better world. If the Supremacists lost the dispute, she would be remembered as the most frightening, vile monster ever encountered by Maedia. She would be written into the pages of their history as someone unworthy of kindness or love.

The village of driftwood structures built of bark-stripped logs as gray, as the sky above and ocean beyond, remained just as she saw it last. Territorial markings of urine soured air that stung with the metallic scent of fresh blood. The putrid odor of Maedian fluid and excrement overpowered the delectable aroma of sex and fear.

As she approached, a raven cleared the first line of roofs then dropped from the sky like the rock that had smacked it. She smirked, suppressing an amused chuckle at the unsuspecting creature's demise. It had been an idiot bird, fueled by that damnable Power of Madius, that had flapped its black wings across the Aver, only to die upon the Madius' hearth. The sky vermin had nearly managed to unravel the careful planning and render useless the precautions taken to completely erase Neo Maedia, uninhibited by the Maedians of the Empire.

The camp bestirred with fewer Lykos than she expected. Those who remained became alert and made themselves known, as she passed on her way to the Alpha's den. She heard every reverent whisper of her title: the fury of blood that paints the world with vengeance – The Crimson Whirlwind. They eagerly waited for the blood that she would spill when she confronted the false Alpha. She knew they wouldn't linger for fear of being swept up, losing life or limb, in the violent storm to come.

Merik Blackdeath waited for her in front of the Alpha's den. He grasped the decapitated, limp corpse of the dead raven in his dirt-caked claws. His lips smacked while he crunched the skull between his teeth. She envisioned dragging him by the tendrils of his matted hair to the surf and shoving his filthy face into the silt. She wanted to feel his body writhe, feel it succumb to her superior strength while he filled his lungs full of salt water and sand. Only after his last, subdued twitch, would she take his own scythe from his belt and slice open his throat. Her packmates would see the ocean turn crimson with his blood, staining the beach of Alpha Whirlwind's home with the color of life and death.

He took another obnoxious bite of the bird carcass. Without swallowing the grit, he spoke. Bits of bird spewed from his mouth with each word. "I see that look in yer eyes - thinkin' you're gonna take me down right here and now. Ya better think twice before ya act on it, Whirlwind. Ya've been gone for a very long time. Much has changed since ya were left for dead."

"Time has passed, as it does. There's nothing I couldn't learn, or guess. I know that Sow Endus wasn't completely destroyed - the Drakeon are unreliable. The ones working with you in Tekton clearly understood the concept of 'annihilation' better than the Hunter and Warrior at my side. I'll assume, the other targets fell jus' like Sow Endus and Tekton. Tekton - your assigned mission - was likely the most successful, and then ya stepped into my place, using the glory of that success as your crownin' token. Perhaps ya prepared and ordered another attack on the smaller town. Perhaps ya have done nothin'. Does it really matter? The point stands, your title has been claimed on false pretenses - especially if ya used the competence of our Drakeon allies to claim it. Submit or bleed out, Merik."

He dropped the remains and spit on the ground, then he belted out a mocking laugh. "We know where ya've been - with the Madius. Ya've spent months at his side. You assisted him in attacking our allies. Unless you're askin' these Lykos, the strongest and most intelligent of the Lykos, to follow the Madius, then it is *you* that needs to submit."

The surrounding Lykos listened, and sure as he spoke, she could sense the truth of his words. The whole pack believed her to be a traitor, a human-sympathizer - a Calyxist at heart. Kaece swallowed, despising the jab at her character. The Lykos could smell her fear, and the guilt of her betrayal.

"In order to track him, befriend him and capture him," she lied.

"Then where is he now?"

She licked her lips and smiled deviously. "On his way to us. Ya know this."

"And when he gets here I have orders to kill the Metakosmos children, and capt– oh, what was that?"

She'd flinched slightly; her heart had beat faster. As long as Kaece breathed, she would never allow him or anyone to harm Rebecca.

"I see now – ya've gone soft. The Whirlwind is but a light breeze. All ruckus but no real danger. You've gotten attached to a human. Why don't ya go take up your woes with your mate, I'm sure he'd understand."

The other Lykos seemed to enjoy his humor, but she didn't find it funny. "I'm no Calyxist, Alpha Blackdeath."

Bowing to the Lykos before her disgusted her as much as sharing a meal with the Madius, but she forced herself to stoke his ego and let him have the small victory. While he used the entire pack as leverage, she had little control over his reign.

His false title, rolling from her tongue, made him glow. "We expect to see proof. Everyone knows ya'd lie and kill to get what ya want."

"Rebecca, one of the Metakosmos, isn't human. She is as superior to them as we are, superior to us, even. She could defeat me, you, any and all of us. He doesn't know. Tell him. Tell him that she is unkillable. Tell him that when she dies, she just rises back from the dead, stronger than before. I witnessed it. Tell him that she is a valuable ally, but she must be converted."

"If she can survive being taken by all of us, then getting stripped of her skin and used again just for the bloody joy of it, then I'll tell him. I, of course, welcome you to join in the fun. Sounds like your kind of game, eh?"

"I do not wish to taste her wrath, my Alpha," Kaece forced herself to say through clenched teeth, "where is the rest of the pack? I count only eight."

"I've put extra guard duty on the facility since ya were out playing with the Madius. We don't need a dozen Lykos on this beach – they are in better use over there."

She disagreed. "If Alpha Timbercut sent three good fighters, this handful of Lykos would be slaughtered. Claw to claw, even a nomadic pack could conquer us while we are off guard. They're keeping track of our movements, don't think they don't pay attention."

"They aren't gonna attack us - they're pacifists! A couple of Lykos, now including the wholly stoppable Crimson Breeze, is more fortified than we'd ever need to be. It's the way I want to do things, and it ain't changing." The last came with an irritated snarl, the snarl of an Alpha whose word was law.

She bowed her head to him, "It's Whirlwind, my Alpha. My title came from a championship, and ya can't undo that unless, of course, ya wish to challenge me?"

He growled. "No, I have business to attend to."

"*Alpha Blackdeath*. I imagine the title ya hold from your Puppy Trial victory, in a year of illness, is not something you are eager to lose. I'd rename ya 'Stinky.'"

"You can't provoke me, Whirlwind. You'll get your challenge, but not until after I've reported. Ya can hold off, keep yourself alive, and away from humans for a day, can't ya?"

She huffed and left him. The other Lykos silently judged her as she passed; their mouths twitched and their eyes gleamed with contempt. The broken heart Rebecca had gifted her served as a badge of shame among the Supremacists.

The night descended on the beach; she sank into the shadows. The waning tide came and went, again and again. Out at sea, she heard the choppy voices of Merik and his mate, Lyriel. Then they were gone. Knowing what they had planned for Rebecca left her waiting for Merik's return. She needed to defeat him and return to her seat of power. That would be her redemption, and her only opportunity to protect Rebecca.

Faint whimpers of pain carried to her ears. The sound led her to the large chamber used to torture Maedian slaves. In the center of the room, too bloody and beaten to discern her features, a young woman hung with her feet barely touching the ground, her wrists secured to the central support pillar. The wood had long since blackened with the blood of the many Maedians tortured before her.

Kaece wiped a thick mixture of blood, semen, and sweat from the girl's face. Only the fresh layer came off with Kaece's touch. The Maedian shuddered, and her heart beat faster. This one had been abused past her breaking point.

She found the supply chest had been ravaged, likely by a nomadic pack, but plenty enough supplies remained. She tossed weapons and chains into the sand. She shuffled through containers of acids and poisons. The girl's fear rose; she panted in ragged sobs.

Kaece loved it once, the fear and the pain. Helpless Maedian terror once felt like a dark, delightful pleasure, but to her own disgust, she'd changed. They were right about her. The great Crimson Whirlwind had become nothing more than a zephyr. She hung her head, feeling remorse for herself as much as for the dying human. This victim, like the others before her, had been captured and tortured as if she had been the one to create the Lykos, and to banish them. The girl may not have even known what a Lykos was, or where they came from, but they'd punished her all the same. They'd used her screams to calm their pain. What they didn't realize, what she hadn't realized before Rebecca, was that no amount of vengeance could ever close the void born of betrayal.

When she at last found the bottle of cleansing fluid and a cloth, she proceeded to clean the grime from the girl's flesh. The wounds were great and numerous, from scrapes and bruises to gashes and burns: the girl had suffered for a long time.

"Please..." she begged in a hoarse whisper, "Please just end it."

Kaece responded by spinning the lock, as coded, open. The chains dropped away and the girl fell into her arms.

"I'm endin' it here. You're free, human-girl."

She lay limp and whispered the words Kaece had heard from so many others before her, "I want to die."

"Look, yer free, I'm not gonna hurt ya more. Ya came from somewhere, didn't ya? Don't ya wanna go home?"

Half starved and left naked, the girl's body felt nearly as cold as Rebecca's. Kaece lowered her to the ground. The girl was free, unchained, and instead of embracing her freedom she hugged her knees and stared at Kaece with unseeing eyes.

She gave the girl comfort in the form of gentle touch and sharing her warmth. The girl soothed slightly while Kaece gently stroked her arm. She'd hoped that she'd realize her freedom, form a reason to escape, and make for the door. The night passed along, but the girl soothed little.

Kaece felt a strange kinship with her as she realized that no amount of patience or time would lead to reason. She wondered aloud, "If ya give up, and ya just die here, then what? It's an eternal end; the dead can't accomplish anything. Why do we long to be undone in our darkest hours of self-pity? There's gotta be something worth living for."

"They killed everyone. They destroyed everything. I see them when I close my eyes. And when they are open I relive everything they've done to me. It's in me, it's a part of me... there is no freedom, not when the chains are inside. Death is the only escape. I keep waiting, but they won't kill me. You won't kill me."

"They say that from the deepest of wounds, comes the greatest strength. Your wounds give you strength, human." Kaece said the words, but she didn't feel strong for all her scars. She'd murdered, raped, and tortured with the strength of her wounds. Trust, faith and love had been far more transformative than all the power brought forth from her inner-strength. She held the girl's hand, reassuringly. "I'm gonna stay with ya until you're ready to go home. I'm not gonna kill ya. I know what happened to ya feels awful, but I can't undo it. No one can. The past is behind ya, I'll protect ya now."

The girl squeezed her hand and sobbed.

Kaece had known Lykos passed by the chamber throughout the night. She hadn't known they'd been spying on her until they closed in for the attack. She crouched, cursing the chamber's builder for making only one entrance.

Kevyn, a broad-chested Lykos, big but nearly brainless, stepped through the door first. Behind him came Autumn, a furry beast of a man with hair the color of dying leaves, and Rozco, Merik's runty littermate. The Maedian screamed and scurried to hide behind the pillar.

"Three? Is that all? Ya know I can kill three of ya with my eyes closed."

"Blackdeath said ya'd lost it. Didn't believe it till we heard ya whispering sweet nothings to the whore," Kevyn said.

The girl's gasps and cries created a palpable fog of terror, though Kaece, herself, felt no fear; she felt only the boiling rage that she had known her whole life.

"Funny, isn't it?" Rozco asked, taking a good long whiff, "They say they want to die, and yet they are still so afraid of it."

They stalked forward, spreading out.

Kaece casually countered, "She's not afraid of death, she's afraid of life. 'Cause life is its own form of torture, yeah? But you three... you're not nearly as afraid as ya should be... Unless you're eager to escape life too?"

"You can't even kill a pathetic injured human anymore, Whirlwind. Why would we be afraid of you? Calyxists are weak."

"But first..." Autumn snatched up the girl. Shrieks echoed into the night, abruptly cut off by a loud pop as he violently broke her neck. "Let's clear out the trash so we have room for your lover when she arrives."

Kaece dove at him with such speed that the Maedian's body hadn't yet hit the floor when her claws ripped through the underside of his bearded jaw. She clamped a fist around his teeth and pulled. Using herself as a counterweight, she swung him around. His jaw broke free, and his body slung into Rozco.

Kevyn slashed at her with his claws, but she moved quicker. She flung the useless flat-toothed jawbone at him, then dashed for a weapon. Her legs flew out from under her and she landed hard on her chest in the sand. Kevyn wrapped a heavy chain around his hand while she kicked at Autumn. With his claws buried in her unarmored flesh, and his face torn he looked like a monster from a pup's night tale. Blood rushed past his lolling tongue as he gurgled and howled. Kaece took hold of a rusty old dagger, just as she felt the muscle of her calf tear.

She screamed, thrusting the blade up into the gaping bloody hole of a face. His heavy body collapsed atop her.

Twisting and crawling, she managed to grasp a coil of razor wire, but not before a shackle smacked into her head. Spots flitted across her vision. She dizzily dodged the second swing of Kevyn's chain. It smacked into the pillar, which caused sand to rain down from the drift log roof. She quickly grabbed the end of the chain, and let Kevyn pull her to him. His wicked wolf grin melted into a grimace; his fate sealed when she whipped the razor wire around his arm.

She smirked at him before she tightened the wire and sliced the flesh from his bone. He wailed like a newborn and ran. Blood spurted, coloring the walls, the ceiling, the sand and the Lykos.

Rozco swallowed and circled wide around her. His confidence had waned, but he still stood to fight because other Lykos waited outside - she could sense them. She tried to stand, using the wall for support and shouting to distract from her mutilated leg.

"You all waitin' out there smell the blood? The Crimson Whirlwind is back, and I'm not gonna stop until all of ya are dead."

She stumbled, and he slashed at her with his axe. She move into his swing, up under his arms and held the wire tight. The axe nicked her cheek, but the razor-wire's bite stopped his attack short of her death. She charged, pushing him into the wall - rage giving her the strength she needed to ignore her wound. The wire split his throat from ear to ear, spraying blood all over her face.

She limped to the entrance. Outside, she could smell the others, but couldn't see them. Kevyn's oozing corpse lay face down. She cautiously knelt down at his side. He hadn't made it very far.

A bolt struck her. Howling at the pain of the wood shaft piercing her side, she ran for cover. Another bolt zipped past. Kaece rarely prayed, but a prayer came to her lips in the moment. She knew she wouldn't live to protect Rebecca, so she could only hope the ancestor spirits or gods cared enough to listen.

"Winds, take my love to her. I give my soul, my blood, my body for her safety. Please let her know, in her dreams, in her heart, that I loved her. The monster that I am... It wasn't all bad."

The bolts had been shot from a rooftop. The climb wouldn't be hard, and once she could see the device, she could dodge the attacks. She'd meet the shooter soon. Her time to die had come, but she swore that before she took her last breath and lay in her final resting place, the Crimson Whirlwind would soak the beach in the traitors' blood.

CHAPTER 32

From the moment she saw the water's edge, Rebecca frantically scanned the horizon, searching the land for any sign of civilization. The morning sun shone through a break in the clouds; a pillar of light cast down on the distant shoreline. As the Hadros sped toward the ocean, her heart jolted: what she sought came into view.

"I see it!" She called down the hatch.

Alex peered up at her, bracing himself on the ladder. "Do you want Sebastian to stop?"

"No. If the Lykos think we're going to plow through their village, maybe we can catch them off guard."

"Okay, I'll tell him." He disappeared from her view.

The desperation burning in her chest couldn't force the Hadros to charge forward any faster; Sebastian already pushed the machine to its limits. The gears gyrated, moving the mechanical legs up and down too fast to see the parts working to propel the machine. She adjusted her grip on the leather strap around her wrist, loosening her white-knuckled fist and trying to relax her tense muscles. Atop the Hadros, the ride was no different; inside and out, the metal body swayed like choppy waves on a stormy sea.

Haphazard buildings studded the grayish sand, the clumsiness of their construction more obvious as they drew near. Windblown sand filled large gaps between the driftwood structures. Rebecca imagined the dwellings served as poor shelter. Trails of dried blood and sun-bleached bones littered the beach. Other than the shreds of cloth that fluttered in the wind, nothing moved.

The Hadros jerked; the force of momentum threatened to burst the legs' hinges as the vehicle ground to a halt; the leather strap bit into her wrist. She hurried down the ladder and threw open the door. She broke into a run the moment her feet hit the ground; the power of Typhos coursed through her veins, her body driven by the need to rescue Kaece from herself. Behind her, Alex called for her to wait. Rebecca ignored the plea and drew her swords, knowing her brother and Sebastian would be in more danger if she didn't get to the Supremacists first. With Typhos' strength raging, she knew she could fell anyone who tried to get between her and Kaece.

The sight of a dead Lykos froze her mid-stride. The woman lay on the blood-soaked ground in front of a hut, her lifeless eyes staring up at the sky. Her throat gaped open, a ragged slit split apart by the weight of her head lolling back. Flies flitted in and out of the carnage.

"Kaece!" Rebecca called out.

She strained to hear anything over the wind; her eyes roamed over the blood splattered hut. The thirsty driftwood had absorbed so much blood that it seeped from the wood's pores like something from a horror film. A thickened red droplet fell from the rooftop and landed in the sand beside the corpse.

Rebecca sank the dagger end of her sword into the wood and pulled herself up to eye-level with the blood-slicked rooftop. Having found nothing, she dropped back down and continued her search for Kaece. The trail of blood led to a young male Lykos. He lay contorted awkwardly as if he'd fallen from the roof. His intestines, pooling under his body, smelled awful. Rebecca backed away.

"Hey Kaece!" Alex echoed. "We just wanna talk! Come on!"

"Go back to the Hadros!" She demanded, even though she couldn't see him amongst the clutter of buildings and gore. "Now!"

"Why?" He asked defiantly.

"Just do it!"

"Go wake Chupita," came Sebastian's voice. "I know the sun is still up, but we may need her. She has proven useful in seeking aid."

She found Sebastian. He looked at her with concern, his eyebrows arched and lips pulled into a cringe.

"You have blood on your hands," he murmured.

Rebecca looked down at her hands, then back to Sebastian. She knew some of it belonged to the woman, some to the young male, but the pit in her stomach told her that some of the blood belonged to Kaece. Tears stung her eyes. "Help me find her. I need to know she's not dead."

"I will search inside. Please be sure to stay within hearing distance, so we may alert one another of our findings, for better or for worse." He then ducked into the first of the ramshackle huts.

The many trails of blood led her around the outside of the huts: some smeared through the dirt, some had splattered.

She found another dead Lykos lying on his side; a river of blood seemed to flow toward his body from a wide opening in one of the largest buildings. Inside, the walls, ceiling, everything dripped with a thick mess of bodily fluids like some huge living creature had exploded. Rebecca stepped in far enough to inspect the female corpse: it wasn't Kaece. She couldn't even tell whether the girl was human or Lykos.

Disheartened, she left. She nearly bumped into Sebastian, who stood silent in wide-eyed horror.

"What?" She asked; fear shot down her spine.

"This Lykos brute died from a strange arm wound... the flesh is cut from wrist to elbow. The wound is deep enough to expose his bone..."

"Is that all?" Rebecca sighed. "I don't care about him. Have you seen any sign of her?"

"Nothing." Sebastian shook his head solemnly. His gaze redirected off into the distance. Alex had returned from he Hadros. They hurried to meet her brother in the middle of the bloody avenue.

"You brought Chupita? Hurry, put her down."

Alex unwrapped the blanket clutched to his chest. The once tea-cup chihuahua sized pup had easily tripled in size since the day Rebecca held her in that same fashion. Chupita's teeth chattered and clicked before her paws hit the ground; her hackles raised.

"I know it's bright out, Chupi," Alex consoled, kneeling down and stroking her coarse fur. "But, we need you."

"Yeah, I need you to find Kaece for me, girl. The Lykos. Can you find her?" Rebecca asked.

Chupita pawed at her own face, blinking rapidly against the light. She scratched around her eyes, ignoring Rebecca's plea completely.

"Please, Chupita?" She persisted.

The Haima Fox Demon only continued to hiss and bat at the blinding light in her vision.

Rebecca frowned, then yelled into the wind again, "Kaece!"

The silence bore down on her, the lack of response threatening to crush her very soul.

"This blood is pretty fresh," Alex observed. He pointed at the trail leading into the room Rebecca had searched.

"I don't want you looking in any of these buildings, Alex. There's a dead woman in there," she said. Then to Sebastian, "I think she might be Maedian."

"I can handle it," Alex quipped. "Better than you. Remember how *I* didn't run away from Tekton?"

Sebastian hushed them both, gesturing to Chupita. The demon's ears twitched and her head raised. She sniffed the air.

"She hears something," Alex blurted. "What is it, girl?"

Chupita barked, a meld of rapid clicks and a deep-throated growl, then she bounded toward the beach. Rebecca broke into a run after the little demon, her hope reignited that Kaece could be found.

At the ocean's edge, the small black pup slowed to check that they still followed, then hopped onto an eroded rock formation half-buried in the sand. Waves crashed against the rocks, sending spray over the lithe Haima Fox. Rebecca gasped when she caught up with Chupita – the demon led them to another Lykos, this one dead in the surf. Blood and gray matter trickled from his split skull; more blood ran from claw wounds in his chest.

Alex lifted a broken crossbow, nearly identical to the one strapped to his arm, out of the water. Sebastian asked him something she couldn't hear, while she clambered

271

across the algae-slick rocks after Chupita. Water lapped up around the tide rocks as she followed the demon. The rock formed a peninsula, but Rebecca wondered how long they had before the rising tide created an island.

Chupita stopped at the highest point of the rock formation, furthest out into the ocean. Between Chupita and Rebecca, the rocks dipped down into a steep slope that leveled to form a tide pool. The stagnant cloudy red water, murky and thick with blood, completely obscured the lower half of Kaece's body. Her head lolled back. Claw marks ran from her forehead to below her slack jaw. Nothing Rebecca could have imagined before, not even her death at Typhos' hands, hurt like the pain of finding Kaece's body. Her legs gave out and she fell to her knees next to the pool. Waves crashed against the rock, rolling in one after the other, showering them both with ice cold sea spray.

Tears streamed down Rebecca's face. She closed her fists around Kaece's soaked leathers and heaved her out of the water. Her tears fell faster; choked sobs burst from her when she saw the arrows jutting from her love's torso.

"Oh, Kaece," she sobbed, stroking Kaece's wet locks of hair. "Why...? Why did you have to leave me...?"

She pulled Kaece into her lap and rocked back and forth, hugging the cold body against herself. Rebecca leaned down and pressed her lips against Kaece's, wishing this wouldn't be their final kiss. She wished those lips would move, would kiss her back like she had kissed her before.

Rebecca sobbed harder. The wonderment of something mutual had been strangled by her own closet of insecurity. She would never know what it was like to share love openly, to experience the happiness such love could bring.

"First time ya push me away, second time ya cry. I must be a bad kisser," Kaece's hoarse voice rasped faintly.

Rebecca gasped, shocked to see the beautiful gold of Kaece's eyes peering up at her. "Kaece!" She kissed her again, then again, and again.

The Lykos started coughing, her lungs heaved and every breath sounded forced. Blood streamed from her mouth, flowing fresh. "Rebecca ya gotta listen, get far away from –" she coughed again, spitting blood that trickled down her chin. Her voice was nearly inaudible. "get away from here. I killed as many as I could but they want ya...they wanna..."

"I'm not going anywhere," Rebecca protested. She tried to stop crying, to stop choking on her strangled words. "I'm here with you until you aren't here anymore. I don't want you to die. I love you, Kaece. I want to be with you – in every way. My heart is yours."

Rebecca sealed her promise with another kiss, but Kaece didn't kiss back. The Lykos' eyes closed again; she wheezed – her whole body shuddered and convulsed with each breath.

"Kaece?" Panic swept over her anew, crushing the momentary respite from her worst fear.

"Oh my. This does not look good..." Sebastian said from behind her. "Would you like me to treat the wounds? It may... help."

She nodded, numbly moving aside while Sebastian pulled supplies from his side bag. Chupita helped him by nosing her way inside, then squeezing her too-large body into the bag and pushing the contents out. The supplies all looked totally foreign, instruments and bottles Rebecca'd never seen. She watched Sebastian gather a few items and felt useless.

"Please save her Sebastian, I'll owe you everything."

"She would fare better against the fates if she were in a medical facility, but I will do what I am capable of."

Rebecca looked out over the ocean. The water's surface churned up waves into the gray sky just like the ocean she'd gawked at in Thalassa Harbor. She flexed her fingers, remembering Sebastian telling her once about a medical facility there. "How far is Thalassa Harbor?"

"It is the closest civilization to us now. How did you know?"

She glanced back at him. His hands were coated in a mixture of blue fluid and Kaece's blood. "How close is it?"

"Three to four days by Hadros. Depending, of course, on the difficulties presented by the terrain. Travel along the shoreline is often very precarious and requires more diligence."

Rebecca looked down the coastline. The beach stretched out as far as the eye could see. At the land's edge, she could see Alex still standing ankle-deep in the incoming tide. He held the broken crossbow and stared out at the ocean. The water crept up his legs a little more with each wave; the spot where they'd been able to climb onto the rock formation was beginning to submerge in the surf.

"The tide is coming in fast," she warned.

"Then we will need to hurry. I am nearly finished. We will have to move her shortly."

Once his patchwork was complete, Sebastian instructed her on what to do. They arrived back on the beach and set Kaece in the sand. Her golden eyes focused on Rebecca, then unfocused. A glassy sheen overtook them as Kaece stared up at the sky, unseeing.

Sebastian rested his fingers against her wrist, checking her pulse. "She is not dead... Yet. She will not come back, though. She has fallen into the Lykos' regenerative coma – she will either begin to recover, or die. All that we can do at this point is to pray to the gods."

Rebecca nodded. She waited by Kaece's side, stroking her hair. Alex approached them, his gaze shifting out to the ocean every few moments.

"How is she?" He asked solemnly, but Rebecca could tell something different was on his mind. She couldn't expect him to really care — he had his own agenda for coming with them after the Lykos celebration, and she imagined it involved hunting the Drakeon.

"Not good. She's going to have to fight to survive, but I believe in her."

"Are we going to stay here?"

"No," Sebastian replied. "When Hesperis departs, so must we. There may be more of these Lykos lurking nearby. We would have disembarked on our travel to Thalassa Harbor if I believed it still stood."

Alex sighed and sat cross-legged in the sand. He laid the new crossbow out in front of him, tracing his finger up and down the brass stock. Rebecca frowned — the Lykos having Demarko's weapon meant there probably weren't any Maedians left to go to for help. She felt the hopeless weight of failure sinking in: Sebastian had failed his mission for peace on the continent just as surely as Rebecca failed to save Kaece. Everything that could've gone wrong, did.

"I think I know where your father is," Alex said after a stretch of silence. "Or at least where he was."

"I am not blind. There are more than enough human bones here, scraps of clothing lie everywhere. I have seen the birds, but please, tell me what I already know — he is dead." Sebastian's strained voice cracked.

Though Sebastian seemed to want to avoid becoming the next emperor, Rebecca thought Sebastian would make a great emperor; he was more intelligent than Demarko, and humbler than Kym.

"I swear I saw a dragon in the distance," Alex said, "There's an island or something out there. You can barely see it, but I know there's something — something big. And that's where the Lykos and Drakeon have to be meeting."

Rebecca squinted, looking into the distance. Was there an island out there? It seemed possible, but the overcast sky and rugged waves made it impossible to know. "I don't see anything."

"If you don't believe me, turn around and tell me why they've got those here."

She glanced back to where Alex pointed. Two large carved canoes leaned up against the side of a driftwood shack. She sighed, "I hate it when you're right."

CHAPTER 33

The sun sank lower in the sky, the shadeless light of high noon stretched into elongated shadows of afternoon. Gray clouds threatened to swallow up the fading light. Rebecca stood at Kaece's feet, trying to convince herself to accept the plan they'd spent hours deliberating over. Urgency pressed at her; it begged her to shrug off the potential of losing Kaece in a torrent of waves out on the open sea. Kaece's state hadn't changed – the Lykos still remained unconscious, unbreathing – while they concocted a plan to investigate the island. Her need to protect Kaece barred their ability to do little more than wait for night to set in and the Supremacists to attack; her need to protect Alex and Sebastian demanded she accompany them to the island. Her self-prescribed ultimatum, leave Kaece behind and lose her or take Kaece along and risk her life, rendered Rebecca powerless. Tears of frustration burned her eyes.

"We do not have to do this," Sebastian offered, touching her lower back.

Alex shifted his weight, his arms crossed over his chest, but remained silent. He wanted them to get to the island and finish their mission. Despite his determination, though, he never moved to rush them into action. Rebecca took comfort in the fact that neither of them pressured her to act faster, but she knew the rapidly setting sun left little room for procrastination.

Rebecca nodded to Sebastian, signaling him to help her move Kaece into the canoe that rested in the sand next to the ebbing tide.

"One-Strike!"

Shanan appeared from the driftwood village. She slowed to a jog as she approached; a male Lykos rejoined Shanan at her side from another avenue. They came to a halt a few paces away from Rebecca as Asher came from another side of the driftwood. Cloven hooves attached to furry legs hung from both of Asher's sides; Hani rode on him piggy-back.

"What are you doing here?" She asked, perplexed. When she left their village, she hadn't expected to see any of them again.

"My brother, Alpha Wildfire, and I wanted to help you negotiate," Shanan replied with a gesture to the male Lykos beside her. "You bested the Alpha Prime in battle, so if you want peace between us... Well, he must consider it deeply. But we want to be reunited with our estranged pack and knew you didn't have time to wait around for him to awaken and make a decision"

"And we woulda been right on yer tail if this overgrown goat hadn't insisted we'd need him after the dust settled," Asher added as he set the Satyr down. "Turns out it's already settled. All his weight slowed us down and made me miss the action."

"There is plenty of action to be had," Hani retorted with a wink.

Wildfire shook his head solemnly. "No, it looks as though there's nothing left to negotiate – Whirlwind betrayed the Supremacists and the blood storm has passed, it seems."

"She did," Rebecca confirmed. "But I don't understand. Did you guys come here looking for peace or a fight?"

Shanan replied, "Peace. But none of us, not even you One-Strike, could've expected Supremacists to come around without a little resistance."

"Right, but like he said, Kaece already took care of them. Can you help us save her life? There is no peace for me without her."

The Lykos looked at one another, exchanging a series of looks and gestures that implied they'd never before encountered a situation like hers. The Satyr stepped up beside Kaece's body and squatted down. He rested his chin in his hand, his elbow on his knee, and peered at her thoughtfully. His lips twitched, his jaw tightened, then he sat back on his haunches and shrugged his shoulders. The tension in his face and body relaxed and Rebecca had no idea what kind of conclusion he'd drawn.

Shanan knelt down too and laid her ear to Kaece's chest. She listened only for a moment before she looked to Rebecca and shook her head.

"Nothing?" Rebecca's heart plummeted into the pit of her stomach, extinguishing the flame of hope their arrival had forged.

"We'd have dragged her off the battlefield and left her to die in this state. It is an honorable death, One-Strike."

"No!" She all but screamed. "Think. Please. What if this was your Alpha? What if it was Kym? You wouldn't just drag him off to die, would you?"

Again the three Lykos exchanged a look, then all three nodded.

"She doesn't feel any pain while she's in the coma," Shanan offered, trying to console Rebecca as if their answer should be readily accepted. "She'll die peacefully."

Wild-eyed, Rebecca sneered at Shanan. Anger burned in her chest – what good were the cavalry when they charged in too late to fight and too agreeable to ward off death?

"What do you have to offer in trade?" Hani inquired casually. "I could, possibly, with the utmost of physically draining effort and self-sacrificing mental exertion, not to mention strenuous exhaustion of my magical healing energies, have a chance at revitalizing this dying Lykos' soul into her usual Lykossasity."

"Anything you can do, please. Do it."

"Well, the ritual will not be cheap, nor easy, for me. I can't do it without a reasonable trade of goods."

"You can have anything I have," Rebecca agreed. She had nothing of real value. With shaking hands, she took out her earrings and unfastened the wolf pendant from around her neck. Then she held the jewelry out to the Satyr.

"You're gonna charge her after I dragged your sorry butt all the way out here on my back? You selfish weasel." Asher scowled.

"Yes." The Satyr said simply as he took the offering. He inspected the silver chain closely, then the pendant, then he bit down on each. "These are something. But I need more."

Rebecca frowned and patted herself down. Nothing. Only the canvas belt around her waist, which held the magical pouch with invaluable swords, remained. She looked to her companions, hoping their answer might be different. "Alex? Sebastian?"

"That's a deal," Hani chirped before either of them could speak. "Add in Sebastian with the silver and I'll have this Lykos up and about faster than an antelope on the run."

"I beg your pardon," Sebastian protested. "You cannot own people – human beings are not trade-able commodities. Although, I am sure I have something of value to you on the Hadros."

"Silly prince," the Satyr chuckled. "I don't want to own you, I merely want to borrow you for my pleasure – say, for one single occasion? You're a very attractive young Maedian man, why, the sheer adventure of –"

"Woah! No! Sebastian would never, ever do that. He's got the Power of Madius, and he'll use it to make you do what Rebecca wants if you don't just agree."

"Shut up, Alex," she snapped. "Sebastian can speak for himself, okay? I'm sure he's got something other than his cute butt to trade."

"Hmmm." Hani examined Sebastian closely, eying him up and down as he circled around them. Her level of discomfort rose as she watched him oggle Sebastian, who stood by in silence as if contemplating the demand. Then Hani's eyes shifted to Alex, roaming over her little brother's body too. Rebecca's anxiety spiked; she wished Sebastian would actually use his Power for once – or at least come up with something else to charm the Satyr into compliance.

"Perhaps the boy?"

"Dream on," Alex scoffed.

"Then we're back to the beginning again, aren't we? I will need more than the silver."

Rebecca's jaw tightened; her eyes stung with tears that threatened to spill over; her heart ached with anger and defeat. The stupid gay Satyr didn't care about helping her, and her friends didn't care enough about Kaece to save her if it meant doing something gay. Why hadn't she kept the diamond-studded engagement ring Brad had given her? At least bartering it for the life of someone she loved would've put it to use.

Hani inserted himself into the long silence. "My material costs are covered by the silver. For my labors, however... I would suppose a full night with a man of such importance is too high a price. I can be reasonable, I will lower my demand to a single, willing, kiss."

Sebastian nodded without hesitation. "One kiss as compensation upon our return and we see that the Lykos is in full health, as promised. She must recover completely, and be the same Maedian-hating scoundrel that Rebecca cherishes so dearly."

Alex's lip curled in disgust, but the Satyr clapped his hands together, with an excited twinkle dancing in his eyes. "Wonderful!"

"Are you sure you can heal her?" Rebecca pleaded.

"This location is an exquisite place for the ritual I'll need to perform. Supposing I have an extra pair of hands to assist with some of the heavy lifting," at this, Hani gestured to Kaece's body. "Then I am sure, yes."

"Here?" Rebecca gestured widely, indicating the blood-splattered village. "She said I was in danger here. That has to mean more Supremacists could come any minute – Shanan, can you guys wait with Hani? Do what you came to do and negotiate with them, and if that doesn't work... Protect Kaece?"

"It would be an honor, One-Strike. Neither tooth nor claw shall harm her while we still breathe." Wildfire assented. At his command, the three Lykos bowed their heads to Rebecca.

The Lykos' reassurance helped soothe her anxiety about leaving Kaece's side, but it didn't erase it completely. The unfairness of having to separate after such a short time together disturbed her as greatly as watching Hani snap off the arrow shafts protruding from Kaece's body. The Satyr worked with diligence, but no care. The wounds began to bleed anew and Rebecca knew she needed to leave. Whatever came next would crack through her calm state of shock, would render her a useless, sobbing mess that could do nothing beyond cling on to Kaece's fading life.

They collected the oars from their distorted place in the sand, then lugged the canoe out into the surf. Sebastian climbed in as the siblings guided it deeper. Once neither could hold their footing against the force of the tide, both Alex and Rebecca clambered into the boat. The same tidal pull helped them drift toward the island with little need to row. The oars served more as guides to keep them facing forward as the canoe bobbed along the choppy ocean surface.

Rebecca noticed the dragon at the same time Alex did; he cursed under his breath. The scaled beasts watched their approach from the clouds as if waiting to swoop on them like vultures on a wounded animal. Ahead, more of the Drakeon Betrayers paced along the water's edge.

The glowing amaranthine color of one dragon's eyes struck a chord deep in Rebecca's chest. She swallowed back the lump in her throat, the choking anger that roused Typhos' passion inside of her veins. They had no excuse for their actions – Typhos would never have condoned such senseless destruction. Righteous anger burned in her core; her nerves tingled with anticipation. She reached for her swords. Her hand hovered just above the magical sheath as she stared back into the eyes of the Hunter that destroyed Sow Endus.

CHAPTER 34

"Cowards," Alex growled. "I wish they had the guts to come face us out here. If we could get 'em in the water, just for a second, they'd be powerless."

"We are nearly close enough to use the Power of Madius," Sebastian mused.

"Yeah, if they don't have earplugs it'll work. You oughta make them walk into the water!"

The dragons paced along the rocky shore. The jungle-like trees set back on the island shook; dense green foliage trembled. As the canoe drew nearer – near enough for Sebastian to use his power – Rebecca heard fragments of Drakeon thoughts.

"Hold the boat steady. I can call out to them from this distance. They should be able to hear me." Sebastian stood up in the canoe. "Drakeon! You will not harm us. You will step away from the shore, and allow us safe passage onto the island. You will allow us to speak to your leader!"

Do as he says. Move away, let them believe we're under his control.

Moments after the command echoed in her mind, the Drakeon stepped back from the shore as if opening a path to the heart of the island.

"It worked!" Alex exclaimed, "Now make them walk into the water."

"I won't," Sebastian said. "I cannot use my power to kill. As much as I may have the desire to, I simply cannot do it."

"It may not *kill* them. Besides, it's not your problem if they happen to die 'cause they're bad swimmers."

"That is the very logic that has justified such practices as banishment – the practices that have made the Lykos our enemy and instigated this entire ordeal. While I am the one who controls the Power, I will not use it to kill, whether it be directly or indirectly."

"The Power doesn't work on them, so it doesn't matter either way," Rebecca interjected.

"Sure it does. Look. They just did what he said." Alex grabbed the oars as if pointing out the obvious validated him. He began to row the canoe toward the island, but Rebecca rowed the opposite direction. She wanted to hear more of their thoughts, know their plan, before her foolish brother forced her into action, again.

They know the power did not affect us.

The Lykos must have told them.

They can't escape now.

We'll kill the Lykos soon.

Capture them.

The disembodied voices jumbled together, a confused mesh of conversations Rebecca struggled to sort.

"Sit down," she snapped at Sebastian. "Something's about to—"

A howling wind kicked up, drowning out Rebecca's warning. Sebastian teetered off balance and landed hard in his seat. The canoe rocked as a wave slammed against the side. Alex yelled out to lean against the rocking boat. Their weight countered the wave, keeping them afloat. Then another wave crashed into them, the momentum throwing them toward a churning whirlpool near the shore.

The boat capsized, the tail end pulled under as the nose raised into the air. Rebecca clung to the sides, abandoning the useless oar. All of their weight bore down on Alex, who held on against the crushing force of the undertow and his companions' bodies. Rebecca tried to brace herself to keep from smashing him. The pull of the swirling water shifted and the force of the momentum changing direction flung them up and out of the canoe.

Rebecca tumbled across rocks. She gripped damp blades of grass in her fist, dazedly trying to figure out how they were on land. An enormous Drakeon claw had pinned her to the ground.

He did say the child was of little importance.

Two of the Drakeon flanked her little brother. She heard them laughing at his attempts to shoot them.

We could report a regrettable casualty and enjoy tearing his flesh from his bones. He does look pleasantly tender.

Rebecca recognized the voice. The Drakeon above her was the same as the cruel dragon who wanted to kill the Lykos. The rune of Force blazed across his chest, an intricate pattern similar to Magnus.

"How did you know they were about to attack?" She heard Sebastian call out to her.

As the Drakeon from the sky circled closer, coming in for a landing, she groped for her swords. Her arms, still pinned by the sadistic Warrior, couldn't reach far enough; her fingers couldn't slip into the magical sheath at her waist. *Move,* she growled to the dragon. The Drakeon Warrior's attention faltered, shifting to her. His purple eyes held only confusion.

Fight, and you will die. Cower, and you will die. The Seal on Typhos' tomb has been broken, it is I who will bring the worlds together and restore the Dragons to their rightful place. Now move – get your talons off me.

The dragon's eyes widened, alight with the same shock of the first Drakeon Betrayer.

That came from you?

I said, get your claws off me! I am the Protector, chosen by Typhos.

The dumbfounded Drakeon lifted his hand. Rebecca stood and dusted herself off dramatically, imagining that Zakhar, if he were trapped in a human body, would do the same.

All of you, come look at this now. This human claims that Typhos' seal has been broken.

280

Rebecca tried to hide her embarrassment; she'd intended to project her message to the entire group.

"Watch out!" Alex shouted, firing bolts at the dragons closing in around her. "Rebecca, duck!"

"Quit wasting your ammo," she yelled back. The dragons didn't scare her, but the idea of Alex getting his arm eaten off because of his annoying toy gun did. "We can handle this without shooting anyone."

Transform.

Agreement resounded throughout the semi-circle of dragons.

"I can't." Rebecca unzipped her hoodie and peeled it off to reveal the glowing band of tribal fire licking up her arm.

The collective gasp of surprise quickly gave way to argument.

No markings so extensive have existed for many centuries.

It's a trick. She isn't a dragon — she can't transform!

Look. The mark is just like that of Typhos. It is of living ember — she has the power.

A human could not contain the power of Typhos. She can't.

We have no proof Typhos' tomb has ever been breached. It will never open, the power lies dormant.

Typhos has abandoned us all.

Then how does she recite his prophecy to us?

Does she?

"I have more than just the rune of Truth," she added. She unsheathed the artifact blades and held them up. "These were forged by Typhos himself. For me."

Impostor! Speak in Drakeon, as he claims you can. Repeat the prophecy, if you know it.

Rebecca sighed. She knew the prophecy by heart, but she didn't know the meaning of the words, they only asked her to repeat it, not to understand it. She concentrated on projecting her voice outward, imagining it booming and powerful like Elder Zakhar's when she heard him for the first time.

Without their magic, Sauros are destined to rest as nothing but bones embedded in rock. Without our magic, Dragons will fade from power. Even the weakest of creatures will rule over the former gods of this world. And creatures there will be many of in the years to come. Fight, and you will die. Cower, and you will die. Kill only those that already walk the path of death. Dragon-kind will cease to exist, if you do not heed this: When the Drakeon fall to darkness, when warm-blooded creatures control the world, you must open the seal on my tomb. All who enter will perish. The one who breaks the seal will release my power. They will bring the worlds together, and restore the Dragons to their rightful place. If the seal is not broken, the warm-blooded creatures will destroy both worlds. All will die.

When she finished reciting the prophecy, she knew her Drakeon voice had been heard; several of the Betrayers bowed to her. She felt awkward for a moment before she steeled herself: A leader, she knew, should expect respect. She needed the Drakeon to believe she commanded all the power of Typhos and had the strength to use it.

281

Get up, you fools! This proves nothing.

Confused shock laced their chaotic flurry of thoughts. They all felt the weight of their betrayal, guilt for destroying the lives of those who flourished rather than only those who walked a path of death. These Drakeon had given up on Typhos, felt abandoned by the millennia spent in his absence. Many refused to take sides; few justified their ways and tried frantically to retain their control.

Enough! Rebecca interjected. She had to protect the Drakeon that would follow her and support her effort to fulfill the prophecy. *This is your final warning. Turn away from the path of senseless destruction you're on, or I will destroy you all – if I must.*

The Hunter from Sow Endus laughed openly at her threat. *Bring your worst, little Typhos. With no Drakeon form, you cannot win a fight against Drakeon.*

Rebecca raised her swords – she knew the Hunter wouldn't hesitate to fight. As she moved to bring the blades up, they pulled against her until she dropped her arms back to her sides. The weight in her swords lifted – then like the counter-swing of a pendulum, the momentum of her swords guided her arms. The weight eased, then renewed in full force that begged her body twist in another direction. Each urge she succumbed to birthed a new, inexplicable, desire to move with her weapons. The swords beckoned her, pulled her into an intricate dance that left trails of magic in her wake.

As Rebecca allowed the magic to overtake her, an overwhelming sense of calm sank into her core. Her arms and legs moved with the power of Typhos in broad, yet controlled motions. Every extension of her body, each contraction of her muscles, amplified the nirvana that muddied the world around her.

Drakeon magic.
We will follow you, Typhos.
Idiots! This girl is not Typhos.
It was our mistake... We have done great harm, we will protect the humans if that's your desire.
I'm going to kill her – you will all see how she's tricked you.
Can't you feel it? This spell is unlike any I've seen. It will destroy us all...
We repent!

The Hunter reared his head; his jaws spread wide. *Crawl back into your grave, Typhos. This is our world now!*

Blazing embers spread across the Hunter's marking, the Drakeon magic breathing life into a fireball. Typhos' power guided her swords, urging her to move faster than the languid, trance-like sway of the dance. She raised the blades and crossed them in front of her face; she didn't shy away from the molten mass speeding toward her.

The fireball crashed into her swords; the viscous sphere erupted into droplets of flame that absorbed into her blades. Heat shot through her arm; her tattoo flared to life as the power of Typhos consumed the Hunter's fire. Pillars of white-hot steam burst

282

from three of the Drakeon. Those dragons exploded into clouds of ash that billowed out into the sky and fluttered down to settle on the eight surviving Drakeon.

Loud cries of repentance filled her head; the pleas flooded her mind, a ruckus of voices she couldn't decipher. None seemed hesitant any longer and each message carried the same meaning.

Let us live as Drakeon once more.

Forgive us, Typhos!

"I'm not Typhos," Rebecca replied as she sheathed her swords. "I am the one that Typhos entrusted with the power to save the Drakeon from their fate. I am Rebecca, the Protector, and I speak for Typhos now. If you truly repent, you will return to Drakeon Peak. Tell the Warlord that I have destroyed the true Betrayers. Share all that you have witnessed today, and ask Elder Zakhar to once again consider you Drakeon. Tell the Elder you agree to suffer any fate he deems fitting of your actions.

"When I need you, I will call upon you. For now, you must leave before I begin to regret my decision to spare your sorry hides."

Thank you for saving us, Rebecca, the Protector!

You will not regret it.

We'll do everything you ask.

The Drakeon lowered their heads, bowing to Rebecca once more. Then each spread their wings and took flight. As they ascended, a wave of relief washed over her — they'd managed to avoid a bloodbath.

Wait! She called out to the departing dragons. *Are there any more Drakeon Betrayers?*

One, Protector. He watches over the caves we dwelled in — before the increase in guard was required.

Tell the Elder all are accounted for — the warrior is dead.

As the Drakeon disappeared into the horizon, Alex shouted, "You told me you weren't a dragon! You're a liar."

She turned to her little brother. His eyes glistened with tears and anger. He crossed his arms over his chest. Sebastian stared, his face blanched and his jaw hanging open. He looked like he'd seen a ghost.

"I said that I was still me," Rebecca assured them both. "I never said anything about what I wasn't. Besides, I *am* still me, which was the truth. I'm just me with Typhos' power. I didn't even want it, by the way. He was supposed to just kill me like every other ritual sacrifice."

Alex shook his head, his pout unwavering. "You're nuts."

"Which is — apparently — the exact reason Typhos picked me. The reason why we were brought to this world. If I wasn't crazy, I couldn't have saved us from certain death."

"A second time," Sebastian added. His pallor seemed just as permanent as her brother's frown.

Rebecca placed her hand on Sebastian's shoulder. She looked into his icy blue eyes, knowing that he would see the Drakeon purple of the dragon god in her own, and asked, "Are you going to be okay with this?"

He nodded. His Adam's apple bobbed as he swallowed some emotion – fear, uncertainty?

"Are you okay with me being part Drakeon? Speak. You're freaking me out, I need you to *tell me* you're okay. I need you to be okay with it."

Sebastian hesitated, then nodded again. "I feel as though I should have known. Perhaps, I did. As you said, you are still yourself. It is simply a lot to take in, logically, that you have spoken with – perhaps have more intimate of a relationship with – a beastial god that I had believed was mere fiction... But your 'side-effects,' as you called them, are quite convincing evidence – remarkable, really – and are more than a little mind-boggling. What could this all mean?"

"I don't know," Rebecca shook her head. "But I'm sorry. I should've been more open with you. I just didn't know what to think. I didn't want you to judge me poorly for being not-quite-human, since you hated Kaece so much..."

"I cannot say I would have taken the information well," he agreed. "But *what* are you, exactly?"

Rebecca frowned. His question demanded she find a label for herself, a word so that he could categorize her in some way. She shifted uncomfortably – she wouldn't have an easy time trying to find a neat sticker to make herself easily identifiable. "Now doesn't really seem like the time to figure that out. I only know what Ardin could guess at based on the prophecy and what I remember from before I died... We can talk about that stuff later, after we've managed to find the Lykos and whatever it is they're guarding. Are you with me?"

Alex interrupted right as Sebastian murmured a quiet assurance of help. "What, don't you even care if I'm okay with you being part dragon?"

"No, because you're not okay with anything I do. I don't expect that to change now." Rebecca rolled her eyes.

"That's not true."

"Really? You didn't like me dating Brad; you freaked out when you thought I was trying to kill myself. You didn't like me relaxing on the Hadros, and yet you got pissed off when I actually went out into the world. Tell me, exactly why would me dying and being reborn half-dragon be acceptable in your book?"

"Because it's cool," he replied defiantly. "I'd kill to be a half-anything..."

Rebecca raised her eyebrow, then gestured toward the thicket leading to the center of the island. "You may get your chance, you never know. Let's keep moving - we have a mystery to solve so I can get back to Kaece."

287

288

292

293

294

295

XXXVI

Time passed. His thoughts circled endlessly, like the ouroboros that consumes its tail. In seclusion, his thoughts alone would drive him to the madness that precluded death. Sebastian collapsed against the wall, his legs exhausted from pacing. The solid iron cell remained dimly lit, brightened by an artificial light that stripped him of any sense of day or night. Without dawn or dusk, he could not accurately mark time's passage, though he estimated many days had come and gone since his imprisonment.

His only sense of a world beyond the iron cage was a barred vent at the apex of the vaulted ceiling. The incessant cawing of ravens that roosted in the vent served as nothing beyond a vexatious reminder of his foolhardy venture to Xiratera. Periodically, as if on a timer, a fan would whir to life inside the duct and force air into the cell. When the fan clicked on, it pulled a raven from its nest and the confused creature plunged into the room to ultimately suffer the same dark fate he expected for himself.

Stephan Madius lay dead on a filth-laden cot. His body, in the latter stages of decomposition, bordered on recognizable. Sebastian was as certain of the corpse's identity as he was that he, too, would decay in the very same cell. Even in death, his father's hair, unkept from long months of imprisonment, held the color of wheat turned gold by the last rays of sunset. The silver embroidery, which gleamed even through the layers of filth in his once-white silk, betrayed his royal heritage. The tattered sleeves of his garment confirmed Sebastian's suspicion about his father's plea for help.

"Why did you send for me? Why summon for help in such a hopeless situation? I would not have lured others to this wasteland of refuse and mutiny. I wonder if you called me here with the sole intent for me to perish beside you. You knew of my wanderlust, of how deeply I wished to explore this land. Why would you to want to see me dead, father? Because that is what you have done. You have ensured that you will not have died alone. The future of Maedia, our entire family line will end here - with us."

No Lykos or Maedian had set foot in the chamber since his arrival. The air thickened with the musk of rot as the artificial breeze ebbed into stillness. A heaviness borne of festering disease encumbered his lungs. Certainly, Sebastian thought, his father died at the hand of illness. The trapped raven battered itself frantically against the ceiling, looking for the opening that had sequestered it to Sebastian's prison. He wondered how long the raven his father sent to its death had done the very same thing.

His father's robes were in such a state that many ravens, he supposed, had been given cloth and commanded to cross the Aver. Stephan's army of messenger fowl were marionettes, completely bereft of their own will to reclaim the freedom that their escape awarded them. As were the Maedian slaves on the other side of the prison walls. The Maedians, however, had fallen victim to a force much more heinous than a man's final

297

act of desperation. Only one other person on the continent possessed the Power of Madius: Overseer Clay Demarko.

The man Sebastian had admired, perhaps envied, had methodically plotted the demise of his own territory. He had sought the enemies of Maedia, allied with the cruelest of Lykos, and turned his brilliance toward the endeavor of bringing war upon the very people he swore an oath to protect. Sebastian shuddered. The last time they had seen one another, Demarko had looked beyond him as if entranced, and he warned Sebastian to leave or die trying. He envisioned the fate Demarko must have been subtly suggesting to the Lykos strapped to the Hadros' roof. It felt inconceivable that, flying overhead on a Pegasus, Demarko had been oblivious to her existence.

Sebastian sighed and rested his head between his knees. Comprehension of the past in retrospect offered no solace in the isolation of his cell. The foreboding that plagued him since their ascension of Drakeon Peak weighed heavier on his shoulders as certainty of his demise in putrid captivity reached insurmountable heights. He wondered if some part of him had known from the beginning that his quest was fated to end in tragedy. Even his earnest attempt at romance amounted to torment. A deep scar born of Earth's violence tore into the Metakosmos' souls. If they still lived, he did not know, but if so, he believed that nothing could undo the hurt caused by such an environment. Their culture seemed obsessed with justification and rationalizations for harming others as a mode of personal satisfaction. Rebecca, though she excelled at masking her iniquity, had revealed the true extent of the Other Side's contamination when she'd forced herself upon him during the Lykos' festival.

Sebastian scrambled to his feet when light from beyond the iron walls spilled into his chamber. A female Lykos stood in the doorway. She held out her clawed hand, a gesture to leave the cell and follow her. Without question, he obeyed. He would do whatever she required of him, so long as it would keep him from the endless torment of seclusion.

"Ya try anything to save yourself or your friends and I'll break each of your joints myself."

He nodded a mindless assent and hurried after her, down a corridor. The striated organic stone walls narrowed around them as the Lykos guided their way.

At the top of a stairwell carved of the same stone, a bronze door opened to a large room. Heat blasted his skin and made his eyes water from the febricity. Within, tremendous forges burned hot. Maedians smelted ore and shaped the cooling metal into parts. His Lykos captor led him past the workers without heed of their presence, and to another bronze door.

Beyond the door lay a massive storage warehouse. The room held ropes and siege ramps, as well as strange flying machines and ros, that had been weaponized by mounting cannons or catapults to their bodies. Sebastian understood without a word spoken that these were all supplies for Demarko's revolt. The Overseer sought a war with Maedia.

Pipes ran along the walls and ceiling. A glass chamber loomed over the air-tight door. Cube-shaped, enormous, and unlike anything Sebastian had ever seen, the chamber allowed daylight to seep in the storage warehouse and stretched beyond the wall into the forge room from which they had come. It was bracketed in bronze, and appeared to be constructed of borosilicate - glass meant to withstand extreme pressures, temperatures and impacts like those one would encounter in the ocean's depths. Inside the glass, chains and belts connected gears to a mechanism. The centerpiece of the chamber was a platform upon a many-jointed ros arm.

The two Metakosmos waited directly below the glass floor, guarded by a single Lykos. Muscular and clean cut, the Lykos wore a sleeveless body suit made of leather. Rebecca had tied her jacket around her waist, but it failed to hide her bare legs or undo the tattering of her shirt.

"Now we wait."

The female Lykos shoved Sebastian up next to the Metakosmos, then took up her post beside the male Lykos. Rebecca patted Sebastian's shoulder.

"What was in the room? We had jail cells. With rats."

"Nothing except my father. He has passed on. Do you know what it is, exactly, that we are awaiting?"

"I don't know, but I really wish I had my pants... or at least my belt."

"Stop jabbering, prisoners. You'll see soon enough."

"I'm sick of being a prisoner. Why should we even listen to you anyways? You killed Sebastian's dad! You ruined the story! We were suppose to save him, and reunite Sebastian's family! Now we're just... Trapped."

The female Lykos pointed upward in response to Alex's accusations. Overhead, a black pegasus pranced across the top of the glass. The gears and chains along the sides of the box began moving and the ceiling of the chamber split into two panes. The panes dropped slowly in mirrored arcs, down and inward, until each rested against an inner glass wall.

"It took him long enough. These Grufoi are worthless for getting quick responses."

"Don't tell him that - hah. He prizes the dumb flying beasts. Won't even let us kill 'em. I bet they taste amazing."

The metal contraption unfurled and stretched vertically until the platform disappeared from sight. It returned, carrying Overseer Clay Demarko. As he descended he moved a lever and the two halves of the ceiling rose to meet one another, sealing him inside of the impenetrable cube.

Rebecca grumbled about never having trusted Demarko. While seeing the man Sebastian had once revered did indeed make him feel quite ill, he also succumbed to the curiosity of how the man had not fallen, but rather, willfully jumped, into dereliction.

"I see he is engaging some kind of voice amplifier... We will be able to hear his words, but will verbal communication be mutual? Will he hear what I have to say?"

"He can hear whatever he wants to hear, he's got the whole building hooked up to that box. He coulda listened to your insane ramblings in the Madius cell, if he wanted to."

The Power of Madius traveled through sound, requiring no other medium to be effective. Demarko could control every Maedian throughout the complex with a single command, all from the safety of his glass chamber in the sky. The implication of the Lykos' intel seemed too immense to fully comprehend.

Demarko gazed at them coldly, unmoving. His appearance had not changed since last they met. He bore the same wild hair and dirty workman's coveralls. The sole difference in the Overseer was that he appeared sober. When he spoke, his voice resonated throughout the gigantic room.

"Well, you have made your point, my Prince. You survived the Drakeon and traveled the length and breadth of this godforsaken continent until you found the cause behind its unrest. I must congratulate you on that small success."

"You could have made my journey considerably shorter, Clay."

"If you had heeded my advice and returned on that ship, you would be safe in Idan by now. You would be ignorant to this loathsome business, just another deaf ear for our cries to fall upon. You had a choice to act in your own best interests, and you chose instead to meddle."

"As Overseer, you were entrusted with this land. You were appointed by the royal committee and given the Power of Madius and the authority of the Empire to allow you to lead with sensibility and justice. You have abused your power in the worst way possible, and you will gain nothing out of doing so. Even if I die by your hand, just as my father did, it will not end here. You will not succeed in overtaking all of Maedia, not even with your machines of war. No misguided alliance with the sentient beasts of Xiratera could ever earn you an empire."

"You've built a false assumption, fool boy. I do not want to rule Maedia."
Sebastian stood in dumbfounded silence.

"Then why the hell are you killing your own people?"

"And building tanks and guns. This room is all about combat stuff!"

"Alex, you are a very clever boy. I am building an army, but that's a recent development. When Old Maedia realizes they are no longer receiving supplies from Xiratera, they will come to investigate - and they will die. This land is nothing more than a yet-uncharted level of Hades. It is not fit to be civilized. We would do better to leave it to the beasts. My plan is to ensure desolation is Xiratera's fate. Going forward, any Maedian who sets foot on this continent will cut us down to conquer it or die trying. It will be recognized and told by all to be the place of nightmares it truly is, and thus no human will ever again be forced to live in this heinous land."

Spit frothed around his mustache and splattered in droplets upon the glass pane overhead. Sebastian watched, perplexed as Demarko continued his monologue in tones of bitter remorse resembling his drunken ramblings.

"In coming here, I lost everything. This continent is cut off from communications. The arts, education, and literature - the very culture of our homeland. It is nothing but a factory for destruction. We farm the lands, mine the ore, and harvest the trees. Then all the materials we have gathered are sent to the mainland to feed its gluttonous appetite for resources. And what do we receive in return? Nothing.

"The children of this continent are all but illiterate. Xiratera's only school, in Thalassa Harbor, is designed to teach labor-intensive trade skills supplemented only by laws and values meant to mold the people into compliant workers for the benefit of their privileged, well-educated counterparts in Old Maedia. That is not an education. The people of this land are not Maedians. Before I ever touched their minds, they were akin to the risen dead. Your grandfather, the glorious Dorian Madius, and his father before him, promised the settlers of Neo Maedia that they would be the future of our civilization. Lies. He spoke meaningless words to inspire hope and servitude. Then, without an educational system, how long does it take to turn Maedians into thoughtless mules? No guesses? Let me tell you then: it took less than three generations."

Sebastian swallowed. He could hear Demarko's voice crack, he could see the tears shining in the man's eyes. Emotion, a hungry demon of the cruelest kind, tore the man apart. Sebastian longed for the naivety he'd clung to when they'd last met. He understood what such pain felt like, but knew vengeance could not mend the wounds.

"My wife couldn't live here. After only four short years on Xiratera, she'd fallen into such a state of depression that she impulsively ended her own life. She was an artist - a beautiful mind that this colony could never give true value to. She had no place among the mindless workforce of the Neo Maedian Empire. How could classless beings such as the drones we bred to work ever hope to appreciate art, appreciate beauty?

"My children watched their mother fall ill, and they could do nothing to help her. Nor could they get the education they deserved. My eldest son became a coal miner. I watched over him as his lungs deteriorated from overexposure to the toxins deep within the caves of this land. These forgotten Maedians, they just accept it as part of life, they accept it when men die at twenty-three years. They are conditioned to call it an honor to have died in the service of Maedia. Yet as their ruler, I see no honor in it.

"My two youngest children are back in Old Maedia, estranged from me forever because I'd rather they have the health and happiness of that land than watch them wither and die here. They were all I had left... but I cannot condemn them, not even for the sake of blood bonds. My family is but a single instance of the reality of life on the Wild Continent. The tragedies of this place are endless, and yet the Emperor ignores our anguish."

"Life is imperfect everywhere. You cannot possibly believe that Old Maedia is free of suffering. Tragedy such as yours has touched my own home - not even the royal palace can escape it. Do not belittle the losses to the Haima Demon raids - which none on Xiratera can comprehend fearing. Allowing the people of this land to live their lives to the fullest extent possible would have been the best you, or anyone, could do in such a circumstance. It was not your place to decide what was best for them."

"Make up your mind, young Madius. Am I to do my appointed job - caring for the people of this land, or am I to let them suffer and feign ignorance like those who are not breaking bread with the commoners? I disagree with the statements of honor and duty fed to us in order to keep control. There is no value in a peace brought about through people suffering abuse in silence. Extreme though it may seem, something had to be done. Old Maedia at least wants for Xiratera's resources for the time being. As you had said, I'll be lucky to see a response at all. Old Maedia will likely continue in its ways - a grinding machine that will not stop until its fuel has all burnt and the gears are rusted. It will continue, deaf to the screaming of the citizens whose blood oil its gears until even that runs dry and nothing remains. But you cannot deny this - if I guard this land and keep from Old Maedia all that which it would consume to keep its peace, then the machine will seize up faster than if I do not."

"Woah, woah. Let's hit pause for a second here, okay? I get your problem with Maedian peace policies - Sebastian tried to take anti-violence way too far. But, dude, you killed the people you were trying to save. Mothers, fathers, children, whole freakin' families... in cold blood! I saw the bodies. It was gruesome. Really, really gruesome. Did you actually see what you did to them?"

Demarko frowned deeply at Alex and shook his head. Alex threw his hands into the air, but it was Rebecca who voiced the meaning of his gestures where he seemed too flustered to find the words that she then spoke.

"If you didn't even see what you did to them, then you're no different than what you're complaining about Emperor Whoever having done. You still let them suffer and feigned ignorance to all those people stranded in Thalassa Harbor while completely failing to care for them."

"Believe me, I know what's been done. I've seen the effects of it - the refugees flooding by the masses into the harbor... But blood debts had to be paid for the alliances necessary to accomplish this act of treason. The Lykos hate the Maedians for the way they treat anything they perceive as a threat. They were abandoned by Maedia in much the same manner as the Maedian colonialists. The Drakeon, until you children nullified my alliance, blamed the Maedians for their decline of power in this world. It disgusted them that such a weak, short-lived species had come so far towards conquering all of Gaeadia. They saw it as beneficial to eradicate humans. It was a common goal among us all to return this continent to the wild state from which it came."

"My god Sebastian, the politics of your world suck. Like, this has got to be worse than anything I've ever heard about - and there are a lot of bad tyrants in our history. This guy is completely insane, and someone gave him the power to mind control people! Months ago, I was like 'Demarko is a bad man' and you both were like 'nah, he's just a quirky stressed out old guy that likes to give kids weapons and booze out of kindness.' And now look at us all."

"Hey, I saved your life with that crossbow."

Under normal circumstances, the Emperor would be able to override Demarko's Power with his own. This was a provision of the Power entrusted to each of the Overseers - it was not irrevocable. Dorian was not among them, however. And one detail had been nagging at Sebastian that made him leery of the possibility of employing that failsafe - the immunity to the Power of Madius apparent in Demarko's allies - Drakeon and Lykos alike.

"How have your allies become unaffected by the Power of Madius? My words go disobeyed, and by your situation in such a protective capsule, I can assume they would disobey yours as well."

"I wanted you captured alive because you forced me to have Stephan killed - my key to immunity - when you failed to leave the continent. You are to be my new Madius training figure. You will use your Power against my allies in small doses until they've become immune to it. It takes daily training for many months in order to build up a resistance, but sure enough, the mind is strong and adaptive; the Power can be trained against. Only your grandfather's Power stands any chance at holding sway, and even that is unlikely now."

"The Power is steadfast, without death. How could such a thing be accomplished?"

"When two opposing thoughts are commanded from two separate Powers, the individual must reconcile the differences. They must let their mind settle at what is most in accordance with their own preservation. With enough exposure, the mind learns how to ignore those traces of Power and work of its own accord. The process is excruciating, but worth it, I've been told."

"If your allies already have resistance, the Metakosmos' power of resistance is useless to you."

"Ah, on the contrary. We do not have natural resistance - and that could have faults. It has not been long enough to see if the resistance grows weak over time. The

Metakosmos' inability to be commanded would make them unstoppable against even the Emperor. They've more than proven their worth. With the prowess to manipulate dragons and kill Lykos, these two are precious assets to have in my army."

"They know the truth, I doubt there is anything you could do to persuade them to join you against our people."

Rebecca made a noise of agreement, her arms crossed over her chest. Alex looked pleased with Sebastian. Demarko, however, appeared completely unfazed. In wordless response, he pushed the lever on his control panel and the celling once again began to split open.

"I know that I am not a very charming man, and your friends may not agree with me or my argument for the necessity of these politics, but that is why I have allies. It was the Lykos who first joined me and helped form a solid strategy to achieve the peace of mind I so desire. The Lykos recruited the Drakeon. They have a very good cause, and I support it - particularly that of my favorite Lykos – one who has the commanding, charismatic presence that I lack. I have her here as a special guest, just for your pleasure, Metakosmos. Welcome my ally in all endeavors, the commander of Lykos forces and head of the Xiratera guard, Crimson Whirlwind."

On Demarko's theatrical sweep upward, Kaece appeared at the edge of the glass ceiling. She slid down one of the two partially opened panels and dropped to stand on the platform next to Demarko, then landed lithely on her feet like a companion cat. Her body was still covered in the same open wounds that had left her on the brink of death mere days before. Some wounds still oozed traces of fresh blood. Yet she moved with no sign of injury, nor did her face betray any pain.

"Alpha Whirlwind... She survived. May she have mercy on us."

"I told ya she'd be back, and doing stupid stuff for Alpha Blackdeath would only end in blood. The Crimson Whirlwind is unstoppable."

"Yes, she does have a rather indomitable quality, that is what made her an astute leader. She, and she alone, has complete authority to execute war tactics. I fear that without her presence, much has gone awry in a very short time. As I know you are already well acquainted, and you won't listen to me, I will allow her once again to spearhead this revolution."

Kaece wordlessly nodded an acknowledgement to her Lykos subordinates. Yet her gaze fixated on Rebecca. She turned Demarko's voice amplifying device towards herself, emotion blazing in her eyes.

"I'm making this clear to all of ya, right now. I want Rebecca returned to me. She's mine, and no one else's for any purpose. Understood?"

"Dream on, Lykos. Rebecca isn't going to join up with Demarko - not even for you!"

"Kaece! You're alive... you still look like you should be resting. How did you get here?"

Kaece leaned forward and reached her hand toward Rebecca, as if despite the impenetrable borosilicate between them, she might touch her. Rebecca mirrored the gesture, their hands an impossible distance apart and yet clearly together in spirit. Sebastian shuddered at the thought of Rebecca's newfound Drakeon powers, still largely unknown, being used against mankind.

"I came in by boat, like you. Asher and the others are unharmed, but I had 'em wait at the driftwood camp. They're eager to start a new pack, somethin' different. The ways of Calyx and his opposition have lost their appeal, for the truth in Drakeon lore has changed the playing field. Here ya all stand before the bringer of Drakeon rebirth. Their ridiculous legends came to be, and the Drakeon cannot be defeated. They will come to power. If we're gonna be on the victorious side in the war, then we must treat 'em with utmost respect. They alone deem which species are worthy of life, and which are not.

"Let's make the Supremacists - the most powerful of Lykos - an ally they treasure. Ya see, Rebecca? We can be great together. It could be me an' you on top of the world. Say you'll join me, say all the words ya cried for me are true."

Lies, or truth - it all muddled together. Empty promises. Poor choices. Regrets. In the end, fighting the inevitable would be futile because it would all happen as the gods intended. Sebastian realized, whether it be in one or one hundred years, the Maedian Empire would fall. That felt as fated as his father's demise, as fated as the romance between the passionate youth of opposing views. Sebastian had truly believed that bringing them together would be for the best - Rebecca's goodness would lead Kaece into the light, and their opposition would be quelled with the peace of her single command to abandon the warpath.

He watched Rebecca's expression as emotions flittered across her face. She seemed to weigh the values, yet he could easily assume it was a choice of Kaece and world destruction, or her typical non-committal stance of neither. He knew she would settle on the former, for Kaece had already experienced the sting of Rebecca's inaction and her love for Kaece had proven much stronger than a need for neutrality.

Sebastian's future held no hope. He would have happily become Emperor to a dying empire, doomed to fall under his ignorant rule, if he could reverse time and never venture to Xiratera, never set foot in the cold iron cell filled with rot and the madness of isolation.

"Please, do what you must, dear friend. The world needs your kind heart, your loving intent, to be at its best when faced with such forceable change. If Maedians are to fall, and the Madius family is a threat, so I must be destroyed in one way or another... I.. I do not wish to become what my father was, nor die as he had died. I cannot control the future. I cannot save the world, nor stop this war... I am powerless, but please, I beg of you, let me control how I die. I repeat this man's puzzling words of wisdom: whatever you do, may you do it prudently, and look to the end. Make it quick, painless, and soon."

CHAPTER 37

"I'm not on anyone's side," Rebecca asserted, indignation burning in her chest. "You know how I feel about it, Kaece."

"I do." The devious smile and mischief lighting Kaece's eyes, the amused tone in her voice, the way she held her ground with a shell of indifference, all of it sparked a curiosity deep in Rebecca's gut. "We don't need to fight if the Maedians leave. We can live an' let live. All I ask is that ya fight to protect Xiratera, the home of the Drakeon, an' only so long as ya feel like your home or your loved ones are threatened."

"She just said she's not gonna join you," Alex spat. "You knew where Sebastian's dad was all along, and you just let him die! You could've helped us save him. Rebecca's a hero, not a murderer. She won the Trials of Domination without killing a single Lykos. I bet you killed as many as you could."

Rebecca shook her head, rolled her eyes and laughed. Alex glared back at her. His upset made sense, she guessed: if normalcy and happiness existed on separate, parallel planes, then when she chose happiness she could probably also choose villainy. She looked back to Kaece and Demarko, safely above them in a protective glass capsule, affirming to herself that being evil strayed pretty far from normal.

"Defeated Kym, eh?" Kaece quirked an eyebrow at Demarko. "All the more reason why she's useful – protection without killin' still meets your needs. Don't ya think?"

"Yes," he agreed with a satisfied clap of his hands. "If we can win without starting a war, it is a welcome strategy."

"There ya have it, my love. We can shape this land however we desire. There's no need for slaughter so long as ya have better ideas, an' I know ya will. For me torture an' death is the only way – killin' is what I do," she laughed a cruel, lilting laugh and every note held Rebecca captive in anticipation. She wondered if Kaece intended to toy with them until she could reunite Rebecca with her swords, her jeans, and her power.

"If I join you –"

"You can't!" Alex cried. "Think of all the people they've killed! They're the bad guys! You can't join them..."

"Are you done?"

"No. Sebastian *loves* you." Alex pushed for his fairytale ending the same way her mother had pushed her toward a fairytale ending with Brad.

"And I love Sebastian. As a friend. That doesn't change how I feel about Kaece, or that I want to be with her more than anything."

"More than keeping your promise to stay with me? We came to this world together... I'm family. Remember how you said you were being selfish and naïve? You swore you'd make it up to me – that you wouldn't do it again... This is worse than suicide, please don't do it."

"It will be as it is fated to be," Sebastian whispered. "They were drawn together despite the Kosmos, their species, their very alignments."

"Thank you, Sebastian." Rebecca smiled weakly, then she pulled Alex close and silenced him the only way she knew how: she muffled his mouth. Kaece waited patiently, her amused smirk unwavering.

"If I join you, what happens to Sebastian?"

"He stays under lock an' key. I'm sure we can make his prison comfortable, fit for an emperor if ya like. When he sees what kinda leader ya are, he'll agree to train peoples' minds to be saved from that wicked power of Madius."

Rebecca raised her eyebrows; Kaece's response had been so quick and thoughtless it seemed practiced. "And if I refuse to join you, then what happens to us? What will you do to them? I want the truth."

"This glass," Kaece gestured to it, "is thick. Solid. I can't smell ya. I can't hear your heartbeat. But I can see ya. I can see that you want to be here, with me, and know ya won't refuse. But, ya have conditions. Give 'em, so we can get past this part and get to the good part - the part where we both get what we want."

Rebecca swallowed. She said, "under no circumstance can *anyone* who isn't a serious, direct threat be harmed in any way. If people come to talk, we let them talk. Then they can go back to where-ever they came from. Since the power of Madius will be useless, we won't have to worry about being manipulated."

"Done."

"That's not all. Sebastian has to be comfortable – he shouldn't have to live in a dungeon like some criminal. Prisoner or not, he shouldn't be treated like one. And I don't want him to feel like one, either. He can't be abused for his power: he has to agree to use it willingly."

"Only if he's willing to be agreeable," Kaece retorted. "It'd be a waste of air to keep him around, fed and healthy to not do what he's here to do."

"I don't think he'll be unreasonable as long as he's treated well," Rebecca waved her hand in dismissal. "If there are still issues, we can talk about it later. But lastly, I don't want you in charge. You can't resist pushing limits, sneaking and lying and manipulating whatever loopholes present themselves. I'd be an idiot not to be prepared for that after all we've been through."

The Lykos peered down at her, wounded by the jab. Though it finally gave Kaece pause, she still nodded her agreement. "As she wishes. I'll drop rank and follow her command; assuming ya agree with her overly Maedian friendly demands."

"Of course," Demarko exclaimed, grinning. "All is well. I couldn't have fathomed my plan coming to such a fruitful conclusion. We can arrange sleeping quarters for our young prince immediately. I trust in the meantime, you are capable of informing your new commander of the urgent air message from Neo Maedia."

"A conversation best had in privacy. It's a twist that the Madius isn't prepared for."

Alex groaned into Rebecca's palm. She felt his tense muscles and knew he was angry, disappointed – just like she expected. When she let him go, he jerked away and rubbed his face. His silence told her that he'd get over it.

Demarko pushed a button on the control panel he'd used to turn on the intercom and the sounds of gears whirring to life filled the room. The loud clanking of metal echoed as the ceiling above him split open like a glass mouth eager to devour the sky. He continued speaking to Kaece as the platform began its ascent, "In your absence, the other Lykos have caused me incalculable problems with injured Maedians. It would have been more humane to finish the job as you would have done, rather than allow them to spread infection and disease as they are. I cannot undo the illness or the noxious waste. There is a freight vessel arriving before our honored guest. We will load it with those who cannot be helped here. Whoever survives the journey will be able to enjoy the Maedia that they should have been born into."

"That journey takes a fortnight!" Sebastian gasped.

The Overseer flipped a switch and the microphone crackled with static then fell silent.

"This isn't going to work if I'm not included in everything," Rebecca growled. "Kaece. I need to know what's happening."

Demarko talked animatedly about something, gesturing with his hands while a heavy chain clanked upward in time with the platform. Kaece's captivating golden eyes focused on Rebecca the entire time, as if whatever the Overseer had to say didn't matter.

Kaece winked at her, then hopped up onto the control panel. Crouching on its edge, she frightened Demarko with a sinister smile. She then pried something from the podium and leapt upward. Prize in hand, she scrambled to hold into the slanted glass. As Kaece hoisted herself up onto the roof, Rebecca remembered to breathe.

"She took the remote-control," Sebastian observed aloud.

The lift ground to a halt. Worry etched on Demarko's face, he beat the control panel with his fists. Sweat beaded on his forehead and his entire face turned red from yelling. As Kaece disappeared from view, his gestures became more and more frantic. The platform held him suspended mid-air. The glass panels reversed direction

"Can he get out of there without it?" Alex asked. "Like, if he tries to break through the bottom or something?"

"It was designed to protect him from the Lykos and Dragons he did not trust... Borosilicate is meant to resist extreme temperatures, pressure changes, and impacts. I do not believe that man or beast could break it."

The male Lykos added, "I tried gettin' in while he wasn't around, but there's only one way in – through the top with that device she's holdin'. She's messin' with him."

While Alex and the Lykos laughed together at the man's plight, Kaece stepped back out onto the glass panel. She jumped effortlessly from one pane to the other across an expansive gap, taunting Demarko with the ease of her escape. He had few options, none of which looked any more promising to Rebecca than standing idle.

Legs wobbling, Demarko clambered up onto the control panel. Then, mimicking Kaece's movements, he crouched and bounded for the glass pane as it rose past him. He fumbled to grasp onto the slick glass. His dirt-caked boots flailed while he tried to hold his grip with the gap between the closing panels quickly narrowing.

She didn't want to watch, but Rebecca couldn't tear her gaze away. Demarko's fingers clung to the edge of the smooth pane, his fingertips all that kept him from plummeting. As he slipped, Kaece dropped onto her chest and snatched him by the wrist. She raised him up - his savior. But his relief morphed into horror as she grabbed him by the hair and held him fast.

He flailed anew as the glass panel pressed into his back and it didn't stop – the gears clanked onward. The soundproof glass did, however, stop the sound of his breaking spine, of his ribs cracking inward and tearing into his lungs, of his blood-curdling scream as the panes bit into his flesh and crushed his throat.

Blood oozed from his neck and drooled down his worksuit. The deep crimson fluid rushed from his body as the mechanized ceiling sealed shut. The winding gears pushed on a few more clicks, then stopped. Demarko's legs and torso collapsed from the ceiling and smacked into the glass floor above them. The already-pooling blood splattered: a messy dark spray of gore spilled from the part of Demarko that failed to escape.

The Lykos' shadow walked away from the contorted mass of Demarko's head and left arm. Nothing about his dark fate elicited sympathy from Rebecca. She'd felt more sorrow for the rotting corpses of strangers in Tekton. No – for the man who started it all, she only held bewilderment and disgust. His was the first blood, other than her own, she felt belonged outside of its flesh-encased prison.

Sebastian gagged, turning away from the gore. "Did you know this was her plan?"

"How could I?"

"No wonder they call her Crimson Whirlwind," Alex remarked in awe.

The female Lykos guard chuckled, "That's nothin' on what she can do. You oughta see when she—"

"Stop," Rebecca interjected. She didn't want to hear about the horrible things Kaece had done. They'd evolved together beyond the people they once were: Crimson Whirlwind existed only as much as Rebecca Silas-Logan ever had.

"As you command," the male Lykos agreed with a fanged grin. "What do you want us to do, then, Alpha?"

The title hardly made her feel any more like a leader than she did before Kaece put her in charge.

"I want to see Kaece. Can you make that happen?"

He nodded, then ushered them into the forge room. The once-zombified Maedian workers gawked up at the mess spilling into their side of the glass chamber overhead.

Sebastian addressed them, "My dear citizen's of Neo Maedia, you have suffered a grave and unforgivable fate at the ill-used power of a madman. Come speak with me, I wish to meet you and hear your grievances, and discuss how we can work together to rebuild our broken nation."

As Sebastian questioned and answered his people, Rebecca followed the Lykos toward the exit. Alex trotted along after her, chattering with the other Lykos about Demarko's attempted jump toward salvation. They eagerly discussed the flaws in his tactics, and what each would have done differently had they been in the Overseer's position. She sighed – Alex's fascination with action, violence and death had been the exact reason she'd been shafted with Typhos' power. The demigod wanted someone who found these "exciting" things to be exhausting rather than enticing. After all, the point of the Eolith was how tiresome fighting became: all the bickering over power, the squabbling over land... Everything amounted to trivial words and trivial rules about rights to places only the earth itself could ever truly own. None of their territories would ever be real; limitations could only be physical boundaries, never the lines etched into a map.

After they crossed the threshold from the industrial building, the Lykos paused. Rebecca frowned; their tense muscles, the female's wrinkled nose, implied trouble that her human senses couldn't preempt. Then she heard it – the faint echo of a Haima Fox's threatening chatter.

"Chupita?" Alex called out, his hands cupped around his mouth like a megaphone. He walked toward the forest.

The chattering stopped. The leaves rustled. Glowing red eyes stared out from the darkness of the underbrush. Then Chupita burst forth from the bushes and bounded straight for him.

He knelt and scooped his puppy into a hug. Holding her close, he exclaimed, "Chupi! I missed you, girl."

Chupita covered her brother's face in affectionate licks.

Strong arms wrapped around Rebecca's neck as she was tackled to the ground.

"Got ya," Kaece laughed.

"Get off me," Rebecca snapped, then she spotted her missing treasure clutched in the Lykos' claws. She dove for her jeans, snatching at the air as Kaece raised the denim out of her reach.

"What's the rush? Ya look good with all that skin showin'." Kaece smirked. "Even Clay noticed."

Rebecca jabbed Kaece in the breastbone, hard. "Is that why you did that to him? Jealous much? He agreed to non-violence."

She gasped as Kaece took her by the wrist and pulled her close. After dropping the jeans, she cupped Rebecca's chin in the comforting warmth of her hands. Those dark-rimmed yellow eyes peered deep into Rebecca's very core; She shivered as she looked back into the loving gaze of a monster – a monster whose expression contorted with gentle affection, whose eyes burned with a mixture of adoration and desire.

"Ya saved my wretched life for a second time. I love you more than the gods themselves could ever understand, my protector, my reason to live."

Kaece leaned in and sealed the confession with a kiss. The feel of Kaece's soft lips sent Rebecca's heart racing.

"Why did you do it?" Rebecca persisted, despite longing swelling up and threatening to burst from her chest when Kaece whispered the promise of mutual desire.

Sebastian emerged from the building and drew everyone's attention to his confounded expression.

Kaece held up her hand. "That human had many reasons to die. But here is one I know ya value -" She gestured at Sebastian then brought her hand to hold Rebecca's forehead to her own. "He would've lived his life in a cage - nice or not. He would've never seen daylight again. Like the Madius before him, he would've suffered, and eventually been destroyed."

Rebecca objected, "That sounds more like an excuse. You hate Sebastian."

"I hate all Maedians equally these days. Truth is, I saw an opportunity to get rid of a harmful one, an' I did. He left himself exposed and he shouldn't've." Kaece chuckled and ran her fingers down Rebecca's bare thigh. "Plus, he put ya in a dungeon, naked. That's my thing."

Rebecca rolled her eyes and pushed Kaece away. She put on the pants she'd been holding instead of wearing for entirely too long. When she pulled the cinch tight on the belt, she felt another wave of relief – finally, she had the comfort of her own clothes, and Typhos' protection securely in the artifact pouch at her hip.

"There are dozens of men here," Sebastian complained, "They came from towns all over Xiratera. How am I to get them to a safe steadfast? I am grateful for my life, and of course my freedom, but the weight of responsibility upon me as to their well beings... well, I hardly know where to begin."

"We have at least one boat," Rebecca shrugged.

"If ya wanna move hundreds of Maedians one-by-one off this island, then by all means. But don't expect me to help ya. You'll be rowin' against the tide 'til your arms go numb."

"Do you have a better suggestion?"

"What about all of Demarko's war machines?" Alex theorized, excitement obvious in his voice. "I bet most or all of them fly or submerse – you can't really walk a Hadros into the ocean when it's time to fight a war, you know?"

Sebastian shook his head. "Even so, flying machines are a fool's ambition. Bronze is not meant to soar."

The male Lykos replied, "The Metakosmos knows the truth of it, these machines all fly and float. They'll get us to mainland."

"See? We'll figure it out." Alex grinned at Sebastian. "It's a solution, right?"

As if her brother's sheer optimism made it so, Sebastian's skepticism slipped away. Sebastian nodded and waved for Alex to follow him back into the building.

When Alex, Sebastian and Chupita disappeared inside of the compound, Rebecca turned to the Lykos who stood as if eagerly awaiting a command. She frowned. "What are you waiting for? Shouldn't you be helping them figure out those machines?"

The male shrugged. "Is that your command?"

She sighed, frustration at the stupidity of his question gnawing at her. Both Kaece and the Drakeon could read her, in one way or another - why were these guards so daft? All Rebecca needed, having been reunited with her pants, was some alone time with Kaece.

"Maybe ya'd better put someone who likes bossin' people around in charge," Kaece chuckled.

"Not you."

"Of course not me. My want is the same as yours - obligation-free eternity alone with you."

Rebecca blushed, dismissing the proposition by focusing on the next task at hand - crossing the vast expanse back to shore. The Lykos proved more useful when she demanded their help locating their boat, and some oars.

Before long, she and Kaece had paddled far from the Island. As Kaece hefted the canoe into the sand of the driftwood shore, the air had started humming as if alive with a thousand dragonflies. Various shaped flying machines scattered across the sky. Some were large, others smaller, some emitted the white smoke of steam power, while the rest appeared to be mechanized and man-powered like Alex's crossbow, but they all were fashioned in the same creepy insect quality that the Hadros embodied.

Rebecca couldn't believe how fast Demarko's inventions flew over the same stretch of ocean they took. Her Lykos guards pulled their boat up on shore just as her Lykos friends approached from the village. The Satyr looked at the sky with an expression of awe.

"Fascinating," He mused aloud. "Loud, but interesting. May I assume that one of them harbors the young Emperor - I intend to collect my debt."

"What Thanos filth is this? I'd run fast if were you, dark-magic trader," the male guard snipped.

"He's Protector One-Shot's friend, traitor. The killing is over. Her reign is of peace," Alpha Wildfire explained, though his threatening body language spoke the exact opposite of peace.

The female guard cackled, "She needs killers - this Commander knows that world peace is a children's fantasy and the truth is in balance. Why else join Alpha Crimson Whirlwind?"

Wildfire replied, "For peace. Bringing Whirlwind back into the fold, it is far braver and more just than anything Timbercut has done in his reign as Alpha Prime. We stand by her for the right reasons."

When Kaece glowered at them all with that dangerous glint in her eyes, Rebecca took it on herself to stop the fighting before it got worse. "I don't care what any of you believed before now. I can't be here to babysit all the time so you have to grow up and get over your issues with each other or just leave now."

The two clusters of Lykos, at ends moments prior, watched, rapt with attention. Only a few nodded their assent.

She pointed to the lithe Lykos guard, that donned a set of red-tipped pale blonde pigs-tails, "You've been with me all day and I never asked. What's your name?"

"Lyriel."

"Good. Lyriel will be the voice for the pack formerly known as the Supremacists. She will speak for you and you will know your view is shared with one of the Alphas. And Lyriel will share her position of power with Shanan, who will represent the Calyxist viewpoint. They have equal authority and should only involve me when they cannot come to an agreement because of those fundamental differences. Otherwise, the Supremacists and the Calyxists are a thing of the past; it's over, let it go. I want us to work together – the Drakeon and the Lykos – as one. You are now the Drakeon Pack."

"I do not mean to offend, One-Strike, but I have no title. I am not worthy of such a status," Shanan said meekly.

Rebecca trusted the collected red-head from Kym's pack could make judgments that would keep quarrels from ever reaching Rebecca - Shanan had decided to leave Kym by her own good sense, after all. "Drakeon are born into their authority - as are the Maedians. On Earth, wealth tended to equate power - but I don't want the elite in charge of this broken world. There are gonna be a lot of changes, while I'm in charge, and this is the first. Typhos saw the leader in me, and I see it in you. You can do this, Alpha Shanan - the only question is, are you willing?"

"I will ensure your confidence is not mistaken, One-Strike." Shanan pulled Lyriel into a hug, "To a new world, Alpha Lyriel."

Surprised, but somehow softened by the gesture, Lyriel returned the hug and gave Rebecca a silent nod.

Leaving the Lykos and locking herself away on the Hadros, Rebecca realized she'd never have imagined the contraption she hated so would be her sanctuary. But, there she sat on the edge of the bed, coaxing Kaece to join her.

She tossed her arms around Kaece's neck and pulled her in close. Her body tingled when Kaece's palms rested on her hips, their bodies pressed together.

"Where were we before I realized you were a lying backstabber?" Rebecca breathed into Kaece's ear.

Kaece reached over to Alex's cluttered pile of junk and grabbed a random Maedian book. "Ya were readin' Sebastian's love notes he left ya."

Rebecca slipped the book from her fingers and casually tossed it backward over her shoulder. "Let's change it. How about this time, I was dreaming about having your hands all over me."

With a wide grin, Kaece obliged by pushing Rebecca down onto the bed. Rebecca pulled Kaece into a kiss, this time without a regret in the world.

CHAPTER 38

The light of dawn spilled in through the blinds, casting a soft golden hue on their naked skin. Rebecca could see every detail of Kaece's smooth, angular jawline, every faint scar etched into her flesh, every fleck of gold in her yellow eyes. Rebecca knew that Kaece, staring back at her, saw even more. For the first time in her life, though, she didn't care — she lusted after the hungry, searching gaze that didn't miss a single blemish. She traced her fingertips along the Lykos' collar, then rested her head on the perfect dip of Kaece's shoulder. She was completely exposed and completely comfortable.

Why did they need her? She felt that surely the ceremony could commence without interrupting her little piece of heaven. A nearly silent whimper — her frustration at the knowledge of Sebastian waiting just outside the door — escaped her lips. Beyond his presence loomed countless Maedians who needed closure, closure they would never have if she gave in to her yearning.

"Forget them," Kaece breathed into her ear. She shuddered against the warmth that tickled along her skin. "Ya know this'll be better than anything ya got out there."

Rebecca sat up and ran her fingers through her tangled hair. "It's time, I have to go."

"I can't go into the Polis," Kaece objected. "As long as ya stay with them, we'll be apart."

Rebecca leaned over and pressed her lips against Kaece's, silencing the protest with a kiss. Her heart raced as Kaece returned the kiss — she couldn't ever get enough, addicted to the feeling of Kaece in every way. She saw the understanding in those dark-rimmed eyes; she felt it in the gentle touch of Kaece's fingers tracing circles on her belly.

She placed her hand over Kaece's, stopping the Lykos from tempting her with those languid touches. Then she moved Kaece's hand down, down, down, until she knew Kaece felt what she felt for her. When Kaece moaned, a throaty purr of excitement, Rebecca pushed her hand away and slid off the bed.

"Wait for me," she commanded.

Rebecca opened her eyes when the cheers erupted from the crowd. Beside her, Alex vibrated with nervous energy. He couldn't keep the look of awe and excitement from his face; the sheer marvel at being held in the same regard as royalty held him captive in a state she could only describe as a stupor. The sun shone high overhead, its warmth radiating against the marble walls of the colosseum. They stood at the back of a platform on the north side of the amphitheater and looked out at the endless sea of Maedian faces. Hundreds of them filled the arena floor, below the platform, while countless more lined every level of the tiered structure. Thousands of eyes were focused in their direction, focused on Emperor Dorian Madius.

A cropped white beard accentuated the squareness of the old emperor's jaw. His long, white hair flowed down into his long white robes and became lost in the pale fabric and neat silver embroidery. Atop his head rested a thin silver circlet that dipped down onto his forehead with an iridescent sapphire jewel set in the center.

Two fierce, armor-clad guards flanked the Emperor. One male, biceps bulging under thick leather; and one dark-skinned female in segmented plate, both baleful. The Emperor had announced his presence and the reason for his journey: to track down his heroic grandson. He apologized at length for the hardships they endured at the hands of an abusive and neglectful overseer; he expressed his condolences for all that they had lost, and offered his deepest sympathies from Old Maedia. He vowed to make amends. Without saying anything of substance, he'd moved them to tears and he'd elicited deafening applause.

As the applause faded, Dorian gestured behind himself to Rebecca and Alex. "We all owe our saviors our sincerest gratitude, and more. They come before you, in full view of the gods, to honor us with their tale of heroism. These two children from the Other Side have saved Neo Maedia, my grandson, and our Empire from a certain end. Come forth, Metakosmos, let your people look upon you and hear your voice."

As Rebecca stepped forward, a guard took her by the arm and forced her up past the Emperor. Her and Alex stood alone, in front of the ruler of the world, at the forefront of the crowd.

Alex beamed and waved energetically. Rebecca swallowed; she felt ill. The spectators all waited for her to say something, expecting her to give a moving speech like the Emperor's.

"We came from Albuquerque, New Mexico. It's a place on Earth across the Kosmos and it's mostly a desert," Alex began. "But that's beside the point. The point is how we got here, so we could be here to help fix everything! It all started on Rebecca's wedding day. A dragon fell from the sky and *crushed* our car – that's what we call our land-version Metaros. We saw the dragon's ghost, and it looked right at us... Then—"

"The dragon we saw wasn't the one that had fallen," Rebecca interrupted. She knew Alex would drag it on for the next decade if they let him exaggerate the truth. "It wasn't even really a ghost. The Drakeon lord, Typhos, sent us a message in the form of that spirit before he pulled us through a rip in the Kosmos. He guided us on our journey. Over the course of our travels we saw all sorts of unimaginable things, so much death and violence. We've suffered injuries, both physical and emotional, that we'll never fully heal from. We've changed, just as Xiratera's changed. Everything we endured has made us a part of this world.

"We witnessed first-hand the mistakes of Maedian ideals, and we saw the consequences of Old Maedia's neglect. A man like Demarko shouldn't have ever gotten away with what he did for as long as he did. Nor should the Lykos be ostracized like the bloodthirsty beasts the Maedian history books say they are – without the help of the Lykos, none of us would be standing here today. They made it possible. But what it all comes down to, all of you, is that your methodology is *not* infallible. Every choice you make, every thing you do – or *don't* do – effects other people, whether it's now or in a hundred years. So before you do something for your people or your country just because someone told you to, you need to *think*. Think for yourself. Make decisions for yourself. Each and every one of you needs to be your own person, with your own self-image. Define your world with your own experiences, your own perceptions, and not with what others expect of you. Know what's right because you decided it for yourself, not because you were told to believe it was right or true."

The people cheered, a roar that burned her ears and made her bones shake. Their ovation took her terror and transformed it into a lightness, the butterflies in her stomach ready to take her up and away. Her face flushed a cold pink.

Alex walked to the edge of the platform and held out his hands. The clamor died out and the crowd fell silent. As they quieted, he announced triumphantly, "So with the help of Sebastian, we vanquished the villainous Demarko and saved Xiratera! We can rebuild and live together in peace!"

The applause erupted again.

Rebecca rolled her eyes. "We, with the help of Sebastian...? Kaece should really be getting the credit for killing Demarko. She's the murderer."

"Hey. Sebastian said we shouldn't mention her – for her safety and all."

"Who is this that you have decided was best to keep secret from me?" The Emperor murmured to his grandson behind them.

Sebastian stammered.

"Kaece," Rebecca answered. She wound up her most impossibly fake smile, and shrugged. "She's my imaginary friend. It's a game me and my brother play, that's all. Sebastian said you were above such childish stuff."

"Ah," the old man nodded, then coughed a wet hack that made Rebecca cringe. He cleared his throat and refocused on Sebastian. "Are you ready to give the announcement?"

"Of course, grandfather." Sebastian replied, then stepped up between Rebecca and Alex. He spoke low into her ear. "I saw your pet lurking in the shadows of the arcade to the east. It is the exit nearest us, and still on the ground level. Use this to your advantage, and get her out. She cannot be in the Polis – I thought we had an understanding."

"I told her to stay on the Hadros," Rebecca defended absently. Despite his scolding, and knowing he was right, she attentively scanned the crowd for Kaece's features.

"Go," he urged. "I will excuse you. The rest of this dreary business has little to do with you."

"That's it, then?"

"While 'our Emperor is ill and when he passes in the next few years, I will be your new Emperor, so nice to meet you officially' is a speech I've known for a long while, I'm not prepared for the 'please do not panic, that Lykos is most likely not going to harm you' speech. Thus, I implore you, handle her."

Rebecca hugged Sebastian. "I know this is your worst nightmare, not a Lykos in the crowd. You're not gonna have to transform into an Emperor overnight, and even if you did you're not going to be alone in it. Everyone believes in you. You're going to be a great Emperor."

"So you have said," Sebastian sighed then pulled away from her embrace. "My good people of Neo Maedia, we must bid my dear friend, Protector Rebecca Silas farewell. She is not fond of crowds and has duties she must attend."

Alex lifted the crowds disappointment, "But I'm not going anywhere!"

Rebecca slipped into the back of the gathering of the Emperor's people. The busty, dark-skinned guard stopped her from leaving.

"You can't leave without this. The Emperor would not be pleased." She pinned a medal on the front of Rebecca's hoodie.

The platinum badge looked heavier than it felt. Rebecca assumed the elaborate engraving was the Madius family crest. A shield in the shape of an eye provided the backdrop to Pegasi rearing up around it. Words she couldn't read encircled the crest.

"What does it say?"

"Voice of Serenity, they say. Having it means that you're a hero among all Maedians. It's a rare and special honor, so at least wave or something before you run off."

"Right…" Rebecca nodded, then turned to the Emperor. She caught his gaze and bowed to him the same way she'd seen the people bow when he'd taken the stage. Then, she made a point of smiling and waving to everyone out in the crowd.

She fingered the medal as she walked away; something about the tangible cold metal in her hand made her feel as if she actually had done something for Maedia. She wondered if Typhos predicted her growing into herself long before she could be worthy of a badge of honor.

Rebecca smiled to herself and shook her head as she crossed through the archway leading into the outer colosseum. The long, curved corridor stretched forever before it rounded out of sight. She hurried down the deserted hall, then crossed back into the inner passageway that led spectators to their seats.

"You shouldn't be here," she called out into the shadows of the arcade.

The pillars supporting the broad succession of arches cast blackness all about. The sun struggled to illuminate the passage, instead a blend of grey and black shadow stood out in stark contrast to the brightness of the corridor she'd just left. Kaece stepped out of the darkness and into the grey haze just enough for Rebecca to see the amused, yet guilty expression on her face. Even in the dim light, Rebecca knew Kaece would stand out. Her yellow eyes, silver hair, the still-healing scar on her face – none of it could be hidden in broad daylight.

Kaece held out her hand, palm up. Even the burn from Rebecca's sword stood out, a white patch of abnormality seared into her flesh.

Rebecca sighed, relishing the feel of Kaece's fingers closing around her own. "How am I ever going to tame you if you can't even follow simple directions? Stay. Not follow."

"With enough of ya, I'm sure I'll get it," Kaece murmured into Rebecca's ear as she pulled her into the shadows.

The annoyance at Kaece's inability to obey rules melted away with Kaece's arms wrapped around her. The Lykos held her close, her hands resting on top of Rebecca's just as they had the night they first met. Rebecca leaned her head back on Kaece's shoulder and entwined her fingers with Kaece's. A shiver ran down her spine as Kaece brushed her lips against her exposed neck. Kaece kissed from Rebecca's collar to her jawline and back, and every kiss felt like ecstasy. In the distance, Sebastian's voice echoed faintly throughout the amphitheater – the dull murmur of an Emperor-to-be in the background paled in comparison to the steady beating of Kaece's heart.

"I love you, you bad, bad Lykos," Rebecca whispered. "You'll get more than enough of me. You couldn't get rid of me if you tried."

YOU ARE AMAZING IN EVERY WAY.

Thank you for existing. I appreciate you!
You've actually read my book, all the way to the end and put all of my effort to a purpose.
Could you take a moment to visit the richardstrife.com website, an author review site or amazon.com to leave a review, letting the world at large know what you thought about *Denial.*

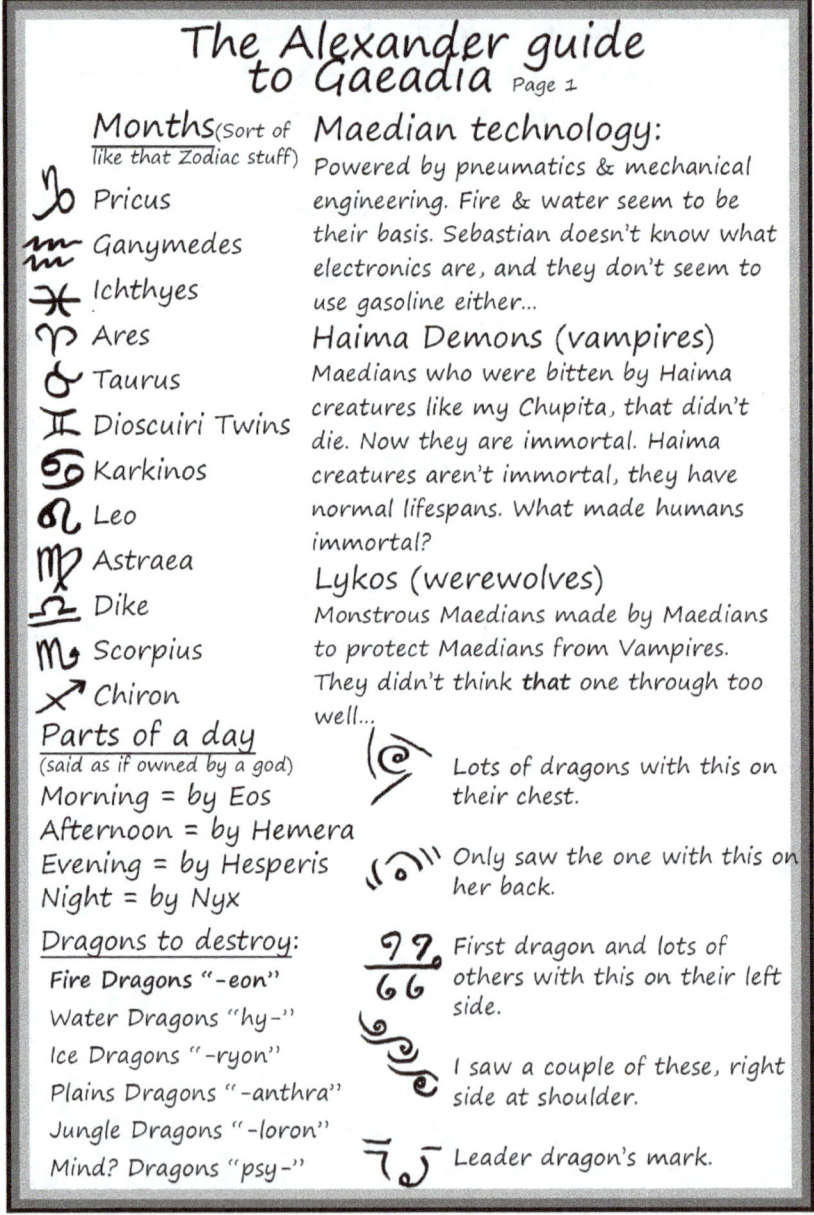

The Alexander guide to Gaeadia Page 1

Months (Sort of like that Zodiac stuff)

- Pricus
- Ganymedes
- Ichthyes
- Ares
- Taurus
- Dioscuiri Twins
- Karkinos
- Leo
- Astraea
- Dike
- Scorpius
- Chiron

Parts of a day
(said as if owned by a god)

Morning = by Eos
Afternoon = by Hemera
Evening = by Hesperis
Night = by Nyx

Dragons to destroy:

Fire Dragons "-eon"
Water Dragons "hy-"
Ice Dragons "-ryon"
Plains Dragons "-anthra"
Jungle Dragons "-loron"
Mind? Dragons "psy-"

Maedian technology:

Powered by pneumatics & mechanical engineering. Fire & water seem to be their basis. Sebastian doesn't know what electronics are, and they don't seem to use gasoline either...

Haima Demons (vampires)

Maedians who were bitten by Haima creatures like my Chupita, that didn't die. Now they are immortal. Haima creatures aren't immortal, they have normal lifespans. What made humans immortal?

Lykos (werewolves)

Monstrous Maedians made by Maedians to protect Maedians from Vampires. They didn't think **that** one through too well...

Lots of dragons with this on their chest.

Only saw the one with this on her back.

First dragon and lots of others with this on their left side.

I saw a couple of these, right side at shoulder.

Leader dragon's mark.

320

www.ingramcontent.com/pod-product-compliance
Lightning Source LLC
Chambersburg PA
CBHW081521050726
47503CB00018B/2934